Kilgorman
A Story of Ireland in 1798

by

Talbot Baines Reed

Kilgorman
A Story of Ireland in 1798
by Talbot Baines Reed

ISBN: 978-93-62760-23-4

Published by

DOUBLE 9 BOOKS

2/13-B, Ansari Road
Daryaganj, New Delhi – 110002
info@double9books.com
www.double9books.com
Tel. 011-40042856

ABOUT THE AUTHOR

Talbot Baines Reed was an English author of boys' fiction who lived from April 3, 1852, to November 28, 1893. He created a type of school stories that lasted until the middle of the 20th century. The Fifth Form at St. Dominic's is one of his most well-known works. He often and regularly wrote for The Boy's Own Paper (B.O.P.). Most of his writing was first published there. Reed became a well-known typefounder through his family's business. He also wrote the standard work on the subject, History of the Old English Letter Foundries. John Reed was a colonel in Oliver Cromwell's army during the English Civil War. The Reed family came from him. Their home was in Maiden Newton, which is in the county of Dorset. They moved to London at the end of the 18th century. Andrew Reed (1787–1862), Talbot Reed's grandpa, was a minister in the Congregational Church and the founder of many charitable organizations, such as the London Orphan Asylum and a hospital for people who could not get better. He was also a well-known hymn writer. His "Spirit Divine, attend our prayers" can still be found in many hymnals today. Talbot Baines Reed grew up in a happy family where Charles Reed was very religious and thought that tough outdoor games were the best way to raise boys.

CONTENTS

Preface

In Memoriam

By the death of Talbot B. Reed the boys of the English-speaking world have lost one of their best friends. For fourteen years he has contributed to their pleasure, and in the little library of boys' books which left his pen he has done as much as any writer of our day to raise the standard of boys' literature. His books are alike removed from the old-fashioned and familiar class of boys' stories, which, meaning well, generally baffled their own purpose by attempting to administer morality and doctrine on what Reed called the "powder-in-jam" principle—a process apt to spoil the jam, yet make "the powder" no less nauseous; or, on the other hand, the class of book that dealt in thrilling adventure of the blood-curdling and "penny dreadful" order. With neither of these types have Talbot Reed's boys' books any kinship. His boys are of flesh and blood, such as fill our public schools, such as brighten or "make hay" of the peace of our homes. He had the rare art of hitting off boy-nature, with just that spice of wickedness in it without which a boy is not a boy. His heroes have always the charm of bounding, youthful energy, and youth's invincible hopefulness, and the constant flow of good spirits which have made the boys of all time perennially interesting.

The secret of Reed's success in this direction was that all through life, as every one who had the privilege of knowing him can testify, he possessed in himself the healthy freshness of heart of boyhood. He sympathised with the troubles and joys, he understood the temptations, and fathomed the motives that sway and mould boy-character; he had the power of depicting that side of life with infinite humour and pathos, possible only to one who could place himself sympathetically at the boys' stand-point in life. Hence the wholesomeness of tone and the breezy freshness of his work. His boy-heroes are neither prigs nor milk-sops, but in their strength and weakness they are the stuff which ultimately makes our best citizens and fathers; they are the boys who, later in life, with healthy minds in healthy bodies, have made the British Empire what it is.

A special and pathetic interest attaches to this story of "Kilgorman," the last that left Talbot Reed's pen. It was undertaken while he was yet in the prime of his strength and vigour. The illness which ultimately, alas, ended fatally had already laid hold on him ere he had well begun the book. In intervals of ease during his last illness he worked at it, sometimes in bed, sometimes in his armchair: it is pleasant to think that he so enjoyed the work that its production eased and soothed many a weary hour for him, and certainly never was other than a recreation to him.

The pen dropped from his hand ere he had quite completed the work, yet, as the book stands here, it is much as he meant to leave it. The figures of Barry Gallagher, and Tim, and the charming Kit will take their places in the delightful gallery of his young people, and their adventures by land and by sea will be followed with an increased interest that they are the last that can come from his brilliant pen.

Talbot Reed came of a right good English stock, both on his father's and his mother's side. His grandfather, Dr Andrew Reed, a Nonconformist minister of note in his day, left his mark in some of the soundest philanthropic undertakings of the century. His thoughtfulness and self-sacrificing energy have lightened the sufferings and soothed the old age of many thousands. He was one of the founders of the London, Reedham, and Infant Orphan Asylums, the Earlswood Asylum for Idiots, and the Royal Hospital for Incurables. His son, Sir Charles Reed, and grandsons, have done yeoman service in carrying on to the present day the noble work begun by him.

Talbot was the third son of the late Sir Charles Reed, Member of Parliament for Hackney, and latterly for Saint Ives (Cornwall). His mother, Lady Reed, was the youngest daughter of Mr Edward Baines, Member of Parliament for Leeds. She was a lady of saintly life, of infinite gentleness and sweetness of heart, with extraordinary strength and refinement of mind, reverenced and loved by her sons and daughters, and by none more than by Talbot Reed, who bore a strong resemblance to her alike in disposition and in physical appearance.

The service that Sir Charles Reed did for his generation, both in Parliament and as Chairman of the London School Board, and in connection with many of the religious and philanthropic movements of his time, are too well known to be recapitulated here.

Talbot B. Reed was born on the 3rd of April 1852, at Hackney. His first schoolmaster was Mr Anderton of Priory House School, Upper Clapton, under whose care he remained until he was thirteen years of age. He retained through life a feeling of warm affection to Mr Anderton, who thoroughly prepared him for the more serious work ahead of him. Only a year or two ago, Reed was one of the most active of Mr Anderton's old pupils in organising a dinner in honour of his former master.

In 1865 Talbot was entered at the City of London School, then located in Milk Street, Cheapside, under the headship of Dr Abbot, where he spent four happy and industrious years of his boyhood. He is described by Mr Vardy, a school-comrade, in the course of a recent interesting article by the Editor of the *Boy's Own Paper*, as being at this period "a handsome boy, strong and well proportioned, with a frank open face, black hair, and lively dark eyes, fresh complexion, full of life and vigour, and with a clear ringing voice ... He was audacious with that charming audacity that suits some boys. On one occasion he had very calmly absented himself from the class-room during a temporary engagement by the French master, who, having returned before he was expected, and while Reed was away, demanded by what leave he had left the class-room. Reed replied with (as he would probably have expressed it) 'awful cheek,' 'If you please, sir, I took "French" leave!'"

Reed was popular at school both with masters and boys. His initials, "T.B.," soon became changed familiarly into "Tib," by which endearing nickname Mr Vardy says he was known to the last by the comrades of his school-days.

It is interesting, in the light of the prominence which in all his school stories he properly gave to out-of-door sports and athletic exercises, to have it, on the authority of his old school-fellow, that he excelled in all manly exercises. He was a first-rate football-player, and a good all-round cricketer; he was an excellent oar, and a fairly good swimmer; and until the last few months of his life no man could enjoy with more zest a game of quoits, or tennis, or a day devoted to the royal game of golf. In the early days of his manhood, with characteristic unselfishness, he risked his own life on one occasion by leaping from a rock into the sea, on the wild north Irish coast, to bring safely ashore his cousin (and life-long friend, Mr Talbot Baines, the distinguished editor of the *Leeds Mercury*), who has told me that he would, without Reed's prompt and plucky aid, inevitably have been drowned.

The large contribution he made to literature in later days amply serves to prove that the more serious studies of school were never neglected for his devotion to sport. He seldom missed the old boys' annual dinner of the City of London School. In proposing a toast at a recent dinner, he reminded Mr Asquith, M.P. (a school-fellow of Reed's) that at the school debating society they had "led off" on separate sides in a wordy battle on the red-hot controversy of "Queen Elizabeth versus Queen Mary." Every boy who has read "Sir Ludar" will remember that the hero of that charming story and Humphrey Dexter fall to blows on the same dangerous subject.

I cannot find that in his masterly pictures of public school life he drew much from his experiences at the City of London School, except, perhaps, in a few details, such as the rivalry which he describes so vividly as existing between the fifth and sixth forms in his delightful book, "The Fifth Form at Saint Dominic's." In Reed's day there was no such "set" among the juniors at the City of London School as the "guinea-pigs" and "tadpoles," who play so important a part in the story; but in a room devoted to the juniors, known as the "horse-shoe," in the old school buildings in Milk Street, many of the pranks and battles of the "guinea-pigs" and "tadpoles" were played and fought.

In 1869, at the age of seventeen, Reed left school, and joined his father and elder brother Andrew in the great firm of type-founders in Fann Street. He threw himself with strenuous application into the new work, maintaining at the same time with equal keenness his interest in football, wishing nothing better than a fierce game—"three hacks on one leg, and four on the other," as he said, and glorying in his wounds. The same strenuous energy applied to his reading at this period. A friend tells me that in a letter about this time he speaks of devouring "five of Scott's novels in a month, resulting in parental remonstrance; history; and a Greek play, in which he is not so 'rusty' as he feared." In Fann Street his practical business energies found free play, although the bias of his mind undoubtedly lay towards literature rather than commerce; but for nearly a quarter of a century he devoted himself to this work with a degree of success that was to be expected of his talents, the conscientious uprightness of his character, and his unceasing industry. At the death of Sir Charles Reed, and of his brother Andrew, Talbot became the managing director of the Type-foundry, and held that position to the time of his death.

Reed had not long left school when his creative literary instincts began to assert themselves. His apprenticeship in literature may be said to have been served in the editing of an exceedingly clever family magazine, called *The Earlsmead Chronicle*, which circulated in the family and among friends.

His earliest printed effort appeared in 1875, in a little magazine for young people, called *The Morning of Life* (published in America by Messrs Thomas Nelson and Sons. It is, by the way, a noteworthy coincidence that his first and last printed work should have been issued by this house). His contribution to *The Morning of Life* was an account in two parts of a boating expedition on the Thames, entitled "Camping Out." It has in it the promise of the freshness and vigour that were in such abundant degree characteristic of all his later descriptions of boy life.

It was in the pages of the *Boy's Own Paper* that Reed found his *métier*. Its editor writes: "From the very first number of the paper Mr Reed has been so closely and continuously identified with it, that his removal creates a void it will be impossible to fill." Any one looking through the volumes of this most admirably-conducted boys' paper will see that Talbot Reed's work is indeed the backbone of it. In Number One, Volume One, the first article, "My First Football Match," is by him; and during that year (1879) and the following years he wrote vivid descriptions of cricket-matches, boat-races; "A Boating Adventure at Parkhurst;" "The Troubles of a Dawdler;" and a series of papers on "Boys in English History." There was also a series of clever sketches of boy life, called "Boys we have Known," "The Sneak," "The Sulky Boy," "The Boy who is never Wrong," etcetera.

These short flights led the way, and prepared him for the longer and stronger flights that were to follow. In 1880 his first boys' book began to appear in the *Boy's Own Paper*, entitled "The Adventures of a Three-Guinea Watch." Charlie Newcome, the youthful hero, is a charming creation, tenderly and pathetically painted, and the story abounds in thrilling incident, and in that freshness of humour which appears more or less in all the Public School Stories. In the following year came a story of much greater power, "The Fifth Form at Saint Dominic's," by many boys considered the best of all his stories. It deserves to take its place on the shelf beside "Tom Brown's Schooldays." Indeed, a youthful enthusiast who had been reading "The Fifth Form" and "Tom Brown" about the same time, confided to me that while in the latter book he had learned to know and love one fine type of boy, in the former he learned to know and to love a whole school. The two brothers, Stephen and Oliver Greenfield, and Wraysford, and Pembury, and Loman stand out with strong personality and distinctness; and especially admirable is the art with which is depicted the gradual decadence of character in Loman, step by step, entangled in a maze of lies, and degraded by vice until self-respect is nigh crushed out.

"The Fifth Form at Saint Dominic's" was followed in 1882 by "My Friend Smith;" in 1883 came "The Willoughby Captains" (by many considered his best work); 1885 saw "Reginald Cruden;" and in the same year appeared "Follow My Leader." This story—an excellent example of Reed's peculiar power and originality in depicting school life—he wrote in three months; a feat the full significance of which is best known to those who were aware how full his mind and his hands were at that time of other pressing work. Yet the book shows no marks of undue haste.

In 1886 came "A Dog with a Bad Name," followed in 1887 by "The Master of the Shell." In 1889 Reed made a new and successful departure in "Sir Ludar: A Story of the Days of the Great Queen Bess." Here he broke away from school life, and carried his youthful readers back to the Elizabethans and the glorious incident of the Armada. There is a fine "go" and "swing" in the style of this story which recalls Kingsley to us at his best.

Following hard on "Sir Ludar" came in the same year (1889) "Roger Ingleton, Minor," a story dealing with young men rather than boys, although Tom Oliphant, a delightful boy, and Jill Oliphant, his sister, take their places among the most lovable of his youthful creations.

In "The Cock-house at Fellsgarth" (1891), and in "Dick, Tom, and Harry" (1892), Reed returned to school life for the materials of his plots, and in these fully maintained his reputation. In addition to these stories, most of which have appeared, or are about to appear, in volume form, he contributed many short stories and sketches to the Christmas and Summer numbers of the *Boy's Own*. These are also, I am glad to learn, being collected for publication in volume form.

In "Kilgorman," the last of the series of boys' books from his gifted hand, as in "Sir Ludar," he displays a fine historic sense—a capacity of living back to other times and picturing the people of another generation. Much of the scene of "Kilgorman" and of "Sir Ludar" is laid in Ireland—in the north and north-western corners of it—of all the localities in the United Kingdom perhaps the dearest to Reed's heart.

To him, in more senses than one, Ireland was a land of romance. The happiest associations of his life were there. There he wooed and won his wife, the daughter of Mr Greer, M.P. for the County of Londonderry; and he and she loved to return with ever new pleasure to inhale the pure air of Castle-rock or Ballycastle, or to enjoy the quiet of a lonely little resting-place in Donegal, on the banks of Lough Swilly, to recuperate after a year's hard work in London. It was something to see the sunshine on Reed's beautiful face when the time approached for his visit to the "Emerald Isle." When he was sore stricken in the last illness, he longed with a great longing to return, and did return, to Ireland, hoping and believing that what English air had failed to do might come to pass there. Three weeks before his death he writes to me from Ballycastle, County Antrim: "I wish you could see this place to-day bathed in sunlight, Rathlin Island in the offing, Fair Head with its stately profile straight across the bay, and beyond, in blue and grey, the lonely coast of Cantire, backed by Goatfell and the lovely hills of Argyle." He loved Ireland.

But for himself and for his family there were in Ireland associations of sadness that made the place sacred to him. His young and beloved brother Kenneth, with a comrade and kinsman, W.J. Anderson, in 1879 started on a canoe trip in Ireland, intending to explore the whole course of the Shannon and the Blackwater, together with the connecting links of lake and sea. In a gale of wind on Lough Allen—known as the "wicked Lough"—the canoes were both upset, and the two young men were drowned.

The shock in the family circle can be imagined. It was the beginning of many sorrows. Two years later, in 1881, Sir Charles Reed died; and in 1883 the family was again plunged into grief by the sad death of Talbot's eldest brother ("my 'father confessor' in all times of trouble," Talbot used to say of him), the Reverend Charles Edward Reed, who was accidentally killed by a fall over a precipice while he was on a walking expedition in Switzerland. Lady Reed, it may be here said, died in June 1891.

While most people will think that Talbot Reed's boys' books are his best bequest to literature, he considered them of less importance in the work of his life than his book entitled "A History of the Old English Letter Foundries; with Notes Historical and Bibliographical on the Rise and Progress of English Typography" (Elliot Stock, 1887), the preparation of which cost him ten years of research and labour. His boys' books were the spontaneous utterance of his joyous nature, and their production he regarded in the light of a recreation amid the more serious affairs of life. He had an ambition, which the results of his labour fully justified, to be regarded as an authority on Typography. I can remember his amusement, and perhaps annoyance, when he had gone down to a Yorkshire town to deliver a lecture on some typographical subject, to find that the walls and hoardings of the town were decorated with posters, announcing the lecture as by "Talbot B. Reed, author of 'A Dog with a Bad Name!'"

But all scholars and book-lovers will regard this work of his on "The History of the Old English Letter Foundries" as being of supreme value. In it, as he himself says, he tells the story of the fifteenth century heroes of the punch and matrix and mould, who made English printing an art ere yet the tyranny of an age of machinery was established. Whatever Talbot Reed's pen touched it adorned, and in the light of his mind what seemed dry and dusty corners of literary history became alive with living human interest.

Besides this great work, he edited the book left unfinished by his friend Mr Blades, entitled "The Pentateuch of Printing," to which he added a biographical memoir of Mr Blades.

All that related to the craft of printing was profoundly interesting to Reed, whether viewed from the practical, or the historic, or the artistic side. His types were to him no mere articles of commerce, they were objects of beauty; to him the craft possessed the fascination of having a great history, and the legitimate pride of having played a great part in the world.

Reed delivered more than one admirable public lecture on subjects related to the art of printing. One he delivered at the Society of Arts, on "Fashions in Printing" (for which he received one of the Society's silver medals), and another on "Baskerville," the interesting type-founder and printer of Birmingham in the last century, to whom a chapter of "The History" is devoted.

Only two years before his death Reed was one of a small band of book-lovers who founded the Bibliographical Society, a body which aims at making easier, by the organising of literature, the labours of literary men, librarians, and students generally. From its start he undertook, in the midst of many pressing personal duties, the arduous task of honorary secretaryship of the young society—an office which he regarded as one of great honour and usefulness, but which entailed upon him, at a time when his health could ill bear the strain, hard organising and clerical work, cheerfully undertaken, and continued until a few weeks before his death. The first two published Parts of the Transactions of the Bibliographical Society, edited by him, are models of what such work ought to be.

Reed was a Fellow of the Society of Antiquaries, and for many years was an active member of the Library Association. His own library of books bearing on Typography, Bibliography, and many a kindred subject, the harvest of many years' collecting, is unique. It was a pleasure to see the expression of Reed's face when he came upon a new book really after his mind, or, still better, an old book, "Anything fifteenth century or early sixteenth," he used to say; any relic or scrap from Caxton's or De Worde's Press; any specimen of a "truant type" on the page of an early book; or a Caslon, or a Baskerville in good condition; or one of the beauties from Mr Morris's modern Press. Charles Lamb himself could not have looked more radiant or more happy in the sense of possession.

Reed laboured successfully also in another department of literature—in journalism. For many years he wrote a non-political leading article each week for the *Leeds Mercury*. His wide culture, his quiet humour, and light, graceful touch, were qualities that gave to his journalistic work far more than an ephemeral value. In politics Reed was a life-long Liberal; he utterly disapproved, however, of Mr Gladstone's latter-day policy in Ireland. Reed was a member of the Reform Club and of the Savile Club.

In these notes I have written rather of Reed's work than of the man himself. This is as he would have had it. There was in him a magnetic charm that attracted all who came near him, and which bound his friends to him as by "hooks of steel." Erect and manly in bearing, he stepped along, never apparently in a hurry, never dawdling. One had only to look in his beautiful face, the bright kind eyes, the high wide brow, and to come under the spell of his winning smile, to obtain a glimpse of the noble soul within.

A calm, strong nature his, facing the world, with all its contingencies, bravely and with constant buoyant cheerfulness. He walked through life with eyes and heart wide open to the joy of the world, brightening and lightening it for others as he went. He was always ready to stretch out a helping hand to the weak and falling ones who came across his path. Never merely an optimist, he yet lived and died in the full, simple faith that—

> "God's in his heaven,
> All's right with the world."

Socially, Reed was the life and soul of any party of friends. There were certain American student-songs which he was wont to sing with a quiet and inimitable drollery, very refreshing to hear, and which those who heard them are not likely readily to forget. His love of music was part of his nature. His reposeful, wooing touch on the piano or organ, either when he was extemporising or when he interpreted one of the masters, expressed the inner working of his own gentle spirit. Whether in his own family, or among friends, or in the midst of his Foundry workmen, he was universally beloved.

A true, loyal, and friendly spirit like his was sure to have "troops of friends." To three friends in Highgate he wrote, during his last sad visit to Ireland, the following beautiful letter. Mrs Reed was at the moment detained in Highgate, nursing their eldest boy, who was ill.

"Westoncrofts, Ballymoney, *October 6, 1893.*

"Talbot, the exile, unto the faithful assembled at the hour of evening service at H—; to H— the beloved banker, and S— our brother, and H— our joyous counsellor, and all and sundry, greeting: peace be with you! Know, brethren, that I am with you in the spirit; neither is there any chair in which I would not sit, nor pipe I would not smoke, nor drink I would not drink, so as I might be one with you, and hear your voices. In good sooth, I would travel far to catch the wisdom that droppeth from the lips of H—, or sit among the philosophers with S—, or laugh with the great laugh of H—. I would do all this, and more also, could I make one with you around the familiar hearth.

"Yet know, brethren, that I shall come presently, and strictly demand an account of what is said and done, what mighty problems are solved, what joys are discovered, what tribulations are endured, in my absence.

"Meanwhile, I would have you to know that I am here, not without my teachers, for I read daily in the great missal of Nature, writ by the scribe

Autumn in letters of crimson and gold; also in the trim pages of the gathered fields, with borders of wood-cut; also in the ample folios of ocean, with its wide margins of surf and sand. These be my masters, set forth in a print not hard to read, yet not so easy, methinks, as the faces of friends. Perchance when *she* cometh, in whose light I interpret many things, I shall have rest to learn more therefrom; for now I am as a sail without wind, or a horn without his blower, or a stone without his sling.

"Yet am I not here to no purpose. There is a certain coy nymph, 'Health' by name, who is reported in these parts—her I am charged to seek. Where she hides 'twere hard to say; whether on the hill-side, golden with bracken, or in the spray of the sea, or on the bluff headland, or by the breezy links— in all these I seek her. Sometimes I spy her afar off; but the wanton comes and goes. Yet I am persuaded I shall presently find her, and bring her home rejoicing to them that sent me.

"Finally, brethren, I pray you, have me often in your remembrance, and report to me such things as concern our common welfare, for I desire ardently to hear of you.

"Farewell, from one who loves you and counts himself your brother.

"T.B. Reed."

Alas! "the coy nymph, 'Health' by name," was never found. Within a week or two of the despatch of this letter, he became so much worse that he was advised by the Belfast doctors to return at once to London. He suffered from a hopeless internal malady, which he bore with heroic patience.

At Highgate, on 28th November 1893, he passed peacefully away.

It was given to him in his short life—for he condensed into the span of forty-two years the literary labours of a long life—to materially add by his charming boys' books to the happiness of the youth of his generation. It was given to him also by his labour and research to make a solid contribution to the learning of his time. He has enriched many lives by his friendship, and by the example of his unceasing thoughtfulness for the welfare of others. To all who had the inestimable privilege of knowing Talbot Reed, there will be the remembrance of a man "matchless for gentleness, honesty, and courage,"—the very ideal of a chivalrous English gentleman.

John Sime.

Highgate, London, *February 1894.*

Chapter One
Wandering Lights

It was the first time Tim and I had fallen out, and to this day I could scarcely tell you how it arose.

We had gone out on to the headland to drive in the sheep; for the wind was blowing up from seaward, and it was plain to tell that the night would be a wild one. Father was away with the trawlers off Sheep Haven, and would be ill pleased should he return to-morrow to find any of the flock amissing. So, though mother lay sick in the cottage, with none to tend her, Tim and I, because of the dread we had of our father's displeasure, left her and went out to seek the sheep before the storm broke.

It was no light task, for the dog was lame, and the wind carried back our shouts into our very teeth. The flock had straggled far and wide in search of the scanty grass, and neither Tim nor I had our hearts in the work.

Presently Tim took a stone to dislodge one stubborn ewe, where it hid beside a rock, and, as luck would have it, struck not her but my cheek, which received a sharp cut.

"Faith, and you'll make a fine soldier when you're grown," said I, in a temper, "if that's the best you can shoot."

Tim often said he would be a soldier when he came to be a man, and was touchy on the point.

"Shoot, is it?" said he, picking up another stone; "you blackguard, stand where ye are and I'll show yez."

And he let fly and struck me again on the self-same place; and I confess I admired his skill more than his brotherly love.

I picked up the stone and flung it back. But the wind took it so that it struck not Tim but the ewe. Whereat Tim laughed loudly and called me a French spalpeen. That was more than I could bear.

"I'll fight you for that," said I, flinging my cap on the ground and stamping a foot on it.

"Come on wid ye," retorted Tim, giving his buckle a hitch.

And there, on the lonely, wind-swept cliff, we two brothers stood up to one another. Con, the dog, limped between us with a whine.

"You might tie the dog to the gate till we're done, Barry," said Tim.

"You're right, Tim," said I; "I will."

It took no long time, but 'twas long enough to cool my blood, and when I returned to Tim I had less stomach for the fight than before.

"Was it 'Frenchman' you said?" asked I, hoping he might say no.

"Troth and I did," said he.

But it seemed to me he too was less fiery than when he spoke last.

So we fought. And I know not how it went. We were a fair match. What I lacked in strength I made up for in quickness, and if Tim hit me hard I hit him often.

But it was a miserable business, and our hearts were sorer than our bodies. For we loved one another as we loved our own lives. And on a day like this, when mother lay dying at home, and father was out with the trawlers in the tempest, we lacked spirit to fight in earnest. Only when Tim called me "Frenchman" it was not in me to stand meekly by.

I know that when it was over, and we parted sulky and bruised each his own way, I flung myself on my face at the edge of the cliff and wished I had never been born.

How long I lay I know not.

When I looked up the day was dark with tempest. The whistle of the wind about my ears mingled with the hoarse thunder of the surf as it broke on the beach, four hundred feet below me, and swept round the point into the lough. The taste of brine was on my lips, and now and again flakes of foam whirled past me far inland. From Dunaff to Malin the coast was one long waste of white water. And already the great Atlantic rollers, which for a day past had brought their solemn warning in from the open, were breaking miles out at sea, and racing in on the shore like things pursued.

As for me, my spirits rose as I looked out and saw it all. For I loved the sea in its angry moods. And this promise of tempest seemed somehow to accord with the storm that was raging in my own breast. It made me forget Tim and the sheep, and even mother.

I tried to get up on my feet, but the wind buffeted me back before I reached my knees, and I was fain to lie prone, with my nose to the storm, blinking through half-closed eyes out to sea.

For a long time I lay thus. Then I seemed to descry at the point of the bay windward a sail. It was a minute or more before I could be certain I saw aright. Yes, it was a sail.

What craft could be mad enough in such weather to trust itself to the mercies of the bay? Even my father, the most daring of helmsmen, would give Fanad Head a wide berth before he put such a wind as this at his back. This stranger must be either disabled or ignorant of the coast, or she would never drive in thus towards a lee-shore like ours. Boy as I was, I knew better seamanship than that.

Yet as I watched her, she seemed to me neither cripple nor fool. She was a cutter-rigged craft, long and low in the water, under close canvas, and to my thinking wonderfully light and handy in the heavy sea. She did not belong to these parts—even I could tell that—and her colours, if she had any, had gone with the wind.

The question was, would she on her present tack weather Fanad Head (on which I lay) and win the lough? And if not, how could she escape the rocks on which every moment she was closing?

At first it seemed that nothing could save her, for she broke off short of the point, and drove in within half-a-mile of the rocks. Then, while I waited to see the end of her, she suddenly wore round, and after staggering a moment while the sea broke over her, hauled up to the wind, and careening over, with her mainsail sweeping the water, started gaily on the contrary tack.

It was so unlike anything any of our clumsy trawler boats were capable of, that I was lost in admiration at the suddenness and daring of the manoeuvre. But Fanad was still to be weathered, and close as she sailed to the wind, it seemed hardly possible to gain sea-room to clear it.

Yet she cleared it, even though the black rocks frowned at her not a cable's length from her lee-quarter, and the wind laid her over so that her mast-head seemed almost to touch them as it passed. Then, once clear, up went her helm as she turned again into the wind, and slipped, with the point on her weather-quarter, into the safe waters of the lough.

I was so delighted watching this adventure from my lonely perch that I did not notice the October afternoon was nearly spent, and that the light was beginning to fade. The storm gathered force every moment, so that when at last I turned to go home I had to crawl a yard or two to shelter before I could stand on my feet.

As for the sheep, unless Tim had driven them in, which was not likely, they would have to shift for themselves for this night. It was too late to see them, and Con, who limped at my heels, had not a yap left in him.

As I staggered home, leaning my back against the wind, I could not help wondering what this strange boat might be, and why she should make for the lough on so perilous a course. She might be a smuggler anxious to avoid the observation of the revenue officers. If so, her cargo must be precious indeed to make up for the risk she ran. Or she might be a foreigner, driven in by one of the king's cruisers, which had not dared to follow her into the bay.

Whatever she was, she was a pretty sailer, and prettily handled. I wondered if ever I, when I grew to be a man, should be able to weather a point as skilfully.

It was night before I reached our cabin, and all there was dark. Neither Tim nor father was home, the fire was out on the hearth, and the poor fevered sufferer lay tossing and breathing hard on the bed.

She was worse, far worse than when we left her in the morning; and I could have died of shame when I came to think that all those hours she had lain alone and untended. I struck a light and put it in the window.

"Is that Barry?" said she faintly.

"Ay, mother, it's Barry," said I, going to the bed and bending over her.

"Bring the light, and let me look at you," she said.

I obeyed. She scrutinised my face eagerly, and then turned her head wearily on the pillow.

"Barry," said she presently.

"Well?" said I, as I took the hot worn hand in mine.

She lay silent a long while, so that I thought she had fallen asleep, then she said,—

"Where is father?"

"Away with the boats."

"And Tim?"

"I can't say. Tim and I fought the day, and—"

"Fought? Ay, there'll be fighting enough before wrong's made right, Barry. Listen! I'm dying, son, but I must see him before I go."

"Is it Tim?" said I.

"No." Then she lifted herself in her bed, and her face was wild and excited as she clutched my hand. "Barry, it's Gorman I must see—Maurice Gorman. Fetch him to me. Make him come. Tell him I'm a dying woman, and must speak before I go. There's time yet—go, Barry!"

"Mr Gorman!" exclaimed I. What could my mother want with his honour down at Knockowen?

"Ay, and quickly—or it will be too late."

Knockowen was across the lough, five miles up above Dunree. It would be hours on a night like this before he could be here. But my mother continued to moan, "Go, Barry—make haste." So, much against my will, I put on my cap and prepared to leave her alone. At the door she called me back.

"Kiss me, Barry," said she. Then before I could obey her she fell to raving.

"Give me back the lassie," she cried, "dead or alive. She's more to me than all Kilgorman! Trust me, Mr Maurice—I'll breathe never a word if you'll but save Mike. It's false—he never had a hand in it! Some day truth will out—if the lad's mine no harm shall come to him. I'll use him against you, Mr Maurice. The truth's buried, but it's safe. There's more than earth under a hearthstone." And she laughed in a terrible way.

After a minute she opened her eyes again and saw me.

"Not gone, Barry? For pity's sake, fetch him, or I must go myself." And she even tried to get up from her bed.

This settled it, and I rushed from the house, whimpering with misery and terror.

What was it all about? Why did she send me away thus on a fool's errand? For Mr Gorman was not likely to come out on a night like this at the bidding of Mike Gallagher's English wife.

If there had only been some one I could have sent to mind her while I was gone! But our cabin on the bleak headland was miles from a neighbour—Knockowen, whither I was speeding, was indeed the nearest place.

For a lad of twelve it was no easy task on a dark stormy night like this to cross the lough. But I thought nothing of that. Most of my short life I had spent afloat, and I knew every rock and creek along the shores.

The boat lay tugging at her moorings when I got down to her, as if impatient to be away. Luckily her mast was up. It would need but the least taste of canvas to run her across. The business would be coming back in the face of the wind.

Sure enough, when I cast off, she rushed through the water like something mad. And again my spirits rose as I heard the hiss of the foam at her bows, and felt her rear and plunge among the big boisterous waves.

After a time I could catch the light at Knockowen as it flickered in the wind, and put up my helm so as to clear the shoal. This would bring me close under Kilgorman rock, whence I could drive before the wind as far as Knockowen.

To my surprise, as I closed in on the shore I saw strange lights at the water's edge, and casting my eyes up towards Kilgorman (which I never did in those days without a qualm, because of the ghost that haunted it) I seemed to see a moving light there also.

I said a hurried prayer, and put round my helm into the wind before my time. Even the shoal, thought I, was less to fear than the unearthly terrors of that awful deserted house.

By good luck the strong wind carried me in clear of the bank and so into fairly still water, and in half-an-hour more I was in under the light of Knockowen, mooring my boat in his honour's little harbour.

It must have been near midnight, and I was wondering how I should waken the house and deliver my message, when a voice close beside me said,—

"Are the guns all landed and taken up to the house?"

It was his honour's voice. But I could not see him in the dark.

"I beg your pardon, your honour," said I, "it's me, Barry Gallagher."

A quick step came down to where I stood, and a hand was laid on my shoulder.

"You! What do you here?" said his honour sharply, for he had evidently expected some one else.

"If you please, sir, my mother's sick, and she sent me to bid you come before she died."

He made a startled gesture, as I thought, and said, "What does she want me for?"

"It's to tell your honour something. I couldn't rightly say what, for she spoke strangely."

"I'll come in the morning if the weather mends," said he.

"I've the boat here for you, sir," I ventured to say, for I guessed the morning would be too late.

"Leave her there, and go up to the house. You may sleep in the kitchen."

What could I do? For the first time that night I knew for certain I hated his honour. My mother's dying message was nothing to him. And she, poor soul, lay in the cabin alone.

Knockowen was a poor shambling sort of house. Strangers wondered why Maurice Gorman, who owned Kilgorman as well, chose to live in this place instead of the fine mansion near the lough mouth. But to the country people this was no mystery. Kilgorman had an evil name, and for twelve years, since its late master died, had stood desolate and empty—tenanted only, so it was said, by a wandering ghost, and no place for decent Christian folk to dwell in.

As I lay curled up that stormy night in his honour's kitchen, I could not help thinking of the strange lights I had seen as I rowed in by the shore. Where did they come from, and what did they mean? I shuddered, and said one prayer more as I thought of it.

Then my curiosity got the better of me, and I crept to the window and looked out. The wind howled dismally, but the sky was clearing, and the moon raced in and out among the clouds. Away down across the lough I could see the dim outline of Fanad, below which was the little home where, for all I knew, my mother at that moment lay dead. And opposite it loomed out the grey bleak hill below which, even by this half light, I fancied I could detect the black outline of Kilgorman standing grimly in the moonlight.

It may have been fancy, but as I looked I even thought I could see once more moving lights between the water's edge and the house, and I slunk back to my corner by the fire with a shiver.

Presently, his honour came in with a candle. He had evidently been up all night, and looked haggard and anxious.

"Get up," said he, "and make the boat ready."

I rose to obey, when he called me back.

"Come here," said he harshly. And he held the candle to my face and stared hard at me. It was a sinister, sneering face that looked into mine, and as I returned the stare my looks must have betrayed the hatred that was in my mind.

"Which of Gallagher's boys are you?" he demanded.

"Barry, plaze your honour."

"How old are you?"

"I think twelve, sir—the same as Tim." For Tim and I were twins.

He looked hard at me again, and then said, "What was it your mother sent word?"

"She said would your honour plaze to come quick, for she felt like dying, and wished to spake to you before."

"Was that all?"

"Indeed, sir, she talked queerly the night about a dead lassie, and called on your honour to save my father, if you plaze, sir."

He went to a cupboard and poured himself out a glass of raw whisky and drank it. Then he beckoned to me to follow him down to the boat.

Chapter Two
A load of turnips

Mr Gorman seated himself silently in the stern, while I shoved off, and hauled up the sail.

The storm was blowing still, but more westerly, so that the water was quieter, and we could use the wind fairly to the point of the shoals. After that it would be hard work to make my father's cabin.

I handed the sheet to his honour, and curled myself up in the bows. Maurice Gorman was no great seaman, as I knew. But it was not for me to thrust myself forward when he took the helm. Yet I confess I felt a secret pleasure as I looked at the breakers ahead, and wondered how soon he would call me aft to steer him through them.

To-night, as it seemed to me, he hugged the eastern shore more than usual, thereby laying up for himself all the harder task when the time came to cross in the face of the wind.

"Begging your honour's pardon," said I at last, "luff her, sir."

He paid no heed, but held on as we went till the shoals were long distanced, and the black cliff of Kilgorman rose above us.

The day was now dawning, and the terrors of the place were somewhat diminished. Yet I confess I looked up at the gaunt walls and chimneys with uneasiness.

Now, as we came nearer, the mystery of the moving lights of the night before suddenly cleared itself. For snugly berthed in a narrow creek of the shore lay the strange cutter whose daring entry into the lough I had yesterday witnessed. At the sight of her the curiosity I had felt, but which my poor mother's message had driven from my head, revived.

Who and what was she? and what was she doing in Lough Swilly?

Then I recalled the strange words his honour had spoken last night in my hearing, about the arms being landed and stowed. And I remembered hearing some talk among the fisher folk of foreign weapons being smuggled into Ireland against the king's law, and of foreign soldiers coming, to help the people to tight against his Majesty.

I was too young to understand what it all meant, or why his Majesty was to be fought with; for we were comfortable enough in our little cabin, what with the sheep and my mother's savings, and my father's fish, and the little that Tim and I could earn ferrying passengers over the lough. I was too young, I say, to know what wanted altering, but the sight of this queer-looking craft set me thinking about it.

"Get out your oar," said his honour suddenly, letting the sheet fly, and running the boat into the creek.

My heart sank, for I hoped we were going across to where my poor mother lay.

I got out the oar, and paddled the boat into the creek till we came up to the stern of the cutter. *Cigale*—that was her name, painted on the stern-board; but there was nothing to show her port or the flag she flew.

At the sound of our bows grating on her side one of her crew ran aft and looked over. He had a strange foreign appearance in his red cap, and curls, and white teeth, and looked like some startled animal about to spring on us. But his honour shouted something in French, and the man scrambled over the side of the cutter with a grin and jumped lightly into our boat, talking rapidly all the while.

I do not think Mr Gorman understood all he said, for he presently ordered the man to hold his peace, and stepped ashore, beckoning me to follow him.

I obeyed after making fast the painter. As we scrambled up the rocks and reached the road which leads down from Kilgorman to the shore, I was surprised to see several carts standing laden with sacks or straw, as though on the way to market. Still more surprised was I when among the knot of men, half-foreign sailors, half countrymen, who stood about, sheltering as best they could from the sleet (for the weather was coming in yet worse from the west), I recognised my father.

If he noticed me at first he made no sign of it, but walked up to Maurice Gorman with a rough nod.

"Is all landed and stowed?" said his honour, repeating the question of last night.

"'Tis," said my father shortly, nodding in the direction of the carts.

"How many are in the house?"

"There's two hundred."

"Father," said I, breaking in at this point, in spite of all the Gormans of Donegal, "you're needed at home. Mother's dying, and sent me for his honour to speak to her."

My father started, and his sunburnt cheeks paled a little as he looked at Mr Gorman and then across the lough. He would fain have flown that moment to the beat, but I could see he was too far under his honour's thumb to do so without leave.

"We cannot spare you, Mike, till the job is finished. We must get the carts to Derry before night."

"I'm thinking," said my father, "Barry here knows the road to Derry as well as me. Who'll be minding a young boy on a cart of turnips?"

His honour mused a moment, and then nodded.

"Can you get the cutter away in this wind?" asked he.

"I could get her away as easy as I got her in," said my father; "but she's well enough as she is for a day or two, by your honour's leave."

"Father," said I, all excitement, "sure it wasn't you ran the cutter into the lough round Fanad yesterday? I knew nobody else could have done it!"

My father grinned at the compliment.

"That's the boy knows one end of a ship from the other," said he.

Mr Gorman looked at me, and a thought seemed to strike him.

"Come here!" said he, beckoning me to him.

Once again he looked hard in my face, and I looked hard back.

"So you are Barry?" he demanded.

"I am," said I.

"And you'd like to be a sailor?"

"No," I retorted. It was a lie, but I would be under no favour to his honour.

His honour grunted, and talked in a low voice to my father, who presently said to me,—

"Take the turnips to Joe Callan's, in Derry, on the Ship Quay. Wait till dark before you go into the city. Tell him there's more where these came from."

"Is it guns you mane?" said I.

"Hold your tongue, you limb of darkness," growled my father. "It's turnips. If any one asks you, mind you know nothing, and never heard of his honour in your life."

By which I understood this was a very secret errand, and like enough to land me in Derry Jail before all was done. Had I not been impatient to see my father and his honour away to Fanad, I think I should have made excuses. But I durst not say another word, and with a heavy heart clambered to the top of the turnips and started on my long journey.

Before I had passed the hill I could see the white sail of our little boat dancing through the broken water of the lough, and knew that my father and Mr Gorman were on their way to set my mother's mind at rest. In the midst of my trouble and ill-humour I smiled to think what a poor figure his honour would have cut trying to make Fanad in that wind. My father could sail in the teeth of anything, and some day folk would be able to say the same of his son Barry.

It was a long, desolate drive over stony hills and roads whose ruts swallowed half my wheels, with now and then a waste of bog to cross, and now and then a stream to ford. For hours I met not a soul nor saw a sign of life except the cattle huddling on the hillside, or the smoke of some far-away cabin.

My mare was a patient, leisurely beast, with no notion of reaching the city before her time, and no willingness to exchange her sedate jog for all the whipping or "shooing" in Ireland.

Presently, as it came to the afternoon, I left the mountain road and came on to the country road from Fahan to Derry. Here I met more company; but no one heeded me much, especially when it was seen that my turnips were a poor sort, and that he who had charge of them was but a slip of a boy, with not a word to say to any one.

"Are you for Derry?" one woman asked as she overtook me on the road.

"So you may say," said I, hoping that would be the end of her.

But she carried a bundle, and was not to be put aside so easily.

"I'll just take a lift with you," said she.

But I jogged on without a word.

"Arrah, will you stop till I get up? Is it deaf ye are?" said she.

"'Deed I am," said I, whipping my beast.

It went to my heart to play the churl to a woman, but I durst not let her up on the turnips, where perhaps a chance kick of her feet might betray the ugly guns beneath.

I was sorry afterwards I did not yield to my better instincts, for the woman was known in these parts, and with her perched beside me no one would have looked twice at me or my cart.

As it was, when I had shaken her off, and left her rating me loudly till I was out of sight, I passed one or two folk who, but that it was growing dusk, might have caused me trouble. One was a clergyman, who hailed me and asked did not I think my beast would be the better of a rest, and that, for turnips, my load seemed a heavy one, and so forth.

To ease him, I was forced to halt at the next village, to give the poor beast a feed and a rest. Here two soldiers came up and demanded where I came from.

"From Fahan," said I, naming the town I had lately passed.

"Whose turnips are these?"

"Mister Gallagher's," said I.

They seemed inclined to be more curious; but as good luck would have it, the clergyman came up just then and spoke to me in a friendly way as he passed, for he was glad to see me merciful to my beast.

And the soldiers, when they saw me acquainted with so reverend a gentleman, took for granted I was on a harmless errand, and went further on to inquire for the miscreant they were in search of.

The fellow of the yard where I fed my horse laughed as he watched me mount up on to my turnips.

"Faith, them's the boys to smell a rat. It's guns they're looking for; as if they'd travel by daylight on the highroad."

"I'm told a great many arms are being smuggled into the country," said the clergyman.

"To be sure," replied the man; "but if they get this length it's by the hill-roads and after dark. Why, I'll go bail they would have looked for guns under this gossoon's turnips if your reverence hadn't known him."

It seemed to me time to drive on, and with a salute to his reverence I touched up my horse smartly, and left these two to finish their talk without me.

By this time it was nearly dark, so that I had less trouble from passers-by. My beast, despite her meal, showed no signs of haste, and I was forced to lie patiently on the top of my load, waiting her pleasure to land me in Derry.

The clock was tolling ten as I came on to the Ship Quay, and tired enough I was with my long day's drive. Yet I was a little proud to have come to my journey's end safely, albeit that story I had told about Fahan stuck in my conscience.

I had been once before with my father to Joe Callan's, who kept a store of all sorts of goods, and was one of the best-known farmers' tradesmen in the city. It was some time before I could arouse him and bring him down to let me in. And while I waited, rousing the echoes, I was very nearly being wrecked in port, for a watchman came up and demanded what I wanted disturbing the peace of the city at that hour.

When I explained that I had brought Mr Callan a load of turnips, he wanted to know where they came from, and why they should arrive so late.

"The roads were bad between this and Fahan," said I.

To my alarm he took up a turnip in his hand and put it to his nose.

"I'm thinking Joe Callan's no judge of a turnip," said he, "if this is what suits him. Maybe that's why you're so anxious to get them in after dark. He'll not wake out of his sleep for the like of these, so you may just shoot them in a heap at his door, and they'll be safe enough till the morning."

My jaw dropped when he proposed this and made ready to lend me a hand.

"Begging your honour's pardon," said I, "I was to spake to Mister Callan about the turnips."

"Sure, I can tell him that. Let the man sleep."

"But the horse has been on the road all day," said I.

The watchman pricked his ears.

"All day, and only came from Fahan?" said he.

Here, to my vast relief, a window opened above me and a head appeared.

"What's the noise about at all, at all?" called Mr Callan.

"'Deed that's just what I'm asking him," said the watchman. "And since you're awake, Mr Callan, you may see to it. To my thinking the noise is not worth the turnips. So good-night to you."

I was never more glad to see a man's back. In due time Mr Callan came down in his night-cap, lantern in hand.

"Turnips," said he, as he looked first at me, then at the cart. "Whose turnips are they?"

"They're from Knockowen, sir," said I. "My father, Mike Gallagher, bade me tell you there's more where they came from."

He pulled the bolt of his yard gate without a word, and signed to me to back in the cart; which I did, dreading every moment lest the watchman should return.

When we were inside, the gate was shut, and Mr Callan turned his lantern towards me.

"You're a young lad to send with a load like this," said he. "Did no one overhaul you on the road?"

I told him about the two soldiers, and what the man at the inn had said.

He said nothing, but bade me unload.

The turnips were soon taken out. Under them was a layer of sacking, and under that some thirty or forty muskets, with a box or two of ammunition.

These Mr Callan and I carefully carried up to a loft and deposited in a hollow space which had been prepared in a pile of hay, which was carefully covered up again, so as to leave no trace of the murderous fodder it hid.

"Tell Mr Gorman—tell your father, I mean, that his turnips are in great demand, and I can sell all he's got."

"I will," said I.

"Now put in the horse and take your rest, for you must start back betimes in the morning."

"Plaze, sir," I ventured to say, "I'd sooner eat than sleep, by your leave."

"You shall do both," said he, for he was in great good-humour.

So I got a bite of pork and a scone, and curled myself up in the warm hay and slept like a top.

Before daybreak Mr Callan roused me.

"Make haste now," said he, "or you'll not be home by night. And see here, I've a message for Mr Gorman."

"Mr Gorman?" said I, remembering what I had been told.

"You are right, sonnie. You do not know Mr Gorman," said the tradesman, slapping me on the back and laughing. "If you did know him, I would have bid you tell him that people talk of him here, and say he lacks zeal in a good cause. If lie is resolved to deal in turnips, he must deal in them largely, and not go behind our backs to them that deal in other trades. Mark that."

I confess it sounded very like a riddle, and I had to say the words over many times to myself before I could be sure of carrying them.

Then, my cart being loaded with straw, I bade Mr Callan good-day, and started on my long journey back to Knockowen.

Chapter Three
Waking

Had it not been for what I dreaded to find at home, my journey back from Derry would have been light enough; for now I was rid of my turnips I had nothing to fear from inquisitive wayfarers. Nor had I cause to be anxious as to the way, for my mare knew she was homeward bound, and stepped out briskly with no encouragement from me.

Indeed I had so little to do that about noon, when we had got off the highroad on to the hill-track, I curled myself up in the straw and fell asleep. Nor did I wake till the cart suddenly came to a standstill, and I felt myself being lifted out of my nest.

At first I thought I was back already at Knockowen, and wondered at the speed the old jade had made while I slept. But as soon as I had rubbed my eyes I found we were still on the hillside, and that my awakers were a handful of soldiers.

They demanded my name and my master's. When I told them Mr Gorman of Knockowen, they were a thought less rough with me; for his honour was known as a friend of the government. Nevertheless they said they must search my cart, and bade me help them to unload the straw.

I could not help laughing as I saw them so busy.

"What's the limb laughing at?" said one angrily. "Maybe he's not so innocent as he looks."

"'Deed, sir," said I, "I was laughing at the soldiers I met at Fahan, who thought I'd got guns under his honour's turnips. I warrant Mr Gorman won't laugh at that. Maybe it's guns you're looking for too. They're easy hid in a load of straw."

At this they looked rather abashed, although they thought fit to cuff me for an impudent young dog. And when the straw was all out, and nothing found underneath, it was not a little hard on me that they left me to put it in again myself, roundly rating one another for the sorry figure they cut.

I was too glad to be rid of them to raise much clamour about the straw, and loaded it back as best I could, wondering if all his Majesty's servants were as wide-awake as the smuggler-catchers of Donegal.

This was my only adventure till about seven o'clock when I sighted the lights of Knockowen, and knew this tedious journey was at an end.

His honour, I was told, was not at home. He had crossed to Fanad to be present at the wake of my poor mother, who, I heard, had died long before my father and Mr Gorman could reach her yesterday. She was to be buried, they told me, on the next day at Kilgorman; and I could guess why there was all this haste. My father was needed to steer the *Cigale* out of the lough, and his honour would be keen enough to get the funeral over for that reason.

With a very heavy heart I left the weary horse in the stable and betook myself to his honour's harbour. Only one boat lay there, a little one with a clumsy lug-sail, ill-enough fitted for a treacherous lough like the Swilly. I knew her of old, however, and was soon bounding over the waves, with the dim outline of Fanad standing out ahead in the moonlight.

My heart sank to my boots as I drew nearer and discerned an unusual glow of light from the cabin window, and heard, carried across the water on the breeze, the sounds of singing and the wail of a fiddle. I dreaded to think of the dear body that lay there heedless of all the noise, whose eyes I should never see and whose voice I should never hear more. I could not help calling to mind again the strange words she had last spoken—of her longing to see his honour, of her wandering talk about a dead lassie and the hearthstone, and of some danger that threatened my father. It was all a mystery to me. Yet it was a mystery which, boy as I was, I resolved some day to explain.

The landing-place was full of boats, by which I knew that all the lough-side and many from the opposite shore had come to the wake. His honour's boat was there among them. So was one belonging to the *Cigale*.

I felt tempted, instead of entering the cabin, to wander up on to the headland and lie there, looking out to the open sea, and so forget my troubles. But the thought of Tim and my father hindered me, and I clambered up to the cabin.

The door stood open, because, as I thought, so many folk were about it that it would not shut. As I made my way among them I was barely heeded—indeed there were many who did not even know me. I pushed my way into the cabin, in which were stifling heat and smoke and the fumes of whisky. There, on the bed in the corner, where I had seen her last, but now lit up with a glare of candles, lay my poor mother, with her eyes closed and her hands folded across her breast. At the foot of the bed sat my father, haggard and wretched, holding a glass of whisky in his hand, which now and again he put to his lips to give him the Dutch courage he needed. At the bedside stood Tim with a scowl on his face as he glared, first, on the noisy mourners, and then looked down on the white face on the pillow. At the fireplace sat his honour, buried in thought, and not heeding the talk of the jovial priest who sat and stirred his cup beside him. There, too, among the crowd of dirge-singing, laughing, whisky-drinking neighbours, I could see the outlandish-looking skipper of the *Cigale*.

It was a weird, woeful spectacle, and made me long more than ever for the pure, fresh breezes of the lonely headland. But Tim looked round as I entered, and his face, till now so black and sullen, lit up as he saw me, and he beckoned me to him. When last we parted it had been in anger and shame; now, over the body of our dead mother, we met in peace and brotherly love, and felt stronger each of us by the presence of the other.

My father, half-stupid with sorrow and whisky, roused himself and called out my name.

"Arrah, Barry, my son, are you there? Faith, it's a sore day for the motherless lad. Howl, boys!"

And the company set up a loud wail in my honour, and pressed round me, to pat me on the head or back and say some word of consolation.

Presently his honour motioned me to him.

"Well?" said he inquiringly.

"All right, sir," said I.

"That's a man," said he. "Your mother was dead before I reached her yesterday."

"She was English," said the garrulous priest, who stood by, lifting his voice above the general clamour. "She never took root among us. Sure, your honour will remember her when she was my lady's-maid at Kilgorman. Ochone, that was a sad business!"

His honour did not attend to his reverence, but continued to look hard at me in that strange way of his.

"A sad business," continued the priest, turning round for some more attentive listener. "It was at Kilgorman that Barry and Tim were born—mercy on them!—the night that Terence Gorman, his honour's brother, was murdered on the mountain. I mind the night well. Dear, oh! Every light in Kilgorman went out that night. The news of the murder killed the lady and her little babe. I mind the time well, for I was called to christen the babe. Do you mind Larry McQuilkin of Kerry Keel, O'Brady? It was his wife as was nursing-woman to the child—as decent a woman as ever lived. She—"

Here his honour looked up sharply, and his reverence, pleased to have a better audience, chattered on:—

"Sure, your honour will remember Biddy McQuilkin, for she served at Knockowen when the little mistress there was born—"

"Where's Biddy now?" asked some one. "She was never the same woman after her man died."

"Ah, poor Biddy! When your honour parted with her she went to Paris to a situation; but I'm thinking she'd have done better to bide at home. There's many an honest man in these parts would have been glad to meet a decent widow like Biddy. I told her so before she went, but—"

Here the fiddler struck up a jig, which cut short the gossip of the priest and made a diversion for his hearers. Some of the young fellows and girls present fell to footing it, and called on Tim and me to join in. But I was too much out of heart even to look on; and as for Tim, he glared as if he would have turned every one of them out of the cottage.

In the midst of the noise and the shouts of the dancers and the cheers of the onlookers, I crawled into the corner behind his honour's chair, and dropped asleep, to dream—strange to tell—not of my mother, or of his honour's turnips, or of the *Cigale*, but of Biddy McQuilkin of Kerry Keel, whom till now I had never seen or heard of.

When I awoke the daylight was struggling into the cabin, paling the candles that burned low beside my mother's bed. Tim stood where I had left him, sentinel-wise, glaring with sleepless eyes at his father's guests. Father, with his head on his arm, at the foot of the bed, slept a tipsy, sorrowful sleep. A few of the rest, worn-out with the night's revels, slumbered on the floor. Others made love, or quarrelled, or talked drowsily in couples.

His honour had escaped from the choking atmosphere of the cabin, and was pacing moodily on the grass outside, casting impatient glances eastward, where lay Kilgorman, and the *Cigale*, and the rising sun.

Presently, when with a salute I came out to join him, he said, "'Tis time we started. Waken your father, boy."

It was no easy task, and when he was wakened it was hard to make him understand what was afoot. It was only when his honour came in and spoke to him that he seemed to come to his senses.

The coffin was closed. The crowd stepped out with a shiver into the cold morning air. The priest took out his book and began to read aloud; and slowly, with Tim and me beside her, and my father in a daze walking in front, we bore her from the cabin down to the boats. There, in our own boat, we laid the coffin, and hoisting sail, shoved off and made for the opposite shore. Father and we two and his honour and the priest sailed together; and after us, in a long straggling procession of boats, came the rest. The light wind was not enough to fill our sail, and we were forced to put out the oars and row. I think the exercise did us good, and warmed our hearts as well as our bodies.

As we came under Kilgorman, I could see the mast of the *Cigale* peeping over the rocks, and wondered if she would be discovered by all the company. His honour, to my surprise, steered straight for the creek.

The *Cigale* flew the English flag, and very smart and trim she looked in the morning light, with her white sails bleaching on the deck and the brass nozzles of her guns gleaming at the port-holes. We loitered a little to admire her, and, seaman-like, to discuss her points. Then, when our followers began to crowd after us into the creek, we pulled to the landing and disburdened our boat of her precious freight.

The burying-ground of Kilgorman was a little enclosure on the edge of the cliff surrounding the ruin of the old church, of which only a few weed-covered piles of stone remained. The graves in it were scarcely to be distinguished in the long rank grass. The only one of note was that in which lay Terence Gorman with his wife and child—all dead twelve years since, within a week of one another.

With much labour we bore the coffin up the steep path, and in a shallow grave at the very cliff's edge deposited all that remained of our English mother.

As his reverence had said, she never took root in Donegal. She had been a loyal servant to her master, a loyal wife to her husband, and a loyal mother to us her sons. Yet she always pined for her old Yorkshire village home; a cloud of trouble, ever since we remembered her, had hovered on her brow. She had wept much in secret, and had lived, as it were, in a sort of dread of unseen evil.

Folks said the shock of the tragedy at Kilgorman, at the time when she too lay ill in the house with her twin babies, had unnerved her and touched her brain. But in that they were wrong; for she had taught Tim and me to read and write better than any schoolmaster could have done, and had read books and told stories to us such as few boys of our age between Fanad and Derry had the chance to hear.

Yet, though her brain was sound, it was not to be denied that she had been a woman of sorrow. And the strange words she had spoken when she was near her end added a mystery to her memory which, boy as I was, I took to heart, and resolved, if I could, to master.

That afternoon, when the mourners had gone their several ways, and the short daylight was already beginning to draw in, Tim and I lay at the cliff's edge, near our mother's grave, watching the *Cigale* as, with all her canvas flying and my father's dexterous hand at the helm, she slipped out of the lough and spread her wings for the open sea. Even in the feeble breeze, which would scarcely have stirred one of our trawlers, she seemed to gather speed; and if we felt any anxiety as to her being chased by one of his Majesty's cutters, we had only to watch the way in which she slid through the water to assure us that she would need a deal of catching.

I told Tim all I knew about her, and of my errand to Derry.

"What are the guns for?" said he. "What's there to be fighting about? Man, dear, I'd like a gun myself."

"There's plenty up at the house there," said I, pointing to Kilgorman— "two hundred."

"Two hundred! and we're only needing two. Come away, Barry; let's see where they're kept."

"You're not going up to Kilgorman House, sure?" said I in amazement.

"'Deed I am. I'm going to get myself a gun, and you too."

"But his honour?"

"Come on!" cried Tim, who seemed greatly excited; "his honour can't mind. I'll hold ye, Barry, we'll use a gun as well as any of the boys."

I would fain have escaped going up to so dreadful a place as Kilgorman on such an errand at such an hour. But I durst not let Tim think I was afraid, so when I saw his mind was made up I went with him, thankful at least that I had his company.

Chapter Four
The kitchen at Kilgorman

The daylight failed suddenly as we turned from our perch on the edge of the cliff, and began to grope our way across the old graveyard towards the path which led up to Kilgorman House.

But that Tim was so set on seeing the hidden arms, and seemed so scornful of my ill-concealed terror of the place, I should have turned tail twenty times before I reached our destination. Yet in ordinary I was no coward. I would cross the lough single-handed in any weather; I would crack skulls with any boy in the countryside; I would ride any of his honour's horses barebacked. But I shook in my shoes at the thought of a ghost, and the cold sweat came out on my brow before ever we reached the avenue-gates.

"What's to hurt you?" said Tim, who knew what was on my mind as well as if I had spoken. "They say it's the lady walks through the house. Man, dear, you're not afraid of a woman, are ye?"

"If she is alive, no," said I.

"She'll hurt ye less as she is," said Tim scornfully. "Anyway, if you're afeard, Barry, you needn't come; run home."

This settled me. I laughed recklessly, and said,—

"What's good enough for you is good enough for me. I'm not afraid of a hundred ghosts."

And indeed I should have felt easier in the company of a hundred than of one.

We halted a moment at my mother's grave as we went by.

"She lived up at the house once," said Tim.

"I know," said I.

"Come on," said Tim; "it's getting very dark."

So we went on; and on the way I tried to recall what I knew of the story of Kilgorman, as I had heard it from my mother and the country folk.

Twelve years ago Terence Gorman, brother of his honour, lived there and owned all the lough-side from Dunaff to Dunree, and many a mile of mountain inland. He was not a rich man, but tried, so folk said, to deal fairly with his tenants. But as a magistrate he was very stern to all ill-doers, no matter who they were; and since many of his own tenants aided and abetted the smuggling and whisky-making on the coast, Terence Gorman had plenty of enemies close to his own door. His household, at the time I speak of, consisted only of his young wife and her newly-born babe, and of my father and mother, who served in the house, one as boatman and gamekeeper and the other as lady's-maid. My mother had come over with the young bride from England, and had married my father within a month or two of her coming. And, as it happened, just when my lady gave birth to her infant, and was most in need of her countrywoman's help, my mother presented my father with twins, and lay sadly in need of help herself; so that Biddy McQuilkin, who was fetched from Kerry Keel to wait on both, had a busy time of it.

What happened on the fatal night that left Kilgorman desolate no one was able rightly to tell; for, except Biddy and Maurice Gorman, who chanced that night to have come over to see his brother, the sole occupants of the house had been Mrs Gorman and her child and my mother and her two infants.

Terence Gorman at nightfall had taken the gig, with my father, to drive to Carndonagh, where next day he was to inquire into some poaching affray. That was at seven o'clock. About midnight my father, half crazy with fright, brought the gig back, and in it the dead body of his master. They had reached the gap in Ballinthere Hill, he said, going by the lower road, when a shot was suddenly fired from the roadside, grazing my father's arm and lodging in the neck of Mr Gorman. It was so suddenly done, and the horse bolted so wildly forward at the report, that before my father could even look round the assassin had vanished.

Mr Gorman was already dead. My father did what he could to stanch the wound, but without avail; and, in a daze, he turned the horse's head and drove back as fast as he could to Kilgorman. My lady, whose bedroom was over the hall-door, was the first to hear the sound of the wheels, and she seemed to have guessed at a flash of the mind what had happened. Weak as she was, she succeeded in dragging herself from the bed and looking out of the window; and the first sight that met her eyes, by the gleam of the lanterns, was the lifeless body of her husband being lifted from the gig.

The shock was too much for her. She was found soon after in a dead swoon on the floor, and before morning her spirit had joined that of her husband. And not only hers—the little hope of the house shared the fate of her parents. And when the day of burial came, Terence Gorman and his wife and daughter were all laid in one grave.

My mother, to whom the shock of the news had been more gently broken, and whose husband had at least escaped with his life, recovered; and with her twin boys, Tim and me, was able in due time to remove to the cabin on Fanad across the lough which Maurice Gorman (who by this sad tragedy had unexpectedly become the heir to his brother's estate) gave him for a home.

That was all I knew, except this: ever since that night Kilgorman House had remained empty, and people said that its only tenant was the wandering spirit of the distracted mother crying in the night for her husband and baby.

These sombre recollections were an ill preparation for our nocturnal visit to the haunted house. As the rusty avenue-gate swung back with a hoarse creak I was less inclined than ever for the adventure.

But Tim was not to be hindered, and paced sturdily down the long avenue, summoning me to keep close and hold my tongue, for fear any one might be within earshot.

Kilgorman was a big, irregular mansion of several stories, with some pretensions to architecture, and space enough within its rambling walls to quarter a ship's company. In front a field of long, rank grass stretched up to the very doorway, having long since overgrown the old carriage-drive. In the rear was a swampy bog, out of which the house seemed to rise like a castle out of a moat. On either side gaunt trees crowded, overhanging the chimneys with their creaking boughs. There was no sound but the drip of the water from the roof, and the sobbing of the breeze among the trees, and now and again the hoot of an owl across the swamp which set me shivering.

Tim boldly marched up to the front door and tried it. It was fast and padlocked. The windows on the ground-floor were closely shuttered and equally secure.

We groped our way round to the rear, keeping close to the wall to avoid the water. But here, too, all was fast; nor was there a sign of any one having been near the place for years. My hopes began to rise as Tim's fell.

"Why not come by daylight?" said I.

"Why not get in, now we are here?" said Tim—"unless you're afraid."

"Who's afraid?" said I, shaking the window-frame till it rattled again.

"Come to the yard," said Tim. "There'll be a ladder there, I warrant."

So we felt our way back to the side on which abutted the stable-yard, and there, sure enough, lay a crazy ladder against the wall. It took our united strength to lift it. To my horror, Tim suggested putting it to the window that overlooked the hall-door—that fatal window from which the poor lady had taken her last look in life.

I would fain have moved it elsewhere, but he was obstinate. The top of the porch was flat, and we could stand there better than anywhere else. So—Tim first, I next—we clambered cautiously up, and stepped on to the ledge. The window was fast like the rest, but it was not shuttered, and Tim boldly attacked the pane nearest to the catch with his elbow. What a hideous noise it made as it shivered inwards and fell with a smash on the floor!

"Mind now," said Tim, as he slipped in his hand and pushed back the catch. "Lift away."

It was a hard job to lift it, for the wood had warped and grown stiff in its grooves. But presently it started, and gave us room to squeeze through into the room.

Even Tim was a little overawed when he found himself standing there in the room, scarcely changed, except for the mildew and cobwebs, from what it had been twelve years ago.

"Whisht!" said he in a whisper. "I wish we had a light."

But light there was none, and the fitful gleams of the wandering moon served only to make the darkness darker.

Once, as it floated clear for an instant, I caught sight of the bed, and a chair, and some withered flowers on the floor, left there, no doubt, since the day of the funeral.

Next moment all was dark again.

Tim had used the gleam to find the door, and I heard him call me.

"Come away. Keep your hand on the wall and feel with your feet for the stairs. It's down below the arms will be."

I am sure, had he looked, he would have been able to see the whiteness of my face through the darkness; but he was better employed.

"Here it is," he said. "Now keep your hand on the rail and go gently down."

"How'll we find our way back to the ladder?" said I.

"We've to get our guns first," said he, shortly.

When we reached the bottom of the stairs, we seemed to be in a passage or hall that went right and left.

In the plight in which we were it mattered little which turn we took, so Tim turned to the right, feeling along by the wall, with me close at his heels. Cautiously as we trod, our footsteps seemed to echo along the corridor, till often enough, with my heart in my mouth, I stopped short, certain I heard some one following. Tim too, I thought, was beginning to repent of his venture, and once more said, "We need a light badly."

Just then the moon peeped in for a moment through a loophole in one of the shutters, and showed us a bracket on the wall opposite on which stood a candle, and beside it, to our joy, a tinder-box.

"These have not stood here twelve years," said Tim, as he lifted them from their place. "This is a new candle."

And I remembered then the moving lights I had seen not a week ago.

The dim light of the candle gave us some little comfort. But for safety we kept it closely shaded, lest we should betray ourselves. At the end of the passage a door stood partly open, and beyond we found ourselves in a large kitchen paved with flagstones, and crowded round the walls and down the middle of the floor with muskets, piled in military fashion in threes and sixes.

Tim's soul swelled within him at the sight; but I confess I was more concerned at the gloomy aspect of the great chamber, and the general sense of horror that seemed to hang over the whole place.

"Begorrah, it was worth coming for!" said Tim, as he crouched down examining the lock of one specially bright weapon.

Suddenly he started to his feet and extinguished the candle. "Whisht!" he exclaimed, "there's a step."

We stood like statues, not even daring to breathe. There, sure enough, not on the walk without, but down at the end of the corridor we had just traversed, was a footstep. Tim drew me down to a corner near the hearth, where, hidden behind a stack of arms, we could remain partly hid. The step approached, but whoever came was walking, as we had done, in the dark. To my thinking it was a light step, and one familiar with the path it trod. For a moment it ceased, and I guessed it was at the bracket from which we had taken the candle. Tim's hand closed on my arm as the sound began again; and presently we heard, for we could not see, the door move back.

I never wish again for a moment like that. If I could have shouted I would have done so. All we could do was to crouch, rooted to the spot, and wait with throbbing hearts for what was to happen. As the footsteps halted a moment at the open door my quick ears seemed to detect the rustle of a dress, and next moment what sounded like a sob, or it might have been only a moan of the wind outside, broke the silence.

Then the steps advanced direct for us. Even the moon had deserted us, and by no straining of our eyes could we detect who the stranger was, even when she (for by the rustling sound we were positive it was a woman) reached the hearth and stood motionless within a foot of us.

Reach out we could not; stir we durst not; all we could do was to wait and listen.

It is strange what, when all other senses fail, the ear will do for one. I at least could tell that this strange intruder was a woman, and that the dress she wore was of silk. Further, I could tell that when she reached the hearth she knelt before the empty fireplace, not for warmth, but as if seeking something. I could hear what seemed a faint irresolute tapping with the knuckles; then just as, once more, the wind fell into a moan without, there came a sudden and fearful noise, which roused us out of our stupor and filled the place with our shrieks.

"Sped the hunted hares down the avenue."

For a moment we could not say what had happened. Then I understood that, in the tension of looking for the ghost I could not see, my foot had stretched against the butt of one of the guns and upset a stack of some six of them on to the stone floor, thereby putting an end to all things, the ghost included; for when we recovered from this last fright, and Tim in desperation struck a light, the place was as silent and empty as it was when we entered it.

If it was all an illusion, it was a strange one—strange indeed for a single witness to hear, stranger still for two. Yet illusion it must have been, begotten of my terrors, and the creak of the stairs, and the sighing of the wind, or the excursions of a vagabond rat. I do not pretend to explain it. Nor, for months after, could I be persuaded that the visitor was aught other than the poor distracted lady of Kilgorman. And it was months after that before I could get out of my mind that she had stood beside us and sought for something in the hearth.

As for us that night, I can promise you we were not many minutes longer in Kilgorman when the spell was once broken. Even Tim forgot the guns. With all the speed we could we ran to the stairs and so to my lady's chamber, against which stood the friendly ladder, down which we slid, and not waiting even to restore it to its place, sped like hunted hares down the avenue and along the steep path, till we came to the harbour in the creek where lay our boat.

Nor was it till we were safely afloat, with sail hoisted and our bows pointing to Fanad, that we drew breath, and dared look back in the dim dawn at the grim walls and chimneys of Kilgorman as they loomed out upon us from among the trees and rocks.

Chapter Five
Farewell to Fanad

After that, life went uneventfully for a time with Tim and me. Now that the cabin was empty father visited us seldom. His voyages took him longer than before, and we had a shrewd guess that they were not all in search of fish; for little enough of that he brought home. Young as we boys were we knew better than to ask him questions. Only when he showed us his pocket full of French coin, or carried up by night a keg of spirits that had never been brewed in a lawful distillery, or piloted some foreign-looking craft after dark into one of the quiet creeks along the coast, or spent an evening in confidential talk with his honour and other less reputable characters, we guessed he was embarked on a business of no little risk, which might land him some fine day, with a file of marines to take care of him, in Derry Jail.

For all that, I would fain have taken to the sea with him; for every day I longed more for the open life of a sailor, and chafed at the shackles of my landsman's fate. What made it worse was that one day, sorely against Tim's will, my father ordered him to get ready for the sea, leaving me, who would have given my eyes for the chance, not only disappointed, but brotherless and alone in the world.

But I must tell you how this great change in our fortunes came to pass.

It was about a year after my mother's death when, one dark night, as father and we two sat round the peat fire in the cabin, father telling us queer stories about the Frenchmen, and icebergs in the Atlantic, and races with the king's cruisers, that the door opened suddenly, and a woman I had never seen before looked in.

"Biddy McQuilkin, as I'm a sinner!" said my father, taking the pipe from his lips, and looking, I thought, not altogether pleased. But he got up, as a gentleman should.

"Arrah, Mike, you may well wonder! I hardly know myself at all, at all. And there's the boys. My! but it's myself's glad to see the pretty darlints." And she gave us each a hug and a kiss.

Somehow or other I did not at first take kindly to Biddy McQuilkin. She was a stout woman of about mother's age, with little twinkling eyes that seemed to look not quite straight, and gave her face, otherwise comely enough, rather a sly expression. And I guessed when she made so much of us that it was perhaps less on our account than on my father's.

As for father, I think he felt pretty much as I did, and had not the cunning to conceal it.

"I thought you were in Paris, Biddy?" said he.

"So I was, and so, maybe, I'll be again," said the widow, taking her shawl from her head, and seating herself on a stool at the fire. "'Twas a chance I got to come and see the folk at home while the master and mistress are in Galway seeing what they can save out of the ruin of their estate there. Ochone, it's bad times, Mike; indeed it is. Lonely enough for you and me and the motherless boys. I've a mind to stay where I am, and settle down in the ould country."

My father looked genuinely alarmed.

"Lonely!" said he with a laugh; "like enough it is for you, poor body, but not for me. I promise you I've plenty to think of without being lonely."

"Like enough," said she with a sigh. "It's when you come home now and again to the empty house you'll be feeling lonely, and wishing you'd some kindly soul to mind you, Mike Gallagher."

But my father was not going to allow that he was lonely even then; for he guessed what it would lead to if he did.

"I'm well enough as I am," said he. "But since you're so lonely, Biddy, why not get yourself a husband?"

She looked up with her little blinking eyes, and was going to speak. But my father, fairly scared, went on, —

"It's not for me, who'll never marry more, not if I live to a hundred, thank God, to advise the likes of you, Biddy. But there's many a likely man would be glad of you, and I'd give him my blessings with you. You need company. I don't; leastways none better than my pipe and my glass."

She turned her face away rather sadly, and sat with her chin on the palm of her hand, blinking into the fire.

"What about the boys?" she said, not looking up.

"They're rightly," said my father shortly.

She gave a short, grating laugh, and was about to speak again, when there fell a footstep outside, and his honour looked in.

He had come to see father, who was to sail again to-morrow, and was fairly taken aback to see what company we had.

Biddy rose and courtesied.

"The top of the morning to your honour," said she. "Faith, I'm proud to see you looking so well."

"What brought you here, Biddy?" said his honour.

"'Deed, I had a longing to see my friends and the ould country, that's why."

His honour looked round the cabin. Tim lay asleep curled up in the corner, and I, wide-awake, sat up and listened to all they said.

"Go down and make fast his honour's boat, Barry," said my father.

I obeyed reluctantly, for I was curious to know what these three had to say to one another.

I found his honour's boat already fast, and returned as quickly as I could to the cabin.

Biddy's shrill voice, as I came near, rose above the other two.

"It served your turn, Maurice Gorman," said she. "You know as well as me one of the two boys is—"

"Whisht!" exclaimed my father; "there he is."

And as I entered the talk suddenly dropped, and I felt quite abashed to see them all look at me as they did.

"Well, well, Biddy," said his honour presently, "you're a decent woman, and I'll help you. You shall have the forty pounds when you get back to Paris. My agent there will see to it, and you shall have a letter to him."

"Your honour's a gentleman," said Biddy with a courtesy. "Maybe you'll make it a little more, to save a poor widow another journey over to see you. Sure, forty pounds wouldn't keep me in France for six months."

"Well, well, we'll see. Come to Knockowen to-morrow evening, Biddy."

Biddy departed with a curious look in her eyes, and somewhat consoled for my father's indifference to her charms.

"You sail to-morrow?" inquired his honour when she had gone.

"I do," said my father. "I'm away to Sheep Haven to join her at cock-crow."

His honour turned and caught sight of me standing by the fire. He beckoned me to him, as he had done once before, turned my face to the light, and stared at me.

Then he looked up at father.

"He's no look of you, Mike."

"So you may say," replied my father, with a knowing glance at his honour. "Tim's liker me, they say."

His honour looked up with a significant nod.

"Well, Mike, I've said I'll see after one of the lads, for their dead mother's sake. Which will it be?"

"I'm thinking of taking Tim with me," said my father.

"Very good. I'll see to Barry then."

"Och, father," I cried, "take me to sea."

"Howld your tongue, ye puppy," said my father. "Can't you hear his honour say he'll see to you? There's many a lad would be glad of the chance."

"But Tim hates the sea, and I—"

"Be silent wid ye," roared my father, so angrily that he woke Tim.

"Tim," cried I, determined to make one more desperate effort, "you're to go to sea, and I'm to be kept ashore at Knockowen."

"Sea, is it?" roared Tim. "I'll run away—no sea for me."

"And I'll run away too," shouted I. "No Knockowen for me."

But it was of no avail; protest as we would, we had to do as we were bid. That very hour, with nothing but a little book that was once my mother's, and a few poor clothes, and Con the dog at my heels, I followed his honour down to the boat and left my old home behind me. And before dawn of day Tim was trudging surlily at my father's heels across country, on his way to join the *Cigale* at Sheep Haven.

Chapter Six
Miss Kit

His honour, saving his presence! was one of the meanest men I ever met, and I have come across many a close-fisted one in my day. There was nothing large about Maurice Gorman. His little eyes could never open wide enough to see the whole of a matter, or his little mouth open wide enough to speak it. If he owed a guinea, he would only pay a pound of it, and trust to your forgetting the rest. If his boat wanted painting, he would give it one coat and save the other. If his horse wanted shoeing, he would give him three new shoes, and use an old one for the fourth. If he ever gave money, it was by way of a bargain; and if he ever took up a cause, good or bad, it was grudgingly, and in a way which robbed his support of all graciousness.

It took me some months to discover all this about my new master.

When first I found myself an inmate of Knockowen, I was so sore with disappointment and anger that I cared about nothing and nobody. His honour, whose professions of interest in me were, as I well knew, all hollow, concerned himself very little about my well-being under his roof. Why he had taken me at all I could not guess. But I was sure, whatever the reason, it was because it suited his interest, not mine. I was handed over to the stables, and there they made a sort of groom of me; and presently, because I was a handy lad, I was fetched indoors when company was present, and set to wait at table in a livery coat.

The Knockowen household was a small one, consisting only of his honour and Mistress Gorman and the young lady. Mistress Gorman was a sad woman, who had little enough pleasure in this world, and that not of her husband's making. The man and his wife were almost strangers, meeting only at meal-times, and not always then, to exchange a few formal words, and then separate, one to her lonely chamber, the other to his grounds.

The brightness of the house was all centred in my little lady Kit, who was as remote from her mother's sadness as she was from her father's meanness. From the first she made my life at Knockowen tolerable, and very soon she made it necessary.

I shall not soon forget my first meeting with her. She had been away on a visit when I arrived, and a week later I was ordered to take the boat over to Rathmullan to fetch her home.

It was a long, toilsome journey, in face of a contrary wind, against which the boat travelled slowly, and frequently not without the help of an oar. How I groaned as I beat to and fro up the lough, and how I wished I was away with Tim and father on the *Cigale*.

At last, late in the afternoon, I reached Rathmullan, and made fast my boat to the pier. I was to call at the inn and find my young mistress there.

And there presently I found her, and a bright vision it was for me that dull afternoon. She was a little maid, although she was a month or two my elder. Her dark brown hair fell wildly on her shoulders, and her slight figure, as she stood there gazing at me with her big blue eyes, was full of grace and life. Her lips were pursed into a quaint little smile as she looked at me, and before I could explain who I was, she said,—

"So you are Barry Gallagher? How frightened you look! You needn't be afraid of me, Barry; I don't bite, though you look as if you thought so."

"'Deed, Miss Kit," said I, "and if you did, I'm thinking there's worse things could happen."

She laughed, and then bade me get together her boxes and carry them down to the boat.

Strange! Half-an-hour before I had been groaning over my lot. Now, as I staggered and sweated down to the wharf under her ladyship's baggage, I felt quite lighthearted.

In due time I had all aboard, and called on her to come, which she did, protesting that the water would spoil her new Dublin gown, and that if I sailed home no quicker than I had come, she supposed it would be morning before she got her supper.

This put me on my mettle. I even went ashore for a moment to borrow a tarpaulin to lay over her knees, knowing I should have to make a voyage all the way back to-morrow to restore it. Then, when I had her tucked in, and set the ballast trim, I hoisted the sail, and sat beside her, with the tiller in one hand and the sheet in the other.

She soon robbed me of the former; for with the wind behind us it was plain sailing, and she could steer, she said, as well as I.

"Keep a look-out ahead, Barry," she said, "and see if I don't get you to Knockowen in half the time you took to come. I'll give you a lesson in sailing this evening."

Here she had me on a tender point.

"Begging your pardon, Miss Kit, I think not," said I.

"Are you a seaman, then?" she asked.

"I'd give my soul to be one."

"Your soul! It would be cheap at the price."

"I don't know what that means," said I; "but if your ladyship will put the helm a wee taste more to port, we will catch the breeze better—so, so. Keep her at that!"

We slipped merrily through the water for a while; but it made me uneasy to see the clouds sweeping past us overhead, and feel the sting of a drop or two on my cheek.

I hitched the sheet a little closer, and came astern again to where she sat.

"You'll need to let me take her," said I; "there's a squall behind us."

"What of that?" said she. "Can I not steer through a squall?"

"No, Miss Kit," said I; "it takes a man to send her through when the weather gets up. Pull the wrap well about you, and make up your mind for a wetting."

She sniffed a little at my tone.

"I see you are captain of this ship," said she.

"Ay, ay; and I've a valuable freight aboard," said I.

Whereat she gave it up, and sat with her hair waving in the wind and her sailor's wrap about her shoulders.

It was a nasty, sudden squall, with a shower of hail and half a cap of wind in it. Luckily it was straight behind us. Had we been crossing it, it would have caught us badly. As it was, although it gave us a great toss, and now and then sent a drenching wave over our backs and heads, we were in no real peril. Our only difficulty was that, unless it eased off before we came within reach of Knockowen, we should have to cross it to get home. But that was far enough away yet.

Miss Kit, who for all her pretty bragging had had little commerce in the mighty deep, sat still for a while, startled by the sudden violence of the wind and the onslaught of the waves behind us. But as soon as she discovered that all the harm they did was to wet her pretty head and drench her boxes, and when, moreover, she satisfied herself by a chance glance or two at my face that there was nothing to fear, she began to enjoy the novel experience, and even laughed to see how the boat tore through the water.

"Why can't we go on like this, straight out to the open sea?" said she.

"We could do many a thing less easy," said I. "It's well Knockowen's no nearer the open sea than it is."

"Why?"

"If it was as far as Kilgorman," said I, "we'd meet the tide coming in, and then it would be a hard sea to weather."

"Kilgorman!" said she, catching at the name; "were you ever there, Barry?"

"Once," said I guiltily, "when I should not have been. And I suffered for it."

"How? what happened?"

"Indeed, Miss Kit; it's not for the likes of you to hear; and his honour would be mad if he knew of it."

"You think I'm a tell-tale," said she. "I'm your mistress, and I order you to tell me."

"Faith, then, I saw a ghost, mistress!"

She laughed, and pleasant the sound was amid the noise of the storm.

"You won't make me believe you're such a fool as that," said she. "It's only wicked people who see ghosts."

"Sure, then, I'm thinking it'll be long till you see one, Miss Kit. But mind now; we must put her a little away from the wind to make Knockowen. Sit fast, and don't mind a wave or two."

Now began the dangerous part of our voyage. The moment we put her head in for Knockowen, the waves began to break heavily over the stern, sometimes almost knocking the tiller from my hand, sometimes compelling us to run back into the wind to save being swamped.

"She was down on her knees on the floor of the boat."

She did not talk any more, but sat very quiet, watching each wave as it came, and looking up now and again at my face, as if to read our chances there. You may be sure I looked steady enough, so as not to give her a moment's more uneasiness than she need. But, for all that, I was concerned to see how much water we shipped, and how much less easily the boat travelled in consequence.

Quit the helm I durst not. Yet how could I ask her to perform so menial a task as to bail the boat? But it soon went past the point of standing on ceremony.

"Begging your pardon, Miss Kit," said I, "there's a can below the seat you're on. If you could use it a bit to get quit of some of the water, it would help us."

She was down on her knees on the floor of the boat at once, bailing hard.

"Are we in danger of sinking?" said she, looking up.

"No, surely; but we're better without water in the boat."

Whereat she worked till her arm ached, and yet made little enough impression on the water, which, with every roll we took, swung ankle deep from side to side, and grew every minute.

We wanted a mile of Knockowen still, and I was beginning to think there would be nothing for it but to put out again before the wind, and run the risk of meeting the heavy sea in the open, when the wind suddenly shifted a point, and came up behind us once more. It was a lucky shift for us, for my little mistress was worn-out with her labour, and a few more broadsides might have swamped us.

As it was, we could now run straight for home, and a few minutes would see us alongside the little pier of Knockowen.

I helped her back to her seat beside me, and drew the tarpaulin around her.

Her face, which had been anxious enough for a while, cleared as suddenly as the wind had shifted.

"I declare, Barry, I was afraid just now."

"So you might be; and no shame to you for it," said I.

"Are you ever afraid?" said she.

"Ay, I was at Kilgorman that night."

Again she laughed.

"I'd as soon be afraid of a real peril as of a silly fancy," said she. "I mean to go and see Kilgorman one day."

"Not with my good-will, mistress," said I.

"Well, without it then, Mr Barry Gallagher," she replied with a toss of the head which fairly abashed me, and made me remember that after all I was but a servant-man in my lady's house. The sea, blessings on it! levels all things, and I had almost forgotten this little lady was my mistress. But I recalled it now, and still more when, ten minutes later, we ran alongside his honour's jetty, and my fair crew was taken out of my hands by her parents, while I was left to carry up the dripping baggage, and seek my supper as best I could.

Chapter Seven
A Book of Fate

The coming of Mistress Kit, as I said before, made life at Knockowen tolerable for me. It mattered little if his honour neglected me, and my lady never looked at me; it mattered little if my fellow-servants ill-used me and put upon me; it mattered little that I had not a friend but Con and the horses to talk to, and not a holiday to call my own.

Miss Kit made all the difference. Not that she concerned herself specially about me, or went out of her way to be kind; but it did one good to see her about the place, with a smile for every one and a friendly word for man and beast. She even beat down the gloom that, in her absence, had weighed both on her father and mother. The former, indeed, was as indifferent as ever to his wife and the latter to her husband. But this daughter of theirs was one interest in common for both—perhaps the one object in the world about which both agreed.

It fell to my lot, as my young lady was an ardent horsewoman, to attend her on many a long ride, riding discreetly twenty yards in the rear, and never forgetting my duty so far as to speak when not spoken to.

One day, some weeks after she had come home, as we were riding on the cliffs near Dunaff, she turned in her saddle and beckoned me to approach.

"What road is that?" she said, pointing with her whip to a grass-grown track which led off the shore.

"That's the Kilgorman road," said I, guessing what was to follow.

"Kilgorman!" repeated she. "I should like to see the house."

"By your leave," said I, "his honour forbids any one to go there without his permission."

She tossed her head.

"I am not any one," she said. "I shall go where I please. Fall behind, sir; and if you are afraid to follow, stay where you are till I return."

And without more words, she flicked her horse and cantered over the turf to the road.

Of course I followed. If I feared the place, it was all the less possible to allow her to go there alone.

It was one comfort to me that it was still broad daylight, so that the mystery, whatever it might be, would lose its chief terror.

She looked round once to see if I was following or not, and then, changing her canter to a trot, turned into the road.

Now his honour's order to me about Kilgorman had been a very strict one, so much so that I suspected he had a shrewd idea who it was, eighteen months ago, had broken the window and knocked over the stand of arms in the kitchen.

"Mind, Barry," said he, "I allow no one on the road that leads up to Kilgorman. No one is to go to the house on any excuse. If my orders are disobeyed, he who trespasses will be sorry for it."

This had prevented my going near the place since. But now I followed the little mistress I felt myself in another case, and, any way, Gorman or no Gorman, I was not going to let her go alone.

The year and a half had made little change about the place. Only I noticed some wheel-ruts on the road that were not old, and saw, as we came nearer, that the window over the porch had been mended.

As we entered the avenue, Miss Kit reined up for me to approach.

"It's a finer house than Knockowen," said she. "I never saw it so near before. Why does my father hate it so?"

"'Deed I cannot say, but it's certain he does hate it."

"Help me down, Barry, and fasten the horses. Where do we go in?"

"Faith, that's the puzzle. When I came before I got in by yon window."

She laughed as she looked up.

"You'll have to go the same way again," said she, "and I'll wait here till you open the door for me."

I was in for the venture now! When I looked for the ladder, though, it was not to be seen. But the thick creeper beside the door served the purpose, and by dint of clambering I reached the porch-top in safety.

To my relief, I found that, though the window was mended, it was not bolted, and that I could lift it without breaking a new pane of glass.

I confess, in spite of the bright daylight, it gave me a turn to find myself once more in that fatal room, and recall the terrors of the night when I saw it last. As quickly as possible I left it, and descended the stairs to the hall.

Here a strange perplexity arose. For though I was certain where the door should be, there was never a sign of it inside—nothing but a row of iron-barred windows along the wall, like the corridor of a jail. When I came to look a little closer, I found that the doorway had been bricked up and plastered, so that by the ground-floor there was positively no entrance to the house.

With some misgivings, I wandered on to the great kitchen where Tim and I had had such a fright. But it was empty now, and the sun, as it glanced through the guarded window, fell brightly on the white hearthstone. Nor, though all was still as death, could my ears catch a single sound, except the stamping of the horses without and the idle tapping of my lady's whip against the pilaster of the door.

I traversed the corridor to the other end. It opened into a large room of the same size as the kitchen, evidently a dining-room, for a long table stood in the middle, and a solitary, moth-eaten stag's head, with antlers broken, hung over the chimney-piece.

Other doors opened off the corridor, and beyond them, along the back of the house and overlooking the boggy lake, ran another corridor, out of which no door opened to the outer world.

There was no sign of life anywhere, and the few pieces of furniture, rotten and withered with time, were more deathlike than if the house had been stark empty.

I returned upstairs, and on my way peeped into this room and that out of curiosity. But all was the same. Only in the last of all, at the end of the landing, did I see anything. There, on the window-ledge, covered with dust, which made it seem part of the woodwork it rested on, lay a little shabby book. How it caught my eye I hardly know, except that, believing in Providence as I do, I suppose it had lain there all those years, like the Sleeping Beauty in the fairy tale, waiting for me to discover it.

I remember, as I lifted it, the under cover stuck fast to the window-ledge and parted company with the rest of the book.

It was a common little volume of English ballads, with nothing much to commend it to the book lover. But the sight of it moved me strangely, for not only was it the same work, only another volume, as that I had brought away from the old home at Fanad, but on the front page, in my mother's hand, was written in faded ink, "Mary Gallagher, her book. A gift from her dear mistress." I thrust the precious relic hurriedly into my pocket, and casting a last look round the room, which I now guessed to be that in which I first saw the light, I hurried back to the chamber over the porch.

My little mistress was very vexed and put about when she found that there was no way into the house except the one. Had she been alone, I suspect she would have been up in a trice, and let dignity go; but my presence hindered her, and she chose, I think rather harshly, to blame me as the cause of her disappointment.

"If I were you," said she, with a frown, "and you I, I warrant I could have found some way to let you in."

"Faith, you wouldn't be sorrier to keep me standing out here than I was," said I humbly. "And indeed there's little enough to pay you for the trouble when you're once in. It's a dull, dismal house."

"And how was the ghost?" asked she.

"Whisht, Miss Kit! It wasn't likely any evil spirit could walk abroad while you're about."

"All very fine," said she. "I'll see Kilgorman before I'm much older, cost what it may. And I'll be my own groom, what's more. Fall behind, Barry."

And she set off, looking very mortified and angry.

I don't know if I was more sorry or glad that things had turned out as they had. I dreaded for her to come across sorrow in any form. And this house of mourning, with its mysterious air of terror, with its prison-like bars and bolts, and its time-devoured relics of a life that had gone out all in one day like the wick of a candle, was no place, then, for the bright sunflower of Knockowen.

His honour, happily, was away in Derry, and no one was there to question us as to our expedition. So I put up the horses, and trusted to God there was an end of Kilgorman.

But that very night, as I curled up in my narrow bed above the stable, I recalled my prayer.

By the light of a candle I took the book I had found from my pocket to look at it again. My mother's hand on the cover called back all the old memories of my childhood—how she sang to Tim and me these very ballads, and taught us to say them after her; how she always seemed as much a stranger in Fanad as this little English book seemed on the ledge at Kilgorman. There, too, between the leaves, were a few pressed flowers, and—what was this?

A little piece of thin paper fluttered down to my feet, written over in my mother's hand, but, oh, so feebly and painfully. With beating heart I held it to the light, and made out these words,—

"If you love God, whoever you are, seek below the great hearth; and what you find there, see to it, as you hope for grace. God send this into the hands of one who loves truth and charity. Amen."

Chapter Eight
A race for a life

My impulse, when I read that sad message from my dead mother, was to rise from my bed and saddle the horse and return, cost what it might, to Kilgorman. Had I done so I might perchance have saved myself months, even years, of trouble.

But in a weak moment I let my fatigue and my irresolution and my fear of the ghost get the better of me, and decided to put off till to-morrow what I should have done to-day. If in after years my worst enemy had to confess that what I did I did quickly, it was due to the lesson which this one act of procrastination taught me.

Putting everything together, the meaning of the letter seemed pretty clear. My mother, distraught by the sudden death of her master and mistress, and believing herself to be dying too, had desired to ease her mind of a secret (I knew not what) which lay upon it; but being in dread of it falling into wrong hands, had written it and hidden it in some place, leaving this slender clue to the chance discoverer of her little book of ballads.

How was it possible to believe otherwise than that Providence had, after fourteen years, placed that clue in the hands of her son, and thereby imposed upon me a duty from which, whatever it was, I should have been undutiful, and a coward to boot, had I shrunk?

But, as I tell you, for one night I shrunk from it, resolving that on the morrow I would obey the summons. But many to-morrows were to come and go before the promise could be fulfilled.

His honour returned at dead of night from Derry, and when, as usual, I presented myself to wait at breakfast, I was surprised to find him seated there with his wife and daughter.

Miss Kit was in her wonted high spirits, and alarmed me by plunging at once into the story of yesterday's adventure.

"Father," she said, "why is Kilgorman all barred and bolted against its future mistress? Here was I, yesterday, standing humbly like a beggar on the doorstep of our own house, and obliged to slink away disappointed after all."

His honour looked up with an angry flush on his pale face.

"Kilgorman!" cried he; "what took you there? Don't you know no one is allowed within the grounds?"

"I didn't know till Barry told me. And even then I did not suppose the prohibition applied to me."

His honour rounded angrily on me.

"What does this mean, sirrah? How did you dare to take her to Kilgorman after the charge I laid upon you?"

"Barry take me, indeed!" broke in Miss Kit, with a mighty toss of her head. "Barry takes me nowhere. It was I took him, whether he would or not; and a very poor adventure he made of it. You shall take me yourself next time, father."

"Understand," said his honour, looking very black, "that no one, not even my daughter, is permitted to go where I forbid.—As for you, you prying fool," added he, turning on me, "you shall see whether I am to be obeyed or not."

I deemed it prudent to say nothing, and retired, pretty determined that were his honour Saint Patrick himself he should not keep me out of Kilgorman. But I had missed my chance.

After that day my position at Knockowen became more irksome than ever, for I was taken from my work in the stables, and a new boy appointed in my place to tend the horses and accompany Miss Kit when she rode out. And I was kept all day within doors, at everybody's beck and call, from cock-crow, when I had to light the fires, to midnight, when I had to see his honour's clothes brushed and laid out in his dressing-room.

My only liberty, if liberty it might be called, was when the boat was wanted. There my seamanship made me necessary. But since no one thought of sailing towards the lough mouth, but only across or up towards Rathmullan, there was no chance of my defying his honour's regulations that way.

For a week or two even my mother's message was driven from my head by hatred of my rival, the new groom—a villainous-looking rascal, some years my elder, who yet had not even the merit of being a good horseman to commend him.

Rightly or wrongly, I suspected that part of his business was to keep a watch on me. And if anything could determine me to defiance that was enough. As to Miss Kit, I humbly hoped she liked the change as little as I; for since her liberty was cut off from one road, and her new lackey had neither looks nor conversation to commend him, her love of riding gradually flagged, and presently Martin—that was the fellow's name—had to lead out her riderless horse for exercise.

The trying thing to me was that Martin would not even do me the compliment of recognising me as his enemy. It was not for lack of invitation, nor was it owing to cowardice. But he was a dogged, short-sighted villain, taken up with his own concerns, and not choosing to trouble his head with those of others.

But one day I had the luck to startle him out of his reserve. Miss Kit came down to the yard that morning, and for the first time for more than a week ordered out her horse.

Martin, who was sitting lazily in the kitchen, rose somewhat sulkily and said,—

"It's not the day for a ride. Sure Juno's that saucy with want of work there'll be no holding her in. Besides, the master—"

But the young lady cut him short.

"Get up, sir, at once, and do as you are bid. There's more than Juno is saucy with want of work. Be quick now."

He went off with a scowl, and presently returned, leading out Juno and the horse on which he was to follow—a great-limbed animal called Paddy.

What he had said about my little lady's mare was very true. High-spirited she was at best of times, but a week's idleness and eating had made her fairly wicked; and as I looked out from the kitchen door to watch them start, I wished it was my business and not Martin's to see her safe on her way.

"Hold her head till I mount," said Miss Kit, after trying for a minute or two to coax the mare into peace. "She will be easy enough when I am up."

But though Martin held her head, the animal yet started and shied and curvetted every time Miss Kit gathered the reins in her hand and lifted her foot to the stirrup.

So I came out to the yard and gave her my hand to mount by.

Martin scowled very black at this.

"Go along away out of that," said he, when my lady was fairly perched on the saddle; "the mare's enough to fright her without you."

"Get you up on Paddy," said I, "and don't talk to me.—So, steady there, Juno lass.—Hold her gently, Miss Kit."

Martin, muttering to himself, let go the mare's head and walked over to where Paddy stood.

Just then, as luck would have it, out came Con the dog with a joyous yap.

This sudden noise was too much for the courage of Juno, who, feeling her head free and only a light weight on her back, gave a wild plunge, and next moment was away at a gallop out of the yard gate and down the avenue.

It was no time for halting. The mare must be caught before she could reach the cliffs, or to a certainty she and her rider were doomed.

Martin stood with his hand on Paddy's mane, gaping after the runaway.

With a sudden spring I dashed him aside and vaulted into the saddle, and before he could expostulate or guess what had happened I was away in full chase.

Even in the terror of the moment I could not help laughing to myself at the thought of poor Martin tumbling across the stable-yard, and finding himself out of the hunt. After that he would at least deign to recognise Barry Gallagher.

Though scarcely half-a-minute had elapsed, Juno and her precious burden were at the end of the long avenue before I was at the beginning of it. Paddy, amazed at all the excitement, lost some seconds in plunging before I could induce him to lay himself out for the pursuit. Then, to do him justice, he needed little coaxing from me. If only his wind was as long as his stride, this hue and cry might prove a holiday freak. If not—

It was a moment of keen suspense when at last I got clear of the avenue and looked round in search of the fugitive. There she was, her light figure thrown back as she strained at the reins, and her face turned to the upland ahead. Just beyond Knockowen, on the south side, is a long stretch of smooth turf, lying along the cliff-tops for a mile or more, and then suddenly cut short by a deep chasm in the coast, into which the waters of the lough pour tumultuously even in fair weather, and in foul, rage and boil as if in a caldron. It was a favourite sport of Miss Kit to gallop along this tempting stretch of grass, and Juno knew the way only too well.

As I came into the open, I could see that, in spite of the rider's efforts, the mare was making straight for the dangerous cliffs, and that in a few short minutes, unless a miracle happened, or unless I could reach the spot first, her mad career was likely to end in a way it made me sick to contemplate.

I stood in my stirrups and gave a loud halloo, and could see Miss Kit turn her head for a moment and then settle down again to the task of keeping her seat and pulling frantically at the reins; while I, aiming direct for the point of danger, put Paddy in a straight line across country.

It was a desperate race, that between the mad, high-mettled mare and the canny, raw-boned hunter. Happily he had but a boy's light weight to carry. For a moment or two I lost sight of the runaways. Then as I cleared a rise I saw them, a quarter of a mile away on my right, our courses closing on one another at every yard.

Presently, with a sickening sensation, I caught sight of the solitary beacon-post which marks the edge of the chasm for the unwary traveller. On clear ground I could have been certain of arriving there in time to stop the mare, but, to my dismay, two tumble-down stone walls, of which I had forgotten the existence, lay between me and the goal. The nearer of them was fairly high; the other, only twenty yards beyond, was lower, but more dangerous on account of the loose stones between the two.

I called on Paddy; and, oh, the suspense as he rose at the ugly wall!

Over! Paddy came down with a stagger, and lost a pace as he gathered himself again for the next. None but a born Irishman could have picked his way as he did among the scattered boulders, or chosen his starting-point for the lower yet longer leap.

I remember, as we rose at it, I saw Miss Kit quite close, very white, with her hat gone, and her stirrup swinging loose, but very resolute still, gripping hard at the pommel with one hand as she tried to wave to me with the other.

Paddy performed his task nobly, and never broke stride as he settled down for the few remaining yards of that great race.

We had won, but only just. I had barely time to rein up at a safe distance from the edge, and turn to meet the oncomers, when there they were.

Juno, finding her way suddenly obstructed, flung up her head and swerved inland, and before she could gather herself I had leaned across and lifted her panting burden in my arm.

Juno might go now for me!

As for Paddy, no one knows how much at that critical moment I owed to his steady help.

The little lady looked up with a half smile as I set her before me on the saddle. Then her head fell back on my shoulder in a faint, and I had the sweetest and (for all we walked the whole way) the shortest ride home I ever knew.

It was with a sore heart that presently I surrendered my burden to her mother's arms, and addressed myself to the task of recompensing my brave Paddy for that day's feat.

While I rubbed him down, up came Martin, and my spirits rose.

"Go along away out of that, you blundering spalpeen," said he, with a cuff on the ear. "I'll learn you to meddle, so I will. Go and clean the pots, and let the horse alone."

"Clean the pots yourself," said I, pretty hot, "and leave the horse to one that can ride him."

He gaped at me in his stupid way.

"You'll swallow it in time," said I, having finished my rubbing down. "Wait out there, like a jewel, till I put the beast away, and then you shall call me spalpeen again."

I think he was more astonished to be defied than he chose to confess. Anyway he waited for me.

"Now," said I, "Mister Martin, I'm waiting for you."

He made a lunge at me, which I dodged, and before he knew where he was I had him on the cheek-bone so suddenly that he slipped and tumbled on the ground.

I was two years older than the day I had fought Tim, poor Tim, on the cliff at Fanad. And to-day I was so uplifted I could have fought an army.

So it was a disappointment when Martin stumbled to his feet and sheered off with a threat of vengeance.

What cared I? Paddy and I had won a race, and my little mistress was safe.

Yet Martin, as will appear presently, was a man of his word.

Chapter Nine
Behind the inn door at Rathmullan

I know not what account of our adventure was given by my little mistress to her parents, but certain it was I found myself risen in the good graces of the mother, if not in those of his honour. As to the latter, his graces, good or bad, were hard to calculate. Perhaps he disliked me less than before, rather than liked me better. He said nothing, except to reprimand me for assaulting Martin. But I suspected it was no special love for Martin which called forth the rebuke.

And now, for a time, things went uneasily at Knockowen. For a sour man, his honour kept a good deal of company; and I, who waited upon them, with eyes and ears open, could see that my master was playing a difficult and dangerous game.

One week certain mysterious persons would drop in, and sit in long confabulation. Another week some fellow-justice of his honour's would claim his hospitality and advice on matters of deep importance. Sometimes a noisy braggart from the country side would demand an audience; and sometimes an officer in his Majesty's uniform would arrive as an honoured guest.

On all such occasions the tenor of the talk was the growing unrest of the country, and the gathering of that great storm which was soon to turn the whole country into a slaughter-house.

But the difficult task which Mr Gorman set before himself was to agree with everybody.

That he was deep in league with the smugglers on the coast I myself knew. But to hear him talk to the revenue officers who visited him, one might think that he spent his days and nights in seeking to put down this detestable trade. That he had a hand in the landing of foreign arms the reader knows as well as I. But when his brother magistrates came to lay their heads with his, none was more urgent than he to run down the miscreants. Indeed, he went to more than empty words; for once, when a rumour spread that a cargo of powder and shot was expected off Malin, he himself led the party which for three days lay in wait to intercept it. And no one knew except himself and me that during those very three days, while he kicked his loyal heels on Malin Head, the *Cigale* ran quietly into Lough Swilly, and after resting a few hours, ran as quietly out, with a good deal less ballast in her than she came with.

I remember that well, for it was a day when I was secretly plotting to take advantage of my master's absence to steal up to Kilgorman. I had indeed got not far from the place when, to my disgust, Martin and another man overtook me on horseback, and ordered me to return at once to Knockowen at my mistress's bidding.

I durst not disobey, or betray my purpose, so turned back sulkily, leaving them to canter on; and, to add to my chagrin, as I looked round presently from the hill-top, I recognised the flaunting sails of the *Cigale* standing in for the shore. This sight filled me with a new longing to see Tim, on whom for two years now I had only once, for an hour, set eyes. Come what would, I must steal away and hail him as soon as ever I could escape for an hour or so. Alas! it was easy to promise.

The reason of my mistress's summons was for me to take an officer, who had just ridden over in hot haste from Carndonagh, by boat to Rathmullan. He was to rejoin his regiment that night, and being a distant kinsman of my lady had presumed on his relationship to beg a passage across the lough by the shortest way.

You may guess if I cast loose the boat with a merry heart, and bade farewell to my chance of seeing Tim, let alone of obeying my mother's call to Kilgorman.

More than that, this voyage to Rathmullan reminded me of another time when my crew was more to my taste than this lumbering trooper; and, as if to complete my trouble, Miss Kit came down gaily to the jetty to speed the parting guest.

"It's a pity we could not keep you, Captain Lestrange, till my father returned. You must come again when times are quieter."

"That'll not be this year or next," said the young officer; "but whenever it is, I could hardly find you looking prettier than you are now, Miss Gorman."

"Wait till you see," said she, with a saucy laugh, waving her hand as we pushed off.

I had it in my heart to upset the boat as the fellow stood and kissed his hand.

"Sit down, sir, if you please, and trim the boat," I said. "By your leave, sir, till I haul the sail."

And before he was aware of it I hauled away, and left him kissing his hand to a sheet of white canvas that interposed between him and my little mistress.

That solaced me vastly.

Once out on the lough I found my passenger, who was little more than a lad of twenty, friendly enough, and inclined to while away the voyage with chat.

"So the master's at Malin, after the smugglers?" said he.

"Troth, yes," said I; "but they're hard boys to catch."

"I wouldn't thank you for fools that ran into your arms," said he.

"'Deed you won't find many such in these parts."

"What's that building on the far point there?" he asked presently, pointing to Kilgorman.

"That's Kilgorman House, colonel."

"Oh! There's some story about that house surely. Somebody was murdered or robbed—what was it?"

"His honour's brother, Terence Gorman, owned it. And he was shot on the hill fifteen years ago; and nobody will go near the place since."

"Oh, I remember now," said he. "And there was something about a lady and child that died too. I heard about it from a cracked body that was servant to my sister-in-law in Paris."

"Biddy McQuilkin," said I. "Sure she's in France still!"

"What, do you know her?"

"She's from these parts, colonel."

"Well, she may be there still, unless they're all dead. Paris is a hot place for any one just now. When they kill kings, and cut off heads like turnip-tops, it's no place for strangers."

"They do say the French will be this length before long," said I, recalling some of the talk I had heard at his honour's table.

He eyed me sharply.

"They do, do they? And how come you to know it?"

"Sure, it's common talk," said I; "and more by tokens, they've sent their guns before them."

"The less you talk about what you don't understand the better," said the officer, looking glum; "but I'd give any one a hundred pounds to tell me where they put the arms when they land them."

Here I thought it wise to be silent. I could have earned a hundred pounds easily that afternoon.

When we reached Rathmullan, a sergeant was down on the pier awaiting Captain Lestrange.

"There's wild work going, captain," I heard him say; "the boys are getting to a head, and every mother's son of them with a gun in his hand. The troop's been ordered over to Letterkenny, and they're away already to watch the fun. Begging your pardon, captain, you must take your dinner in the saddle this day."

The captain took this news, especially the end of it, bravely, and tossed me down a shilling.

"Good-bye, my lad; and carry my respects to your young mistress."

And he strode away to the inn where the horses waited, and in a few minutes was clattering at full speed down the road that leads to Letterkenny.

Now, thought I, was my chance, with a favouring breeze, to slip down the lough and carry out my purpose of speaking the *Cigale*.

I would spend my shilling, or part of it, in drinking his Majesty's health, by which time it would be dusk enough to enable me to pass Knockowen unobserved.

In the inn, however, I found a great disturbance going on; so much so that I was crowded behind the door, and forced to stay there, first because I must, and presently because I would. What the trouble was I could not at first ascertain; but it soon came out that at Sheep Haven a gang of smugglers had been trapped, and their skipper swung at his own yard-arm. That was bad enough; but what was worse, he was a Rathmullan man, and the warrant for his capture had been given a week ago by a magistrate across the lough.

"I'll warrant you that was Maurice Gorman did it," said some one.

At the name I crept further back behind the door, and stood like a mouse.

"The very man," said another. "He's a dirty thraitor. He can let the boys well enough alone when he loikes."

"Whisht!" said another; "he's away at Malin this very week after more, and his men with him. I tell you what I'm thinking, Larry," continued the speaker, who had drunk somewhat, "this—"

"Howld yer tongue," said the first speaker in a whisper. "Do you know no better than blather at the top of your voice like that?"

"I'm thinking," continued the other, retreating towards the door, and beckoning the others around him, "that it'd do Maurice a world of good to have his winders broken."

"Ay, and not by pebbles. There's lead enough to spare in the country, praise God."

"And fire enough to warm his bones if he should be feeling cold," said another.

"He's to be back to-morrow. I heard that from Martin, who's been left to take care of the place."

"Sure, Martin's a right boy for us. He'd never spoil sport for the likes of Gorman."

"Not he. I warrant you Martin will be waiting on us, for I'll step across and tell him myself. There's no one else to mind but the women and a fool of a boy."

"Begorrah, thin, we'll stand by you, Larry. If Pat Corkill swings to plaze Maurice Gorman, Maurice shall roast to plaze us. But whisht! I'll have a boat for the eight of yez at this time to-morrow."

Then, one by one, they slunk off out of the dark shanty, leaving me behind the door in a fever of excitement and impatience.

I durst not go all at once, or be seen in the place; so I waited on till the road was clear and the host was away putting up his shutters.

Then I slipped out, and slouched quietly down to the pier. By good luck I had moored my boat under the side of an old hull that lay there, where she could hardly be noticed by any who did not look for her. I was thankful, aided by the friendly night, to reach it safely, and was soon speeding up the lough as fast as my sail would carry me, with my big budget of news for Knockowen.

Chapter Ten
A night attack

I think, had the wind only favoured, I might have been tempted, notwithstanding the risk of it, to venture up in my boat as far as Kilgorman for the sake of getting a word with Tim, even if I could not hope to follow my quest up to the house itself. But the breeze dropped slack before I was well clear of Rathmullan, and it took me many hours of hard pulling, with the chance aid of an occasional puff, to make as far as Knockowen; and by that time the dawn was beginning to show in the east, and my chance of passing undetected was gone.

Besides, the news I bore, and the importance of it to the little, unprotected family at Knockowen, would hardly allow of delay. I slipped into the house and curled myself up in my corner, but not to sleep. Supposing, as was likely, his honour was not back by night, it would be left to me to defend the house and the women as best I could. And how was I to do it?

The first thing I saw when I arose at the summons of the cock was the white sails of the *Cigale* in the distance standing out for the mouth of the lough. So there was an end of Tim for the present. I confess I was almost glad; for had he been still within call, I should have been tempted all day long to desert my post to get at him. Now I had nothing to take my mind from the business of the night that was coming.

By mid-day his honour had not returned. And then it seemed to me I must do something, if the danger was to be averted. So I saddled Juno (who, by the way, had quietly trotted home to her stable the morning after her runaway race with Miss Kit three months ago), and despite Martin's questions and objections, to which I replied that I was on my lady's business, rode as hard as the mare would carry me to the barracks at Fahan.

There I boldly reported what I knew, and in my mistress's name bade the sergeant in charge send half-a-dozen armed men to protect the house. The sergeant answered that all his men were away, and that unless they returned soon he would have no one to send.

Then I demanded a brace of guns, and a promise that, failing any others, he would come himself. To this he agreed that he certainly would, and bade me keep my own counsel and not alarm the women. As to Martin, I would do well, he said, to make sure of him before he could do any harm. He gave me the guns done up in a truss of straw to avoid detection, and with this clumsy parcel slung across the mare's back I trotted home.

As I came near the avenue I noticed a skulking figure step quickly behind the trees, and guessed this was probably the messenger who had promised to come over to warn Martin of what was in store. I doubted whether I ought not to attack him there and then. But had I done so I might have given an alarm, and lost my guns into the bargain. So I pretended to see nothing, and passed on, whistling to myself, up to the house.

The afternoon was already well advanced before I dismounted in the stable-yard. Martin, as I expected, stood there waiting for me. It was as much his object to get me disposed of as it was mine to dispose of him. My only chance was to seem to know nothing, and keep a sharp look-out on him.

"You're fond of riding," said he with a sneer; "it's worth a ride to Fahan to fetch a truss of straw when there's plenty in the stable."

"There's more than straw in this," said I, lifting it up and carrying it up to the house. "Man, dear, it's full of guns."

He was not to be taken in by chaff like that, he said. And indeed he fully believed, as I hoped he would, that I was making a fool of him.

"Since you don't believe me, you might carry it indoors for me, while I put up the mare," said I, risking a little more to make sure of him.

"You may carry your own litter," said he, "and hold your tongue over it."

So I carried the truss into the kitchen, and laid it in the corner there, and presently returned to the yard.

He had taken Juno into the stable, and was unsaddling her there.

"Come here," he called, "and put up your own beast."

I guessed pretty well what he meant by that. The stable was a small one, with only one little grated window high up, and a thick door. Could he lock me in there, I should be quiet enough for the rest of the evening.

Happily for me Martin was a dull fool as well as a great villain, and he betrayed his purpose by the glitter of his eye too clearly for any one to mistake him. I strolled carelessly up towards the door, and as I did so he left the horse and came to meet me.

"Come in here," said he, "and let's see how you can rub down a horse."

"I don't need you to show me," said I. "Look at her there, with her mane all in a twist and her fetlock grazed by your clumsy pail."

He turned round to look, and in that moment I had the door shut on him and the key turned on the outside. I knew that the door, which was thick enough to stand a horse's kick, had nothing to fear from his. And as to his noise, there would be no one to heed that. He would be safe there till morning, and there were oats enough in the place to keep him and Juno both from starving.

This business done, I hastened back to the house, and sought Miss Kit, to whom I told everything.

"Father will not be home to-night," said she bravely. "We must do the best we can, Barry."

"We'll do better than that, plaze God," said I.

Then followed an anxious council of war. Besides our two selves, there were my lady and three maid-servants in the house. Mistress Gorman was too nervous and delicate to count upon for help, but the maids were all three sturdy wenches. So our garrison was five souls, and, counting the two guns I had brought, there were eight stands of arms and ammunition to match in the house.

The danger to be feared was not so much from the invaders' shooting as from the possibility of their carrying out their threat to fire the house. Our only hope seemed to lie in frightening them off at the onset by as formidable a show of resistance as possible. Failing that, we should have to protect ourselves as best we could.

Fortunately we could at least prevent their surrounding the house; for by closing and barricading the garden doors on either side, all approach would be limited to the water-front, unless a very wide circuit was made outside the grounds. The drawing-room in which the family usually spent their evenings was on the first floor at this side, and here no doubt the enemy would direct their first attack.

I therefore resolved to have the candles lit as usual and to keep the blinds up, so as to give no hint that we were forewarned of their visit.

Below, on the ground-floor, there were two windows on either side of the door, with shutters in which we bored some hasty loopholes, at each of which we could station one of our party. And the more effectively to keep up an appearance of being in force, I placed a loaded gun, pointed towards the door, on the outer wall at each side, which, by an arrangement of string attached to the triggers, I should be able to let off from within, and so give the party the discomfort of believing themselves taken in the rear.

For the rest, we removed everything inflammable, such as curtains and bedding, as far from the windows as possible, and trusted to a supply of well-filled buckets stationed in every room to help us in case of fire. And as an additional defender against a forcible entry from any unexpected quarter, I brought Con the dog (who seemed to understand all that was going forward) into the house, and stationed him in the hall.

By the time these preparations were all complete it was quite dark, and I knew we might expect our visitors at any moment.

I begged Miss Kit to see her mother disposed of in an apartment as far from the point of danger as possible, while I lit the candles in the drawing-room, and stationed the maids at their posts in the darkened hall below.

My little mistress came to the drawing-room to report her task done.

"If you are not afraid," said I, "it would be well to move about in this room near the window for a little, so as to let ourselves be seen by any one who approaches. They may be in view of us already."

She seated herself boldly at the window, while I, in my livery coat, waited on her with a tray.

"Afraid!" said she, taking up my words; "that would be difficult. I do not forget that afternoon in the boat, or the gap in the cliff."

If anything could have put me more on my mettle, these words and the smile that accompanied them sufficed. I could have received an army single-handed.

We waited silently after that. Presently Con below gave a low growl, and Miss Kit's eyes met mine. "Listen, and you'll hear them," said I. Sure enough, through the open window there came the steady plash of oars, and the sound of voices across the water.

It was an uneasy moment, especially when we heard the grating of the boat alongside the jetty.

"It's time now we went below," said I. "Leave me here to close the window and pull down the blinds. And, Miss Kit," said I as she rose, "if any one is hurt this night it shall not be you."

She laughed a brave little laugh, and replied, "You want too much for yourself, Barry. We'll share and share alike."

Then with her cheeks somewhat pale, and her eyes very bright, she went below, and groped her way to her station in the hall.

Meanwhile, as ostentatiously as I could, I closed the window and lowered the blinds; and after moving from one place to another between them and the candles so as to throw as many shadows as possible, I slipped from the room, and ran down the stairs.

At first nothing could be seen, and we only had Con's growing uneasiness to warn us of the danger approaching. Then through my loophole I saw among the trees a moving light, evidently a lantern, and presently seven or eight dark forms moving doubtfully along the little jetty.

They halted at a little distance to reconnoitre, and perhaps to wonder why Martin, on whom they depended to conduct them, did not appear.

At last we could discern a movement and the sound of footsteps crunching on the gravel. My orders were that no sign should be given by any of us in the house till they had expended their first shot. And this, as it happened, turned out to be good advice.

Presently we could see them ranged in a row, about twenty yards from the house. Then one stepped forward cautiously, and rapped at the door behind which we stood.

His only answer was a growl from Con.

"Boys," whispered he, "there's not a sound stirring. You'll need to rap at yon window to find if his honour's at home. All together now."

Whereupon, with a hideous noise, seven guns were let off, and we heard the bullets crash into the room overhead.

One of the maids lost her nerve, and shrieked. But if they heard it, they thought nothing of it.

"Are you a goose?" cried Miss Kit angrily. "Stand steady now, like a woman."

This reassured the girl, and at the same time I gave the order to fire.

Our object was not to kill but to frighten. And I knew well enough the women would aim wild. But for myself, I confess I had no scruples in covering the man who carried the lantern.

The effect of our volley was amazing. The villains had barely grounded their arms, and were proceeding leisurely, with their eyes still upturned to the shattered windows, to reload, when we let fly.

My man fell back with a yell, so did one of the others. The rest yelled in chorus, and stood a moment stupified. Quick as thought I pulled my strings right and left, and completed their consternation by a flank fire, which, had it been aimed by a marksman, could not have been more decisive. For one other of the party fell without even a cry, and at the same moment the rest rushed gasping and stumbling over one another down to the boat.

It was the shortest battle I ever took part in. Within three minutes of the first attack the invaders were flying for their lives across the lough. Three of their number were left on the field senseless, and for all we knew stone dead.

I confess that victory is sometimes more terrible than defeat, and any relief our little garrison felt in the danger averted was lost in the counting of the cost. My little mistress, especially, was not to be held till the door was opened, and she could go out to where the victims lay.

Of the three, one—he who had caught the fire of the gun on the wall— was dead. The other two were senseless, but only slightly wounded. The one, whom I had brought down, was bleeding from a wound in the forearm; and the other, who was shot with no will of her own by the frightened servant-maid, was deeply grazed on the cheek.

We had scarcely carried the two wounded men inside, when a clatter of hoofs in the avenue warned us that the sergeant, true to his promise, had come to our succour, and not alone. He was not well pleased to find himself too late for the fighting, and only in time to tend a couple of bruised men, and carry off the body of another. But for this duty he might at least have given chase to the fugitives, and gained a little credit to himself by their capture. As it was, my lady, who in her husband's absence, and then only, spoke with his authority, would hear of no such attempt, and ordered the immediate removal of the body to Fahan, pending the necessary inquiry, while two of the soldiers were to be left in the house to protect it and see to the wounded.

As for these, a little whisky and bandaging soon set them right; and when next morning his honour, who had already been met by the news of the night's adventure, reached home, he was able to send them off to jail in the custody of the soldiers.

"There'll be trouble enough to us out of all this," said he to me that day, as we followed to the court of inquiry. "I wish to God I had left you where I found you."

That was the least I expected of his honour. His gratitude counted for very little beside the look Miss Kit had given me the night before, when the danger was yet to come.

Chapter Eleven
Fugitive but not vagabond

His Honour was quite right; there was trouble enough out of that night's business. But more for me than for him.

For him, as he was then situated, playing a fast and loose game between the side of order and the side of treason, the fact that his house had been attacked by friends of the latter party stood him in good stead with the former. And if any of his brother magistrates had been inclined to suspect him of half-heartedness before, this outrage might be counted on to confirm his zeal for the right cause.

Under cover of this new security he was able to play even more than before into the hands of the lawless party. His first act was to hush up the affair of the night attack and procure the release of the two prisoners. His next was to abandon me to the tender mercies of those who sought vengeance for the blood of the dead man.

Once as I crossed the lough in a boat on his honour's business a shot across the water, which buried itself in the gunwale, made me look round, and I perceived one of the Rathmullan long-boats, manned by four of the party I had overheard in the inn weeks before, in full chase. The wind was slack, and escape was almost impossible. Could I only have used my sail I might have led them a pretty dance out into the open. As it was, without arms, one to four, and in a little, broad-beamed tub, I could do nothing but haul down my sail and wait their pleasure.

"Martin was right this time," I heard him who had fired the shot say, as he leisurely reloaded.

I was in doubt whether I was to be made an end of then and there, or allowed the mockery of a trial.

"What's your will?" said I, as they came alongside. "You've no need to scratch the paint of his honour's boat, anyway."

They said nothing, but hauled me bodily into their own craft, and tied me hand and foot.

"Save your breath," said one presently, "till it's wanted."

And I was flung like a sack on the floor of the boat.

"What'll we do with yon?" said another, knocking his oar against the Knockowen boat.

"Capsize her and let her drift," said the leader of the party.

So my old craft, which had carried me so often, and not me only but my little lady whom it seemed I was never to see more, was upset and turned adrift, to carry, for all I knew, the message of my fate to any whom it might concern.

It was almost dark already, and by the direction my captors rowed I concluded I was to be taken, not to Rathmullan, but to a landing-place nearer the lough mouth. They cruised about till it was quite dark, and then put in for a point called Carrahlagh, some miles south of my old home on Fanad. Here my feet were loosed and I was ordered to march with my company inland. The man with the gun walked by my side. The others, who as we went along were joined by some half-score of confederates at various points, who all gave a watchword on joining, talked among themselves eagerly.

Presently we came to a hill—one I knew well—and here the stragglers began to muster in larger numbers, till as we came to the hollow basin below the top I counted nearly fifty. A few of them I recognised as old gossips of my father's, but for the most part they were strangers who seemed to have come from a distance.

About ten of the number carried guns, the rest were all armed with either clubs or sticks, while one or two carried rude pikes.

I noticed that one of my captors, not he who guarded me, was looked up to as the leader of the gathering; and when by common consent a circle was formed, and sentinels posted, one on either side of the hollow, it was he who stepped forward and spoke.

If he was an Irishman, his voice did not betray him. Indeed, he spoke more like an Englishman, with a touch of the foreigner at the tip of his tongue.

The first part of his speech was about matters I little understood—about some Bill before the Irish Parliament at Dublin, and the efforts of the friends of the people to defeat it. Then he went on to talk of the great events taking place in Paris:—How the whole people were up in arms for liberty; how the king there had been beheaded, and the streets were flowing with the blood of the friends of tyranny. From end to end of France the flag of freedom was floating. Was Ireland to be the only country of slaves in Europe? She had a tyrant worse than any of whom France had rid herself. The English yoke was the one secret of the misery and troubles of Ireland, and so on. "Boys!" cried he, "the soldiers of liberty are looking at you. They're calling on you to join hands. Are you afraid to strike a blow for your homes? Must I go and tell them that sent me that the Irishman is a coward as well as a slave? There's fighting to be done, if there's only men to do it—fighting with the men who wring the life's blood out of you and your land—fighting with the toadies who are paid by England to grind you down—fighting with the blasphemers who rob your priests and your chapels—fighting with the soldiery who live on you, and tax you, and insult your wives and daughters. It's no child's play is wanted of you. We want no poltroons in the cause. We know the people's friends, and we know their enemies; and it's little enough quarter will be going on the day we reckon accounts. Arrah, boys!" cried he, letting go his foreign air for a moment and dropping into the native, "it's no time for talking at all. There's some of yez armed already; there's a gun for any mother's son here that will use it for the people, and swear on the book to leave the world with one tyrant less upon it. Come up, boys, and take the oath, and shame to them that hang back."

Instantly there was a forward movement in the audience, as with shouts and cheers they pressed towards the speaker.

He held aloft a book and recited the oath in a loud voice. As far as I remember it bound every one to be a loyal member of the society organised in that district to put down the tyrant and free Ireland from the English yoke. It bound him, without question, to obey any command or perform any service demanded of him in the cause. It pledged him to utter secrecy as to the existence and actions of the society. And it doomed him to the penalty of death for any breach of his vow.

In fours, each with a hand on the book, the company advanced and took the vow, each man's name as he did so being written down and publicly announced. Even the two sentinels were called from their posts and replaced, in order that they might join.

Finally the leader cried,—

"Is that the whole of ye?"

"No," cried my custodian, pushing me forward with the butt-end of his gun. "There's a boy here, plaze your honour, captain, that we took this day. It's him that gave Larry Dugan his death that night we visited Knockowen."

The leader turned me to the moonlight and scrutinised my face sharply.

"I had forgotten him," said he; "he should have been left behind.—That was a bad business at Knockowen."

"'Deed, sir," said I, plucking up a little heart at the mildness of his manner, "I did no more than your honour would have done in my shoes; I defended the women. And as for Larry Dugan, it was a mischance he was hit."

A hurried consultation took place among the chief of the confederates, during which I was left standing in suspense.

It was against me that I had been present and overheard all this business of the oath. That, it was evident, weighed more against me than the part I had taken in the defence of the Knockowen women. Were they to let me go now, the society would be at the mercy of my tongue. It would be simpler, as some advised, to put me out of harm's way then and there with an ounce of lead in my head.

Presently the consultation ended.

"Give him the oath," said the leader; and the book was held out to me, while a couple of guns were pointed at my head.

It was an ugly choice, I confess. Little as I understood the nature of the work in hand, I had gathered enough to know that the oath sold me body and soul to men who would stick at nothing to gain their end, and that in taking it I became not only a traitor to the king, but an accomplice of murder and outrage.

Yet what could I do? Young life is sweet, and hope is not to be thrown away like a burned-out match. Besides, I longed to see Tim once more before I died, and—I blushed in the midst of my terror—my little mistress.

"Loose my hands," said I, "and give me the book."

The muzzles of the guns laid their cold touch on my cheeks as the cord was unfastened.

Then in a sort of dream I held the book and began to repeat the words. I know not how far I had gone, or to what I had pledged myself, when a sudden shout from one of the sentries brought everything to an end.

"Whisht—soldiers!" was the shout.

In a moment the hollow was almost empty. Men scuttled away right and left like sheep at the alarm of the dog. Those who guarded me let me go and raced for the gap. The clerk left paper and pen and lantern on the ground and slunk towards the rocks. I was left standing, book in hand, with but one of the party, and that one the leader, beside me.

"Kiss the book," said he in a menacing tone.

I looked at him. He was not armed, and I was as free a man as he. Quick as thought I seized the list which the clerk had dropped on the ground.

"Your secret is safe," said I, flourishing it in his face, "so long as the women at Knockowen are unhurt. But my soul and my hand are my own."

So saying I flung the book and struck him a blow on the breast which sent him reeling back against the rock. And off I went among the bracken, thanking God for this peril escaped.

As I have often proved many a time since, the road to safety lies often on the side of danger. Most of the fugitives had made for the hills in an opposite direction to that towards which the sentinel had pointed. I went the other way, and hid myself under a broad flat rock near the roadside, guessing that no one would ever look for lurkers there.

And in so doing I was able to discover what the others would have given something to be sure of:—that the sentinel's alarm had been a false one altogether, and that what he took for soldiers was no more than a party of revellers returning from a harvest dance in high good spirits along the road. I even recognised some of the familiar faces I had known at Fanad in the old days, and was sorely tempted to claim acquaintance.

But prudence forbade. As sure as daylight came no effort would be spared to hunt me down. For had I not the secret of this society in my own hands, down to the very list of its members? A word from me could smoke them in their holes like rats in a drain. It was not likely I should be allowed to remain at large; and when caught next time, I might promise myself no such good luck as had befallen me to-night.

So I lay low till the road was clear, and then struck north for Fanad, where I knew nooks and crannies enough to keep me hid, if need be, for a month to come.

For a week I lodged uncomfortably enough in one of the deep caves that pierce the coast, which at high tide was unapproachable except by swimming, and at low so piled up with sea-weed at its mouth as to seem only a mere hole in the cliff. Here, on a broad ledge high beyond reach of the tide, I spent the weary hours, living for the most part on sea-weed, or a chance crab or lobster, cooked at a fire of bracken or hay, collected at peril of my life in the upper world.

Once as I peeped out I saw a boat cruising along the shore, and discovered in one of its crew no other than he who had acted as leader of the gathering of a week ago. So near did they come that I could even hear their voices.

"You're wastin' your time, captain, over a spalpeen like that. Sure, if he's alive he's far enough away by this time."

The leader turned to the speaker and said, —

"If I could but catch him he would not travel far again. Was there no news of him at Knockowen?"

"'Deed no; only lamenting from the ladies when his empty boat came ashore."

Then they passed out of hearing, never even looking my way. At last, when I judged they had abandoned the pursuit for a time and were returned to Rathmullan, I ventured out on to the headland, and one day even dared to walk as far as to the old cabin at Fanad.

It had become a ruin since I saw it last. The winter's winds had lifted the thatch, and the wall on one side had tumbled in. There was no sign of the old life we lived there. The little window from which the guiding light had shone so often was fallen to pieces. Even the friendly hearth within was filled with earth and rubbish.

I left it with a groan; it was like a grave. As I wandered forth, turning my way instinctively to the old landing-place, a flash of oars over the still water (it was a day of dead calm) sent my heart to my mouth. The place was so desolate that even this hint of life startled me. Who could it be that had found me out here?

Quick as thought I dropped on my hands and knees and crawled in among the thick bracken at the path-side. There was one place I remembered of old where Tim and I had often played—a deep sort of cup, grown full of bracken, and capped by a big rock, which to any one who did not know it seemed to lie flat on the soil. Hither I darted, and only just in time, for the boat's keel grated on the stones as I slipped into cover.

I peered out anxiously and as best I could without showing myself. By their footsteps and voices there were two persons. And when they came nearer, and I caught a momentary glance as they climbed the path to the cabin, I recognised in one of them the face of one of my late captors.

Whether they were here after me or on some other mischief I could not guess. But I hid low, as you may fancy.

Then a sudden thought came to me. The boat was down at the pier. Why should I stay where I was, hunted like a partridge, while across the lough I should at least be no worse off, and have seven clear miles of water between me and my pursuers? Now was my time if ever. Besides—and once more I think I blushed, even under the bracken—on the other side of the lough was my little Lady Kit.

So while the two men walked up the steep path to the cabin I slipped from my hiding-place and ran down to the boat. And a minute later I was clear of the land, with my bows pointing, as they had pointed so often before, for the grim turrets of Kilgorman.

Chapter Twelve
How I joined the good ship "Arrow"

It was a still, sultry afternoon, and as I lay on my oars half-a-mile from shore I made up my mind I had little help to look for from the breezes; nor, as the tide was then running, could I afford to drift. I must row steadily, unless I wished to find myself out in the open, without supplies, before nightfall. However, that was no great hardship, and after my idle week in the cave I was glad enough (had my stomach only been a little less empty!) of a little hard work.

Whether the two men whose boat I had borrowed discovered their loss sooner or later I do not know to this day. But they might have left me a handier craft. I knew her of yore, an old Rathmullan tub, useful enough to ferry market women across to Inch, but ill-suited for a single rower on a windless sea.

For all that I was glad enough to have her, and feel myself once more my own master.

I would fain have put her head to Knockowen had I dared. But there I knew I could not look for safety. His honour, no doubt thankful to be allowed to consider me dead, would resent my return, and a way would soon be had of handing me over to the League, who by this time were in hue and cry to have my life. Martin, fool as he was, could be trusted to see to that business, while his honour received the compliments of his brother magistrates on his loyalty and sacrifices.

No; if I landed anywhere it must be at Kilgorman, where I should hardly be looked for, or if I was, should possibly pass for one of the ghosts of the place.

It was a dark night, without even a moon, before the distant light of Knockowen far up the lough showed me I must be coming within reach of my destination. A little breeze was now coming in from the open, which would, did I only dare to take it, carry me to my little lady's side in less than an hour. Alas, it was not for me! and I pulled toilfully on.

It was not without some groping that at last I found the little creek into which the *Cigale* was wont to creep on her secret visits; and here at last, worn-out with fatigue and hunger, and still more with care, I ran my boat and landed.

What to do next I hardly knew. Food was what I needed most; after that, sleep; and after that, safety. It seemed as if I was to sup off the last, which was poor comfort to an empty stomach. I felt my way as quietly as I could up the track which led from the creek, and found myself presently on the cliff above, close to my dear mother's grave. I might as well sleep here as anywhere else, and when they found me dead in the morning they would not have far to carry me.

Was I turning coward all of a sudden—I, who had looked down the barrel of a gun a week ago and not quailed? The gleam of the white cross on the Gormans' tomb made me start and shiver. I seemed to hear footsteps in the long grass, and detect phantom lights away where the house was.

Presently I felt so sure that I heard steps that I could stay where I was no longer, and hurried back by the way I had come towards the boat. Then gathering myself angrily together, and equally sure I had heard amiss, I turned back again and marched boldly up towards Kilgorman House.

Whether it was desperation or some inward calling, I know not, but my courage rose the nearer I came. What had I to fear? What worse could happen to me in the house of my birth than out here on the pitiless hillside?

Even when I found the avenue-gate locked and barred I did not repent. It was easily climbed.

Soon I came under the grim walls, and, as if to greet me, a wandering ray of the moon came out and fell on the window above the hall-door. It even surprised me how little fear I felt as I now hauled myself up by the creepers and clambered on to the porch. But here my triumph reached its limit.

The window this time was closely barred. His honour had no doubt guessed how, on my former visits, I had found entrance, and had taken this means to thwart my next. No shaking or pulling was of any avail. Kilgorman, by that way at least, was unassailable.

Yet I was not to be thwarted all at once. My courage, I confess, was a little daunted as I clambered down to earth, and proceeded to feel my way carefully round the house for some more likely entry. But entry there was none. Every window and door was fast. The moonlight, which swept fitfully over the stagnant swamp, struck only on sullen, forbidding walls, and the breeze, now fast rising, moaned round the eaves to a tune which sent a shudder through my vitals.

My courage seemed to die away with it. But I determined to make one more round of the walls before I owned myself beaten. I tried the bar of every window. One after another they resisted stiffly, till suddenly I came on one (that below the room where I had found the strange relic of my mother months ago) which yielded a little in my hand, and seemed to invite me to test it again. The second time it gave more, and after a while, being eaten through with rust, it broke off.

The bars on either side of it proved equally yielding, and though some cost more trouble than others, I succeeded in about half-an-hour in breaking away sufficient to effect an entrance. The window behind the bars was easily forced, and once more I found myself standing inside Kilgorman.

It would be a lie to say that I felt no fears. Indeed every step I took along the dark passage helped to chill my blood, and long before I had reached the door of the great kitchen I wished myself safe outside again.

But shame, and the memory of that pathetic message from my dead mother, held me to my purpose. And, as if to encourage me, the candle stood where I had found it once before on the little ledge, and beside it, to my astonishment, a small crust of bread. It must have stood there a week, and was both stale and mouldy. But to my famishing taste it was a repast for a king, and put a little new courage into me.

It surprised me to find the great apartment once again crowded with arms, stacked all along the sides and laid in heaps on the centre of the floor. What perplexed me was not so much the arms themselves as the marvel how those that brought them entered and left the house.

But just now I had no time for such speculations. I was strung up to a certain duty, and that I must perform, and leave speculation for later. My mother's letter, if it meant anything, meant that I was to seek for something below or behind the great hearth; and as I peered carefully round it with my candle I could not help recalling the ghost which Tim and I had both heard, years ago, advance to this very spot and there halt.

Save the deep recess of the fireplace itself, there was no sign above or below of any hiding-place. The flagstones at my feet were solid and firm, and the bricks on either side showed neither gap nor crack. I pushed the candle further in and stepped cautiously over the crumbled embers into the hollow of the deep grate itself.

As I did so a blast from above extinguished the light, and at the same moment a sound of footsteps fell on my ear, not this time from the outer passage, but apparently from some passage on the other side of the wall against which I crouched.

I felt round wildly with my hands for the opening by which I had entered. Instead of that I found what felt like a step in the angle of the wall, and above it another. An instinct of self-preservation prompted me to clamber up here, and ensconce myself on a narrow ledge in the chimney, some six feet above the level of the ground.

Here I waited with beating heart as the footsteps came nearer. I could judge by the sound that they belonged not, like the last I had heard, to a wandering woman, but to two men, advancing cautiously but with set purpose, and exchanging words in whispers.

Presently, to my amazement, a ray of light shot through the blackness of the recess below me, followed by a creaking noise as a part of the floor of the hearth swung slowly upwards, and revealed to my view a dimly-lit, rocky passage below, slanting downwards, and leading, as I could judge by the hollow sound that came through it, towards the shore of the lough.

I could now understand how it came that a house so closely barred and bolted was yet so easily frequented. And, indeed, the whole mystery of the smuggled arms became clear enough.

The two men who now clambered up, carrying a lantern, which illuminated the whole of the recess, and (had they only thought of looking up) the very ledge on which I sat, were sailors; and in one I recognised the foreign-looking fellow who, years ago, had commanded the *Cigale* and attended my mother's wake. I knew from what I had overheard at his honour's that, since my father had given himself up to the smuggling of arms, and received charge of the *Cigale*, this worthy fellow had left, that ship and devoted himself to the more perilous occupation of robbing his Majesty's subjects indiscriminately on the high seas. His companion was evidently, by his villainous looks, a desirable partner in the same business.

"I told you so," said the latter, turning his lantern into the room. "Guns enough for a regiment. Luck for us."

"We have room enough for the lot," growled the Frenchman in pretty plain English. "Monsieur Gorman shall find that two can play at one game. He smuggles the guns in in the *Cigale*, I smuggle them out in the *Arrow*. *Parbleu*! we are quits."

And he laughed a loud laugh at his own jest. Then they proceeded to count their booty, and while so engaged it seemed to me that I had better escape before my position became more exposed, as it would be sure to be as soon as the business of carrying the guns through the recess began. So I took advantage of the darkness, when they were engaged at the far end of the kitchen, to drop from my perch and slip through the trap-door.

The peril of this movement only dawned on me when I found myself in the narrow, rocky cave. If this secret passage were guarded at the other end, as was most likely, by sentinels from the ship, what was to become of me? However, there was no retreating now. So I groped my way forward, down the ever-widening passage, till at last I found myself in a great wide-mouthed cave, full of water, in the middle of which ran a smooth causeway of stones, forming a kind of natural pier and landing-place. The rocky ledges running out beyond on either side formed a little harbour, in which, in the roughest weather, the water was fairly calm; and a further tongue of rock beyond that, rising some thirty or forty feet, and seeming to any one approaching it from without to be part of the cliffs, offered a safe riding-place for a ship of moderate draught.

As good luck would have it, the cave was empty. The *Arrow* must have come in after I had crossed the lough that evening. And the French skipper and his mate had evidently left their crew to anchor and clear the vessel in the roads while they reconnoitred the house.

I could see very little of the ship through the darkness, and, indeed, was too busy making myself scarce to heed her.

Nor had I much time to spare. For almost before I had got round the ledge and clambered partly up the cliff at the top of the cave mouth, I heard a boat putting off and voices making for the little harbour.

After that, fatigue and hunger did their work with me, and despite the peril of my position I fell asleep, and never woke till the sun was high and hot in the heavens.

Then, when I looked out, I saw as pretty a little schooner as I had ever set eyes on lying in the roads. I used to think it hard to beat the *Cigale* for looks, but the *Arrow* was her superior in every way. She was a bigger vessel, and armed at every port. Her lines were both light and strong, and by the cut of her rigging I could fancy she had the speed of a greyhound.

The sight of her set all my old sea-longing aflame. Pirate as she was, it would be good, I thought, to be on her and face the open sea, far away from my persecutors and enemies—away from Knockowen, and Kilgorman, and—

Here I stopped short. Knockowen, next to the *Cigale* where Tim was, held what counted most to me of this world's good. Kilgorman held the spirit of my dead mother, waiting to be relieved of its trouble. How could I desert the one or the other and call myself a brave man?

What I could not decide, fate decided for me. The cave below me was guarded by the pirate's men, who clattered their muskets on the stones and kept a keen look-out on all sides for any chance intruder. To quit my present perch would be certain death. So I lay and watched the boat as she plied backwards and forwards with the guns, and wondered how soon the task of loading would be done.

It went on all the day, and every hour I felt myself grow fainter and more sick with hunger. For nearly two days, except last night's crust, I had tasted nothing; and before that, sea-weed had been the chief article of my diet. The scene presently seemed to swim before me, and at last, what with the heat and famine, I fairly swooned away.

When I came to, two curious faces were bent over me, and my bed was no longer the rocky cliff side, but the hard floor of a boat as it danced over the waves.

"He looks a likely lad," said one voice.

"He's safer with us than ashore," said another. "I warrant he was put there to spy on us."

"Come, lad," said the first speaker, shaking me not altogether roughly; "we have you safe this time."

"'Deed, sir," said I, "as long as you give me some food you may do what you like with me."

And with this I rolled over again and all grew dim. When I opened my eyes next it was dark, and by the motion under me I guessed I was on the ship. A lantern swung dimly overhead, and a loud snoring below me showed me I was not alone in my bunk. What was of more interest just then, a piece of a loaf and some salt meat stood within reach of where I lay, and had evidently been put there for my use. You may guess if I let them stand long.

This refreshment, with the sleep I had had, and a few drops of rum in the tail of a bottle that stuck from my messmate's pocket, made a new man of me. And I sank back to my rest with a sense of comfort I have rarely known the like of since.

In the morning a rough hand roused me.

"Come, you have had enough coddling, my hearty. The captain wants you. And, if you'll take my advice, you'll say your prayers before you go on deck, as he'll likely drop you overboard."

This failed to frighten me, as it was meant to do; and I gathered myself together and climbed the hatchway, feebly enough, I confess, but with good cheer, and stood on the deck of the *Arrow*.

The coast of Donegal was clear over our stern, and a smart breeze from the east filled our sails and sent us spanking through the water.

The skipper was sitting aft, pipe in mouth, and waiting for me. I resolved to take the bold course and not wait to be spoken to.

"The top of the morning to you, captain," said I, saluting; "and it's well you're looking since you were at my mother's wake."

He stared at me, and then seemed to understand.

"You—you are Gallagher's boy, then?"

"The same, captain," said I; "and I'm obliged to you for this day's food."

"Gallagher was no friend of mine," said he; "but since he is dead, that shall not be against you, if you sail with me."

"Dead!" I exclaimed. "Is my father dead?"

"The *Cigale* went down off Foreland Head a month since."

"And Tim, my brother, was he drowned?"

"Likely enough, if he was aboard. Only two of the crew escaped.—So you sail under my orders?"

"I have nothing else to do," said I.

"You may swing at the yard-arm, if you prefer it," said he.

"Thanking you all the same, I'll sail where I am," said I.

So, with a very heavy heart, I found myself one of the crew of the *Arrow*.

Chapter Thirteen
The guard-house at Brest

Captain Cochin—for so the commander of the *Arrow* styled himself, though I always had my doubts whether he had any right to one title or the other—was too well aware of the value of his cargo to risk it in pursuing his ordinary calling of a pirate on the present voyage. So he stood well out to sea, ostentatiously flying the English flag, and giving friendly salutes to any chance vessels that came in his course.

"*Parbleu!*" said he, "England owes me one debt for taking the guns away from those who would have used them against her, and selling them to my poor countrymen, who will use them against one another. But there is no gratitude in England, and if I want payment I must help myself. But not this voyage—by-and-by."

As for me, the joy I should have felt at finding myself free and at sea was damped by the news of the loss of the *Cigale*, and with it, of my father and Tim. The hope of seeing Tim again had kept me in heart during many a trouble and danger, and now I felt more alone than ever.

In the whole world, except Con the dog, there was left me but one friend; and she, if she ever thought of me, did so as of one below her, and already dead. But that I was young and clung hard to life, I would as soon have dropped over the side of the *Arrow* as anywhere else, and so ended the bad business of my little history.

In a day or two, however, as the wind freshened and the great Atlantic waves pitched the *Arrow* like a plaything from one to the other, my spirits began to rise once more, and the cloud on my mind gave way before the cheery influence of a seaman's life.

One of the first things I discovered was that I knew far less about seamanship than I gave myself credit for. Sailing the *Arrow* was a very different business from sailing his honour's lumbering tubs across Lough Swilly, and I had to own that I had a great deal to learn and very little to teach before I could call myself a complete sailor. Still, I was handy, and not afraid to lend a hand at anything, from holding the helm to cooking the mate's dinner. And so, before many days were over, I had taken my place without much ado as one of the crew.

For a ship of that size, engaged in such a trade, a crew of thirty men was small enough. Most of them were foreigners, a few, like myself, Irish, and the rest English. The one thing that kept them all from quarrelling was the hope of plunder; and it was easy to guess that, in the matter of the stolen guns, although the credit of that achievement belonged to Captain Cochin alone, the men would not have agreed on this peaceable journey to France if they had not been promised a share in the fruits of the cargo when sold.

Captain Cochin found out that it is as hard to avoid the enemy's ships when you do not want them as it is to fall in with them when you do.

We had been out nearly a week, beating about against fitful winds down the west coast of Ireland, when one evening just before nightfall we sighted land on our weather-bow, and between us and it a sail bearing down our way.

As far as we could make out the stranger was a cruiser, in all probability one of the government vessels at that time stationed off Bantry Bay, on the look-out for some of the foreign smugglers and privateers that made it their hunting-ground. The light fell too suddenly to enable us to see more, but Captain Cochin flew the English colours at his mast-head, and held on his course until night hid us completely.

Then we put out into the wind and ran for the open sea, and waited for the morning.

The short midsummer night left us little waiting; and as soon as day broke, the first thing we saw, within a league of us, and bearing right across our course, was the stranger in full chase. She was a brigantine fully armed, and carrying a great spread of sail, but to our surprise she flew not the English but the French colours.

On seeing this, Captain Cochin quickly hauled down the English flag, and ran up that of his own country; but he disregarded the stranger's signal to come to, and held on with every breath of wind he could get into his canvas.

"Set a thief to catch a thief," they say. And so, the French privateer suspecting the French pirate to have good reason for running away, pressed on all sail, and gave full chase.

What surprised me most was to see that she was fast coming up on us. I had never contemplated such a thing as the *Arrow* being caught by anything on water; but I had to admit now I was wrong. If the *Arrow* was a hare, the Frenchman was a greyhound.

However, there was no time to speculate on questions of speed. The question was, should we show fight, or lie-to and explain ourselves? There was no hope of a ship like ours, so slenderly manned, being able to capture or even disable our heavily-armed pursuer. On the other hand, to surrender meant losing all our booty, and possibly our ship into the bargain; for the French, when it suited their purpose, were ready enough to take advantage of a chance of pressing a smart craft like the *Arrow* into their own service, especially as she bore an English name, and was known to have preyed pretty impartially on friend and foe alike.

An eager consultation took place on deck, some urging one course, some another, while some proposed to throw the cargo overboard, and one or two to scuttle the ship.

However, as good luck would have it, there was a fifth way out of the difficulty which we had little dreamed of.

"A sail on the weather-quarter!" suddenly shouted our watch.

The captain and mate went aloft to view her, and presently reported an English frigate in full sail bearing down in our direction. She seemed to be coming fast, across the wind, and by the look of her was a regular line-of-battle ship, with a double row of guns snarling from her ports.

"That settles us," said Captain Cochin, rapidly recovering his spirits. "While the lion and the tiger fight, Mister Fox slips off with the booty. Way there; keep her as she goes, master; and good-day to you, monsieur."

He spoke the truth. The Frenchman, as soon as she caught sight of the English frigate, altered her course abruptly, and instead of being the hunter became the hunted. So, for an hour or more, each of us held her own way, the Englishman closing on the Frenchman, and the *Arrow* sailing clear of both. Towards afternoon, the distant sound of a gun behind us told us the battle had already begun, and before nightfall the two were no doubt at it broadside to broadside.

After that, we gave the land a wide berth, and met nothing we need fear, till at last, with the French flag flying, we sailed merrily into Brest Harbour, safe and sound, without a scratch on our hull or a hole in our canvas.

But here Captain Cochin's good luck suddenly deserted him; for no sooner was he berthed, with sails stowed and anchors out, than he discovered that the French merchantman next him was none other than a vessel which on his last voyage out he had attempted to board in mid-channel, and, but for a sudden squall, would have captured and plundered. The captain of the merchantman had already reported his wrongs to the authorities; and now, finding himself cheek by jowl with the offender, lost not a moment in taking his revenge.

So, just as we were about to lower our boat for a jaunt on shore, to refresh us after our voyage, the port-admiral sent off a galley to board us, and summon us to attend on shore in irons, and show cause why we should not, each one of us, be hanged by the neck.

It was a pretty end to our jaunt, and so suddenly done that there was nothing for it but to surrender and follow where we were bidden. No doubt a smart craft like the *Arrow*, with a cargo of guns, was a good enough excuse for the French admiral, quite apart from our delinquencies; and at a time like this, when France lived under a reign of terror, the only excuse needed for any act, just or unjust, was the force to perform it.

You may imagine, out of all the hang-dog prisoners who marched that day through the streets of Brest, I felt myself the most ill-used; for I had sailed in the *Arrow* by no will of my own, and had taken part in no act of violence against any Frenchman, dead or alive. And yet, because I chanced to be among the crew, I was to be hung by the neck! I knew well enough, from what I had heard of French justice, that any excuses would be but breath wasted. Indeed, as one of the few English of the party, I should probably be spared even the farce of a trial. My only hope was that Captain Cochin, who had not been unkind to me so far, would speak a word in my favour.

We were marched to a dismal, white-washed guard-house on the edge of the town, and were there locked up by half-dozens till it suited the admiral's convenience to consider our case, and that was not till next day. The cell in which I and five of my shipmates were confined was a small, underground cellar, reeking with damp and foul smells, and lit only by a narrow grating in the ceiling, through which all night the rain poured steadily, forming a huge puddle in the middle of the earth floor.

There was one narrow bench on which we sat huddled together, to eat our scanty portion of black bread, and pass the dismal night as best we could. For my part, that night reconciled me to the prospect of a French gallows as much as anything.

In the morning we were ordered to march once more, and were brought into the presence of some official who acted as judge to try cases of misdemeanour on the high seas. With the exception of Captain Cochin and myself (I was able to speak the language a little) few of us understood French, and the formality of having the proceedings interpreted to us was not even allowed. The captain and certain of the crew of the merchantman were present and told their grievance, and with a large sweep of assumption swore that we were each as bad as the other. The judge demanded what Captain Cochin had to say, and cut him short before he had well opened his mouth.

I made a feeble effort to put myself right, not so much in any hope of moving the tribunal as of reminding Captain Cochin of my claims on his good offices. But he was too savage and perturbed to take the hint.

Then it came out that we were bringing arms into France, and were called to prove that they were not for the use of the enemies of liberty. Whom were they consigned to? They were not consigned.—Where did they come from? Ireland.—Ireland was in sympathy with France in her war against tyranny. To rob Ireland was to rob the friend of France. To whom were the arms about to be sold? To any that would buy them.—None but the enemies of France needed arms. Her sons were all armed already. Therefore the traffic was not only wicked but treasonable, and for treason there was but one punishment—death.

At this the audience, who had crowded into the court, cheered loudly.

Had we any defence? any witnesses? Of course we had none but ourselves.

Then the sentence of the court was pronounced. Captain Cochin was to be guillotined next morning. The rest of us were to be hanged in chains that afternoon, and our bodies left exposed to view for three days as a warning to pirates and traitors.

So ended our trial; and had it not been so tragic in its ending, I could have laughed at the farce of it.

We were marched back to our prison to spend the few hours that remained of our lives; and on the way our attention was directed by a friendly guard to a great gallows with accommodation on it for at least ten persons side by side. I only hoped, if it came to that, I might be in the first batch.

This time I was placed in a different cell from that I had occupied the night before. It was above ground, and lit by a larger window. Indeed, it was not intended to be used as a cell at all; but, as my jailer explained in a jocular way, he had so many guests that day that he was obliged to accommodate some of them in the soldiers' quarters, and begged monsieur (that was I) would accept his excuses for not having made more elaborate preparations for his reception. In half-an-hour or so, he said, there would be more room. If monsieur could kindly wait till then, he should have an apartment suited to his dignity.

"Monsieur is too good," said I in the politest French I could muster, thinking it wise to humour him; "but I should take it as a favour to be allowed to give up my apartment."

"By no means," said the other, slapping me on the back; "we cannot spare your company a moment before the time.—Meanwhile, make yourself at home, and receive the assurance of my profound esteem."

"There is one favour I would beg, if I might be so bold," said I. "In the short time left me I would like to write a letter to a friend."

"If it is a lady friend," said the Frenchman with a wink, "it might be allowed—provided she is fair, and I may have the honour of delivering it."

"She is fair," said I, trying hard to keep up the jest; "and I will gladly trust you with what I write to her."

The fellow was, after all, of the good-natured kind, and I think meant no harm by his jests. At any rate, after some demur, he agreed to loose my handcuffs for half-an-hour while I wrote; and having fetched me in pen and paper, left me to myself, double locking the door after him.

This was what I wanted. I waited till his footsteps died down the passage, and then crept silently to the window. It was above my reach, but by jumping I could just catch the bars and haul myself up. Not being intended as a dungeon, the bars were loosely fixed, and I found that it would be possible to remove one, and so allow room through which to squeeze. The casement itself was of the ordinary kind, and opened outwards with a simple catch-fastener.

Outside was a courtyard at the back of the guard-house, in which were scattered sundry brooms and buckets, and a pile of rubbish in one corner. By mounting this I calculated I could get my hands to the top of the outer wall; and once over that, my chance was come.

I returned to my table and pretended to be occupied with writing, while really I was listening with all my ears for any sound that might show on which side of the prison the guard was set.

The Frenchman, I believe, had been quite correct in saying that the company at present being entertained in the place was inconveniently large; and if so, the guard set over them was probably dangerously small. And if the executions were to begin at once, it was conceivable they might be still smaller as the afternoon wore on. So, though I knew that my precious half-hour was slipping by, I waited patiently for a good part of it, till presently I heard a word of command, and a confused tramp of footsteps down the passage.

This was the first batch of my luckless comrades being marched to their death, and I shuddered as I thought how near I stood to their fate.

But cost what it would I would make a dash for freedom first. I sprang to the window and hauled myself up on to the ledge. The loose bar gave way after a very little coaxing, and next minute I was out of the casement and in the little courtyard. One or two windows overlooked it, but either these were too high for any one to look from, or there was no one to look, or if there was, the attraction of the ghastly scene going on at the other side took them the other way. And to this same attraction, no doubt, was due the fact that no sentry was patrolling the back of the prison.

I succeeded by means of the rubbish heap in scaling the wall. But before leaping down on the other side, the thought occurred to me that if I could hide somewhere near till night, I should have a better chance of escaping with my pursuers ahead of me than behind me.

By following the line of the wall I found I could reach a corner of the prison where there was a blank wall, up which a gutter pipe ran to the rambling, gabled roof, where, if I could only reach it, I should hardly be looked for.

The clamber was a perilous one, especially as the heavy rain rendered the iron pipe more than usually slippery. But I was sailor enough to understand how to grip with hands and feet, and succeeded with no great difficulty in reaching the top and hiding myself away in a deep angle of the roof—not safe, indeed, but with time at least to breathe and consider what next.

Nor was I too soon; for I had not lain there two minutes before I heard a sudden shout and rush of feet in the yard below, and knew that my escape had been discovered and that a price was upon my head.

Chapter Fourteen
The wood near Morlaix

As I expected, the hiding-place I had chosen was about the safest I could have had. For my jailers, taking note of the trampled dust-heap in the corner, and finding, moreover, my half-written letter (which I had taken the precaution to drop on the far side of the wall before I doubled on my steps), had no doubt that I had fled either towards the open country or to the harbour, where possibly I might succeed in smuggling myself on board a ship.

So, instead of increasing the sentries round the house, they actually reduced them in order to reinforce the pursuing party. My policy was to get away while the coast was comparatively unprotected, and trust to night and my good angel to get clear of the place. So, when the excitement had subsided a little, and the remaining soldiers on guard were summoned to assist at the hanging of the second batch of my shipmates, I stole from my hiding-place and, covered by the sea-mist which came with the sundown, slid down the pipe and crossed the wall, and set off as briskly as I could in an easterly direction through the outskirts of the town.

The streets were moderately crowded with wayfarers and loungers, and as I sauntered along with a big French cigar in my mouth, which had cost me two of my few remaining sous, no one paid me any particular heed. A few of the soldiers eyed me suspiciously as a doubtful character, but they were too accustomed to queer sea-dogs prowling about the place to consider me worth the trouble of a challenge.

At last I came to one of the posting taverns of the town where the coach for Paris was beginning to take up passengers in the presence of the usual curious crowd of idlers. At the present time, when everybody went in terror of his life, and to be suspected of any design against the liberties of France was the same thing as being condemned for it, it was no easy task even for the most innocent and well-conducted traveller to get clear of a town like Brest.

The few merchants and tourists and nervous women who ventured were made to pass through a row of soldiers, who examined their passports narrowly, and sometimes ordered them to stand aside for further inquiry; a command which sent the blood out of the cheeks of him who heard it, and made him think no more of the mail-coach but of the low tumbrel on which the victims of the guillotine took their last dreadful drive.

Even while I stood, there was one woman—a would-be traveller—who failed to satisfy the officer on guard, and who, on being ordered back, fell on her knees with shrieks and begged for mercy. And not one of those who stood gaping beside me but said she would be in luck if she got it.

Still more fuss was made about a horseman who demanded leave to ride forward to Paris on an errand of hot haste. He was, to all appearance, a gentleman's lackey, and, from the little I heard of the talk, spoke English easier than French. He was ordered to dismount while the officer carefully read his passport by the light of a lantern and inspected his letters of introduction and even of credit. Finally, after much suspense, he was allowed to remount, which he did in less than a moment, and clattered away through the pouring rain out into the wet night.

The sight of him made me envious indeed. What would I not give for a sound horse under me and a sound passport in my pocket!

At last the diligence was nearly ready. The luggage was stowed in the boot, and two great mail baskets were swung and padlocked on the bar underneath. The four horses were brought out and put to, and driver, guard, and officer retired to the hostel for a parting glass.

An impulse seized me then to slip out of the crowd and creep forward on the road under the deep shadow of the wall. Far I could not go, I knew, for at the barrier I should be detected and stopped. But the coach, having been so carefully inspected at its starting-point, would, I judged, be allowed through the barrier without further challenge. It should not be my fault if I did not go through with it.

The rain was pouring in sheets, and on such a night no one would be likely to walk abroad for pleasure. Nor between the hostel and the barrier was it probable that any sentinel would patrol the empty street. At any rate I met nothing, except a market-cart coming in, the occupants of which were too busy discussing the handling they had received at the barrier to look under the shadow of the wall for a vagrant boy.

At last I found a convenient place, where the road was dark as night, and where a sharp turn made it likely that the horses would be taken slowly past. Here I crouched, dripping from head to foot, for a long ten minutes.

Then my heart beat as I heard the dull rumble of the wheels, and caught the lurid glare of the two lamps coming. By the brief glance I got I saw that the guard (as I had hoped) had crouched in for shelter under the driver's hood, and that the sole occupant of the back *coupé* was buried under his tarpaulin.

Now was my time. I had carefully selected my point of attack. The two baskets I spoke of underneath the coach swung on double iron bars, and between the two, could I only scramble there, there was just room for me to perch, completely hidden, at any rate while night lasted, from the keenest of eyes.

I saw the driver throw himself back and pull in the reins for the corner, and in the momentary check of the speed I darted out from my hiding-place, and clambered in under the tail of the coach and reached the bars between the baskets. But for Providence I should have fallen between the wheels. As it was, the start forward of the horses carried me dragging on my toes twenty yards before I could haul myself up and lie face upwards across the bars, with my head on one basket, my feet on the other, and my nose almost rubbing the bottom of the coach.

I have, I own, travelled many a mile more comfortably, but few more happily. I had but one terror, and that was short-lived. At the barrier the coach pulled up, and the guard got down to hand in his papers, and to help himself to a spare wrapper out of the boot. Then, with a cheerful "Hi! hi!" he clambered back to his place, the barrier swung open, and we were out of Brest in the open country outside.

Little I cared that the mud plastered my back with a coat as thick as that I had on. Little I cared that the drippings of the coach fell in my mouth and eyes, and the stench of stale straw almost choked me. I was free! The noose on the gallows would remain empty for me. I was so gay I believe I even laughed under the coach.

Presently, however, I began to realise that this security was not to be for ever. When daylight came, or even sooner, should we reach the end of our first stage before, I should be able no longer to hide myself. It would be wiser to escape half-an-hour too soon than be discovered half-an-hour too late.

So when, some four hours out, I judged by the toiling of the horses we were approaching the summit of a hill, I slipped from my perch, and after running some little way under the boot, cast loose just as the driver cracked his whip and the horses started at a spanking trot down the incline.

It frightened me to find myself standing in the open road and hear the diminishing sounds of the friendly diligence. In front of me I could see the grey break of dawn struggling among the heavy clouds. Behind me swept the rain, buffeting me forward. Somewhere or other I must find shelter from the night.

No sooner had I resolved upon this than the sound of a horse approaching at full gallop sent my teeth chattering in real earnest. I had barely time to dart to the roadside and hide below the hedge when a horseman swept by. By his look he was not a soldier or an ordinary traveller, such as the courier I had seen set out from Brest. I cared little who he was, provided he rode on and let me alone. But till I lost all sound of him I spent an uneasy time in the ditch.

As soon as the August dawn gave me a view, I found myself on the top of a great exposed heath, across which the road reached for a mile or so, and then plunged downwards into a thick wood. Towards this wood I hastened with all the speed I could. Here at least I could lie hid a while till my next chance turned up.

That chance was nearer than I thought. About half-way through the wood the road forked into three, one way on either hand striking deep among the trees; that in the middle holding straight on, and by the marks of wheels being evidently the highroad. I struck to the right some way, and then quitted the road altogether for a glade in the wood which seemed to lead to denser shelter.

I had scarcely left the track when I was startled by the sound of a voice and a groan close by. Had I wanted to retreat I could hardly have done so unseen, but a glance in the direction from which the sound proceeded held me where I was.

A horse stood quietly nibbling the grass, and on his back, fallen forward, with arms clasping the beast's neck, and head drooping helplessly downward, was his rider, bleeding from a pistol wound in the neck, and too weak even to disengage his feet from the stirrups. In a single glance I recognised the horseman who had ridden ahead of the coach.

A pistol, evidently dropped from his hand, lay on the grass, and his hat lay between the horse's feet.

If life was not already extinct, it was fast ebbing away. I lifted him as gently as I could and laid him on the grass. He opened his eyes, and his lips moved; but for a moment he seemed choked. I tried with some moss to stanch his still bleeding wound, but the groan he gave as I touched him caused me to desist.

Then he tried to speak something in French.

"What is it?" said I, in English.

A look of quick relief came into his face.

"Ride forward with the letters—for God's sake—promise."

Even in the feeble, broken words I could recognise a countryman.

"Yes," said I.

"Horses—at each post—my purse," he gasped.

"I promise I will do as you ask—as I am an Irishman and a Christian."

That seemed to satisfy him.

"Your hand," said he, at last.

I gave it to him, and as it closed on his he groaned, and died.

It had all happened so suddenly that for a minute or two I knelt where I was, with my hand still in his, like one in a dream. Then I roused myself, and considered what was to be done.

The dead man was a good-looking youth, scarcely twenty, dressed in the habit of a gentleman's groom, and evidently, by the smartness of his accoutrement, in the employ of some one of importance. As to how he had come by his death I could only guess. But I suspected the horseman I had seen galloping back towards Brest in the morning twilight had had something to do with it. The highwayman had met the traveller, and shots had been exchanged—the one fatal, the other telling enough to send the bandit flying. The poor wounded fellow had had strength enough to turn his horse into the wood and cling to his seat. How long he had stayed thus, slowly bleeding to death, I could not say; but the diligence must have passed that way two hours ago, and he must have been well ahead of it when his journey was thus suddenly stopped.

Then I recalled his dying words, and after tethering the horse set myself to look for the papers he spoke of. I found them at last—the passport in his breast pocket, whence he could easily produce it, the others in his belt. The former described the bearer as John Cassidy, travelling from Paris to Dublin and back on urgent private business, duly signed and countersigned. It gave a description of the bearer, even down to the clothes he wore: I supposed to enable any official who passed him from one point of his journey to another to identify him. The letters were two in number, one addressed to Citoyen Duport, a Deputy of the National Convention, and marked with the greatest urgency. The other—and this startled me the most—to one George Lestrange at Paris, with no other address. Lestrange! The name called to mind one or two memories. Was not the gay young officer I had once ferried across to Rathmullan a Lestrange—a kinsman of my lady; and was not Biddy McQuilkin of Kerry Keel, who once set her cap at my father, in the service of this same Lestrange's aunt in Paris? Strange if this hot errand should concern them! All things considered, I decided that the wisest thing would be for me to put on the dead man's clothes, and make myself in general appearance as near to the description of the passport as possible. In fact, for the rest of this journey I must be John Cassidy himself, travelling post to Paris, with a horse waiting on him at each stage, a purse full of money, a pistol, and a belt containing two urgent letters of introduction. Little dreamed I when I sneaked out of Brest under the belly of that lumbering diligence that I was to go to my journey's end in this style!

Before I started I buried the dead man, and along with him my cast-off clothes, in a pit in the wood, which I covered over with leaves and moss. Then I mounted my horse, stuck my loaded pistol in my belt, commended my ways to Heaven, and cantered on in the face of the rosy summer dawn towards Paris.

Chapter Fifteen
A Rat-trap in the Rue d'Agnès

The worth of my credentials was very soon put to the test; for an hour's ride brought me to Morlaix, where, as I had learned from a hastily scrawled list of places on the cover of the passport, I was to expect my first fresh horse.

Here there was some grumbling at my lateness and wondering as to the cause of it. For the diligence guard had reported that I (or rather he whom I represented) had started ahead of the coach from Brest, and should have passed Morlaix three hours in front.

Whereupon I explained that I had been attacked by a highwayman, and obliged to hide in the woods till daylight. At which they laughed, and said if I chose to travel to Paris alone on horseback, instead of journeying as most honest citizens did, I must expect to be shot at. Then I was ordered into the *conciergerie* while my passport and papers were examined.

It was lucky for me I had put on the dead man's clothes, and that the description chiefly related to these. As regards personal appearance I was described as young, beardless, with blue eyes, brown hair, and "nothing remarkable," which equally well described me as it did poor John Cassidy.

"Who is your master?" demanded the officer.

"Citoyen Lestrange," said I boldly, "an Irishman resident in Paris."

"Where have you been?"

"To Dublin, to see my master's agent, Mr Patten."

"Is this Monsieur Patten's letter?"

"That to my master is his. That to the Citoyen Duport is from a French gentleman in Dublin whose name I do not know."

It hurt me to tell so many lies in one breath. But I must needs have some story to tell, and prayed Heaven to forgive me for this.

To my relief the officer seemed satisfied, and I gathered that the Citoyen Duport must be a man of consequence in Paris.

"Pass, John Cassidy," said he, handing me back my papers.

The same ceremony awaited me at each halting-place, and I realised before I was half-way to Paris that it was no easy matter for a stranger to travel in France in those days. What would have become of me but for the accident in the wood near Morlaix it were hard to say.

But though I had much to congratulate myself on, I confess that as I drew near to the capital I had much to perturb me. At every halting-place on the way there were some who shrugged their shoulders when they heard I was going to Paris. Paris, I heard it whispered, was no safe place just then even for a Frenchman, still less for a stranger. The streets were flowing with the blood of those whose only crime was that they were suspected of not being the friends of the people. As to my passport, it would be of little use to me unless I could give a fit account of myself and my masters. As for Citoyen Duport, if I once put my head in his jaws I need not expect to see it on again. And as for my letter to Citoyen Lestrange, I had better carry it in the sole of my stocking, and let no one know I bore a missive to any Englishman or Irishman in Paris. My wisest course, so one frank official at Alençon told me, was to know no French, to have no errand but my letter to Citoyen Duport; that delivered, he thought I should save trouble if I shot myself through the head.

All this was very alarming; and I began to doubt, when at last I caught sight of the towers and domes of Paris in the distance, whether I should not have been better off after all hiding in the caves under Fanad, or dangling on the gallows beside Brest harbour.

At the barrier, however, things fell out easier for me than I had feared. For, just as I arrived, a common cart on the way out had been stopped and searched, and in it, hidden in a wood packing-case, had been unearthed some notorious enemy of the people, over whose detection there was great rejoicing, and the promise of a famous execution in the morning. For all these reasons the soldiers and officials into whose hands I fell were in high good-humour, and after scanning my passport and the letter to the deputy let me go by.

I had followed the advice of my late counsellor, and forgotten all the little French I knew, and had hidden the letter to Citoyen Lestrange in my stocking. Whether I was to carry out the rest of his advice remained to be seen.

The officer at the barrier retained my passport, saying it was done with, from which I concluded that now I was in Paris there was little hope of getting out of it again. So, feeling like a mouse in a trap, I parted company with my horse, my passport, and even my pistol (of which I was also relieved), and walked forward into the noisy city, wishing I only knew where to go next.

Presently I came into a long narrow street, where the houses overhead slanted towards one another and nearly shut out the light of heaven. Poles stuck out from the windows, on which hung clothes or signs or legends; the sight of which, swaying in the wind, mingled with the foul odour and the noise and the jostling crowd, fairly dazed a country boy like me. How, in such a place as this, was I to find what I wanted—namely, a meal and a night's lodging?

At last, in front of me, there swung a flaunting sign—"A l'Irlandois"— at which I cheered up. Here, at any rate, in the midst of this noisome babel, seemed to come a whiff from the old country, and I felt like a castaway in sight of land.

But before I had time to reach the place the whole street seemed suddenly to go mad. First there was a yell and a roll of drums at the end by which I had entered. Then every window seemed alive with people, straining forward with howls and execrations and clenched fists. From every door below poured forth a crowd, who fought with one another for a place next the roadway, waved their red caps, and shouted in a wild sort of chant some French song. In the rush stalls and barrows were overturned, but there was no one to heed; children were trampled on, but no one heard their cries; pockets were picked, but there was no one to miss their loss; windows were smashed, but there was no one to feel a draught. To my wondering fancy, all Paris had suddenly turned into this narrow Rue d'Agnès and there run mad.

I noticed that the one thing all were agreed upon, was to keep a clear space in the roadway, and strain their necks impatiently in the direction of the drums; and soon enough the reason of all this excitement became clear. Drawn by a single horse, and escorted by a troop of National Guards, came a low open cart, in which sat two persons, deadly white, gazing in a dazed vacant way at the scene around them, and sometimes casting a reproachful glance at the slowly plodding horse. One of the two was an old man, of fine, aristocratic presence, which the coarse clothes he wore could not disguise. The other was a low ruffian, with swollen face and bleared eyes, in the dress of a butcher. Between the two, except that they were on their way to death, there was nothing in common. Till to-day they had never met, and after to-day they would never meet again. The crime of one, so I heard, was that he was related to an aristocrat; that of the other, that he had murdered his own daughter. For both offences the law of France just then had but one penalty. And of the two, he who was most execrated and howled at and spat upon was the gentleman.

In less time than it takes to write it the show had passed. A few of the crowd followed to see the end of the business. The rest, for the most part, returned to their callings, and before the drums were out of hearing the Rue d'Agnès was once more a plain, dirty, ordinary Paris street.

With a heart a good deal weighted by what I had seen, I turned into the Cabaret "à l'Irlandois." If I had expected to find anything there to remind me of my own country, I was sorely disappointed. A few blouse-clad idlers sat at a table, smoking and drinking sugar and water, and discussing the news of the day with their host, a surly-looking fellow, who, whatever his inn might be, was himself a common type of Frenchman. "Now?" demanded he as I approached. "Monsieur," said I in English, "I desire a bed and some food."

"Speak French," said he in English. "I speak no French," replied I in French. Whereupon one of the idlers was summoned as interpreter. I knew French enough to hear in the words that passed between him and mine host the two expressions "spy" and "money," and I wished I had never come into the place. But it was not easy to get out now without confirming the suspicion, and I deemed it wise to appear indifferent.

"If monsieur can give me a bed, I will put up with him," said I to the interpreter; "if not—"

"Citizen Picquot sees his money before he sells his wares," said the other.

I laid a gold piece on the table. "Citizen Picquot is a wise man," said I.

Then followed a cross-examination of me, prompted by the cautious Picquot and interpreted by his ally.

"Who was I? Where did I come from? Why did I seek a lodging at his house of all others? How long was I going to stay? What was my occupation in Paris? How much more money had I got?" and so on.

To all of which I answered my best; and when I produced my letter to the Deputé Duport they treated me more ceremoniously. I was shown to a room, the like of which for filth I had never slept in before, and shall never, I hope, sleep in again. It was a large chamber, the boards of which were furred with mildew, and the valance on the bed was dropping off with rottenness. Generations of cats had haunted it and slept on the coverlet. The dungeon at Brest was fresh and sweet compared to it. Yet Citizen Picquot smilingly demanded two francs a night and the price of my candle.

"Monsieur is safe here," said he, forgetting, as did I, that I knew no French. "I had a guest, a week ago, who was found by the Guards and taken before the Tribunal and guillotined. He would have been safe too, but we had a difference about money, and I denounced him. It was only a week ago. They will not search my house again for a month to come. Monsieur will be quite safe; but if, alas, he perish (and who is quite safe in these days?), I will myself protect his effects, and see his letter to the depute duly forwarded."

All this was vastly consoling.

"Apropos," said I, "cannot I deliver my letter this evening?"

"This evening," said my host with a shrug; "it is death to approach a député à la Convention Nationale after the séance is closed. The last who did it was Mademoiselle Corday, and she— In the morning, monsieur, when the Convention sits, you shall deliver your letter; till then, peace and sound repose." And he bowed himself out.

I knew not much of the world, but I knew enough to wish myself out of this rat-trap. To try to escape just now would, I saw, be futile. Yet to spend the night there meant, if not murder, at least robbery and pestilence. A brave face was the only thing to put upon the business, and I followed Citizen Picquot downstairs and called for food and drink, in which I invited not him only but his gossips to join me.

I noticed that the door was carefully locked when any one came in or went out, and that any chance motion of mine in that direction was quickly intercepted. So the evening wore on, and presently the lights of the cabaret were extinguished, and my host passed me my candle and again bade me good-night.

I went up by no means gaily. Three other men, I observed, were still in the house, and would in all probability join in the attack upon me. I had parted with my pistol. The door was without a lock. The window was shuttered from the outside. My only arms were a small pocket-knife and my belt.

I took the precaution to secrete my letter to the deputy, along with that to Mr Lestrange, in my boot, and the little money I had left I tied up in the tail of my shirt. Then I considered that the only safe place for me that night was to sit on the floor with my back against the door and my heels against the foot of the bed, which chanced to stand at just the required length. In this posture, even if I fell asleep, any attempt to force the door would arouse me; and if the door was reasonably sound I could reckon, with my back and feet, on keeping it fast against the four, at any rate for a while.

I had a long time to wait. They evidently meant to give me time to fall asleep, and themselves, perhaps, time to consume some more of the cognac which my money had provided. I was indeed almost dozing when my ears caught the sound of an unsteady footstep on the stairs and a whispering of voices below. Then the footstep stopped outside my door, and a hand cautiously turned the handle.

"The young dog smells a rat," muttered my landlord, with a hickup which gave me some hope.

"True for you, monsieur," replied I, in as good French as I could muster. "I can shoot rats as well as smell them." And I made the blade of my knife give a click that sounded for all the world like the cocking of a pistol.

"Armed!" ejaculated the tipsy scoundrel. "God have mercy! Pardon, monsieur, I came to see if you were comfortable."

"Monsieur citoyen is too good. I am most comfortable, and beg to be waked at cock-crow. *Bonsoir.*"

I knew of course that was not the end of him, but while he stumbled downstairs to take counsel with his comrades I had at least time to breathe. I peeped out of the door. All was dark, and there was no sound but the ticking of the great Dutch clock in the shop below.

The clock! I had noticed it that evening—a great unwieldy structure like a coffin on end, and a dial above. If I could but get down to it, while my assailants were up despatching me, I might yet have a chance of eluding them. I could hear them discussing together at the foot of the stairs, and presently advance once more to the charge, not this time with my host as an advance-guard, but all together. I slipped out into the passage, and hid in a dark corner at the head of the stairs, so close, indeed, that they all but brushed against me in passing.

"*Alors, il dort,*" said my host, listening for a moment. "No; he moves. All together now."

And with one accord they hurled themselves against the door, which of course offered no resistance, and admitted them toppling one over the other into the room.

I waited no longer, but slipped down the stairs and into the clock. I had to displace the pendulum to do it, but trusted to the muddled condition of the enemy not to miss the ticking.

After a while they came down in a towering rage, blaming one another for what had happened. They were just in the humour to be quarrelsome, and as I stood motionless in my narrow sentry-box I heard as pretty a battle of words as it has ever been my lot to listen to.

Their one comfort was that I could not be far away. Either I had gone out by the window, in which case I had undoubtedly broken my neck;

or I was down in the cellar, in which case I would keep till morning. "Meanwhile, comrades, let us drink long life to the Republic, and down with the Girondists."

So to drink they fell, but were hardly settled when a loud summons came at the outer door, and a shout of, "Open, in the name of the Republic One and Indivisible!"

Then did mine host quake in his shoes, and his comrades turned pale.

"To bed!" whispered my host with trembling voice. "Go up and sleep."

They were not long in obeying, and that night the bed that was meant for me held three of the soundest sleepers in all France.

The knocking continued, and mine host, feigning a great yawn, took down his key and asked who was there.

"Citoyen Picquot, open to the National Guard."

The door opened, and half-a-dozen soldiers trooped into the shop.

"Produce your lodgers," demanded the soldier in command.

"I have but three, citizen soldier. Follow me, they shall be at your service."

The officer followed my host upstairs; the others remained below. Presently I heard a loud outcry and scuffling of feet above, and a shouted word of command. The soldiers instantly rushed up the stairs.

But no speed of theirs could equal that with which I darted from my hiding-place and out at the open door into the street, thanking Heaven that whatever rats might be caught that night in the Rue d'Agnès I was not one of them.

Chapter Sixteen
"Vive La Guillotine!"

It was midnight when I got clear of the Auberge "à l'Irlandois" in the Rue d'Agnès, and being a fine, warm autumn night I was by no means the only occupant of the street. This was fortunate for me, for the guards posted at either end would have been more inquisitive as to a solitary stranger than one of a company of noisy idlers.

That night there had been a great performance in one of the theatres in Paris, which had lasted far into the night, and was only lately over. Those I overheard speak of it said it had been a great patriotic spectacle, in the course of which National Guards and cadets had marched across the stage, unfurling the banner of the Republic, and taking the oath of the people amid scenes of wild enthusiasm and shouting. To add to the enthusiasm of the occasion a party of real volunteers had appeared, and after receiving the three-coloured cockade from their sweethearts, had shouldered their guns and marched, singing the Marseillaise, straight from the theatre to the road for La Vendue, where they were going to shed their blood for their country.

The audience had risen, waving hats and handkerchiefs to bid them God-speed, and then poured forth into the streets, shouting the chorus, and cheering till they were hoarse and tired.

It was into a party of such loyal revellers that I found myself sucked before I was half-way out of the Rue d'Agnès; and yelling and shouting at the top of my voice I passed safely the guards, and reached the broad Rue Saint Honoré. Here the crowd gradually dispersed, some one way, some another, while a few, with cries of "*A la Place,*" held on in company. With these I joined myself, and presently came to a great open square, where on a high platform stood a grim and terrible looking object. "*Vive la guillotine!*" shouted the crowd as they caught sight of it.

It was strangely lit up with the glare of the torches of some workmen who were evidently busy upon it. I could see the fatal knife being raised once or twice and let fall with a crash by way of experiment. And each time the crowd cheered and laughed, and invited one of their number to ascend the platform and put his head in the empty collar. It made me sick to watch it, yet for safety's sake I had to shout *"Vive la guillotine!"* with the rest of them, and laugh with the loudest.

Presently some one near noticed me and caught me by the arm.

"Here is one that will do, Citoyen Samson. Lift him up, comrades. Let us see if the knife is sharp enough."

At the touch of his hand I broke into a cold sweat, and clung to his knees amid shouts of laughter. It was all very well for them, who were used to such jests. I was new to it, and fell a victim to a panic such as I have never known since. A herculean strength seemed to possess me. I flung my tormentors right and left, and darted away from them into the dark recesses of the surrounding gardens. They began by giving chase, but in the end let me go, and returned to their more congenial spectacle, and presently, tired even of that, went home to bed.

It was an hour before I durst look out from my hiding-place in the midst of a clump of thick bushes. I could still see the guillotine looming in the moonlight; but the workmen, like the sightseers, had gone. The only living persons were a few women, who had seated themselves on one of the benches in front of the instrument, evidently determined on a good view of to-morrow's spectacle.

I retreated to my hiding-place with a shudder, glad I was too far away to overhear their talk.

But if I heard not theirs, I heard, oddly enough, another conversation, so near that had it been intended for my ears it could not have taken place in a better spot.

One of the speakers, by his voice, was an Englishman, of more than middle age; the other, a woman, who also spoke English, but with a foreign accent.

This is what I heard, and you may guess how much of it I comprehended:—

"No news yet?" said the old man anxiously.

"None. I expected to hear before this."

"Who is the messenger?"

"A trusty servant of madame's, and an Irishman."

"So much the worse if he is caught."

There was a pause. Then the old man inquired,—

"What hope is there for Sillery?"

"Absolutely none. He is as good as guillotined already."

"Has Edward no influence then?"

"Not now. Duport is no longer a man, but a machine—deadly, mysterious, as yonder guillotine. He would denounce me, his wife, if the Republic demanded it."

"God forbid! for you are our last friend."

Then there was another pause, and the man spoke again. He was evidently broken-down by terror, and engrossed in his own safety.

"My fear *now* is," he said, "that, if Sillery is doomed, the messenger should deliver Edward's letter to Duport at all. It will only make matters worse for us."

"Very true. It is no time for appeals to mercy," said Madame Duport. "But you said you expected a letter for yourself."

"Ay; money to escape with. That's all I live for."

"Money from Edward?"

"No. From my kinswoman, Alice Gorman.—Hush! what was that?" he cried, breaking into a whisper.

"Only a falling leaf.—How was she to reach you?"

"She was to send it to Edward, and he would forward it by the same messenger that carried his letter to Duport."

"Pray Heaven that be lost too," said the lady. "You are safer in Paris. Besides, money without a passport will avail nothing."

The old man gave a bitter laugh.

"They all desert me," said he querulously. "My nephew never shows sign; Sillery is to perish, you fear to speak to me; even my poor wife chides me."

"Surely Madame Lestrange—"

Here I started again, and slight as was the sound it broke up the conference. They separated, one in either direction, the lady gliding towards the benches in front of the guillotine, the old man (whom I now knew to be Mr Lestrange) creeping under the shadow of the trees, and presently lying at full length on a seat apparently fast asleep.

I curled myself up on a seat not far off, where I could watch him without being seen by him. A little before dawn he got up, and after carefully looking up and down the road, walked hurriedly back towards the Place de la Revolution, where he lost himself among the now increasing groups who mustered in the grey light for an early seat at the spectacle of the hour.

I dropped into a seat not far off, and in the distance, among a row of pale, hard, fatigued faces, I could see the deputy's wife, who never looked our way, but sat with her eyes fixed on the dreadful machine.

The old man looked across at her once and again, and then tried nervously to join in the general talk, and nod assent to the loyal sentiments of those who crowded near.

As for me, I was too sick even to keep up appearances, and was thankful when one rough interloper shouldered me from my place and sent me sprawling down among the feet of the onlookers.

"Shame! Let the young citoyen have a view," called some one.

"We are all equal," said the usurper. "Let him take the place from me, and he may have it."

I declined the challenge, and slunk off at the back of the crowd, which was all too busy and expectant to heed whether I got a view or not.

What I heard that morning was bad enough. There was the sound of the drums and the dull rumble of wheels, drowned by yells and shouts from the men and screams from the women; then a silence, when no one stirred, but every neck was craned forward to see; then a sudden tap of the drum; then the harsh crash of the knife; then a gasp from a thousand throats, and a great yell of "*Vive la Liberté.*" Three times I heard it all. Then the spectacle was at an end, and the crowd dispersed.

I kept a keen look-out among the groups that straggled past me for the bent figure of Mr Lestrange, but no sign of him could I see. After all, thought I, this errand of mine to Paris was to be all for nothing, when close by I perceived Citoyenne Duport walking aloof from the crowd and bending her steps towards the gardens. I resolved, cost what it might, not to lose sight of her, and followed her at a distance till the paths were quite deserted.

Then I quickened my steps and came up with her.

"Madame Duport," said I boldly, "I am the messenger you and Mr Lestrange expect."

She looked round at me with blanched face, and held up her hand with a gesture of silence.

"No, no," said she, "I am not Madame Duport. You mistake, my friend."

"Madame need not fear me; I am no *mouchard*. I overheard all you and Mr Lestrange said last night. Here is the letter I bear to Deputé Duport. Either I must deliver it myself or ask madame to do so."

She held out her hand for it.

"We are at your mercy," said she. "Is this from Lord Edward himself?"

"I know nothing of it, madame," said I, and recounted the story of how I had come by the missive in the wood near Morlaix.

She sighed, and said,—

"John Cassidy is happier where he lies than we are. Is this your only missive?"

"No; I have a letter for Mr Lestrange, and beg you to tell me his address."

At that moment she looked round, and gave a little scream as first a footstep, then a voice, fell on her ear.

"Adèle," said a lean, bilious-looking man, with a hard, pinched face and knit lips, approaching from one of the side-walks—"Adèle, what do you here?"

"My husband," said the lady, so far recovering her composure as to smile and advance to meet him, "you are come in a good moment. This lad bears a missive for you, and, having discovered me in the crowd, was begging me to deliver it for him. Here it is."

Duport took the letter with a frigid glance at me as if to say he believed not a word of the story, and mechanically tore it open.

I watched his eyebrows give a sudden twitch as he read the contents.

"Who gave you this?" demanded he.

I repeated my story, which once more he received with an incredulous stare.

Then turning to his wife he said, half to himself, half to her,—

"From Edward Fitzgerald on behalf of his kinsman, Sillery. But too late. Come, Adèle. The twenty-two are before the Tribunal to-day, and I have a place for you in the gallery."

And without heeding me further (for which I was devoutly thankful), he drew his wife's arm in his own and walked off rapidly in the direction of the Tuileries.

Lest my reader should suppose that my letter to Deputé Duport was one of great moment to my own story, let me say at once it was not so, at least directly. It was, as the deputy had said, a letter addressed by Lord Edward Fitzgerald, a young Irish nobleman (of whom more hereafter), to Duport, claiming, for the sake of old comradeship, his good offices on behalf of one of the twenty-two impeached Girondist deputies, Sillery by name, whose adopted daughter, or, rather, the adopted daughter of whose wife, Lord Edward had lately married. Many letters of the kind were no doubt constantly coming into the hands of powerful members of the Convention just then; and many, like it, came too late.

Next morning, so I was told, the whole of the accused, and Sillery first of the batch, were guillotined; the headsman doing his work with such dexterity that in thirty-one minutes the twenty-two were all disposed of.

My letter to Mr Lestrange (which I still carried in my stocking) was another matter, and concerned me considerably, especially now that I understood it was from my lady at Knockowen. Where to find him I knew not, and to be found with the letter on me might compromise not merely me but him and his Irish kinsfolk.

All things considered, I decided to read the letter and commit it to memory, and then destroy it, hoping my good intentions might be excuse enough for the breach of faith. And, indeed, when that afternoon I sought a sheltered place in the woods and produced the soiled and stained letter from my stocking, I was glad I had done what I did.

"Dear Cousin," wrote my lady at Knockowen, "I hear there is a chance of getting a letter to you by the messenger who is to carry back Lord Edward's petition on behalf of the poor Marquis Sillery. Your nephew, Captain Lestrange, told us of his trouble when he was here in the summer, and gave us to understand there was little to be hoped for. If Sillery perish, your position in Paris will be painful indeed. I would fain send you the money you ask for, but Maurice keeps me so low in funds that I cannot even pay for my own clothes. I trust, however, your nephew may bring you some relief, as he spoke of going to Paris this autumn on a secret mission for the English Government. Affairs with us are very bad, and, indeed, Maurice succeeds so ill in winning the confidence of either party, loyalist or rebel, that he talks of sending me and Kit over to you till times are better here. Take the threat for what it is worth, for I should be as sorry as you would, and I hear Paris is a dreadful place to be in now. But you know Maurice. Kit is well, but all our troubles prey on her spirits. I suspect if your nephew were in Paris, she would be easier reconciled to our threatened pilgrimage than I. Between ourselves, my dear cousin, as Maurice now holds all the mortgages for your Irish estates, it would be well to keep in with him, even if the price be a visit from your affectionate cousin,—

"Alice Gorman."

"P.S.—I forget if you are still in the Quai Necker, but am told Lord Edward's messenger will know where to deliver this."

Such was my lady's letter, and you may guess if it did not set the blood tingling in my veins, and make Paris seem a very different place from what it was an hour before.

I carefully read and re-read the letter till I had it by heart, and then as carefully tore it into a thousand pieces and scattered them to the wind. The one sentence referring to Captain Lestrange's visit as an agent for the British Government was (little as I yet knew of the state of affairs in Paris) enough to hurry the innocent folk to whom it was addressed to the guillotine. What if my little lady and her mother were by this time in this terrible city and liable to the same fate?

I spent that afternoon wandering along the river on both banks, seeking for the Quai Necker, but nothing of that name could I find. The names were mostly new, and in honour of some person or place illustrious in the Revolution. At last, in despair, I was giving up the quest, when on an old book-stall I lit upon a plan of Paris dated ten years ago.

The *bouquineur*, a sour fellow whose trade had evidently suffered in recent months, would by no means allow me to look at it till I had paid the five sous he demanded, which I was glad enough to do. And after a very little study I found the Quai Necker marked down near the cathedral; and having carefully noted its bearings, I carried my map to a stall higher up, where I sold it for eight sous, thus making one of the most profitable bargains I ever struck.

Before dark, and while all Paris was ringing with the news that the twenty-two unfortunate Girondists were to be executed next morning, I found myself standing in a shabby passage beside the river, under the shadow of the great cathedral of Notre Dame.

Chapter Seventeen
The overturned diligence in
the Rue Saint Antoine

For a night or two I haunted the Quai without success. If Mr Lestrange really lived there, he was either too fearful of venturing out, or some misadventure had already befallen him. I durst not make any inquiries, for fear of attracting attention to him, which was the last thing any one desired just then.

At last one night, after a week's patient waiting, and when the lightness of my own, or rather poor Cassidy's purse reminded me that I should soon have to seek, among other things, for my daily bread, I was skulking off for my lodging, when a woman hurried past me, whom, in the momentary glimpse I got of her, I recognised as Biddy McQuilkin, my father's old gossip of Kerry Keel.

"Whisht, Biddy," said I, laying my hand on her arm, "is it you? Sure, I'm Barry Gallagher, and I'm looking for your master, Mr Lestrange."

She gave a gasp of terror as she felt my hand on her.

"Saints help us! what a fright you gave me, Barry, my boy. Sure, it's not safe to be seen speaking with any one in the streets. I'm told there's fifty more to die to-morrow!"

"I'll follow you; you needn't fear me; and I've a message for the master."

"Thank God for that, if it's a good one!" said she. "Keep close on the other side, and mark where I go in. I will leave the door open; we are on the top stage." And she darted across the road.

I kept her well in view, till she disappeared at the door of a tall, dingy house of some six stories high. The bottom floor was occupied by a seller of wreaths and candles for worshippers at the cathedral—a poor enough business in those days. Above him was a dresser of frills and lace shirt-fronts; and above this were various tenants, some with callings, some with none, all apparently needy, and glad of the chance of hiding in so economical a tenement. A list of the occupants was hung on the door, by order of the

Convention, and the names of *Lestrange, femme, et domestique*, duly figured upon it. A common staircase led to all the floors, but I encountered no one as I toiled to the top of all, where stood Biddy, with her finger up, motioning to me to be silent.

It went to my heart to see the two poor rooms into which I was ushered—one occupied as a bedroom and sitting-room by the old couple, the other as a kitchen and bedroom by Biddy. The walls were plain plaster, behind which you could hear rats running. The ceiling was low and black with smoke, the windows small and broken. The furniture, once good, was faded and in rents; and the few luxuries, such as books and pictures, looked so forlorn that the place would have seemed more comfortable without them.

All this I took in as I advanced into the room at Biddy's heels.

"Plaze, yer honour, this is Barry Gallagher from Knockowen with a message for yez."

Mr Lestrange sat dozing beside the fire, with a *Moniteur* on his knee. His wife, a sweet and placid-looking woman, sat opposite him knitting.

At the sound of Biddy's announcement both started to their feet.

"A message!" exclaimed Mr Lestrange; "what message?"

"None too cheery," said I, anxious not to raise false hopes.

I then recounted my adventures by the road, and ended up with reciting the contents (or most of them) of the letter from my lady at Knockowen. I took care to omit the little sentence about Miss Kit's interest in Captain Lestrange's movements, which did not seem to me worth recalling.

Mr Lestrange's face fell heavily as he heard me out.

"No money!" he groaned. "We are still penned here. Yes, to be sure, you did well to destroy the letter. I thought Alice would have sent something—"

"Maybe she will bring some help with her," said his lady.

The selfish old man laughed bitterly.

"She brings herself and her girl—a pretty help in times like these. Thank God, there is no room in the house for them!"

"You forget they cannot have heard of our losses. When last they heard of us we had received Gorman's money for the mortgage, and were in comfort. It is since then that all has been confiscated."

"That mortgage was robbery itself," said Mr Lestrange. "Gorman knew I was hard hit, and not likely to stand out for a bargain, and he took advantage of it. The estates are worth treble what he gave."

"That is past and gone," said the lady. "We must be patient. Perhaps Felix will help us."

"My nephew is a selfish man," said the old gentleman; "besides, he has but his pay. And now he has no expectations from us we need not expect him to come near us."

All this talk went on while Biddy and I stood near, hearing it all. At last the sturdy Biddy could stand it no longer.

"Hoot! take shame to yourself, Mr Lestrange. Thank God you're not one of the fifty that ride in the tumbrel the morrow; thank God you've got a sweet wife that will bear with your grumblings; and thank God you've got a body like me that's not afraid to tell you what I think of yez. Hold yer tongue now, and get to your beds."

Biddy, as I learned later on, had stuck of her own accord to her master and mistress through all their troubles, and presumed on her position to take her chicken-hearted lord severely to task when, like to-night, the grumbling fit was upon him.

As for me, I was dismissed with little thanks from anybody; but Biddy bade me call now and again to have a crack with her.

"I had a liking for your father, poor soul!" said she, wiping a corner of her eye, "and thought he might have done worse than make me a mother to you and Tim, rest his soul! But it's as well as it is, maybe. Poor Tim! I always liked him better than you. He was his mother's son. Well, well, he's dead too. Barry, my boy, we can't all just have what we've not got; we all have to stand out of our own. Good-night to yez, and come and see an old body sometimes that held you in her arms when you were a fine kicking boy."

I confess Biddy puzzled me a little by her talk. Whenever she spoke of old days she had the air of keeping a secret to herself, which roused my curiosity, and made me recall my poor mother's dying words to myself. That set me thinking of Kilgorman and the strange mystery that hung there; and that set me on to think of Knockowen, and his honour and my lady and Miss Kit; and so by the time I had reached my shabby kennel in the Rue Saint Antoine, I was fairly miserable and ready to feel very lonely and friendless.

However, I was not left much time to mope, for in the night the street was up with a rumour that a "federalist" deputy, who was known to be in the pay of Pitt, the English minister, had been traced to some hiding-place near, and that a strict house-to-house search was being made by the soldiers for him.

"*A bas les mouchards! à bas Pitt! à bas les étrangers! Vive la guillotine!*" shrieked the mob.

Whereat I deemed it prudent to join them and shriek too, rather than await the visit of the soldiers. Not, thought I, that any one would do me the honour of mistaking me for an agent of Mr Pitt; but there was no knowing what craze the Paris mob was not ready for, or on what slight pretext an innocent man might not be sent to the scaffold.

So I sneaked quietly down the stairs, where, alas! I found I had fallen from the frying-pan into the fire.

A file of soldiers was ready for me, and received me with open arms.

"Your name, your business, your destination," demanded they.

"Citizen soldiers, my name is Gallagher; I am a stranger in Paris in search of occupation."

"Enough. You are arrested. Stand aside!"

"But, citizen—"

A stroke with the flat of the soldier's sword silenced me, and I gave myself up for lost. But as a prisoner of the Revolution I should at least not be lonely, and on the guillotine itself I should have company.

The soldiers were too intent on watching for further fugitives to do more than keep me in sight of their loaded pistols. That was bad enough, however, and would have sufficed to land me in the Conciergerie, had not an alarm of fire, followed by volumes of smoke, just then proceeded from a house opposite that in which the fugitive deputy was supposed to be hidden. A rush took place for the spot and the loud sounding of the tocsin down the street, and in the midst of the confusion I dived between the legs of my captors, upsetting the one who covered me with his pistol, so that the weapon went off harmlessly over my head, and next moment I was safe in the thick of the crowd, struggling for a view of the fire.

It was a strange, motley crowd, composed not only of the rascality of Paris, but of a number of shopkeepers and respectable citizens whom the rumour of the fire and the arrest of the notorious deputy had called on the scene at this midnight hour. Many of the faces lit up by the lurid glare of the flames were haggard and uneasy, as if they belonged to those who, like me, found a crowd the safest hiding-place in those days. A few seemed drawn together by a love of horror in any form. Others were there for what they might steal. Others, sucked in by the rush, were there by no will of their own, involuntary spectators of a gruesome spectacle.

Among the latter were the unfortunate occupants of a travel-stained coach, who, after surviving all the perils of the road between Dieppe and Paris, had now been suddenly upset by the crowd, and were painfully, and amid the coarse jeers of the onlookers, extricating themselves from their embarrassing position. Just as the tide swept me to the spot, a male passenger had drawn himself up through the window and was scrambling down on to *terra firma*.

"Help the ladies!" cried he, glad enough evidently of his own escape, but not over-anxious to return to the scene of his alarm; "help the ladies, some one!"

Just then, first a hand, then a pale face appeared at the window, which, if I had seen a ghost, could not have startled me more. It was the face of Miss Kit, with the red light of the fire glowing on it.

"Help us!" she said, in French.

Need I tell you I had her in my arms in a moment; and after her her mother, who was not only frightened but hurt by the shock of the overturn.

That little moment was worth all the perils and risks of the past months; and if I could have had my own way, I would have stood there, with my little lady's hand clutching my arm, for a month.

It was impossible they could recognise me, with my back to the light, happening upon them in so unlooked-for a way. But when I said, "Trust to me, Miss Kit," her hand tightened on my sleeve with a quick pressure, and she said,—

"Barry! thank God we are safe now!"

I was a proud man that night as I fought my way through the crowd with two distressed ladies under my wing, and a fist and a foot for any one who so much as dared to touch the hem of their garments.

Mrs Gorman became so faint in a little that I was forced, as soon as we were out of the thick of the crowd, to call a vehicle.

The soldiers at the end of the street, when they saw who our party was, and heard that we were passengers in the overturned carriage, let us go by; "for we had been already well overhauled at the barrier," said they.

Once clear—and she kept her hand on my arm all the time—Kit said,—

"Then you are alive still, Barry?"

"Ay, Miss Kit; and ready to die for you."

"This is a dreadful place!" said she with a shiver, looking up at the high houses we passed; "but it was worse before you found us."

How could I help, by way of answer, touching her hand with mine, as if by accident?

"We are to go to the Hotel Lambert, Rue Boileau," said she; "and to-morrow we are to seek our kinsmen the Lestranges."

"I have found them," said I.

Here Mrs Gorman looked up.

"Found them? That is good; we shall have shelter at last."

"Alas, mistress," said I, "they have lost all their goods and are living in great poverty. It will be poor shelter."

Here the poor lady broke down.

"O Kit!" moaned she, "why did your father send us on this cruel journey? Did he want to be rid of us before our time?"

"Nonsense, mother; he thought we should be safer here than among the Leaguers in Donegal. So we shall be—at least we have Barry to protect us."

Whereat we drove up at the Hotel Lambert.

Chapter Eighteen
Days of terror

I confess, delighted as I was to find again my lady and my little mistress, I could have wished them anywhere but in Paris at such a time as this. How they reached the place at all it was difficult to understand, till I heard that they had crossed from Dublin under the escort of a prominent member of the Jacobin Club, with whom his honour had large dealings in the matter of arms, and who had provided the necessary passports.

"Indeed," said Miss Kit, "the soldiers everywhere were so respectful to us that I think Monsieur Cazin must have passed us off as his wife and daughter. At any rate he accompanied us into Paris, only quitting us at the barrier, and has promised to call on us at the hotel to-morrow. See here is his letter to the *maître d'hôtel*, in which he states that we are French ladies, kinswomen of his own."

The *maître d'hôtel*, when he read the letter, made no difficulty about admitting "*les citoyennes Cazin*" as he entered them in his book, and their valet. So for that night, at least, we were safe. And as both ladies spoke French fluently, and I tolerably, we passed well enough for what we were not.

But I disliked the whole business, still more when I heard from some of the attendants in the hotel that this citizen Cazin was a man looked askance upon by some of his own party, and reputed to be both greedy and heartless.

If I could have had my own way, I would have tried that very night to get them out of the city they had been at so much trouble to reach. But they were worn-out with fatigue and anxiety, and were fain to lay their heads anywhere. Before the night was out their baggage, rescued from the overturned diligence, was brought to the hotel, labelled (as I could not help noticing) with the name "Cazin," which only involved us all in deeper complication and trouble.

Next day we waited for the promised visit from my ladies' travelling companion, but he never came. And in the evening we discovered the reason. The *maître d'hôtel* demanded admission to their apartment and announced, with a roughness very different from his civility of the night before, that at the Convention that day several suspected persons had been denounced, among others the citizen Cazin, for having been in traitorous treaty with the enemies of the Republic. In a few hours it would become known that he had travelled to Paris with two ladies, and it was as much as his (my host's) neck was worth to allow those ladies to remain another hour in his house. Indeed his duty was to inform the authorities at once who his guests were.

Happily for us his hotel had been visited by the police only the night before—ere the travellers arrived—and he had not yet exposed their names on his list. But it was known that the baggage, delivered last night, bore the name of the suspected Cazin, and that was enough to ruin us all.

You may fancy the distress of the ladies at this news. All they could do was to hand one of their little rolls of *assignats* to the landlord, and promise that within an hour he should be rid of them.

"But the baggage," said mine host, who, in the midst of his perturbation, saw his way to a *solatium* for himself; "I must detain that, and hand it over if required."

"But it is not Monsieur Cazin's; it is my lady's, who is no connection of the suspect," said I.

"If the ladies cannot part with their baggage," said mine host, fumbling the notes, "they must remain here with it. I confiscate it in the name of the Republic One and Indivisible."

It was no use arguing or appealing; our only hope lay in civility.

"Citizen host," said I, "is quite right, and the ladies are grateful for his consideration. Their name is Lestrange. They know nothing of Citizen Cazin or his baggage, and they bid adieu to the Hotel Lambert forthwith."

The cunning landlord, having gained his ends, returned to his civility.

"The ladies," said he, "are wise. But they will do well to put on the garments of plain citoyennes, which I can provide, in exchange for what they wear; otherwise they may be traced. That done, they will do well to leave my poor house on foot with the young Citoyen Lestrange," (here he pointed to me), "and forget to return."

It was good advice, though it went to my heart to see my mistresses further robbed. But when presently they appeared in the plain garb of common Parisiennes I confess I felt relieved, for no one who saw them would suspect them of being foreign ladies, though any one would be bound to admit they were two very fair women. As for me, I was not long in bartering my livery coat for the blue blouse of a workman; and thus that afternoon, as the light was beginning to fail, and all the world was talking of the execution of the beautiful Madame Roland, which was to take place in the morning, three humble persons quitted the side door of the Hotel Lambert and bent their steps dolefully towards the bridge that led across to the Quai near the Island of the City, once known as Quai Necker.

We hoped that here at least we should find a retreat until it was possible to consider what next should be done.

Leaving the ladies to inspect the stalls which lined the river, I ascended first to announce their arrival; but half-way up the long stairs I encountered a middle-aged woman with sour, haggard face, who demanded my business.

"I desire to see Madame Lestrange, who lives on the highest stage," said I.

"Madame Lestrange lives there no longer," said she with a shrug. "Last night she and her husband and their servant were put under arrest on the accusation of Deputé Duport, for holding connection during his life with the traitor Sillery."

"Arrested!" exclaimed I, staggered at the news.

"Arrested," said she dryly, "and are now at the Austin Convent. To-morrow, perhaps, we may hear of them at the Place."

This was too terrible, but I durst not betray my horror.

"Then," said I, "if that is so, the top stage is vacant. I am seeking lodgings for my mother and sister and myself, and had hoped Madame Lestrange could have helped me."

"The top floor is vacant," said the woman, brightening up, for the calamity of the day had robbed her of her tenants, "to any one who can pay five francs a week."

"We can do that," said I, "and can pay you in advance."

"Enough," said the woman, holding out her hand greedily.

I brought the ladies up, breaking the news about their kinsfolk on the way, and imploring them to keep up appearances. The landlady scrutinised them sharply, and demanded what their occupation was.

"We are seamstresses, my child and I," said my lady; "and my son earns what he can at the stables."

"If you are good workers," said the woman, "I can give you some employ. Come up and see your rooms."

It was a sad introduction, that of these delicate ladies to the squalid apartments of their arrested kinsfolk. But they kept up bravely; only when the woman departed with her first five francs in her hand, they fell on the little shabby sofa and broke into tears.

But miserable as we were, we were at least safe for a while; and as the weeks followed one another—terrible weeks for Paris—we grew not only more reconciled to our lot, but sometimes almost happy.

We gave ourselves the name of Regnier, and in a little time our sour landlady fulfilled her promise of finding work for the ladies' needles. As for me, I lit on occupation close by, with a man who let horses for hire, and here once more I found myself engaged in the old familiar occupation of the Knockowen days. The ladies rarely ventured out, and when they did it was usually after dark, and always under my escort.

Somehow or other our common lot, the common garb we wore, and the common dependence we felt on one another, made our make-believe little family into something very like a real one. When the day's work was done, and the candle was lit and the log thrown on the fire, it was hard not to forget that I was after all only a poor serving-man to these two ladies. They were so grateful and gentle to me, and my little lady's eyes, when sometimes they met mine, were wont to light up so brightly, that, had I been less strict with myself, I should have been—tempted, many a time, to presume on all this kindness, and give myself the airs and privileges of an equal. But Heaven kept me in mind of what was due to her; and though I loved her secretly, she was always my little mistress when we were together.

I was not long in hearing, among other things, the news of what had happened at Knockowen since I left. When my overturned boat had drifted ashore, they all set me down as dead, some with regret, some with indifference, some with relief.

Among the latter, I guessed, was his honour, who never took kindly to me, and bestowed more dislike on me, I always thought, than my importance deserved. However, my absence did not make much difference.

"It was dreadful after you had gone," said my little mistress. "We never knew what would happen next. Father could not keep friends with both sides, and yet he durst not break with either. The house was fired into from time to time by the Leaguers; and yet he continued to obey their biddings and wink at all the smuggling of arms and secret drilling that went on, which he, as a magistrate, ought to have stopped. Oh dear, it was hard to know what to wish! And one day he was summoned by some other magistrates to lead a party to capture the crew of a smuggling ship. He sent Martin off secretly to give them warning; but somehow Martin failed to deliver his message in time, and the smugglers were caught. Then he was in dread lest they should betray him, and used all his efforts to let them escape. Then, when one night they broke bonds, he led a hue and cry after them for appearance' sake, but, of course, in a wrong direction, and in consideration of all this he was let alone by the League. Mr Cazin then came over and stayed at Knockowen a week, collecting all the arms he could get, and making himself polite to mother and me. My father, who desired to be rid of us that he might follow his own plots, saw a way, at last, of getting out of his difficulty, and handed the Frenchman over a large number of guns which had been intended for the Donegal men, on condition he would see us safe to Paris."

"And where is his honour, meanwhile?" I asked.

"I can't say, Barry. Not, I think, at Knockowen. He has written us not a line, though we have written several times to him. I sometimes wish we were safe back at home," said she with a sigh.

Well might she wish it, for that winter Paris was a hell upon earth!

For a time I succeeded in keeping away the shadow of "the terror" from that little top storey in the Quai Necker. The ladies knew that blood was being shed, that liberty was being extinguished, that holy religion was being spurned, in the world below them. But the tumbrels that made their daily ghastly journey did not pass their way. They heard nothing of the roll of drums, of the shrieks of the mob, of the dull crash of the knife, of the streams of blood, in the Place. They saw nothing of the horrors of the prison-houses, in which, day by day, and week by week, the doomed citizens made their brief sojourn on the road to death. They did not even know, as I did, that one evening, in one of the sad batches which rode from the Austin Convent to the Conciergerie, and next morning from the Conciergerie to the guillotine, rode a broken-down couple called Lestrange, and beside them, in the same cart, the *ci-devant* Citizen Cazin.

As the Citoyennes Regnier sat patiently and knitted red caps for the blood-drunken citizens without, their gentle ears may have caught occasional shouts and rushings of feet, and they may have guessed something of the tragedies that were being enacted below. But they kept their own counsel, and looked out seldom from the little window, and talked in whispers of the shadows that flitted across Lough Swilly, and the happy life that was to follow after all this buffeting and exile.

Alas! that was not to be yet. For all their courage, their cheeks grew daily more pale; and into that little damp, cold attic, from which they never ventured except at night, and where, as poverty gradually entered by the window, the fire went out on the hearth, the stress of "the terror" at last penetrated.

Our hostess, the grim woman of whom I spoke, was the first to lose nerve, and during the day, when I was away, would come and retail some of the horrors she herself had witnessed. I could tell by their blank looks when I returned that some one had been tampering with their peace, and I fear the warmth with which I expostulated with the disturber did us all no good.

Another day, also when I was absent, the police made a visitation; and though my two mistresses passed muster, they carried off one shrieking victim from the floor below—a widow, whose only crime was that her husband had once been in the service of his king. Her cries of terror, as they dragged her to her doom, rang in my lady's ears for weeks, and unnerved her altogether.

" Miss Kit's face was as white as marble."

A still worse fright befell them, one early morning, when we sought the fresh air in the direction of the Champ de Mars, where I hoped we should be safe from crowds of all kinds. At a turning of the road we suddenly encountered, before there was time to avoid it, the most terrible of all crowds—that which escorted a *condamné* to his execution. It was in vain I tried to draw the ladies aside; the mob was upon us before we could escape. I had seen many a Paris mob before, but none so savage or frantic as this. The poor doomed man, one Bailly (as I heard afterwards, formerly a mayor of Paris), stood bare-headed, cropped, with hands tied behind him, and with only a thin shirt to protect him from the cold. His face, naturally grave and placid, was so marred and stained with mud and blood as to be almost inhuman. At every step of the way the people hurled dirt and execrations upon him, laughing at his sorry appearance, and goading on one another to further insult. By sheer force they were carrying him, guillotine, executioner, and all to a great dirt-heap by the river-bank, where only they would permit the deed of death to be performed.

Just as this ghastly procession passed us, a missile, better aimed than most, sent the poor wretch staggering to his knees, and in the rush that followed he was happily hidden from our sight.

But the two poor ladies had seen enough. Miss Kit's beautiful face was white as marble, her lips quivered, and her hands clenched in a spasm of self-control. Her mother, less strong, tottered and fell heavily on my arm in a faint.

It was a terrible position just then, for to be suspected of pity for a *condamné* was an offence which might easily place the sympathiser on the tumbrel beside the victim. I observed one or two faces—brutal, coarse faces—turned our way, and overheard remarks not unmingled with jeers on the lady's plight. Happily for us, a new humour of the crowd, to make their poor prisoner dismount and carry his own guillotine, swept the crowd in a new direction, and in a moment or two left us standing almost alone on the path.

It was some time before my lady could recover enough to leave the place. Still longer was it before we had her safe in the attic on the Quai Necker; and ere that happened more than one note of warning had fallen on my ears.

"Save yourselves; you are marked," whispered a voice, as we came to the Quai.

I looked sharply round. Only a lame road-mender was in sight, and he was too far away to have been the speaker. The voice was that, I thought, of a person of breeding and sympathy, but its owner, whoever he was, had vanished.

"There they are," said another voice as we entered the doorway.

This time I saw the speaker—a vicious-looking woman, who stood with her friend across the road and pointed our way with her finger.

"So," thought I, as Miss Kit and I carried our fainting burden up the stairs, "we have at least one friend and one enemy in Paris."

Not a word did my little mistress and I exchange as we laid my lady on the bed, and took breath after our toilsome ascent. She tried to smile as I left her to the task of restoration, and retired to my kitchen to prepare our scanty breakfast.

While thus occupied I was startled by a tap at the window, followed by a head which I recognised as that of the road-mender I had lately seen. He must have crawled along the parapet which connected the houses in our block, or else have been waiting where he was till he could find me alone.

His cap was slouched over his eyes, and his face was as grimy as the roads he mended. His finger was raised eagerly to his lips as he beckoned to me to open the sash.

An instinct of self-preservation impelled me to obey. He clambered in and shut the window behind him. Then, turning to face me, I encountered a double shock. The lameness had gone; the figure was erect; the face, in spite of its grime, was youthful and handsome! That was the first shock. The second was even greater. For I suddenly recognised in the form that stood before me my old acquaintance, Captain Lestrange himself.

Chapter Nineteen
The courtyard of the Conciergerie

"Hush!" said Captain Lestrange, before I could utter a word. "The ladies are not safe here; they are marked down by the spies. They must escape at once."

"My lady is still in a faint," said I.

"Faint or no, she must come. Tell them I am here."

He spoke as a soldier with authority; and a pang of jealousy smote me as I looked at his handsome presence in spite of its disguise.

I went to my lady's room and announced him. She lay half stupified, with her eyes open, her bosom heaving, and a choking sob in her throat. Miss Kit kneeled at the bedside and held her hand.

Both were too numb and dazed to express much amazement at the news I brought; and when Captain Lestrange followed me in, no breath was wasted on empty greetings.

"I lodge in an attic six houses away. If you could only get on to the roof," said he, "you would reach it easily."

"We are not far from the roof already," said I, pointing to a corner of the ceiling through which, even as we spoke, flakes of snow were drifting into the room.

Captain Lestrange took a log of fuel and poked the hole, till it was large enough to let a person through.

He bade me tear the sheet, make a band of it, and fasten it round my mistress, while he clambered through my window on to the roof. It was a perilous climb, but the captain was lithe and active as a cat. In a minute we saw him looking in through the hole in the ceiling.

"Now hand me the end of the band," said he, "and come here and help me to haul.—Nerve yourself, cousin, and all will be well."

Between us, we had no difficulty in drawing the poor lady through the opening on to the roof; and when we let down the band for Miss Kit, her light, little form followed readily enough.

"Down," said the captain, crouching in the gutter of the parapet and beginning to crawl along it.

We followed painfully and slowly, finding the journey very long, and expecting any moment to hear the pursuer behind.

Presently we came to a halt, and saw our conductor remove some slates and discover an opening into the house below.

Once more the linen band came into requisition. The ladies were lowered into the room. The captain and I paused to set the slates, so that no one should be able to detect the place of our entrance. Then he swung himself over the parapet on to the ledge of the little window below, bidding me follow. Next moment we stood, all four of us, in a tiny chamber, no bigger than a cupboard, with nothing in it but a little bed, a chair, and a shelf, on which stood a loaf and a bottle of wine.

"Welcome to my humble quarters, cousins," said he. "They are neither large nor water-tight, but I natter myself they are airy and command an extensive view. We will be safe here till night, but then we must seek something more spacious and secluded."

And with all the grace in the world, he poured out a glass of wine for my lady and begged her to drink it.

Presently Miss Kit said, with the first smile I had seen on her face that day,—

"I am too bewildered to ask questions, otherwise I should like to know how all this has come to pass."

"Not now," said he. "I am as bewildered and perplexed as you are.— Gallagher, go to your daily work, but return early; and bring with you,"— here he handed me a gold piece—"provisions for a journey."

It was hard to be dismissed thus at a moment of peril. But my little lady's words and the smile that accompanied them made up for it.

"Yes. Come back early, Barry. We shall feel short of a protector while you are away."

And she held out her hand, which I kissed with a glare at the captain, who only laughed, and said,—

"Don't forget the provisions."

Little I thought as I groped my way down the tumble-down staircase how many weary months were to elapse before I was to hold that gentle little hand in mine again.

I had reached the stables, and was rubbing down a spent horse, when I became aware that a woman was standing at the gate. I recognised her at once as the woman who had pointed us out that morning when we entered our house, and my heart filled with forebodings as I saw her.

It was a relief when my employer presently ordered me to take a horse round to the house of a citizen in the suburbs. The woman had gone when I started, and after half-an-hour's trot I almost dismissed her from my mind. My orders were, after delivering the horse at its destination, to return on foot, calling on my way at the hay merchant's with an order. This I duly performed; and was hastening back by way of the Rue Saint Honoré, when two muskets were suddenly crossed in front of me, and a harsh voice said,—

"Regnier, you are arrested by order of the Committee of Public Safety."

"On what charge?" faltered I.

"On the accusation of the Citoyenne Souchard, who denounces you as the friend of royalism and of the miscreant Bailly."

"I am no friend of either," I exclaimed. "I do not—"

"Silence! march!" said the soldier.

Resistance was hopeless, escape impossible. In a daze I marched on, pointed at and hooted at by the passers-by, amid cries of,—

"*A bas les mouchards! Mort aux aristocrates!*" (Saint Patrick! that I should be taken for an aristocrat.) "*Vive la guillotine!*"

I cared not what became of me now, but when presently my conductors actually turned towards the Island of the City, and I caught sight of the high roofs of the houses on the Quai Necker, a wild hope of seeing my little mistress once more took hold of me. Alas! it was but for a moment. The cold muzzle of the soldier's gun recalled me to myself.

I longed to know if the accuser, who seemed to know my name and all my movements, had joined the names of the ladies in my denunciation. If so, woe betide them and all of us. In the midst of my trouble the one thought that cheered me, despite the pang of jealousy that came with it, was that they were not without protection; and that Captain Lestrange, who had shown himself so ready of resource in the morning, might succeed even without my help in rescuing those innocent ones from the bloody hands of "the terror."

A chill went through me when it dawned upon me at last that I was being conducted to the fatal Conciergerie—that half-way house between life and death towards which so many roads converged, but from which only one, that to the guillotine, led.

An angry parley took place at the door between the jailer and my captors.

"Why here?" demanded the former; "we are packed to the bursting point."

"To-morrow you will have more room by fifty," said the other.

"This is not to-morrow," growled the hard-worked official.

"The *détenu* is your parishioner," said the soldier.

"It is scandalous the slowness with which the Committee works," said the jailer. "Fifty a day goes no way; we want one hundred and fifty."

"You shall have it, Citizen Concierge. Patience!—Now, Regnier, enter, and adieu," said he, with a push from the butt-end of his gun.

Beyond entering my name and assigning me my night's quarters, no notice was taken of me by my jailers. I was allowed to wander on into the crowded courtyard, where of the hundreds who prowled about like caged animals none troubled themselves so much as to look up at the new unfortunate. Men and women of all sorts were there: gentlemen who held themselves aloof and had their little *cercle* in one corner, with servants to attend them; rogues and thieves who quarrelled and gambled with one another, and made the air foul with their oaths; terrified women and children who huddled together for shelter from the impudent looks and words of the ruffians, who amused themselves by insulting them. Sick people were there with whom it was a race whether disease or the guillotine would claim them first. And philosophers were there, who looked with calm indifference on the scene, and jested and discussed among themselves.

Among this motley company I was lost, and, indeed, it would have troubled me to be anything else. I found leaning-room against the wall, and had no better wish than that the promised fifty who to-morrow were to feed the guillotine might count me in their number.

As soon as the short February day closed in, we were unceremoniously ordered within doors. Some of the more distinguished and wealthy retired to their private apartments; the women (though I heard they were not always so fortunate) were shut up in quarters of their own. Others retired in batches to chambers, for the use of which they had clubbed together in bands of twenty or thirty. The rest of us, comprising all the poorer prisoners, were huddled into great foul, straw-strewn rooms to sleep and pass the night as best we might.

Rough countryman as I have been, the thought of those nights in the Conciergerie turns my stomach even now. The low ceiling and small windows made the atmosphere, laden as it was with dirt of all sorts, choking and intolerable. The heat, even on a winter night, was oppressive. The noise, the groaning, the wrangling, the fighting, the pilfering, were distracting. Only twice in the night silence, and that but for a few moments at a time, prevailed.

Once was when the guard, accompanied by great dogs, made their nightly round, kicking us who lay in their way this side and that, and testing every bar and grating of our prison with hammers and staves. For the sake of the dogs, who were stern disciplinarians, we kept the peace till the bolt was once more turned upon us.

The other time the hush was of a more terrible kind, as I discovered that first night. A jangle of keys without imposed a sudden lull on the noise. The door opened, and in came the concierge and his turnkeys. Every eye turned, not on the man or his myrmidons, but on the paper that he held in his hand. It was the list of prisoners who to-morrow were to appear before the Tribunal—that is to say, of the victims who the day after to-morrow were to ride in the tumbrels to the guillotine.

A deadly silence prevailed as the reading proceeded, broken only by the agonised shriek of some unfortunate, and the gradual sighs of relief of those whose names were omitted.

The ceremony over, the door (on the outside of which a turnkey had chalked the doomed names) swung to, and all once more was noise and babel. The victims drew together, embracing their friends and uttering their farewells. The others laughed louder than ever, like schoolboys who have escaped the rod. Morning came, and with it the summons. Those who quitted us we knew we should never see again. They would spend that night in the dungeon of the *condamnés*; the next day the lumbering roll of the tumbrels would announce to us that they were on their way to the Place de la Revolution.

The first night, I confess, I was disappointed that the fatal list did not contain my name; but as days, and then weeks, and then months passed, the love of life rose high within me, and I grew to tremble for that which I had once hoped for. Day by day I scrutinised the new arrivals in the vague expectation of seeing among them those I loved best. But they never came.

I made few, if any, acquaintances, for I resolved to keep my mouth shut. Spies, I knew, infested the prisons as they did the streets, and many a chance word uttered in the confidence of the dungeon was reported and used as evidence against the victim. Now and again we were thrown into excitement by the arrival in our midst of some notable prisoner, before whose name, a few short weeks since, all Paris, nay, all France had trembled, but who now was marked down and doomed by his rivals in power. And sometimes rumours of convulsions without penetrated the walls of our cells, and made us hope that, could we but endure a while, the end of "the terror" was not far distant.

I remember one night when a new prisoner whispered to me that the great Robespierre, at whose nod any head in Paris might drop into the dreadful basket, had been blown upon within the walls of the Convention itself.

"Death is marked on his face," said he; "and when he falls there is hope for us, for the people are sick of blood."

Alas! this same poor whisperer heard his name called out that very night, and fell grovelling at my side, as if I could help him.

Still my name was held back. Either they had overlooked it in the crowd, or had marked it through as dead already, or considered it less important than others who had more pressing claims on the executioner's knife.

Hope rose within me. I became so used to being passed that I ceased to expect anything else, and only counted the days till the blood-red cloud should have drifted past and left me free.

When, therefore, on the very night that news had come in that Robespierre had indeed fallen, and was even then before his judges, I heard the name "Regnier" read off the fatal list, I broke into a cold sweat of amazement and terror, and fancied myself in a dream.

My name was the last on the list. With a dreadful fascination I watched the turnkey chalk it on the door and the governor fold up his paper and stick it in his belt. Then as they turned to the door despair seized me. But before they could leave, a sudden clamour at the far end of the room detained them. One of the condemned, driven mad by the announcement of his doom, had sprung to the window and was tearing at the bars with such superhuman force that they promised at any moment to yield.

The jailer and his men made a dash to seize him, and in that moment I slipped out of the half-closed door, stopping only to wipe out my name with my cap as I passed, and crept into the courtyard.

No one could have seen my departure, for though I lay hid an hour under the shadow of the wall, and even saw the jailer and his men cross the court, there was no hue and cry or alarm of an escape. Nor, I surmise, did any one even of my fellow-prisoners, distracted as they were by their own concerns and the excitement of the madman's attempt, miss me.

My only hope now lay in patience and prudence. To scale the wall I knew was impossible. To steal through the governor's office would mean instant detection. But to wait where I was was my only chance.

I had studied the ways of the place enough to know that on the stroke of six the outer gates swung open to admit the carts which were to carry to the scaffold the victims of the day. I knew, too, since the horse-master I had served had often supplied carts on an emergency, that these vehicles were usually sent in charge of common carters, one man often being in charge of two or three. These men, having deposited their carts in the yard, were wont to go off to breakfast and return in an hour to convey their freight under an escort of Guards to the place of execution.

Their daily arrival was now so common an occurrence that it attracted little attention inside or out. Indeed, the gate was often left standing open a minute or two while some parley was taking place; for no prisoners were allowed in the court till after the departure of the procession, and no precautions therefore seemed necessary for closing it with special celerity.

This, then, was my hope. Could I but lie *perdu* beside the gate till the time of opening, I might in a happy moment slip out. As if to favour me, a cart of straw intended for the floors of the prison rooms had been admitted into the court the night before, and stood drawn up close to the gate. It was not difficult to conceal myself at the tail of this, under the straw, and so remain unseen, not only by the carters that entered, but by the turnkey that let them in. By equal good fortune, the owner of the cart had left his coat and whip and cap behind him, thus giving me just a disguise that suited me best.

The night—it was July then—seemed interminable; and with morning a drenching rain set in that found its way through the straw and soaked me to the skin. I heard the city without gradually waking up. Market-carts rumbled in the roads, the shrill cry of the street vendors sounded in the air, and above all was the heavy splash of the rain.

At last a long low sound fell on my ear, which I knew only too well to proclaim the approach of the carts crawling in our direction. Nearer and nearer they came till they stopped at the gate, and the familiar bell tolled out. I heard the footsteps of the warder plashing across the yard, growling at the rain. Then I heard the grating of the bolts as they were slowly drawn back, and the creaking of the gates on their hinges. Then the rumble began again, and one by one the carts drew up into the yard. There were eight of them, and as I peeped out I could see that the last three were all in charge of one driver, who rode on the leader. The warder, impatient to return to shelter, called to this man to see the bolts made fast after him, which the man, a surly fellow and hardly sober, grumblingly promised to do at his own convenience.

Now was my chance. I slipped from my hiding-place, clad in the driver's blouse and peaked cap, with a whip over my shoulder and a straw between my lips, and strolled quietly and to all appearance unconcernedly out into the street. If any saw me come out, they probably set me down as one of the tumbrel drivers on his way to breakfast, and paid me no more heed than such a fellow deserved; indeed less, for on that day of all others Paris was in a tremendous ferment. The tocsin was ringing from the steeples, there was a rush of people towards the Tuileries, and cries of "*A bas Robespierre*" — the most wonderful cry Paris had heard yet.

In the midst of it all I walked unchallenged to the Quai Necker. Alas! any hopes I had of comfort there were vanished. The familiar top storey stood empty, with the hole still in the roof, and six doors away, where I had left them last, the attic was empty too.

Chapter Twenty
A voice in the dark

All Paris seemed up that morning, hurrying to the scene of the day's wonder. There was a rumour of fighting in the streets, of guns being pointed against the sacred doors of the Convention, of tyrants fallen and heads to fall. To Paris, sick of blood and strained by terror, it seemed like the end of all things, and the people with one accord rushed eastward to witness the dawn of their new revolution.

I, who had had enough of revolutions, wandered disconsolately westward along the river-bank till the rush was over and the sounds behind me grew faint in the distance. Where next? I asked myself. Whether Citizen Robespierre fell or not, there was not much quarter to be hoped for by a runaway from the Conciergerie. Paris was a rat-trap still, and though large, I should be cornered sooner or later.

As I ruminated thus, I came to a bridge below which was moored a barge, laden with goods and spread over with its great waterproof sheet, ready to drop down the stream. How I envied the two men in charge of her, to whom the barrier of the city would offer no obstacle, and who were free to go in and out of the rat-trap as they pleased!

Apparently they were not so sensible of their good fortune as I was, for they were quarrelling angrily, and filling the air with their insults and recriminations.

"Villain! robber!" I heard one say, who seemed to be assistant to the other, "I demand what is due to me."

"It will be paid you at Rouen, fool," said the other.

"I shall not be there to receive it," snarled the other. "I will have it here, or nowhere."

"What, you will dare to desert! It is treason against the Republic whom we serve. I will denounce you."

"Idiot, I defy you," exclaimed the man, stripping off his jersey and flinging his red cap on the deck. "I spit on your Republic which does not pay its debts!"

"I promise you shall receive all arrears at Rouen," replied the other. "I am under penalties to reach Havre in a week."

The mutineer laughed savagely.

"Pay me what you owe me, and you shall reach it."

"At Rouen," persisted the skipper.

"No! here, I tell you."

The skipper's reply was to make a grab at his companion, who, however, was quick enough to elude him and jump ashore.

"There, thief and robber, villain and assassin, I wash my hands of you! I have done with you. Reach Havre when you like. Adieu!" and he spat at the barge.

The skipper looked as if he would have followed him, but thought better of it. He shrugged his shoulders and pulled out a cigar. The other, after standing insultingly on the bank for some minutes, heaping all sorts of imprecations and taunts on his late employer, swaggered away, and was presently caught up in a knot of belated sightseers hastening to the scene of the insurrection.

I waited till the coast was clear, and then descended to the river side.

"Citizen bargee," said I, with a salute, "do you want a man to-day?"

The skipper looked up at me and took his cigar from his lips.

"Can you sail a barge?" said he.

"Ay, and tow it too if you like," said I. "And as for wages, suit yourself, and give me what you like at the journey's end."

"I serve the Republic," said the man.

"*Vive la République*," said I. "She does not desert her sons."

"Your name?" demanded he. "Belin," said I, inventing a name for the occasion. "You are engaged, Belin," said the skipper; "we start this minute."

With a grateful heart I stepped on board and busied myself with casting loose the rope.

"Observe, Belin," said my new master, noticing approvingly that at least I knew how to handle a rope, "your name under me is Plon, that of a vagabond scoundrel who has just deserted me, and who is named on the way-bill. There are his jersey and his cap; put them on, and keep your counsel."

"Pardon, my captain," said I, when I had obeyed him, "what is our business for the Republic?"

"We carry coats and boots for the Army of the North."

"Long live the Army of the North," said I devoutly.

We soon reached the bridge which marked the boundary of the city. Here our bill of lading was carefully scrutinised, and our cargo inspected to make sure we carried no fugitive hidden in the midst of it.

As for me, I took my skipper's advice, and sat smoking my cigar and saying nothing while the ceremony lasted.

But when at length we were ordered to pass, you may guess how thankfully I cast off the rope and found myself gliding down the quick current of the Seine out of that horrible city in which for nearly a year I had been cooped, expecting every day to be my last I showed my gratitude by undertaking any hard work my skipper chose to put upon me; and when he found me so willing, and on the whole so handy, he was content enough, and we became tolerably good messmates. Only I had learned enough to keep my mouth pretty close respecting matters which did not concern me. I professed to know very little of what had passed in Paris during the past few months, and in what I did to agree entirely with the opinions of Citizen Benoit, my captain. I cumbered him with few questions or opinions of my own, and was never backward to take an extra watch or trudge an extra mile on the bank beside the occasional horses which here and there we engaged to help us on.

It was a tedious and dull journey, threading our way through endless twists and between numerous islands, halting only between the late summer dusk and the early summer dawn, quitting our barge only in search of provender or a horse, parleying only with officials and returning barges.

One or two of the skippers on the latter inquired of Benoit what had become of his former assistant, and alarmed me somewhat by questioning me as to my previous calling. But my skipper's explanation was generally enough, and I was admitted into the noble fraternity of Seine bargees without much objection. The few who did object sailed the other way, so that their objection mattered little.

Our longest stay was at Rouen, where once more my master reminded me that I was Citizen Plon, and that my policy was to hold my tongue and lie low.

The police here were very suspicious, and insisted on searching our cargo thoroughly for fugitives, of whom reports from Paris said there were a good many lying hid in boats and barges.

However, they found none with us. How I toiled and sweated to assist their search! and what a reputation poor Plon acquired for zeal in the service of the Republic One and Indivisible!

After leaving Rouen we used our sail a good deal in the broad reaches of the river. Monsieur Benoit (who had quite forgotten my pay) was good enough to compliment me on my skill in handling canvas, and as we neared our destination his civility became almost embarrassing. He sought to engage me as his permanent lieutenant, and promised to make all sorts of excellent reports on my behalf to the officials. I humoured him as best I could; but the scent of the sea-breezes as we gradually reached the wide estuary and saw before us the masts and towers of the city of Havre, set me longing for old Ireland, and determined me, Benoit or no Benoit, to set my foot once more on Fanad.

I requested of Benoit a few days' leave of absence, after our stores were duly delivered at the depôt, which he agreed to on the understanding that my wages should not be paid me till I returned to the barge. In this way he imagined he made sure of me, and I was content to leave him in that simple faith.

But now, as I wandered through the squalid streets of the city of Havre, and looked out at the great Atlantic waves beating in on the shore, I began to realise that France itself was only a trap on a larger scale than Paris. True, I might possibly find a berth as an able-bodied sailor on a French ship; but that was not what I wanted. As for English ships, it was a time of war, and none durst show their prows in the harbour, save under a false flag. Yet the longing for home was so strong in me, that I think, had I found one, I would even have seized a small rowing-boat and attempted to cross the Channel in it single-handed.

For two days I prowled hither and thither, vainly looking for a chance of escape, and was beginning to wonder whether after all I should have to return to Benoit, when I chanced one evening on a fellow who, for all his French airs and talk, I guessed the moment he spoke to be an Irishman. He was, I must confess, not quite sober, which perhaps made him less careful about appearances than he should have been.

It was on the cliffs of La Hève we foregathered. He was walking so unsteadily on the very margin that I deemed it only brotherly to lend him an arm.

"Thank you, my lad," said he, beginning the speech in French, but relapsing into his native tongue as he went on; "these abominable French cliffs move about more than the cliffs at Bantry. Nothing moves there—not even custom-house runners. Bless your dear heart, we can land our bales there under their very noses! Steady, my friend, you were nearly slipping there. You French dogs never could walk on your hind legs. There she lies, as snug and taut as a revenue cutter, and just as many teeth. What did I come ashore for now? Not to see you, was it? 'Pon my word, monsieur, I owe you a hundred pardons. I quite forgot. You look a worthy fellow. I press you into the service, and the man that objects shall have an ounce of lead through him. Come, my lad, row me aboard. The anchor's apeak, and we're off for the ould country, and a murrain on this land of yours!"

So saying he stumbled along, down a zigzag path that led to the foot of the cliff, where lay moored a small boat and two men in her.

"Belay there, hearties! I've got the villain. Clap him in irons, I say! He tried to send me over the cliff, but— how are you, my friend? Give us your hand. You're one of the right sort.—Pull away, boys. The wind's in the east, and the tide's swung round the *cap*. This time to-morrow we shall be scraping the nose of ould Ireland—glory to her!"

The men, who evidently were used to their captain's eccentricities, made no demur, and laid on with their oars. Presently I volunteered to lend a hand, which was readily accepted. The captain meanwhile lay in a comfortable slumber in the stern-sheets, uttering occasional greetings to the world at large, and to me in particular.

"Where does she lie?" said I presently to the man in front of me in plain English.

He turned round sharply.

"What! you're not a Frenchman then?" said he.

"Heaven forbid! I'm as good an Irishman as you."

"How came you to know Captain Keogh?"

"Sure he found me out and engaged me."

"It's no lie," gurgled Captain Keogh from the bottom of the boat. "I should have been over but for him. Enter him as sailing-master or cook, for he's the right sort."

"We're for the *Kestrel*. She lies a mile or two up the coast, with a cargo for Bantry."

"Lace; I know that. I've been in the business before," said I.

This completed my recognition as a proper shipmate, and no more questions were asked.

When we reached the *Kestrel* it was pitch dark, but we could tell by the grating of the chain as we came up that no time was to be lost in getting under way.

Not a light was shown, only a whistle from our men, answered by another from the ship and a voice over the bulwarks,—

"Boat ahoy!"

"*Kestrel* ahoy!" sang out our men, and in a moment a rope was thrown to us and we were alongside.

Captain Keogh, happily asleep, was hauled up the gangway, and we followed.

"A new hand, lieutenant," said my comrade, pointing at me with his thumb over his shoulder.

"All right. Send him forward to help with the anchor."

At the sound of this voice in the dark I staggered like one struck. It called to mind days spent under the drifting clouds at the edge of Fanad, boyish quarrels and battles, winter nights over the peat fire of our little cabin. Who but Tim had that ring in his voice? Whose voice, if it was not his, could set my heart beating and swelling in my breast so that I could scarcely hold it?

Just now, however, I was hurried forward to the business of weighing anchor, and the lieutenant had gone aft to take charge of the helm.

In a minute or two the *Kestrel* floated free on the water. The sails spread out to the wind, the welcome splash of the bows proclaimed that we had way on us already, and the twinkling lights of Havre in the distance reminded us that France, land of terrors, was dropping astern at every pitch we took.

But the excitement of all this was as nothing to the echo in my ears of that voice in the dark.

Chapter Twenty One
The wreck of the "Kestrel"

The crew of the *Kestrel* consisted of less than fifty men, most of them Irishmen. While the work of setting sails and making all snug lasted I had little chance of looking about me, but the impression I formed was that the schooner was not at all worthy of the praise her tipsy captain had bestowed upon her. She was an old craft, with a labouring way of sailing that compared very unfavourably with the *Cigale* or the *Arrow*. Her guns, about a dozen in all, were of an antiquated type, and badly mounted, and her timbers were old and faulty. As long as we had a sharp east wind astern we had not much to concern us, but I had my misgivings how she would behave in dirty weather with a lee-shore on her quarter.

That, however, concerned me less just then than my impatience to get a glimpse of the face of the lieutenant. I volunteered for an extra watch for this purpose, and longed for some excuse to take me aft.

Sure enough it came. The same voice rang out again through the darkness:—

"Hand there! come and set the stern light."

"Ay, ay, sir," cried I, hurrying to the place.

For the first hour or so after slipping our moorings off Havre the *Kestrel* had remained in perfect darkness. But now that we were beyond sight of the lights ashore there was no occasion for so dangerous a precaution. I unlashed the lantern and took it down to the galley for a light, and then returned with it to the helm.

As I did so I could not help turning it full on the face of the man at the tiller.

Sure enough it was Tim, grown into a man, with down on his chin, and the weather wrinkles at the corner of his eyes. Every inch a sailor and a gentleman he looked as he stood there in his blue flannel suit and peaked cap; the same easy-going, gusty, reckless Tim I had fought with many a time on Fanad cliffs, loving him more for every blow I gave him. When I thought

I had lost him, it seemed as if I had lost a part of myself. Now I had found him, I had found myself.

"Look alive, my lad," said he.

Without a word I fixed the light in its place. I had never, I think, felt so shy and at a loss in my life.

At last I could stand it no longer.

"Tim, old man, is that really you?"

He staggered at the sound of my voice, just as I had staggered at the sound of his, and let go the helm.

"Saint Patrick! it's Barry."

And I felt his hand on my shoulder, and heard him give a little laugh of wonder.

"Fetch that light! Let me have a look at you!"

I obeyed, and it would be hard to say which side of the lantern, as it swung between us, witnessed the greatest wonder.

"Look to the helm," said I. "She's falling off a point or two."

"Ha, ha!" said the joyous Tim, "to think of me manning the helm with you on the ship. Take you it, you dog you, and spin us your yarn."

"Not till you tell me how you came to life again. I heard the *Cigale* was lost with all hands."

"Except one," said Tim. "Father might have escaped too, but he was so ashamed to have run the ship on the rock that nothing would drag him from her. I held on to a spar for a whole day, and drifted to within a swim of Tory Island, where for a whole month I waited to get across. I heard you had been drowned in the Swilly, and Knockowen was empty, so I made my way to Sligo, and Keogh, an old mate of father's, gave me a berth on this crock of a boat. As I could talk French and knew something of the business, he called me lieutenant—me that hates the sea like the very mischief, and French lace worse than that! I tell you, Barry, even if I hadn't found you, this would have been my last voyage. There's other work for you and me."

"What work is that?"

"The work of Ireland! There's a new age dawning there, and you and I will be in it. The chains are dropping right and left, and the poor prisoner is struggling from his knees to his feet. We shall live in a free country of our own before long, Barry, my boy—free because she has learned to help herself, and will remain the plaything or the slave of others no longer. France is free; she has learned to help herself. We in Ireland have our Bastille to storm and our feudalism to destroy."

He spoke with a glow on his cheeks and a fire in his eyes that quite took me aback, and made it hard to recognise the Tim of old days.

"I could tell you something about this glorious freedom in France," said I, with a jerk of my head in the direction of that accursed land.

"You shall; and mark me, Ireland will not be a pace behind her."

"God forbid!" said I.

"But you haven't told me your story yet," said he, carrying the lamp back to its place, as if he were the seaman and I at the helm the officer.

Then I told him all, not omitting my love for Miss Kit, or my disgust for the Republic One and Indivisible.

He heard me with evident disquiet.

"I am sorry about the girl," said he bluntly. "She may be all you say, but Ireland wants you heart and soul just now. It is no time for dancing attendance on ladies."

"For all I know she lies buried under the guillotine," said I.

"Oh no, she does not," said Tim. "She and her mother are back at Knockowen, so I was told a month ago, before we sailed on this voyage."

I seized his hand so eagerly at this news as almost to startle him.

"Watch her helm, she's falling away," said he, almost sharply. "Ay, she's back, but no nearer your reach for that. I hear Gorman has become a rich man since. The English estates that belonged to the master of Kilgorman have yielded a great profit, and besides that he has got hold of the Lestrange property too. The young lady is an heiress, and this Captain Lestrange you spoke of, who saved them out of Paris, is not likely to lose the chance of getting a wife and his family estates back into the bargain. Don't be a fool, Barry. You and I are only sailor lads. It does not become us to be hankering after heiresses. But the freedom of Ireland we may and must strive for; and, Barry, brother," (and what a whack he caught me on my back), "we'll get it!"

I turned in that night with my head in a whirl. It seemed as if every joy I had was destined to crumble in my hand. No sooner had I found my little lady in Paris than a cruel hand swept us asunder. No sooner had I found my brother than I found him estranged from me in a hopeless cause. No sooner had I heard of the safety of her I loved than I heard she was lifted further out of my reach than ever. I could have wished I had never met Tim again.

I should at least have slept better had I lain in my bunk with no thought but that of the French coast dropping league by league astern. Now, even Ireland seemed to have its terrors ahead.

But sleep came to my rescue, and with sleep came courage and hope. Why should I be afraid? What had I to hang my head at? Was I, who had come through a reign of terror, going to mope at troubles in advance? Sufficient unto the day should be the evil thereof!

So I met Tim with a smile in the morning, and asked him to report me to Captain Keogh.

That worthy officer had quite slept off the debauch of last night, and was apparently looking forward to the next, for a bottle of rum stood on the cabin table. He had not the slightest recollection of me, but when he heard I was his lieutenant's brother, he poured out three glasses and proposed luck all round.

"Sit down, Gallagher," said he to Tim. "I can't ask your brother to sit, for the sake of the discipline of the ship; but I'm pleased to see him, and if he's a handy lad like you I'll make a seaman of him."

"Barry's worth any dozen of the likes of me," said Tim, "when it comes to sailing. If any one can get an extra tack out of the old *Kestrel*, he can."

"Don't talk disrespectfully of your ship, lieutenant," said Captain Keogh. "To be sure, the carpenter has been pestering me this morning about the timbers; but I told him he'd probably only make things worse by patching. You can't put new wine into old bottles, you know,"—here he poured himself out a fresh glass—"and we shall hold well enough together till we reach Bantry."

"Sligo," said Tim.

"Well, Sligo. We must keep clear of French privateers and give the coast a wide berth. That's the very thing. This wind must have been turned on to suit us. I positively thought the *Kestrel* was sailing fast to-day."

"She's well enough as she is, but if we get into dirty weather, we ought to run in for the nearest port we can reach."

"We are much more likely to run into dead calms, and have to sit whistling for the wind—dry work at best, but in this weather terrible." And he gulped down his rum, and nodded a dismissal.

The captain's forecast, as it turned out, was pretty near the mark. Off the Cornish coast we fell into a succession of calms, which kept us practically motionless for half a week. Even the light breezes which would have sufficed to send the *Arrow* spinning through the water, failed utterly to put way upon our cranky tub; and every day the carpenter was growing more persistent in his complaints. At last Captain Keogh ordered him to do what he pleased so long as he held his peace, whereupon the sound of hammering and tinkering might be heard for a day across the still water.

During these lazy days, Tim and I talked a great deal. He was full of visions and hopes of an emancipated Ireland, and all the glories which should belong to her.

"Think of it, Barry. Every man's land will be his own. We shall have our own army and navy. There will be no England to tax us and bleed us to death. We shall have open arms for the friends of liberty all the world over. Irishmen will stay at home instead of carrying their manhood to foreign climes. Nay, we shall stand with our heel on the neck of England, and she who for centuries has ground the spirit out of us will sue to us for quarter."

"How will you manage all this?" said I.

"The people are armed, only waiting the signal to rise and throw off the yoke. England is not ready, she is beset on all sides, her fleet is discontented, her armies are scattered over Europe, her garrison in Ireland is half asleep. Our leaders are only waiting their time, and meanwhile Irishmen are flocking to the banner daily. And more than that, Barry," added he, with a thump on the bulwark, "at the first blow from us, France will be ready to strike for our liberty too. I know that for certain, my boy."

"France!" said I. "If there are innocents to be slaughtered, and blood to flow, and fiends to be let loose, you may depend on her."

"She at least is more our friend than men like Gorman, who one day, when they are poor, with nothing to lose, are for the people, and the next, when they are rich, are for the crown and the magistrates and the Protestant ascendency. It will be a sorry look-out for such as these when we come into our own. — There comes a breeze surely!"

"South-easterly," said I; "that will suit us."

It was a moderate breeze only, but it brought us on our way opportunely, until one day, as we looked out, there was land on our weather-beam.

Then fell another calm, longer and more dead than the last. The sea was like glass, the horizon hazy, and the heat oppressive. The carpenter, as now and again he looked up at the lifeless sails, muttered between his teeth.

"I hear," said Tim, "our timbers above the water-line have sprung here and there. The old tub is quite rotten, and every day we lie idle like this she grows worse."

"This time to-morrow, by all signs, we shall not be lying idle," said I, glancing up at the metallic sky, and following the line of a school of porpoises as they wheeled across our stern.

"So much the better. We must run before the wind wherever it comes from. We could not live through a cross-sea for an hour."

The storm came sooner than I expected. The metallic sky grew overcast, and a warning shudder fell over the still surface of the water. Then a sudden squall took us amidships, and sent us careening over on our beam, before we even knew that the calm was at an end.

We had no more than time to shorten our courses and turn her head, when the tempest struck us from the south-west, lashing up the sea at our stern, and making our cranky masts stoop forward and creak like things in mortal pain.

The carpenter's face grew longer than ever.

"For mercy's sake, captain," said he, "keep her in the wind, or she'll crack to pieces. You can't afford to take a point. We're only sound under calm water-line; above it, she's as thirsty as a sieve."

"More shame to you," growled Captain Keogh. "We're all thirsty here."

"You'll have water enough presently," muttered the carpenter to himself as he went below.

"Gallagher, you and your brother take the helm. Keep her out a taste, whatever yonder fool says. My! she's spinning along for once in a way. At this rate we shall make Achill by night."

"Better try for Galway, sir," said I.

"Hold your tongue, you French fool," cried the captain, who was greatly excited. "Save your advice till it's asked, or go aloft. —I tell you," said he, turning to Tim, "it's Sligo or nowhere. There's not a cruiser there to interfere with us, or an exciseman that we can't square. I reckon there's profit enough in this lace to pay an admiral's prize-money. Galway! You might as well try to land at London Bridge."

Here the carpenter once more rushed on deck. He looked up at the canvas, then at the compass, then at the helm.

"I declare, after what I told you, you're two points out of the wind, sir. The ship won't stand it, I tell you. She's leaking already. You need all that canvas down, and only your jibs and foresails; and even then you must let her run."

Captain Keogh turned upon him with a torrent of abuse.

"Saints help us! Am I the captain of this ship, or are you, you long-jawed, squint-eyed, whining son of a wood-chopper you? First it's a French stowaway wants to tell me my business, then it's you. Why doesn't the cabin-boy come up and take charge of the ship? Way there take in the courses, and let the helm go. Give the fool what he wants, and give me a dram for luck."

All that day we flew through the water in front of as fierce a south-wester as I was ever out in. The carpenter reported that the pumps were holding their own and no more, but that a dozen cross-seas would split us open like rotten medlar. When night fell, the weather promised to grow worse, and the rain and hail at our backs made it almost impossible to keep up our heads.

"It's all very well," said Tim, who had been down to the cabin to inspect the chart, "but this can't go on. We've had water-room all day, but I reckon we are closing in on the land every yard now, and if we don't put out her head we shall find ourselves on the Connemara coast."

"Better run for Galway, and say nothing," said I.

"Too late now. I wish we had."

"Out she goes then," said I; "it's a question between going down where we are or breaking to pieces against Slyne Head."

"That's just it," said Tim. "The captain's dead drunk below. Call all hands aft, Barry; let them choose."

The men crowded aft, and Tim spoke to them.

"We're in for an ugly night, my lads, and we're on a rotten boat. The carpenter says, unless we run before the wind, we shall go to pieces in half-an-hour. I say, if we do run, we shall be on Slyne Head in two hours. Which shall it be? I don't mind much myself."

"Put it to the vote," said one.

So a vote was taken, and of forty men who voted, twenty-five were for death in two hours, and fifteen for death in an hour.

"Very good," said Tim. "Get to your posts, and remember you are under orders till we strike. Then shift for yourselves; and the Lord have mercy on us all!"

"Amen!" said the sailors, and returned to their duties.

It was a terrible night, and, to make matters worse, as black as pitch. We should not even have the help of daylight for meeting our doom.

"Barry," said Tim, "I don't think we shall both perish. If it's I, promise me you will fight for Ireland till she is free."

"If you die, Tim, I don't care what I do. I promise. And if I die, promise me—"

"Not to go near that girl?"

"No," said I, with a groan.

"What, then?"

"Search below the great hearth at Kilgorman, and do whatever the message you will find there bids you. It is not my message, but our mother's."

"I promise that. But hold on now," said he, catching me by the arm, "the old ship's beforehand with us. She's going to pieces before we reach shore."

Sure enough she was. The rough water into which we were plunging loosened her already warped timbers, and she gradually ceased to rise on the waves, but settled down doggedly and sullenly as the water poured in on this side and that and filled her hold. Captain Keogh, suddenly roused to his senses, staggered on deck, and took the helm, not for any good he could do, but from the sailor's instinct to be at his post at the end.

All hands came on deck, and the order was given to lower the boats. For the credit of these Irishmen be it said that no man stepped in till he was ordered by name. The first boat capsized before she even reached the water, and swung with a crash that shivered her against the side of the ship. The other was more fortunate, and got clear just before we foundered.

Tim, who might have joined it, preferred to stand by me. The other men provided themselves with spars or corks, and prepared for the end.

"Keep near me," said Tim with a tremble in his voice, not of fear but of affection.

That was all I heard; for at that moment the *Kestrel* gave a dive forward, which cleared her decks, and sent her, captain, lace, and all, to the bottom.

"Jump!" cried a voice at my side.

I felt an arm round me as the water closed over us; and when, struggling hard against the suck of the foundering ship, I rose to the surface, Tim was beside me with one arm still round me, the other clinging to a floating spar.

Chapter Twenty Two
On His Majesty's Service

How long Tim and I clung to the spar I know not. The next thing I remember was opening my eyes and finding myself in the bottom of a boat crowded with men from the *Kestrel*. The sea was running mountains high, and the boat, without rudder or oars, was flung like a cork from wave to wave. The dawn was just beginning to show in the sky, and the thunder of surf and wind was deafening.

"Where is Tim?" said I.

No one heard me, or, if they heard, heeded me. I raised my head and looked anxiously from one to another of my comrades.

"Where is Tim?" I asked again, louder, and with a pluck at the sleeve of the man nearest me.

"Where all the rest are," replied the man, "if you mean the lieutenant."

I crawled from where I lay and came beside him on the bench.

"Drowned?" I asked.

"There was only room for one of you when we picked you up. He made us take you, and it was all we could do to get you aboard."

"And Tim?"

"We gave him a rope to lash him to his spar, and lost sight of him."

Half-drowned and bruised as I was, this blow sent me back to the bottom of the boat like one already dead. What had I to live for now?

When I came to myself next a change had come over the scene. The sea had quieted down, the afternoon sun was striking across the waves, and ahead of us, on the northern horizon, was a low, grey line of coast.

But it was not at that that all eyes were turned, but at a noble-looking ship hove-to in the offing, not a mile away, and flying a signal from her peak.

Our men had sighted her an hour ago, and rigged up an oar with a rag at the end, which the ship had observed. And what all eyes were now intent on was her pinnace, as she covered the distance between us.

It was always my luck to be rescued when I had least heart for life, and I confess if I had seen the boat capsize that moment I should have been well enough pleased.

But she had no notion of capsizing. Long before she came up we could see that she was manned by smart English blue-jackets, and belonged to a line-of-battle ship in the king's navy—one of the very ships, no doubt, that Captain Keogh had been so anxious to avoid in Galway Bay.

Half-an-hour later we were on the shining deck of his majesty's ship *Diana*, thirty-eight guns, standing out, with all sails set, for the wide Atlantic. My comrades were too thankful to find themselves alive, with food to eat and dry clothes to put on, to concern themselves as to the ship's destination. But I, who yearned to know and share the fate of those I loved, groaned as I saw the coast-line drop astern, and realised that, after all, I was as far from home as ever.

As soon as we were revived and fed—and I am bound to confess we were humanely treated in that respect—a ship's officer came forward and questioned us.

I, as brother to the lieutenant, was put forward to answer; and I told him all, not omitting our contraband cargo, or the manner of my own joining the *Kestrel*.

"Well, lads," said the officer, "you've paid for your bit of fun. If the *Diana* had had her full complement of men, you might have been whistling in the breakers still. Now you belong to his Majesty, and your names are entered on the books of his ship. It's more than you deserve, but that can't be helped. Report yourselves to the boatswain."

"Begging your pardon," said I, "I have business in Ireland that presses, and—"

"Hold your tongue, sir," said the officer, turning on his heel.

The land was now out of sight; the ship's course was due west; every sail was full. The boatswain's whistle was calling to quarters. Tim, and Miss Kit, and Fanad, and Kilgorman were part of an ended life. There was nothing for it but to grin and bear it.

So I reported myself, and wrote my name on the books, and became a servant for life of his Majesty.

Now it is no part of my story to relate all that happened to me during the year or two that followed. Not that it was without adventure or peril, or that it would not bear the repetition. On the contrary, if I only knew how to write a book (which none of those who read what I have written so far would be cruel enough to impute to me), I could fill a volume with adventures which not many sea-dogs could show a match to.

But somehow those years, save in a few particulars, never seemed to rank as part of my life. Just as when you come to the old cabin at Fanad, and want to reach Kilgorman, you find a mile or two of water in your way, which, though it has to be traversed, belongs neither to one side nor to the other, so I reckon those years as years by themselves, making only a break in the coast-line of my story.

The *Diana,* spent most of her time in foreign waters, whither no news of any of those I desired to hear of reached me. For a year we cruised in the West Indies, fighting Frenchmen and yellow fever and pirates. Then a summons came to take a convoy into Indian waters, where we were engaged in protecting English merchantmen from the depredations of French and Spanish privateers. Then, just as the welcome order to return to Europe arrived, an engagement in the Persian Gulf disabled us, and compelled us to put into the nearest port for repairs. And before we were fit to sail again, a sudden demand for reinforcements in the West Indies called us back there, where we fought the Frenchmen every other day.

That was the one part of the business I liked best. Every broadside we poured into the enemy helped to wipe out my scores against the Republic One and Indivisible. I am told I distinguished myself more than once in the course of the cruise, though I can take little credit to myself for disinterested gallantry if I did. I had only to call to mind the vision of my dear little mistress as I saw her last, pale and scared in the squalid attic in the Quai Necker, with her bright eyes turned on mine, with her hand on my arm, and her voice, "Come back early, Barry," to make a demon of me, as with my cutlass in my teeth I sprang on to the enemy's rigging, and dashed for his hatchways.

I cared so little for my life in those days that I was ready for any reckless or desperate adventure, and was pretty sure to be selected as one of the party when any specially critical exploit called for volunteers. If I bore a charmed life it was no credit of mine, and if I had more than my fair chance of distinguishing myself it was because the adventure always comes to the adventurous, not that I was greedy of what belonged to others.

On one occasion—it was an evening towards the end of our long term of service in foreign waters—I found myself not only lucky but famous, in a way I had never dreamed of. We were lying off Chanson, a French island, embayed by a strong gale of wind, and uncomfortably near the range of a fort, with which for some hours we had been exchanging distant shots of defiance. Captain Swift, our commander, would have liked, had it been possible, to secure himself more sea-room; but as the wind then blew it did not seem safe to attempt to shift our anchorage, and incur the risk of getting further under the guns than we were.

Captain Swift was in the act of debating with his officers as to the advisability of sending an expedition ashore to deal with the fort, when the look-out man announced two French sail in the offing bearing down on us.

This decided the question. To stay where we were was to wait to be caught between the two fires of the ships and the fort. We must get out of the bay somehow, and to do it we must make a desperate effort to silence the fort.

Two boats were ordered out, each in charge of a midshipman and a petty officer. Twenty men were told off for each boat. Our instructions were, as soon as night fell, to put off for shore, land at two different points a mile apart, and approach the fort from opposite sides. The *Diana*, meanwhile, was to slip her cables and attempt the perilous feat of warping out of the bay, so as to be ready for the French ships.

Much depended on the promptitude and success with which the expeditionary force tackled the fort. For if morning dawned with its guns on our lee-side and the two enemies to windward, there was little chance of getting out of the dilemma.

The lieutenant in charge of the first boat selected me among his crew. With cutlasses and pistols in our belts, a coil of rope over our shoulders, and spiking gear handy, we took our places silently, and waited impatiently for the dark. The sun as usual in those parts toppled down suddenly into the sea, and almost before the last edge of his orb dipped, we were on our way for the shore. Our only difficulty in landing was the heavy surf, which nearly stove in our boat. We managed to beach it, however, without much damage, and then started at a run for our destination.

Before we reached it we heard shouts and the sharp crack of muskets, which told us our manoeuvre had been detected and prepared for.

Then followed a regular race, led by the officers. While some fell, others would get in; but that we should all return to the *Diana* was not to be hoped for.

The guns of the fort were so placed that once under them they could do little harm. Our danger came from the enemy's infantry, who were evidently in reserve to protect the guns.

Now I had spent part of the day in carefully studying the fort through a telescope, and had come to the conclusion that a few nimble fellows, by aid of ropes and the trees whose branches almost overhung the wall behind, could enter it by the rear, and possibly, by creating a diversion in that quarter, help the main body who attacked it from the front. As soon as the order for a rush was given, I called on a few of my comrades—among them one or two of the *Kestrel* men—to follow me and make the attempt. We made a long détour, and, as I expected, found little or no difficulty in reaching the trees.

Once up these, it was not a very difficult feat to swing ourselves on to the top of the broad wall and so gain the yard, where we could even now see the gunners hard at work.

"Now, lads," whispered I, "each pick your man, fire when I give the signal, and then for the guns."

There were but six guns, each manned by two men, and so intent were they on the attack in front that they had not so much as the tail of an eye for the rear. There were five of us in all. We kept well in the shadow till we covered each our man. Then I gave the signal. The pistols rang out, followed by a loud British cheer, as we rushed forward, cutlass in hand, on the gunners. Aided by darkness and surprise, and the good aim of our first volley, we were soon on equal terms as regarded numbers; and after that there was of course no question as to whom the guns belonged. Two of our fellows were killed and one wounded, leaving but me and one other to haul down the French flag.

Our orders had been to spike the guns, but as things had turned out it seemed better now to hold them, and if possible turn them on the enemy. All had been done so quickly that those without knew nothing of what had happened. We could hear the firing grow feebler and more distant, and guessed that our men had been outnumbered, and were being chased down to their boats. In the present darkness we could do nothing to help them; for even if we could have lowered the guns enough to cover them, our shot might have hurt them more than the enemy.

Our only hope was in the faint glow of dawn on the horizon, and the prospect, in a few minutes, of sufficient daylight to work by. Meanwhile we loaded, and reconnoitred the fort, in readiness for the moment of action.

Day came at last, and showed us the *Diana* with the two French ships close-hauled, trying to keep their weather-gage. Our men ashore were still hemmed in between the fort and the troops, who, now we came to look at them, were posted in force behind some earthworks which commanded the passage from the shore to the fort. One of our boats was stove in, and the other was in the hands of the enemy.

Without a glass it was hard to read the signals on the *Diana*; but she must have noticed that the French flag on the fort was down, for we saw her set her sails and prepare to meet her two assailants in the open. If she could only get the weather-gage, we would startle the Frenchmen in a way which would amaze them.

As for our own fellows ashore, a pounding shot from one of our guns, which we contrived to lower sufficiently to command the earthworks, soon apprised them what was in the wind, and with a rush they made for the now friendly fort. The enemy followed, but too slowly to prevent their entrance. The few shots they sent were wild and high. Only one took effect, and that, alas! was on my faithful comrade; so that when the gate was opened, I was the only man left to hand over the fort to his Majesty's officers.

After that, we made short business of the Republic One and Indivisible in the island of Chanson. The *Diana* slipped out cleverly in the wind's eye, with a broadside a-piece to her opponents, who, when they found themselves caught between the two fires, thought better of their enterprise, and tried to get out of it.

Only one of them succeeded; and our fellows spent a merry morning and afternoon with the other, boarding her and running the king's flag to the top of her mainmast.

This adventure—though, as I say, I deserved no more credit for it than the score of gallant fellows who lost their lives—gained me no small renown; and when presently the *Diana* was ordered home to British waters, one of the first pieces of news that met me when we landed at Portsmouth was that I had been recommended to the Admiralty as a suitable person to receive his Majesty's warrant as boatswain to my ship. Meantime, as necessary repairs to the *Diana* would necessitate a full month in dock, leave of absence for a week or two was granted to most of her crew in consideration of their long service.

Chapter Twenty Three
Lord Edward

Captain Swift, himself an Irishman, when he understood that I was desirous of spending my leave of absence in Donegal, was gracious enough to appoint me his secretary for the time being, and thus made easy what might otherwise have been a difficult journey. The captain's destination was a few miles south of Derry, where his family resided, so that I was brought well on my way.

Our journey took us through Dublin, in which city the captain remained some days, to confer with the naval authorities there as to the future service of the *Diana* in Irish waters. During that short halt I had time to look about me, and form some impressions of a place of which I had so often heard but never yet seen.

I am not going to trouble my readers with those impressions. Indeed, when it came to looking about me, I found my attention taken hold of by matters far more important than streets and edifices.

On the day before our departure for the north, one of my first errands was to the coach-office, to engage places for the captain and myself for the journey. I had done this, and was about to quit the yard, when a private travelling coach, evidently about to start (for it was piled with baggage on the top), drew up at the gate, to take on board a sack of corn for the horses.

It was evidently the equipage of a wealthy man. Two passengers were inside—a lady and a gentleman—both well cloaked, for it was a cold spring day. I could not see their faces, and should probably not have troubled myself twice about them, but for two strange incidents which happened, just as, having taken up what they called for, the carriage started on its journey. A man on the pavement, who had evidently been watching the halt, uttered a howl of execration and shook his fist at the window. A moment after, a young gentleman of military bearing, mounted on a grey horse, cantered up the road and overtook the coach on the other side. He carried a small bunch of flowers, which he stooped to pass in at the window to the lady, receiving in exchange a wave from one of the prettiest hands I ever saw.

Next moment the coach was rattling down the street; and the gentleman having accompanied it a short distance, kissed his hand and wheeled up a side street and disappeared.

Unless I was greatly deceived, that gentleman was Captain Lestrange.

"Who are the travellers?" said I to the man who had shaken his fist.

He was apparently a countryman, dressed in an old frieze coat, with a slouching hat.

He ground his teeth as he turned on me.

"The greatest villain on earth," said he. "I know him."

"I suppose so," said I, "or you would hardly excite yourself about him."

"Excite, is it? Man, dear, if there is a Judas on this earth, that's him! Excite? you'd be excited too."

The man talked like one tipsy, but I did not think it was with drink.

"What has he done to you?" said I.

"Done? Isn't that the boy who's lured us all on, and then comes to Dublin to denounce us? Man alive, did you never hear of Maurice Gorman in your life?"

It was as much as I could do to stand steady under this shock.

"I was never in Dublin before," said I; "how should I? Is he an Englishman?"

"Englishman? he's worse. He's an Irish traitor, I tell you, and feeds on the blood of his people. He was the toad that made fools of us all, and wormed himself into our secrets, and then turned and stabbed us in the back. But we're not dead yet. We'll be even with him."

"Where has he gone now?" said I.

"Away home with his girl, who's as bad as himself. Sure, you saw her coquetting with the young dandy just now. He's in the very middle of the nest of vipers that are plotting to grind the life out of Ireland. Maybe," said he, stopping suddenly and looking hard at me, "you're one of that same nest yourself?"

"God forbid!" said I; "I love Ireland."

"That's good hearing. You're one of us?"

"Of the friends of my country, yes."

"A sworn friend?"

"I was sworn, yes," said I, determined at all cost to hear more of the business.

"Come this afternoon to the printer's house in Marquis Street; you'll hear more of Gorman then, maybe. *Pikes and hemp* is the word. No questions will be asked—not if you are Ireland's friend."

"I'll be there," said I; "and God save Ireland!"

"Amen!" said he, and we parted.

It was, as I learned presently, the babbling of foolish talkers like this poor fellow that wrecked the Irish conspiracy.

As for me, I confess I felt misgivings. I was a servant of his Majesty, and had no business with secret conspiracies. Yet, when a life so precious to me was at stake, how could I help trying to do something to save it? Besides (and this salved my conscience a little), had I not promised Tim, in the last hour I was with him, to strike a blow for my country?

For hours that morning I paced the streets of Dublin debating with myself, trying to reconcile dishonour with honour, and love with duty; determining one hour to fail in my appointment, in another to keep it and report all I heard to the government.

Finally, anxiety and curiosity got the better of me, and at the appointed hour I stood at the door of the printer's office in Marquis Street.

No one challenged me as I entered or passed through the outer shop, where a lad was at work folding pamphlets. But at the inner door, leading to the press-room, a little shutter slid back and a face looked out.

"*Pikes and hemp*," said I.

"Name."

"Barry."

"Pass, friend."

I found myself in a large apartment, in one corner of which stood the printing-press, and in another an iron table and a can of ink.

My friend of the morning, looking restless and haggard, was there, and greeted me, I thought, somewhat anxiously, as though he doubted the prudence of his invitation. He did not, I am sure, feel more anxious than I, who every moment found the act in which I was engaged more intolerable.

At last, when about a hundred men, most of them of the class of my friend, had dropped in silently, and stood talking in knots, awaiting one further arrival, I could stand it no longer.

"I told you a lie this morning," said I in a low voice to my companion; "I am not sworn."

He turned as white as a sheet.

"Then you are here to betray us?"

"No," said I. "Let me go, and no one shall hear a word of this."

"You cannot go," said he excitedly, "it would be death to me if it were known, and to you too. Stay where you are now."

"I don't want to stay," said I; "I was a fool to come."

"You will be still more a fool to go," said he. "Sit down; eyes are on us already. Life may be nothing to you, but it is everything to me."

He spoke so eagerly, almost piteously, that I felt sorry for him, and for his sake more than my own took the seat at his side.

At that moment there entered the room a noble-looking young man, at sight of whom every one present rose to his feet and uncovered.

"It's Lord Edward himself!" exclaimed my companion, still trembling.

Lord Edward! I had heard of him before. It was he whose letter I had carried four years ago to Deputé Duport on behalf of the unfortunate Sillery; and it was he on whom just now the eyes of all Irish rebels were turned for guidance and hope in the desperate enterprise on which they were embarked.

There was something fascinating in his open frank countenance and the half reckless, joyous air with which he carried himself. The assembly, which, till he arrived, had been sombre and mysterious, lit up under his presence into enthusiasm and eagerness.

He had news to give and receive; and as I sat and listened I came to learn more of the state of Ireland in half-an-hour than a week in Dublin would have taught me.

The fuel was ready for the torch. The United Irishmen were organised and drilled in every county. The English garrison was becoming day by day more slack and contemptible. What traitors there were were known and marked. The dawn was in the sky. A little more patience, a little more sacrifice, a little more self-restraint, and the hour of Ireland's liberty would soon strike.

But it was not in generalities like these that the speaker moved my admiration most. It was when the meeting came to consider the state of the rebel organisation in various parts that the soldier and general shone out in him, and convinced me that if any man could carry the movement through he would. The present meeting, as I understood, consisted of delegates from the north, where people were beginning to grow impatient for the signal to rise; and where, as some one boasted, one hundred thousand men were ready even now to move on Dublin and drive the English garrison into the sea.

"What of the Donegal men?" inquired Lord Edward, looking at a paper before him. "I see there is a question of treachery there."

"By your lordship's leave," said my companion, starting up, "I denounce Maurice Gorman of Knockowen as a traitor to the cause. He has been in Dublin within the last week in conference at the Castle."

Lord Edward's brow clouded.

"Was it not through him the Donegal men got their arms?"

"It was; and it's through him many of them have lost them, for he's as busy now disarming as he was a few years back arming."

"What is the reason of the change?"

"Money, my lord. He's grown a rich man; he must keep in with the government, or his estates will be taken."

Lord Edward shrugged his shoulders.

"We have not much to fear from a poltroon like him; but let the Provincial Directory of Ulster deal with the matter. Meanwhile we want to know that Donegal is as ready as other parts. We have some good men there surely. Order a return of all secretaries and officers in a month," said he to the clerk.

Then other matters were talked of, including the prospect of a French landing; and presently the meeting broke up. At the end of it Lord Edward walked straight up to me.

"Yours is a new face here," said he.

"It is, my lord," said I. "I am a Donegal man who has been abroad for four years; yet we have had dealings together before now."

"Were you at Hamburg or Basle?" said he.

"Neither; but I had the honour of carrying a letter from your lordship to a French deputy in '93, as well as another, franked by your lordship, for a certain Mr Lestrange in Paris."

He looked hard at me.

"You are not John Cassidy?" said he.

Then I told him the story of my adventure in the wood near Morlaix, and how I delivered the letters of his dead messenger in Paris.

He clapped me on the back.

"You are a good fellow," said he, "and I thank you. Little came of my letters; but that was no fault of yours. So you are one of us in Donegal?"

"No, my lord," said I. "I am here on false pretences, though not wholly of my own accord. I cannot expect you to be troubled with my explanations, but they are at your service if you require them. If not, here I am at your mercy."

He looked at me suspiciously for a moment, then he smiled.

"Walk a little way home with me," said he.

So I followed him out, the members present saluting as he passed through them, and wondering, no doubt, what high official of the society was this whom the leader of Ireland chose thus to honour.

"Now," said Lord Edward, as we got to the end of the street, "what is this mystery?"

"Shortly, my lord, I am in love," began I.

He laughed pleasantly at that.

"There we agree entirely," said he.

"I am a servant to his Majesty, and have sworn him allegiance," I continued.

"His Majesty has more than he deserves."

"I am a sailor, sir, on leave. I arrived only yesterday in Dublin after four years' absence. To-morrow (unless you or your society shoot me through the head) I start northward, hoping to get a glimpse of her I love. By chance to-day I heard her father's name mentioned in the street as a man whose life was in peril. In a weak moment I so far forgot my duty to my king as to pass myself off to my informant as a United Irishman, in the hope of obtaining information which might enable me to help him."

"I trust you got it," said his lordship.

"I did not," said I; "the Provincial Directory of Ulster is to deal with the case."

Lord Edward stopped short.

"You don't mean—" began he, and stopped.

"I mean that I love Maurice Gorman's daughter—a hopeless quest perhaps—but the prize—"

"The most charming lady in Ireland," said he. "Your name is Barry, I believe?"

"Barry Gallagher, my lord."

"Are you a kinsman of Tim Gallagher of Fanad?"

"Twin-brother. Is he alive then?" and in my eagerness I seized his lordship's arm.

He did not resent the liberty at all.

"He is, and is a trusty member of our society, as I hope you will be even yet."

"Pardon me," said I; "had Tim been dead, I promised him to fight for Ireland. As it is, I am bound to my king."

"Well," said he, with a shrug, "that is no concern of mine. As to your spying on our meeting—all's fair in love and war. You will, no doubt, make use of what you have heard against us."

"That I certainly shall not do," said I. "I am a poor man, but I am at least a gentleman. To protect the lady I love I shall certainly try; but to betray those whose gallantry and chivalry have spared me to do it, I certainly shall not. Besides, apart from my obligations to you, I am already sworn to secrecy." And I told him how I had once been forced to take the oath of the society, and had already got the length of pledging myself to secrecy before a happy diversion saved me from the rest.

"Well, Gallagher," said he, stopping short and extending his hand with that engaging smile which, rebel as he was, knit my soul to him, "I do not say but, were I in your shoes, I should feel compelled to act as you do. It is a delicate position. When we meet again it may be with drawn swords. Meanwhile, luck go with your wooing, and may it turn out as happy as my own."

This kindness quite humbled and abashed me. I had been guilty of meanness and disloyalty, and this noble way of passing it over took all the conceit out of me.

I returned crestfallen, with slow steps, to the captain's hotel. Even the news of Tim's safety failed to inspirit me. "The most charming lady in Ireland," were the words that rang in my ears; and who was I—common seaman, sneak, and cadger—to aspire to such as her? Would she, I wondered, ever care to take a flower from me as she had taken one from Captain Lestrange that morning?

I was half minded to beg Captain Swift for leave to remain behind in Dublin. But then the thought of the peril that threatened her urged me to go forward. At least I could die for her.

At the door of the hotel a person in plain clothes, but evidently a soldier, touched me on the shoulder.

"I see you are a friend of Lord Edward Fitzgerald," said he with a smirk.

I did not like the looks of the fellow, and replied shortly,—

"What if I am?"

"Only that you can earn five hundred pounds as easily as you ever earned a shilling," said he.

"Indeed! how?"

"By giving the government some information."

"As to what?"

"The plans of the United Irishmen."

"Who are they?" said I.

"Come, don't pretend to be innocent. The money's safe, I tell you."

"And I tell you," said I, bridling up, "that I know no more of the United Irishmen or their plans than you do. I saw Lord Edward for the first time in my life to-day. Our business had nothing to do with politics; and if it had, I would not sell it to you or your masters for ten thousand pounds. If you want news, go to Lord Edward himself; and wear a thick coat, for he carries a cane."

The man growled out some sort of threat or defiance and disappeared. But it showed me that, as matters then were, there was no doing anything in a corner, and the sooner I was north the better for every one.

So when next morning my captain and I, on the top of the coach, rumbled out of the gate at which only yesterday my little mistress had waved her hand, I was glad, despite many forebodings, to find myself once more on the wing.

Chapter Twenty Four
What I found under the
hearthstone at Kilgorman

Our journey northward was uneventful. Captain Swift and I parted company at Derry. My orders were to join the *Diana* at Dublin at the end of the month, which allowed me only a little over a fortnight for my business in Donegal.

You may fancy with what mingled feelings I found myself one evening standing once more on the quay at Rathmullan, looking down the lough as it lay bathed in the shifting colours of the spring sunset, trying to detect in the distance the familiar little clump of trees behind which nestled Knockowen House. Was this journey one of peace or of war? Did hope lurk for me behind yonder trees; or had I come all this way to discover that the old comrade was forsaken for the new, and that the humble star of the sailor boy had been snuffed out by the gay sun of the gentleman soldier?

Then as my eye travelled further north and caught the bluff headlands towards the lough mouth, other doubts seized me. My mother's message had burned holes in my pocket ever since I set foot again on Irish soil. And that sacred duty done, what fate awaited me among the secret rebels from whose clutches, when last I saw the Swilly, I was fleeing for my life, but who now, if I was to believe what I had heard, counted Tim, my own brother, in their ranks?

Late as it was, I was too impatient to postpone my fate by a night's rest at the inn, and hired a boat for a sail down the lough.

Few men were about, and those who were could never have recognised in the tall, bronzed, bearded boatswain the poor, uncouth lad who four years ago rowed his honour's boat. One or two that I saw I fancied I knew, one particularly, who had changed little since he held his gun to my head that night on the hills when I half took the oath of the society.

It was market day, and many boats were on the water, so that little notice was taken of me as I hoisted my sail and ran down on the familiar tack for the point below Knockowen.

The light soon fell, and I watched eagerly for the window lights. Once or twice on the road north I had heard of the travellers in the private carriage, and knew they had reached home a day or two ago; and to this news one gossip that I encountered on the road to Rathmullan added that Mistress Gorman, my little lady's mother, had died two years ago, and that the maid was now her father's only companion and housekeeper.

Presently the well-known twinkle of light shot out, and towards it, with a heart that throbbed more restlessly than my boat, I turned my keel.

When I came up level with the house it was all I could do to refrain from running my boat alongside the landing-place as of yore. I lowered my sail and let her drift as close under the bank as possible. No one was stirring. There were lights in the upper room, and one above the hall-door. Towards the former I strained my eyes longingly for a glimpse even of her shadow. How long I waited I knew not—it might have been a minute or an hour—but presently she came, her figure, more womanly than when I last saw it, dark against the light within, and her hair falling in waves upon her shoulder. She stood for a moment at the closed window, then opened it and looked out. The night was cold and dark; but she braved it, and sat humming a tune, her hand playing with the ivy that crept up to the window-sill.

The air was one I knew. Many a time had she crooned it in the old days as I rowed her in the boat. Once, on a specially happy evening, she had sung it in the attic on the Quai Necker in Paris, and had laughed when I put in a rough bass.

I could not help, as I stood and listened, repeating the experiment, first very softly, then less so, and finally loud enough for her to hear.

What fools we men are! At that instant, with a savage howl, a dog—my own dog Con—rushed down the garden to the spot. The window closed abruptly; there was a sound of voices in the yard and a drawing of bolts at the hall-door, and a hurrying of lights within. I had barely time to cast off from the stake by which I held, and let my boat into the rapid ebb, when footsteps sounded on the gravel, and a shot fired into the night woke the echoes of the lough.

So much for my serenading, and so much for the life of security and peace my little mistress was doomed to live in her father's house.

I cared not much where the tide took me after that, till presently the tossing of my boat warned me that I must be on the reef off Kilgorman cliffs. In the darkness I could see nothing, but my memory was strong enough to serve for moon and compass both. On this tide and with this wind ten minutes would bring me into the creek.

Why not? Why not now as well as any other time? I was a man, and feared ghosts no longer. Love had been warned away from Knockowen;

duty should welcome me at Kilgorman. So I put down my helm, let out my sheet, commended myself to my Maker, and made for the black rocks.

I was determined to avoid the creek and make for the house by the narrow cave which, as I had discovered at my last visit, led up from the shore to the great hearth in the kitchen of the house, and which, as it then seemed, was a secret passage known only to his honour and the smugglers in his employ. It needed some groping about in the dark to find the ledge of rock behind which was the small crack in the cliff that marked the entrance; but I hit on it after a little, and, shoving through, found myself inside the cave. I moored my boat beside the rocky ledge, and then clambered up to the entrance of the narrow gallery. Once there my course was clear; only I wished I had a light, for I knocked first my head, then my knees, then my elbows, and finally had to complete the journey in humble fashion on my hands and knees.

It surprised me greatly, when after long groping I supposed myself close to my destination, to perceive the glimmer of a light at the end of the passage, still more to hear the sound of voices. Were they ghosts or smugglers, or what?

If ghosts, I was disposed to venture on. That they were smugglers I could hardly believe, for there had been no sight of a ship anywhere near, nor of a boat in the cave. Whoever they were, they must have entered the place by the ordinary way above ground, and if so were probably unaware of the secret passage. At any rate, I had come so far, and would not turn back till I saw good reason. I had a pistol in my pocket and a tolerably handy knife, with which, even if surprised, I could give a good account of myself. So I crawled on, and presently came to a place where I could stand upright, and crept close under the corner of the upright stones that flanked the great hearth.

The mystery of the light and voices was soon explained. About a dozen men were assembled in the kitchen, lit up by the glare of a common candle, engaged in earnest consultation. Among the few faces which the light revealed to me I recognised some of my old foes of the secret society, and in the voices of others whose faces were hidden I recognised more.

The subject under discussion was twofold, and as its meaning gradually dawned on me I felt no compunction in listening.

The first matter was a letter, which had evidently been read before I arrived, from the leaders of the United Irishmen in Dublin, calling for a return of the members and officers and arms in each district. From what I could gather, Donegal was not a hopeful region. It numbered, indeed, a few branches of the society scattered up and down the county like that now in session, and was supposed to possess a few arms, and to be able when called upon to put into the field a few drilled men; but compared with other districts it was ineffective, and more given over to smuggling and unorganised raids than to disciplined work for the cause of Irish liberty.

This, as far as I could gather, was the subject of the somewhat upbraiding letter which had arrived from headquarters.

"Arrah, thin, and it's the truth they're spakin'," said one voice, "and we'll need to be moving."

"Move, is it? How'll you move when only the half of yez—and that's some of yez as are not here the night—come to the meetings? Sure we could move fast enough if all the boys that's sworn would jine us."

"Anyhow, here's the paper. It'ud be a shame if Donegal was not to have a hand in the turn-out when it comes. Bedad, I'd move across to Antrim if it came to that."

"And as for officers, sure we're well off for them. Isn't Larry Flanagan here a rale born secretary; and Jake Finn makes an iligant treasurer; and as for captain—"

"Ah, I can name you the man for that."

"Who now? for it's not iverybody that'll suit."

"Tim Gallagher's your man."

If I started at this, the sound was lost in the general acclamation which the proposal evoked.

"Faith, and you've named the very boy. Young as he is, his heart's in the business."

"And more by tokens, he's well spoke of by them that know. I'm even told Lord Edward has a good word for him."

"If there's anything against him, it is that he's brother to that scurvy informer that set Gorman on to us, and who, I hear, is still about. Tim will have to go the whole hog if he's to lead us. There's hunting down to be done, I warn you, as well as fighting."

"Anyhow, Tim's the boy for us, and I propose him. He's due back this week, if he's not caught by his honour's ferrets."

"That brings us to the other matter," said the man already spoken of as Flanagan, the secretary, in whom I recognised one of my old persecutors, "and it's about that same vermin. I've a letter from the Ulster Committee bidding us deal with Gorman in a way that's best for the good of Ireland."

"That means a bullet in him," said one man bluntly.

"Faith, and you've hit it, my lad. We've been squeamish enough."

"It's got to be done, and soon, or he'll get the upper hand of us. There's men of his away seizing the arms in Rathmullan and Milford this week— him as was the manes of bringing them in too!"

"It's one man's job. His house is too well guarded for a raid; he must be met on the hillside. I say, let's draw lots. To-morrow he's to ride to Malin by the Black Hill road."

"Ay, that's the road Terence Gorman rode the night he paid his debts. It's a grand place for squaring up is the Black Hill."

"Come now," said Flanagan, who had been busily marking a piece of paper, "there's a paper for each of yez, and the one that draws the cross is the boy for the job. Come, one at a time now; draw out of my ould hat, and good luck to yez all."

One by one they advanced and drew, and the lot fell on one they called Paddy Corkill, whose vicious face fell a little as he saw the fatal mark.

"Arrah, and it's me hasn't aven a gun," said he.

"Take mine—it's a good one," said the secretary; "and more by tokens it was Tim Gallagher's once, for he gave it me, and his name's on it. To-morrow noight we meet here to hear your news, Paddy, if we're not on the hill, some of us, to see the job done."

"Faith, if it must be done it must," said Paddy. "It's no light thing setting a country free."

"Away with yez now," said the secretary, "or the ghost will be hunting yez."

On which the meeting dispersed. I could hear their footsteps die away down the passage, and presently pass crunching on the gravel outside, while I remained crouched where I was, as still as a mouse, hardly knowing if I was awake or dreamed.

There was no time to be lost, that I could plainly see. But how to prevent this wicked crime was what puzzled me. I could not hope to gain admittance to Knockowen at this time of night; or if I did, I should probably only thwart my own object, and subject myself to arrest as the associate of assassins. His honour, I knew, was in the habit of starting betimes when business called him to Malin. If I was to do anything, it must be on the Black Hill itself; and thither, accordingly, I resolved to go.

But before I quitted Kilgorman I had another duty scarcely less sacred than that of saving a life from destruction. I stood on the very spot to which my mother's last message had pointed me, and nothing should tear me now from the place till that wandering spirit was eased of its nightly burden.

"If you love God, whoever you are," (so the message ran), *"seek below the great hearth; and what you find there, see to it, as you hope for grace. God send this into the hands of one who loves truth and charity. Amen."*

Even while I repeated the words to myself, my ear seemed to catch the fluttering footstep advancing down the passage and hear the rustle of the woman's dress as she passed through the door and approached my hiding-place. A beam of moonlight struck across the floor, and the night wind-swept with a wail round the gables without. Then all was silence, except what seemed to my strained senses a light tap, as with the sole of a foot, on the flagstone that stretched across in front of the fireplace. After that even the wind hushed and the moonlight went out.

I advanced cautiously over the embers, and felt my way down the room and into the passage without. There, where the conspirators had left it, stood the candle, and the tinder-box beside it. I carried the light back to the hearth, shading it with my hand for fear any one without might see it, and set it down beside the flagstone. All over this stone I groped without finding any trace of a rift or any hint of how to lift so formidable a weight. It seemed fast set in the boards, and gave no sound of hollowness or symptom of unsteadiness when I tried it.

I was almost beginning to lose heart, when I knelt by chance, not on the stone, but on a short board at the side, which ran at right angles with the general planks, and seemed intended as part of a kind of framework to the stone. This board creaked under my weight; and when I looked more closely at it, I discovered a couple of sunk hinges let deep into the plank adjoining, and covered over with dust and rust. With my sailor's knife I cleared away at the edges, and after several trials, one of which broke my blade, I managed to raise it and swing it back on its hinges.

The slight cavity below was full of dirt and rubbish, and it was not till I had cleared these away that I found it ran partly under the adjoining flagstone. The hole was too small to look into, but I could get in my hand, and after some groping came upon what I wanted.

It was a small leather packet, carefully folded and tied round, not much larger than an envelope, and fastened on either side with a wafer. Slipped under the outer string was a smaller folded paper, on the cover of which I recognised, to my great amazement, my own name.

I thrust both packet and paper into my pocket, and after satisfying myself that the hole contained nothing more, filled it up again, and restored the hinged board to its old position. Then I extinguished and replaced the candle, and a few minutes later was hurrying, with my precious freight, down the rocky corridor towards the cave where I had left my boat.

I was not long in getting into the outer world once more. My boat I left where it was, and scrambled up the rocks to the place from which I had once watched the *Arrow* as she lay at anchor. Here I flung myself on the turf and waited impatiently for daylight.

It came at last, and at its first glow I took the packet from my pocket. The small outer paper addressed to me was in Tim's hand, and was very brief. "Dear Barry," it said, "I searched as I promised, and have read this letter. Time enough when Ireland's business is done to attend to yours and mine.—Tim." From this I turned with trembling curiosity to the packet itself, and took from it a faded paper, written in a strange, uncultured hand, but signed at the end with my mother's feeble signature, and dated a month after Tim's and my birth.

This is the strange matter it contained:—

"I, Mary Gallagher, being at the point of death,"—that was as she then supposed, but she lived many a year after, as the reader knows—"and as I hope for mercy from God, into whose presence I am summoned, declare that the girl-child who was buried beside my Mistress Gorman was not hers but mine. My twins were the boy who lives and the girl who died. My lady's child is the boy who passes as twin-brother to mine. It was Maurice Gorman led me to this wrong. The night that Terence Gorman, my master, was murdered and my lady died of the news, Maurice persuaded me to change my dead girl for my lady's living boy, threatening that unless I did so he would show that Mike, my husband, was his master's murderer. To save my husband I consented. Had I been sure of him I would have refused; but I feared Mike had a hand in that night's work, though I am sure it was not he who fired the shot. Thus I helped Maurice Gorman to become master of Kilgorman and all his brother's property. But they no more belong to him than the boy belongs to me. And if this be the last word I say on earth, it is all true, as Maurice knows himself, and Biddy the nurse, who writes this from my lips. God forgive me, and send this to the hands of them that will make the wrong right.

(Signed)

"Mary Gallagher."

"N.B.—The above is true, every word, to my knowledge.

(Signed)

"Biddy McQuilkin."

Chapter Twenty Five
On the Black Hill road

This, then, was the mystery which for eighteen years had hung over Kilgorman. My mother's letter cleared up a part of it, but the rest it plunged into greater mystery still. That Maurice Gorman was a villain and a usurper was evident. But who was the rightful heir my mother, either through negligence or of set purpose, had failed to state. Was it Tim? or I?

I recalled all I could of my mother's words and acts to us both—how she taught us our letters; how she sang to us; how, when need be, she chid us; how, with a hand for each, she took us as children to church; how she kissed us both at nights, and gave us our porridge when we started for the hills in the morning. In all this she never by a sign betrayed that one of us was her son and the other a stranger. Even to the last, on the day she died, the words she spoke to me, I was convinced, she would equally have spoken to Tim, had he, not I, been there to hear them.

Could it be possible that she did not herself know? Any mother who reads this will, I think, scoff at the notion; and yet I think it was so. Weak and ill as she was when it all happened, bewildered and dazed by the murder of her master and the terrible suspicion thrown on her husband, lying for weeks after in a half swoon, and believing herself at the gate of death, I think, in spite of all the mothers in Ireland, that when at last she came back to life, and looked on the two little fellows nestled in the bed at her side, she knew not the one from the other.

My father, I was sure, if he even knew that one of us was not his own boy, neither knew nor concerned himself which was which, so long as he kept his honour in good-humour.

But as regarded Biddy McQuilkin, it was different. She was not ill or blind or in mortal fear when it all happened. If any one could tell, it was she. And she, unless all reports were false, slept in the pit of the guillotine in Paris, beside her last master and mistress. It was not likely that the Republic One and Indivisible, when it swept away the old couple, would overlook their faithful and inseparable attendant.

So, after all, it seemed that mystery was to hang over Tim and me still. I could have been happy had the paper said outright, "Tim is the son of Terence Gorman." But to feel that as much might, with equal probability, be said of me, paralysed my purpose and obscured my path. How was I to set wrong right? As for Tim, it was evident from his brief note, written at a time when he did not know if I had survived the wreck of the *Kestrel* or not, that the matter concerned him little compared with the rebellious undertaking on which he was just now unhappily embarked.

Tim was, I knew, more of a natural gentleman than I, which might mean gentler blood. On the other hand, I, of the two of us, was less like Mike Gallagher in looks. Who was to decide between us? And meanwhile this Maurice Gorman—

That reminded me with a start of last night's business. This very man, robber of the widow, unnatural brother, and oppressor of the fatherless, was appointed for death that very morning, and might already be on his way to meet it. I confess, as I then felt, I could almost have let him run on his doom; yet when I recalled the vision in the kitchen last night of Paddy Corkill shouldering the borrowed gun, my humanity reasserted itself. How could I stand idle with a human life, however worthless, at stake? As to his being Miss Kit's father, that at the moment did not enter into my calculations; but as soon as it did, it urged my footsteps to a still more rapid stride as I made across the bleak tract for the Black Hill.

The morning was grey and squally, and the mists hung low on the hill-tops, and swept now and then thickly up the valleys. But I knew the way well. Tim and I had often as boys walked there to look at the spot where Terence Gorman fell, and often, in the Knockowen days, I had driven his honour's gig past the spot on the way to Malin.

The road ascends steeply some little way up the hill between high rocks. Half-way up it takes a sharp turn inward, skirting the slope on the level, and so comes out on to the open bog-road beyond. Just at the angle is a high boulder that almost overhangs the road, affording complete cover to any one waiting for a traveller, and commanding a view of him both as he walks his horse up the slope and as he trots forward on the level. It needed not much guessing to decide that it was here that Terence Gorman's murderer had lurked that fatal night, and that here Paddy Corkill would come to find his victim this morning.

As I came to the top of a hill that gave a distant view of the road by which the traveller would approach, my heart leaped to my mouth. For there, not a mile and a half away, appeared, in a break of the mist, a black speck, which I knew well enough to be his honour's gig. In half-an-hour or less it would reach the fatal spot, and I could barely hope to reach it before him. The ground in front of me was littered with boulders, and in places was soft with bog. Rapid progress was impossible. A false step, a slip might lame me, and so stop me altogether. Yet on every moment hung the fate of *her* father!

It was a wild career I made that morning—down hollows, over rocks, through swamps, and up banks. I soon lost all sight of the road, and knew I should not see it again till I came above the boulder behind which the assassin probably lurked. Once I fancied I heard the clatter of the hoofs very near; and once, on the hill before me, I seemed to catch the gleam of a gun-barrel among the rocks.

"*Stretched on the boulder, with his gun levelled, lay Corkill.*"

A minute more brought me in view of the boulder and the road below. Stretched on the former, with his gun levelled, lay Corkill, waiting the moment when his victim should reach the corner. On the road, still toiling up the hill, came the gig, and to my horror and dismay, not only his honour in it, but Miss Kit herself.

Even in that moment of terror I could not help noticing how beautiful she looked, her face intent on the horse she was driving as she sat, inclined a little forward, gently coaxing him up the hill. His honour, aged and haggard, leaned back in his seat, glancing uneasily now and then at the rocks on either side, and now and then uttering an impatient "tchk" at the panting animal.

I had barely time to whip out my ship's pistol from my belt—luckily already loaded—and level it at the assassin. Almost at the instant of my discharge his gun went off; and in the moment of silence that followed, I heard the horse start at a gallop along the level road.

Paddy lay on his face, hit in the shoulder, but not, as I judged by his kicking, fatally so. I was less concerned about him than about the occupants of the gig. As far as I could see, looking after them, neither was hurt, and the assassin's gun must have gone off harmlessly in the air. The horse, who seemed to know what all this meant as well as any one, raced for his life, and I was expecting to see the gig disappear round the turn, unless it overturned first, when a huge stone rolled down on to the road a few yards ahead, and brought the animal up on his haunches with such suddenness that the two travellers were almost pitched from their seats.

At the same moment two men, armed with clubs, leaped on to the road, one making for the horse's head, the other for the step.

All this took less time to happen than it takes me to tell it, and before the gig actually came to a standstill I was rushing along the road to the spot. My discharged pistol was in my hand, but I had no time to reload. I flung myself at the man on the step just as he raised his club, and sending him sprawling on to the road, levelled my weapon at his head.

"Move, and you're a dead man!" said I.

Then turning to his honour, I thrust the pistol into his shaking hand, and said, —

"Fire if he tries to get up, your honour. Let me get at the other one."

He was easily disposed of, for the terrified horse was jerking him off his feet and dragging him here and there in its efforts to get clear. I soon had him on the road beside his companion, helping him thereto by a crack on the head from his own club; and I then took the horse in hand, and reduced it, after a struggle, to quietness.

Till this was done I had had neither time nor heart to lift my eyes to the occupants of the gig. His honour, very white, kept his eyes on the men on the road and his finger on the trigger of the pistol. But Miss Kit had all her eyes for me. At first her look was one of mere gratitude to a stranger; then it clouded with bewilderment and almost alarm; then suddenly it lit up in a blaze of joyful recognition.

"Barry, it's you after all?" she cried.

And the light on her face glowed brighter with the blush that covered it and the tears that sparkled in her eyes.

At the sound of her voice his honour looked round sharply, and after staring blankly for a moment, recognised me too.

"How came you here?" he exclaimed, as I thought, with as much disappointment as pleasure in his voice.

"I'll tell you that by-and-by, when I've tied up these two scoundrels.— Come, stand up you two, and hands up, if you don't want a taste of cold lead in your heads."

They obeyed in a half-stupid way. One of them I recognised at once as the man who had acted as secretary at last night's meeting. No doubt he and his fellow had had their misgivings as to Paddy Corkill's ability, and had come here to second him in case of failure.

"So, Mr Larry Flanagan," said I, "there'll be grand news for the meeting to-night!"

"Who are you? I don't know you. Who's told you my name?"

"Never mind. The same as told me that Paddy Corkill borrowed your gun for this vile deed. Come, back to back now."

I had already got the tether cord from the boot of the gig, and in a few minutes had the two fastened up back to back as neatly as a sailor can tie knots.

"There," said I, dragging them to the roadside, "you'll do till we send the police to fetch you.—Your honour," said I, "I chanced to hear of this plot against your life last night. Thank Heaven I was in time to help you and the young mistress! Maybe you'll do well to take a brace of police about with you when you travel, and leave the young lady at home. She will be safer there."

"Stay, Gallagher," said his honour, as I saluted and turned to go; "you must not go like this. I have questions to ask you."

"And I," said Miss Kit. "Don't go, Barry."

"The gig will only hold two," said I; "but if his honour gives me leave, I'll be at Knockowen to-morrow."

"Certainly," said Gorman. "And, Barry, say nothing of this. Leave me to deal with it."

"As your honour pleases. Besides these two by the roadside, you'll find a boy on the top of yonder boulder who wants a lift to the lock-up."

"Don't forget to-morrow, Barry," said my lady with her sweetest smile and wave of the hand, as she gathered the reins together.

I stood cap in hand till they had disappeared round the bend, and then took a final look at my captives.

"So you are Barry Gallagher?" snarled the secretary.

"What of that?"

"Just this, that unless you let me go, and say not a word, your brother Tim shall swing for a rebel before a week's out."

It must have been satisfaction to him to see how I was staggered by this. I had never thought that what I had done to-day might recoil on the head of my own brother. However, I affected not to be greatly alarmed at the threat.

"Tim can take care of himself," said I, sitting down to load my pistol; "but since that is your game, I'll save the hangman a job."

And I levelled the weapon at his face.

"Mercy, Mr Gallagher," he cried all in a tremble. "Sure, I was only joking. I wouldn't let out on Captain Tim for the world. Come now, won't you believe me?"

His face was such a picture of terror and panic that I was almost sorry for him. His fellow-prisoner, too, who stood a good chance of the fag-end of my bullet, was equally piteous in his protestations.

"Mark this," said I, lowering the pistol, to their great relief, "there's more eyes on you and your confederates than you think. Murder is no way to help Ireland. Tell on Tim if you dare. My pistol can carry in the dark, and the first of you that has a word to say against him may say his prayers."

And I left them rolling back to back on the roadside. As for Paddy Corkill, when I went to look for him where he had fallen, there was no sign of him but a pool of blood and a track of footsteps, which presently lost themselves in the bog.

Chapter Twenty Six
Martial Law

I spent the rest of that day in wandering over the familiar haunts on Fanad, in the vain hope of encountering Tim. Towards night, worn-out with weariness and excitement, I abandoned the quest, and dropped back on the tide to Rathmullan.

The place was full of reports of the new orders which had come from Dublin for the disarming of the people, and of the military rigour with which soldiers and magistrates between them were putting their powers into force. Nearly a hundred stands of arms had, it was rumoured, been captured the day before at Milford, and one man who resisted the search had been hung summarily on the nearest tree.

As I sat screened off in a quiet corner of the inn over my supper, a new-comer entered and joined the group who were discussing the news of the day in the public-room.

"Well?" was the greeting of one or two as he entered.

"Whisht, boys! we're done intirely," said the new-comer.

"How done? Did he not pass that road?"

"He did; but never a hair of him was singed."

"I knew Paddy was a botch with the gun," said one; "there should have been better than him for such a job. Was he taken?"

"'Deed, I don't know how it all happened, but you're out about Paddy. He did his best, I'm told, and there were two to second him. But the job had got wind, and Paddy got a shot in the arm before he could let fly. And they tell me the other two are taken."

A cry of consternation went round the audience. "If Flanagan's one of them—"

"The very boy."

"It'll be a bad job for us all, then, for Flanagan will save his skin if twenty others swing for it. Where is he?"

"At Knockowen for the night."

"No news of Tim Gallagher?"

"Not a word. It's a wonder what's keeping him. He's badly wanted."

"'Deed, you may say so. He's the only gineral we have."

"As for Flanagan," said some one else, "I'm thinking he may not have toime to turn king's evidence. They're making quick work of the boys now. Is there no getting him away out of that before he tells?"

"Knockowen's guarded like a fort, with a troop of horse quartered in it."

"Dear, oh! Do the rest of the boys know of it?"

"Ay, and they've scattered. And I'm thinking that is what we'd best do, in case Flanagan names names."

"You're roight," said the chief speaker, rising. "By the powers, there'll be a big reckoning for all this when Tim comes home."

And they trooped out into the road.

All this was disturbing enough, and decided me to be early at my appointment with his honour in the morning.

"Yet," said I to myself, "men who can talk thus above their breath in a public inn are not the sort of men that will turn the land upside down. What would Lord Edward say if he could hear them—or Tim, for the matter of that?"

It was scarcely eight o'clock next morning when I pulled boldly up to his honour's pier and moored my boat.

At the garden entrance stood a trooper on guard, who brought his gun to the port and demanded what I wanted, "I am here to see his honour, at his bidding."

"What is your name?"

"Barry Gallagher."

The soldier gave a whistle, and a comrade from within approached, to whom he spoke a few words.

"Wait there!" said the sentinel to me, closing the gate as if I were a beggar, and resuming his pacing to and fro.

I swallowed my pride as best I could. If I had been fool enough to flatter myself I was to be welcomed with open arms and made much of for yesterday's exploit, this was a short way of undeceiving me. For a quarter of an hour I kicked my heels on the narrow causeway, looking up sometimes at the windows of the house for a chance glimpse of my little lady. How would she meet me after all these years? Would it be mere graciousness to one who had done her a service, or something more? I should soon know.

The sentinel presently opened the gate and beckoned me to approach.

"Pass, Gallagher," said he, motioning me to follow his comrade.

The latter conducted me up the garden, and round the house to the yard, where a strange scene met my eyes.

A soldier stood on guard at each doorway. In the middle of the open space was a table, and at it three chairs, in which sat his honour, another gentleman, and a choleric-looking man in the uniform of a captain of horse. Standing before the table handcuffed, and in the custody of three policemen, stood Flanagan and his comrade, whom I had last left back to back on Black Hill Road.

His honour recognised my arrival with a cold nod, and Flanagan, who was apparently under examination at the moment, scowled viciously. The other prisoner, who seemed as much fool as knave, looked with white face first at his judges, then at the doors, and finally with a listless sigh straight before him.

"How many does your society consist of?" his honour's fellow-magistrate was inquiring of Flanagan as I arrived.

"Och, your honour, there you puzzle me," began the shifty informer; "it might be—"

The officer brought his fist down on the table with a sound which brought all the soldiers about the place to attention, and made the prisoners start.

"Speak out, sir, or you shall swing on that hook on the wall in two minutes."

"Arrah, colonel dear, sure I'm telling you. There's forty-eight sworn men, and that's the truth."

"You are the secretary," said the magistrate. "Give me a list of their names."

"'Deed, sir, my memory is not what it was, and the book—"

"Here 'tis, captain," said a soldier, advancing with a salute, and holding out a small copy-book; "it was found on him."

"That will do," said the magistrate, putting it down without examining it. "Who is your captain or leader?"

"Who's the captain?" repeated the prisoner vaguely.

"You hear what I say," replied the magistrate. "Answer the question at once!"

"The captain? Sure, sir, it's Tim Gallagher, own brother to the man who's standing there."

Here all eyes were turned on me, and I found it difficult to endure the unfriendly scrutiny with composure. Had I walked into a trap after all, and instead of thanks was I to find myself implicated in this plot and suspected as a rebel?

"Tim Gallagher," said the magistrate, turning to his honour. "Do you know him, Gorman?"

"I do," replied Mr Gorman shortly, and evidently uneasy. "His father was once a boatman on my place."

"Ah, and a smuggler too, wasn't he? We used to hear of him at Malin sometimes."

"Likely enough. He was drowned some years ago."

"And his two sons are rebels?"

"One is by all accounts," said his honour; "the other is here, and can speak for himself."

"I am no more a rebel than you," said I hotly, without waiting to be questioned. "I am a servant of the king. His honour here knows if I ever joined with them."

"It is true," said his honour, as I thought rather grudgingly, "this rough-spoken young man was the one who frustrated the attempt on me yesterday. I know of nothing against his loyalty."

"Yet," said the presiding magistrate, who had been turning over the leaves of the secretary's book, "I find Barry Gallagher's name down here as having taken the oath. How's that?"

"It's false!" exclaimed I, betraying more confusion at this sudden announcement than was good for me. "I was once forced, years ago, with a gun at my head, to repeat the words or some of them; but I was never properly sworn!"

"How did you hear of the attempt that was to be made on Mr Gorman?" demanded the officer suspiciously.

"By accident, sir. I overheard the whole plot."

"Where?"

"That doesn't matter. I'm not under arrest?"

At this the officer glared at me, his honour drummed his fingers on the table, and the other magistrate looked sharply up.

"We can remedy that in a moment," said he; "and will do so unless you treat this court with more respect. We require you to say if you know the meeting-place of this gang."

"Sure, your honour, I'm after telling you—" began Flanagan, when he was peremptorily ordered to be silent.

"Answer the question!" thundered the officer, "or—"

Mr Gorman looked up. He had his own good reasons for preventing any revelations as to the secret uses to which Kilgorman had been put in past times.

"Pardon me, captain, would it not be much better to take information like this in a more private manner, if we are to run these villains to earth? At present, what we have to decide is as to the two prisoners; and there seems no question as to their guilt. I identify them both as the men who attacked my car, and whom Gallagher here helped to capture."

The officer growled something about interfering civilians, but the other magistrate adopted his honour's view.

"Perhaps you are right, Gorman; but we must find out their hiding-places for all that later on.—Have you any questions to ask, Captain Lavan?"

"Only how long is this formality going on? It's as clear a case as you could have, and yet here have we been sitting an hour in this draughty yard trying to obscure it," said the soldier gruffly. "I'm sent here to administer martial law, not to kick my heels about in a police-court."

The two magistrates took this rebuke meekly, and the president proceeded to pronounce his sentence.

"Cassidy," said he to the prisoner who had not spoken, and who had evidently refused to answer any question, "you have been caught red-handed in a cowardly attempt to murder an officer of his Majesty, and have admitted your guilt. You have also been proved to be a sworn rebel against the king, and engaged in a conspiracy to overturn his government in Ireland. According to the law, your life is forfeited, and I have no alternative but to hand you over to the military authorities for immediate execution."

"Guards!" cried the captain, rising, "advance! Take the prisoner outside and shoot him. Quick march!"

Cassidy, who heard his sentence without concern or emotion, shouted,—

"Down with the king! Down with informers!" and fell in between his executioners, as they marched from the yard.

"As for you, Flanagan, your guilt is equally clear and heinous; but you have given evidence which entitles you to more lenient treatment. You will be taken to Derry Jail, till arrangements are made to send you out of the country—"

"Faith, I'd start this day!" said Flanagan, on whom the perils of remaining within reach of his late comrades were evidently beginning to dawn.

"Silence! Remove the prisoner!"

At this moment the report of a volley in the paddock without sent a grim shudder through the party. Flanagan, with a livid face, walked off between his guards, and the three magistrates turned to enter the house.

His honour beckoned to me to follow, and took me into his private room.

"I owe you something for yesterday," said he in his ungracious way. "Take a word of advice. Get out of these parts as soon as you can, and warn your brother to do the same."

"Why should I go?" said I. "I've done nothing to be ashamed of."

"Unless you are prepared to tell the authorities everything you know, and assist in hunting down the rebels, you are better away. You are a marked man already among the rebels. Unless you assist our side you will be a marked man among the authorities."

"If it comes to that, your honour," said I, "there is no man more marked in these parts than yourself. The boys could forgive you for being on the English side, but they can't forgive you for having encouraged them once and turned against them now."

His honour turned white at this.

"How do you know that?" he demanded.

"How does every one know it?" replied I. "Your enemies are not likely to let you off with yesterday's attempt."

His honour looked at me as if he would read in my face something more than my words expressed. I was older now than I once was, and I was my own master, so I had no reason to avoid his scrutiny.

"I have given you the advice of a friend," said he coldly; "take it or leave it. Meanwhile, your business here is at an end."

"May I see Miss Kit?" said I, in a milder tone, which his honour at once observed. "She desired to see me when I came to-day."

"Miss Gorman is not at home."

This was a blow to me, and I had not the art to conceal it.

"Will she be back to-day?" I ventured to ask.

"No; she has gone on a visit to friends," replied his honour, who evidently enjoyed my disappointment.

"She expected to be at home when I saw her yesterday."

"And what of that? Pray, what matters it to you?"

"Only this," said I, warming up, "that I would lay down my life any day for Miss Kit; and it is for her sake, and for her alone, that I would be sorry to see harm come to a man to whom I owe nothing but harshness and injury."

I repented as soon as I had said the words, but he gave me no chance of drawing back. He laughed dryly.

"So that's at the bottom of it? The son of a boatman and smuggler aspires to be son-in-law to the owner of Knockowen and Kilgorman—a pretty honour indeed!"

Here I flung all prudence to the winds, and glared in his face as I said,—

"Suppose, instead of the son of a boatman and smuggler, the man who loved your daughter were the son of him whose estates and fortune you have stolen, what then, Mr Gorman?"

He looked at me attentively for a moment, and his face turned so white that I thought him about to swoon. It was a moment or two before he could master his tongue, and meanwhile he kept his eyes on me like a man fascinated.

"Fool!" he gasped at last. "You don't know what you are talking about." Then with a sudden recovery of composure, and in a voice almost conciliatory, he added, "Miss Kit is about to visit her friends in Dublin, and will not be back here for weeks. Take the advice of a friend, Gallagher, and get away from these parts. To give you the chance, you may, if you wish to serve me, ride to Malin instead of Martin, and escort my daughter as far as Derry."

"Miss Kit might prefer some other escort," said I.

"She might. You are not bound to wait upon her. But I can give you a pass if you do."

"When does she leave Malin?"

"To-morrow forenoon."

"And what of Tim if he is caught?" said I.

"Warn him to keep on Fanad. He will be safe there."

"Let the horse and the passport be ready as soon as it is dark to-night," said I. "I will be here."

"Very good. And see here, Gallagher," said he, "what did you mean when you said just now that I had stolen any one's land and fortune?"

"What should I mean?" said I. "It's an old story you've got hold of," said he, "that was disposed of twenty years ago by the clearest proofs. Do you suppose, if you had been what you are foolish enough to imagine, I would have brought you up in my own house, eh? Wouldn't it have been simpler to drop you in the lough? It was only my esteem for your poor mother, Mary Gallagher, that prevented my letting all the world know what you may as well know now, that Mike Gallagher, your father, was the murderer of my brother."

"That is a lie," said I, "and some day I'll prove it."

"Ay, do," said he with a laugh. "It will take a good deal of proof."

"Not more than Biddy McQuilkin can give," said I.

He staggered at this like a man shot.

"Biddy is dead long ago," he exclaimed.

"Are you so sure of that?" said I. "Any way, I'll be here for the horse and the pass at dark. And take my advice, Maurice Gorman, and see that not a hair of Tim's head is hurt. You are safe as long as he is, and no longer."

And not waiting to take food or encounter the other officials, I went down to my boat and cast myself adrift on the dark waters of the Swilly.

My most urgent business was to find or communicate with Tim, and for that purpose I set sail once more for the headlands of Fanad.

As to his honour's curious behaviour, I knew him and distrusted him enough not to think much of it. He was a coward, cursed with a guilty conscience, and would fain have passed himself off as a righteous judge and powerful patron. He was anxious to conciliate me, not so much, I thought, because of my hint about the property, which he was satisfied was incapable of proof, as from a fear I might compromise him with the authorities about his past dealings with the rebels. He was nervously anxious to get me out of the country, and was willing to promise anything, even Tim's safety and Miss Kit's society, to get rid of me.

But it would go hard with Tim if he had no security better than his honour's word; and my dear little mistress, if she was to be won at all, was not to be won as the price of a political bargain.

All the morning and afternoon I searched up and down in vain, meeting not a soul nor any sign of my brother. With heavy misgivings I returned to my boat, and set sail once more towards Knockowen. Half-way down the lough it occurred to me that I would do better to pay a visit first of all to Kilgorman. After the scare of this morning's business the rebels would hardly have the hardihood to meet there to-night; and although there was little chance of finding Tim there, the place contained a spot known to both of us, in which a message could be safely deposited.

So I tacked about, and soon found myself once more in the deep cave. The place was empty and silent, and as I crept along the rocky passage nothing but the echoes of my own feet and of the dull waves without disturbed the gloomy stillness of the place.

The big kitchen, already darkening, was deserted. Everything was as I had left it two nights ago.

I lost no time in lifting the board and depositing in the recess below the hearth my brief message for Tim:—

"Beware, Tim! You are marked down, and there's martial law after you. Informers are at work, and the names are all known. Keep on Fanad. I serve on H.M.S. *Diana*.—Barry."

This done, and the board replaced, I was about to retire so as to be in time at Knockowen, when, taking a last glance round the gaunt room, my eye was attracted by the flutter of a paper pinned to the woodwork of one of the windows.

It contained a few words roughly scrawled with the end of a charred stick. This is what it said, and as I read my heart gave a great bound within me:—

"She's safe at Malin. The Duchman sails on the flud to-night.—Finn."

This, if it meant anything, meant foul play, and crushing the paper into my pocket, I lost not a moment in regaining my boat and making all sail for Knockowen.

Chapter Twenty Seven
What I found at Malin

It was nine o'clock when I came alongside his honour's jetty, and once more demanded entrance of the sentry. This time I was received even more suspiciously than in the morning, and was allowed to wait for nearly half-an-hour before it was decided that I might safely be admitted into the premises. For this irritating delay I had probably to thank the impatience with which I met the sentinel's questions; for when at last I found myself at the house, his honour met me with an inquiry why I had delayed my coming to so late an hour.

"It is four long leagues to Malin," said he, "and on such a road you are not likely to be there before midnight, when the inn will be closed. However, get Martin to saddle Tara for you. I wish Miss Kit and her maid to start for Derry at daybreak."

"Where is she now?" I asked.

"At the house of Mr Shannon, the magistrate who is with me here."

"And where is she to be taken in Derry?"

"To the Foyle Inn, where she will find instructions from me as to her journey to Dublin."

"Have you the pass?"

He handed me a paper, which read:—

"The bearer rides on my orders. Pass him, and two ladies.—Monsieur Gorman of Knockowen."

I was turning to the stable when he called me back.

"Remember my advice of this morning. Don't return here if you value your liberty. There are warrants out against all the men named in the list. The authorities are in earnest this time."

The tone in which he said this, coming from a man who had paltered with treason for years, struck me as contemptible; but I had no time just then to let him see what I felt.

"I will take care of myself," said I; "and your honour will do well to remember what I said about Tim. When the reckoning for all this business comes, it will stand you in good stead." And not waiting to hear his reply, I went off to the stables.

Martin, whom the reader will remember, and who, despite his connection with the marauders and his bad odour with the police, continued to retain his place in his honour's service, was nowhere to be found. He had been absent, said the boy, since the afternoon, when he had taken off Tara for exercise.

I was obliged, therefore, to put up with an inferior animal, and to saddle him myself. But I was too impatient to be off to allow of any further delay.

"At what hour is the tide full?" I asked of one of the servants.

"Half-an-hour after midnight," was the reply.

As he spoke, the clock in the hall struck half-past nine.

"In three hours," said I to myself, as I galloped down the avenue, "the Dutchman at Malin weighs anchor."

It was well for me I was no stranger to the rough, mountainous road I had to travel, for the night was pitch dark, and scarcely a soul was afoot at that late hour. I did, indeed, encounter a patrol of troopers near the Black Hill, who ordered me to halt and dismount and give an account of myself. But his honour's passport satisfied them, as it did the sentry who challenged me on entering the little town of Carndonagh. Thence to Malin it is but two leagues; but my wretched beast was so spent that, unless I wished to leave it on the road, I was compelled to take it most of the way at a foot's pace; so that when at last I pulled up before the little inn at Malin, it was on the stroke of midnight.

"Faith, Mr Gorman's fond of sending messengers," said the landlord. "There was another of his here two hours since."

"What!" I exclaimed, springing up from the bench at which I was partaking of a hurried supper.

"Ay; he came with a message for the young lady up yonder at Mr Shannon's."

"What sort of man was he?"

"Much like yourself—a common-looking man, with a shaven face and a nose that turns up."

"Did he ride an iron-grey mare?" said I.

"Faith, a beauty."

"It's Martin!" I exclaimed, confirmed more than ever in my suspicions of foul play. "Show me Mr Shannon's house, like a decent man," said I to mine host.

"There'll be no one stirring there at this hour. His honour's away with Mr Gorman, and the women folks will be a-bed long since."

"Never mind about that," said I; "show me the house."

The landlord grumblingly turned out and walked with me to the Hall, which was some half-mile beyond the village.

"Yonder's the house," said he, stopping short, and pointing to a clump of trees just discernible in the darkness. "You'll not be wanting me further?"

I hastened on, and was presently knocking loudly at the door of the Hall. The house was quite dark, and every one had evidently retired for the night. Nearly ten minutes elapsed before a window opened, and a surly voice called out,—

"Well? Who's there, disturbing decent folk at this hour?"

"A messenger from Mr Gorman. Is the young lady at home? I must see her instantly."

"Young leddy! There's none younger than the mistress, and she sleeps at night like a decent woman."

"Has Miss Gorman gone, then?" I exclaimed.

"Why not, when she was sent for?"

"Who sent for her? When did she go? Where has she gone? Let me in, I say. There's foul play, and I must see your mistress instantly."

My agitation succeeded in convincing the fellow that something was amiss, and he put in his head and presently unbarred the front door.

"Mercy on us! what's the meaning of all this?" said the old man-servant as I stepped into the hall.

"Let me see Mrs Shannon," said I.

"What is it?" said a voice on the stairs before the butler could answer.

I explained my mission, and inquired if it was true that Miss Kit had already departed.

"To be sure," said the lady. "Mr Gorman's groom, Martin, rode over from Knockowen this evening with a message—"

"Written?" I interrupted.

"No; Mr Gorman was too busy to write. It was to say that a passage had been taken for Miss Kit and a maid on a brig that happened to be lying off the Five Fingers; and that, as he found the ship was to sail for Dublin with the flood to-night, he had sent over Martin to see her safely on board. I confess it seemed a little unusual; and Miss Kit was very reluctant to start on such short notice, saying it had been arranged she was to travel overland by way of Derry. But tell me, what's amiss?"

"Foul play; nothing less!" cried I. "That ship is bound, not for Dublin, but for Holland; and this is a vile plot of the rebels to be revenged on Gorman, and decoy away his daughter as a hostage. Where did Martin say the ship lay?"

"At Five Fingers, west of the headland; two leagues from here."

"When did they start from here?"

"Ten o'clock."

"On foot?"

"No. They rode; and will have been there an hour ago."

"Can you lend me a horse? Mine at the inn is spent."

"There's the cart-horse," said the butler.

"That wall do. Mrs Shannon, I beg you will send over a man at once to Knockowen and let his honour know how matters stand. I will ride to Five Fingers and see if anything is to be done or learned. What sort of girl is the maid?"

"A soft creature enough. She and this Martin have been courting a year past."

With a groan of despair I followed the butler to the yard, and bridled the unwieldy beast I found there.

"It's a fool's errand you are on," said the old retainer; "but maybe you'll have the luck to come within arm's-length of that blackguard Martin. I always doubted him. Are you armed?"

"I have a pistol."

"Take yonder old sword," said he, pointing to a rusty weapon suspended on the stable wall. "It has seen service before now."

Thus mounted and accoutred, I dug my heels into the flanks of the great horse, and, in the breaking dawn, made along the rocky track which the butler had pointed out as leading to Five Fingers.

"If nothing can be done," said I, as I left, "I will return here."

"Dear send we shall see you no more then," said the old man.

Along the road which led from Malin village to the promontory rapid progress was impossible, and but that I hoped to have better use for my horse later on, I could almost have gone as well on foot.

As the early May dawn lifted, I could get glimpses of the sea lying calm on my left, with a light breeze off the land stirring its surface.

"That is in favour of the Dutchman," groaned I.

Not a human being, scarcely a wayside hut, did I see during that tedious ride, as my lumbering beast stumbled over the loose stones and plashed his way, fetlock deep, through the bog. At length I came to the place which the butler had described as the spot where I was to turn off the road and make by a grass track for the sea-level.

A short way down this latter path brought me to a corner which opened a sudden view of the sea to northward. Gazing eagerly in that direction, the first sight which met my eyes was a brig, with all sails set, standing out to sea before the wind, about a mile or two from the shore.

Too late! I had expected nothing else, but the certainty of it now drove me into a frenzy of wrath. I flung myself from the horse and strode, pistol in hand, towards the deserted shore. There, except for hoof-marks, which convinced me three horses had passed that way, there was no sign of living being. By the tracks I could almost fix the spot at which the party had put off, doubtless in one of the brig's boats. Of the return track of the horses I could find nothing, and judged that they had been taken off either at the edge of the water, which the tide had subsequently covered, or up one of the hard rocky tracks towards the foreland.

Along one of these, which seemed the most likely, I went for some distance. It brought me out on to the cliff-top, but disclosed no trace of what I sought.

I took my red scarf, and fixing it on the end of the sword, waved it defiantly at the receding ship. Whether it was seen or not, or whether, if seen, it was understood by those who alone would be likely to understand it, I could not say.

I was about to return to Malin when a thin curl of smoke from behind a rock advised me that there was at least one human habitation within reach, where it might be possible to get information. It was a wretched mud hovel backing on to the rock—its roof of sods being held at the corners by stones—and boasting no window, only the door out of which the smoke was pouring.

An old man, with the stump of a clay pipe in his lips, was turning his pig out to grass as I approached. He looked at me suspiciously, and went on without replying to my salutation.

"Good-morrow, father," said I. "You've had a ship in overnight, I see."

"Like enough," replied he in Irish. "Thrt—thrt!" and he gave the pig a switch.

"Was she English?" I asked.

"'Deed I know nothing of her," said he with a cunning look which convinced me he was lying.

"What does she carry?" I continued, playing with the butt of the pistol in my belt.

He was quick enough to notice this gentle hint.

"Bad luck to the ship!" said he; "she's no concern of mine. What are you looking for? The trade brings me no good."

"Hark here," said I, pulling the weapon from my belt and balancing it on my fingers. "I'm no custom-house runner. Your cabin may be full, as it probably is, of rum or bitters for all I care," here he gave a wince of relief. "I want to know what yonder brig carried off, not what she left ashore."

"Sure, I thought your honour was from the police," said the man with a leer.

"Tell me," said I, "who went off in the ship's boat early this morning."

"Three just—a man and two females."

"Did you know any of them?"

"Maybe I did, maybe no. One of the ladies was maid to Mistress Shannon, away at Malin."

"And the man?"

"He's the boy that's courting that same maid, and comes from Knockowen."

"And the other lady?"

"I never saw her before; but I'm thinking she was a rale lady."

"Who rowed them out to the ship?"

"Some of the crew, by the lingo they talked."

"Did they leave the horses?"

"They did. It was me took them and turned them back over the hill. They'll find their ways home."

"What is the ship's name?"

"That I can't say, except that she was Dutch."

"How long had she been lying off here?"

"Since yesterday morning just."

"What was her cargo?"

"Sure, your honour said that was no matter at all."

"Was it Dutch goods?"

"It was; and if you'll wait here I'll fetch a drop of it to you," said he nervously.

"Stay where you are," said I. "Tell me, who is there can say what the ship's name is and where bound?"

"No one, unless it's Hugh Henry at the inn below."

"Did the young lady say anything as they took her on the boat?"

"Sure, she asked to see the captain, and to know when they were to reach Dublin, and seemed to mislike the voyage altogether. But I heard Martin say it was her father's orders, and that he would be in Dublin to meet her."

This was all the news I could gather, but it was enough to confirm my worst suspicions. Leaving the old man still in doubt as to the motive for my questions, I returned as rapidly as I could to Malin, and presented myself at the inn.

"Sure, I thought you were away," said the host, who came down half-dressed to admit me.

"I want to know something about the Dutch ship that was in here overnight," said I. "Not," I added, as I noticed the conscious fall of his face, "that I care what she carried. No doubt she was a smuggler, and that you and she had your business together—"

"'Deed, sir," he began, "may the—"

"Whisht!" said I, "that will do later. Just now I must know her name, and whither bound. The young lady at the Hall has been decoyed away in her, and must be found."

His amazement convinced me that at least he had been no party to the abduction, which had probably, and wisely so, been confided to no one beyond Martin and the officials of the secret society.

"The young leddy, Mr Gorman's daughter, carried off!" and he indulged in a long whistle. "I always said his honour would get into trouble with a kittle girl like that."

"Hold your tongue, you scoundrel," shouted I, "unless you want it crammed down your throat, and tell me the ship's name and her port."

"No offence, sir," said the honest landlord, taken aback by my anger, and by the gleam of the pistol which I set down on the table—"no offence, sir. She was the brig *Scheldt* from Rotterdam, a well-found craft that's been this way before with messages from the Irish in Holland to those at home."

With this I made once more for the Hall, where I found the household up, and in a state of anxious expectation. When they heard my story, great was the distress of the lady of the house to discover how she, in whose charge Miss Kit had been left, had been imposed upon. She implored me to wait till Mr Shannon returned from Knockowen; but as it was doubtful when that would be, such delay seemed useless.

Before I left I wrote a letter to Mr Gorman giving him all the particulars I could. He would no doubt receive an official notice from the rebels, naming their conditions for restoring their hostage. But so cowardly and shambling a creature had this father become, that I doubted very much whether he would risk much even to recover his child.

I then returned once more to the inn, where already the news of the night's adventure had attracted a group of gossips. The landlord seeing me, took me aside and handed me a paper.

"Here's a song of another tune," said he. "It was left by the Dutch skipper, and may be news to some of you."

I read it. It was a proclamation to the people of Ireland, couched in bombastic language, and stating that the hour of deliverance was at hand. A foreign fleet was about to descend on our northern coasts. Any day now the signal might be given for Ireland to rise. All was ready, and trusty leaders would accompany the friendly fleet. A strong blow well struck would end Ireland's ills for ever. And so on.

"What do I want with this?" said I, giving back the paper. "Give it to those who want it. I've had enough of the Dutch for one night."

And saddling my horse I started, in what sort of humour my readers may imagine, towards Derry.

Chapter Twenty Eight
Two old acquaintances

Save to turn my back on a region which had now become full of gloomy associations, I had no very definite purpose in view in that morning's ride. There was nothing to be done. The mischief to her I loved was beyond recall. Even those who had made themselves the agents of this vile conspiracy had placed themselves out of reach. Tim, my own brother, was nominal chief to the hated band, and though he was absent, and would, I knew, have had no hand in this business, to denounce the whole company would be only to strike at him. From Maurice Gorman, coward and time-server, there was nothing to be hoped. Not a friend was there on whom I could count, not an enemy on whom I could have the sorry satisfaction of being revenged.

As, however, the gallop through the bracing morning air produced its natural effect, it occurred to me to offer my services, during the remainder of my leave of absence, to Captain Swift, or, should he desire it, join the *Diana* forthwith, and try to forget my trouble in hard work.

His honour's passport took me safely past the numerous patrols which beset my way between Malin and Derry, and which spoke much for the rigour with which the new *régime* of martial law was being enforced. Once or twice I was questioned as to the two ladies named in the pass, to which I replied that I was to foregather with them presently—which I devoutly wished might be true.

At Derry more than usual ceremony awaited a stranger at the gates. I was conducted to the guard-room, and there detained under a kind of friendly arrest for half-an-hour or so, until it suited the pleasure of the officer on guard to inspect me.

When this gentleman made his appearance, I recognised, not altogether with delight, my old acquaintance and supposed rival, Captain Lestrange. He failed to recognise me at first, but when I reminded him of our last meeting in Paris, he took in who I was.

"Those were hard times," said he. "How I ever got the ladies out of that terrible city I scarcely know to this day. I see you travel on Mr Gorman's business, and escort two ladies. Where are they?"

"I wish I knew," said I, and gave him a full account of my ride to Malin and all that happened there.

He heard my story with growing attention and consternation.

"Decoyed!" he exclaimed vehemently. "The dogs shall pay for this! I remember that scoundrel Martin."

"Shall you go to Rotterdam?" said I.

"I?" said he, looking at me in surprise. "I am no man of leisure just now."

"But report says you have a particular interest in Miss Gorman's welfare."

"Rumour commits many impertinences," replied he with an angry frown. "For all that, I am not master of my own movements just now. I am here to hunt down rebels; and among them, unless I mistake, a brother of yours holds a prominent place."

I winced.

"At least," said I, "he never had hand either in murder, or pillage, or meanness to a woman. He is an honest soldier, though, alas! on the wrong side."

Captain Lestrange laughed.

"It is the fashion of these rebels," said he, "to dignify themselves as soldiers and claim the honours of war. But when we get hold of them they will learn that there is a difference between felony and warfare. Can you not persuade your brother out of it? I hear he is a fine fellow."

"I have tried," said I, mollified by this compliment; "but it is useless, and at present he is not to be found."

"That's the best place for him. As to Miss Gorman, I will go over to Knockowen and see if anything can be done to intercept the Dutchman. Meanwhile what of you?"

"I go to join my ship."

"Good. We may meet again, Gallagher. Our paths have met strangely before now. Heaven grant they may bring us out into fair weather at last."

I left him on the whole in good cheer. There was a blunt frankness about him which led me to believe that were I ever to be called upon to meet Captain Lestrange as an enemy, it would be as an honest and generous one. His affected indolence had already been disproved by the service he had rendered to the ladies in Paris. His regrets as to Tim showed that he was a man in whom the kindlier instincts were not all wanting. What, however, comforted me most was his tone with regard to Miss Kit. There was nothing of the lover about the words, and too little of the actor about the man to lead me to suppose he was deluding me. Why should he? He was my superior in birth and rank. He had claims of kinship and property which pointed him out as the natural squire for the heiress of Kilgorman. The idea of my being a rival had probably never entered his head; and if it had, would have done so only to raise a smile of incredulous pity. But that a lover could receive the news I brought as he did seemed quite impossible. So I went on my way, if not cheered, at least with a less heavy weight on my mind than before.

I found Captain Swift in bed with an attack of jaundice, and in a state of high excitement.

"How did you know I wanted you?" he said when I presented myself.

"I did not, sir," said I. "Have you any orders for me?"

"A despatch has come from the Admiralty," said he, "cancelling all leave of absence. The *Diana* being still under repair, I am appointed to the *Zebra*, now off Dublin, and ordered to sail on Saturday to join the fleet watching the Dutch off the Texel."

I hope he put down to zeal for the service the whole of the satisfaction with which I received this announcement. No work just then could fit in better with my humour than watching the Dutchmen.

"Be ready to start by to-night's coach," said he. "I shall follow to-morrow, with or without my doctor's leave. Here is a letter I wish you to deliver at the Admiralty. Then report yourself on board. I hear she's an ill-found craft, and no one knows what sort of crew they will rake up for us. I wish the *Diana* hands were within call," he added to himself.

Next day I was in Dublin, and duly left my captain's letter at the Admiralty. I was instructed to report myself on board the *Zebra* before sundown, as there was much work to be done getting crew and stores in order ready for our immediate departure.

Having an hour or two at my disposal, I took a walk through the streets. Dublin, to all outward appearance, was in an orderly and peaceable state, and gave few signs of being, what it actually was at that time, the hotbed of a dangerous rebellion. It was only when I dived into some of the lower streets near the river, and saw the mysterious and ominous groups which hung about at the corners, and noticed the menacing looks with which they greeted any chance passer-by who was known to be a servant of the government, that I realised that I walked, as it were, on the edge of a volcano. How soon I was to experience for myself the terrors of that coming explosion the reader will hear.

I had got beyond the streets and into the Park, attracted thither by strains of martial music, when, in a retired path, I encountered a gentleman dressed in a close-fitting, semi-military coat, with a green scarf round his neck, and switching a cane to and fro as he paced moodily along. I recognised him as Lord Edward.

He looked up as I approached and at once recognised me.

"Ah, Gallagher, what news from Donegal? How is the charming fair one?" said he.

"The charming fair one," said I, with a bitterness that startled him, "is a victim in the hands of your lordship's followers. She has been decoyed away and carried off to Holland as an act of reprisal against her father."

"What?" said he. "Tell me what you mean."

And I told him my story. He listened, switching his cane against his leg, and watching my face with keen interest.

"It is part of the fortune of war," said he, "that the innocent suffer for the guilty. But this must be seen to at once. The *Scheldt* will probably make for Holland by the north route. If so, she will not arrive at Rotterdam for a week or two. By that time I will communicate with some one I know near there, and see she is taken care of. Hang the fools!" muttered he. "What good can come to any one by such an act?"

"Indeed, my lord," said I, "if I may venture to say so; Ireland has little to look for from her professed friends in Donegal, where private spite and greed are the main support of your confederacy."

"You are not the first who has told me that," said he gloomily. "No doubt you are glad to see our weakness in this quarter."

"I should be but that my brother, although absent, is the nominal head there, and it's little credit to him."

"Tim Gallagher is too good a man to be wasted."

"Do you know where he is?" I inquired.

"Abroad on his country's service," said Lord Edward. "You must be content with that. Here our ways part. Good-bye, my lad." And he gave me a friendly nod.

"Your lordship will pardon me one question. Have you any objection to tell me the address of the friend in Holland to whose care you propose to commend Miss Gorman?"

"She is an old retainer in a kinswoman's family, one Biddy McQuilkin. She keeps a little inn on the outskirts of the Hague, called the 'White Angel.'"

"Biddy McQuilkin!" exclaimed I with excitement. "Why, she was servant to the Lestranges in Paris, who perished in 'the terror.'"

"The same. This Biddy was overlooked, and finally escaped, and by the interest of Madame Sillery got to Holland, and set up at this small inn, frequented by English and Irish visitors."

It was difficult to disguise the joy which this unexpected discovery afforded me. I bade adieu to his lordship with a grateful salute, and then betook myself in a state of wonder and jubilation to the harbour.

In Biddy McQuilkin were centred any hopes I entertained of righting the wrong which had been done at Kilgorman, and so of carrying out my mother's sacred bequest. Moreover, the thought that Miss Kit would find so stalwart a protector at the end of her unhappy voyage lifted a heavy weight from my mind.

And all this relief I owed to the man whom, of all others, I, as a loyal subject of his Majesty, was bound to consider as my country's most dangerous enemy! Alack! I was not born to be a good hater. For as I strode that evening through the streets of Dublin I counted this Lord Edward as one of the few men for whom I would gladly have given my life.

When in due time I procured a boat to row me out to the *Zebra*, I found that Captain Swift's forebodings as to the state of the ship were only too well founded. The *Zebra* was a second-rate frigate, which for some years had been out of regular commission, doing duty on coast-guard service, or cruising under letters of marque. She was not an ill-looking craft; though, to judge by her looks as she rode at anchor, her lines were better adapted to fast sailing than hard knocks.

When I reported myself on board, however, I was better able to understand my captain's misgivings. The first lieutenant in charge was a coarse, brutal-looking fellow, who, if he spared me some of the abuse which he measured out to the ordinary seamen, did so because he looked to me to take some labour off his hands.

"It's high time you came," said he; "and unless you can lick a pack of wolves into shape, you may as well swing yourself up at the yard-arm at once. They seem to have emptied all the jails in Dublin to find us men; and as for stores—well, the less said about these the better."

I was not long in discovering that he had good reasons for his gloomy opinions. The hands, whom presently I piped on deck, were as ill-assorted and ill-conditioned a lot as boatswain ever was called upon to overhaul. Many were raw hands, who did not know one end of a mast from the other. Others, who knew better, appeared to be the refuse of crews which had rejected their worst men. And the few old salts of the right kind were evidently demoralised and dissatisfied, both at their enforced association with their present messmates and with the abrupt termination of their leave ashore.

As to the officers, with the exception of the first lieutenant and a few of the petty officers who took their cue from him, they seemed a decent and fairly smart set, although few of them had been tried in active service, and fewer still, I fancy, had had charge of so ill-found a ship as the *Zebra*.

One of the first complaints I was called upon to hear and report to my officers was as to the ship's food, which was truly as scurvy and unsavoury a provision as I ever saw. Biscuits and grog and pork were such as the lowest slop-shop in Letterkenny would have been ashamed to sell.

"It's good enough for hounds like them," was all I could get out of the lieutenant. "They can take it or leave it."

The next complaint I made was on my own account, and referred to the ship's stores. We had barely our complement of anchors and cables, still less any to come and go on. For reserve spars and sails and other tackle we were almost as badly off; while the ammunition and arms were certainly not enough for a service involving any considerable action.

The officer in charge received all these representations with the utmost indifference.

"Get better if you can," said he; "it's all of a piece, and quite proper for a service that's gone to the dogs. Hark at those demons now! The rum seems good enough, anyhow."

And indeed all that night the *Zebra* was more like a madhouse than one of his Majesty's ships. What authority there was was maintained at the end of the cat-o'-nine-tails. As for the enthusiasm and patriotic ardour which are usually supposed to hail the prospect of close-quarters with the enemy, one would have had to listen long and hard for any sign of either below decks that night.

"The best that can happen to us," said I to myself, as I turned in at last, "is a hurricane up Channel, and the Dutch fleet at the end of it. These may hold us together; nothing else will."

When Captain Swift came on board next evening things mended a little, for our gallant officer was a man whose name and manner both commanded respect. At the last moment some few additional stores were brought off; and the little speech he made to the crew, reminding them of their honourable profession, and holding out a prospect of distinction and prize-money in the near future, was listened to with more respect than I feared it would meet. The men, through one of their number, made a formal complaint of their grievances, which Captain Swift received on his part without resentment. The order was then given to weigh anchor, and half-an-hour later the *Zebra* was standing out to sea on as ill-starred a voyage as vessel ever made.

Had Captain Swift's health been equal to his gallantry and tact all might even yet have gone well. But he came on board ill, and two days after we sailed he was confined to his berth with a dangerous relapse, and the fate of the *Zebra* was left in the hands of the worst possible man for the duty—Mr Adrian, the first lieutenant.

Chapter Twenty Nine
Mutiny

A week of light and fickle winds brought us through the Channel and well on our way to Yarmouth Roads, off which we understood Admiral Duncan was lying. As we passed the Downs, strange and ugly rumours of trouble ahead met us. One night, as we lay anchored waiting for our wind, I was on deck at my watch when I caught the sound of oars approaching the *Zebra*. Shortly after several missives were pitched on deck, one of which alighted just at my feet.

I examined it with some curiosity. It was a bundle of printed papers addressed to the sailors of England, calling upon them to insist on the redress of grievances, and to stand by their brethren who at that moment were in a state of mutiny at the Nore. Other papers described the success which had attended a similar mutiny at Spithead a week or so previously. Another was a flaring proclamation, signed "Parker, President," on board H.M.S. *Sandwich* at the Nore, announcing that the fleet was in the hands of the men; that all the obnoxious officers were under arrest; that the Thames was under strict blockade; that conditions had been offered to the Admiralty; and that, if these were not accepted within a given time, it was the intention of the leaders of the mutiny to put to sea and hand the ships in their possession to the enemy. Further, it was stated that the fleet at the Nore was being daily recruited by deserters from the North Sea squadron and elsewhere; that arms and supplies were abundant; and that England was at the mercy of those whom up till now she had treated as veritable slaves. And so on.

All this greatly troubled me; for, from what I knew of the crew of the *Zebra*, such seditious stuff furnished just the fuel required to set the spirit of the men in a blaze. The other missives thrown on board, no doubt containing the same or similar matter, had pretty certainly fallen into the hands of those who would read the call to mutiny with different eyes from mine. If so, the mischief was already far gone.

I hastened with my papers to Lieutenant Adrian, who glanced over them contemptuously.

"All bunkum and wind," said he, pitching them into a corner. "We have heard this sort of thing before."

"If it is true, sir," I ventured to say, "that the ships at the Nore have mutinied, we had better give them a wide berth, for it's a catching thing."

"Pooh! there's no more in it than the cat and a noose or two at the yard-arms can cure," said he. "However, keep your eyes open, Mr Gallagher, and report the first sign of mutiny. There's nothing like nipping it in the bud."

For all the lieutenant's assumed indifference, further consultation with the captain and the other officers resulted in some needful precautions being taken. The watches were increased, the ammunition was placed under extra guard, and picked men were told off to man the helm. As the south-easterly breeze was rising, too, orders were given to weigh anchor at once and put to sea.

The men obeyed the orders to set sail in a sullen, mechanical way, which did not grow more hearty as they saw that every officer carried his pistol in his belt, and watched the execution of every command with suspicious keenness.

It was only when the order to turn in gave them the opportunity of congregating in larger numbers and discussing the proclamation that they took heart, and arrived at something like a united policy. Had I had my own way that night, convinced as I was of the inevitable outcome of delay, I would have clapped down the hatches and left them there to deliberate till doomsday, or such time as they chose to beg for release on the captain's terms. As it was, there was nothing to do but to speculate moodily on what the morrow would bring forth, and meanwhile make what use we could of the favouring breeze to put as many leagues as possible between ourselves and the treasonable neighbourhood of the Nore.

The worst of it was that the honest grievances of the seamen were so patent, and the injustice they suffered at the hands of officers like Lieutenant Adrian so flagrant, that had they been fairly stated and fairly met nothing but good could have come of it. But put forward as they were likely to be by a crew like ours, and encouraged and fomented by agitators such as those who had drawn up the proclamation, what issue was probable but one of desperate struggle and probably bloodshed?

It was plainly seen, when hands were piped next morning, that the temper of the men had changed for the worse. As they strolled indolently up on deck, and glanced up at the well-set sails, and saw the bows pointing due north, and as their eyes fell on the bright pistols and side-arms at the officers' belts, it was evident they were in some doubt as to what course to pursue.

They talked together in surly groups, arguing probably that on the high sea, away from support, and in the presence of a forewarned and forearmed body of officers, their chances of seizing the ship were not promising; and one or two were bold enough audibly to regret their folly for not having struck their blow and hoisted the red flag while the *Zebra* lay in friendly company in the Downs.

Finally, as I supposed, it was decided to wait till we reached Yarmouth Roads, and claim the support of the mutineers there. Meanwhile orders were obeyed with ominous silence; and worse still, the few loyal men on whom the officers had counted to stand by them were got at and drawn into consultation with their messmates, and some of them were seduced into taking part with the malcontents.

Next afternoon we sighted sails to northward; but as just then the breeze fell dead, we were unable before nightfall to ascertain whether they were ships of Admiral Duncan's squadron or not. While Lieutenant Adrian was deliberating with the other officers as to whether we should put off a boat to get word of them, the men came aft in a body and demanded a conference.

Their spokesman was an Irishman whom I recognised as one of the new hands brought on board at the last moment off Dublin. He was a glib, noisy fellow, clever most likely at anything but seamanship, of which he knew nothing, and very little acquainted with the seamen's grievances of which he elected himself to speak.

Lieutenant Adrian, who was in an ill-enough temper at the time, ordered him to take himself and the dogs at his heels to the place they came from, unless he wanted to taste the lash.

The men, who had expected some such reception, stood their ground, and ordered Callan, for that was the leader's name, to say on.

"It's not yourself we need to speak to," said Callan, "it's the captain. Let us see him."

"My lads," said the ship's surgeon, who was one of the officers present, "you are like enough to see your captain in his shroud before morning, for he is this moment at death's door."

"So much the worse," replied Callan. "There was hope of justice out of Captain Swift; there's none at all out of the lieutenant."

"There's precious good hope of a rope's end," retorted the enraged lieutenant hotly.—"Mr Gallagher, see that the fool is put in irons at once, and any one else that joins with him. We'll soon put an end to this, even should a man dangle at every yard-arm for it!"

The only reply to this was a cheer from the men, and, what was quite unexpected, a sudden click of pistols as they drew up in two lines across the deck.

"Look'ee here, Mr Adrian," said Callan, "we're not the fools you take us for. While you have been drinking, we have not been idle. The powder-magazine is ours, and the forward guns are loaded and primed and turned this way.—Stand aside, lads, and let them see for themselves."

The ranks opened, and sure enough in the forecastle we could see the muzzles of two twenty-four pounders pointed at the quarter-deck, and manned by some of the very men of whose loyalty until yesterday there had been least question.

Lieutenant Adrian, although a bully and a brute, was not lacking in animal courage, and betrayed no sign of dismay at this discovery.

"If you think we are to be frightened, hang you," said he, "you are much mistaken. What is it you want?"

A coarse laugh greeted this tame ending to his speech. One old tar put himself forward before Callan could reply.

"It's like this," said he, with a salute. "We mean no disrespect to the captain or the service, but—"

"Hold your tongue," said Callan, pushing him aside.—"What do we want? That's easy told."

And he took a paper from his pocket and read:—

"*First*. The first lieutenant, the third lieutenant, the master, the master's mate, the boatswain, and Midshipmen Gamble and Brock, to leave the ship and be put ashore.

"*Second*. The ship to be taken to the Nore, and placed under the orders of Admiral Parker.

"*Third*. The remaining officers either to take the oath or be placed under arrest.

"*Fourth*. Two delegates, chosen by the men, to attend the admiral's council, and act and vote on behalf of the ship."

Lieutenant Adrian listened with an ill-concealed smile, in which, I confess, he was by no means alone.

"And what if we reject your precious first, second, third, and fourth piece of infernal impudence?"

"Then we shall take what we want without asking," replied Callan with cool effrontery. "You may take an hour to decide.—Come, boys."

The men gave another cheer, and retired singing "Rule, Britannia." They left, however, a strongly-armed picket to cut off access from the quarter-deck to the rest of the ship.

The night was still dead calm, and the *Zebra* lay like a log in the sea, her sails drooping, and her head swinging idly with the tide.

"Well?" inquired one or two, looking at Lieutenant Adrian.

"Well?" retorted that officer. "If you want to know what I intend to do, I mean to drink a bottle of port below. There is but one answer to give, and nothing to discuss. So you may fetch me in an hour."

"Shall we tell the captain?" asked Mr Felton, the second lieutenant, who, if he had only been superior to Mr Adrian, would have seen us through the crisis with more credit than we were likely to get.

"Certainly not," said the doctor authoritatively. "The consultation in his cabin yesterday was a fatal mistake as far as he is concerned. Let him at least die in peace now."

"How many loyal men do we muster, Mr Gallagher?" said Mr Felton.

"Twenty-five, all told, sir," replied I. "We cannot count on any of the men for certain, though one or two may join us if it comes to a fight."

"It will certainly come to that," said Mr Felton quietly. And no one entertained the least question on that score.

"We have one ally more," observed the master, who had for some time been sniffing the night air. "Unless I mistake, there's a sou'-wester coming up in a jiffy."

"I think you are right, master," said Mr Felton. "That will put us over to the Dutch side, anyhow."

"And there's another ally yet, sir," said I. "They've got possession of the two casks of rum that were last shipped at Dublin."

"In that case," said the second lieutenant, laughing, "we may count on a full hour before we are disturbed. If we are to make a fight of it, let it be a good one. Gentlemen," said he, addressing the company, "the quarter-deck is still ours; twenty-five loyal men are a match for two hundred and fifty scoundrels any day. Bring the stern-guns into position, and throw up a barricade here. Look to your pistols and swords, and don't waste bullets or powder. The worst they can do is to blow the ship up, and that they won't do.—Master, you were right about the breeze. Bring her round as soon as she moves.—And some of you young gentlemen," said he to the midshipmen, "be ready to bear a hand aloft with the sails.—Mr Gallagher, watch your chance of getting round to the forecastle and doctoring the guns there. You are not a new hand, I hear, at such a job.—Now, gentlemen all, we can but die once; let us do it well while we are about it."

This spirited address had a great effect, and whatever sense of helplessness had been caused by the disparity of our numbers and the strong position of the mutineers, gave way to a desperate resolve to give a good account of ourselves before we yielded up the ship.

I could not help believing that some of the older and more experienced hands, though now borne down by the general feeling of insubordination, would side with us if only we could show a strong hand. If so, there would not be seamanship enough in the rest to set a topsail or read a chart; and every moment the breeze was freshening and promising us a lively morning.

The *Zebra* still hung listlessly in the water, but any moment now she might get under way. There was no time therefore to be lost in getting unobserved at the forward guns, which I was convinced was only to be done by dropping overboard and swimming round to the stem, where there was sufficient hanging tackle to help oneself on board with.

I secured the services of the master's mate in this perilous venture—a tough sea-dog who was ready for anything, provided it was out of the commonplace. This business, I promised him, would at least be that.

The quartermaster had charge of the helm.

"Look alive, my lads," said he, as we prepared to let ourselves overboard; "her head may go round any moment. As she lies you can drop on to it easy. Take a line with you, and pay out as you go, as you'll need it to come back by. Over you go."

We secured our pistols as best we could against the water, and then one after the other dropped over the stern and struck out for the peak. The ship was already beginning to sway on the breeze, and once or twice as we kept close under her side we were in peril of being sucked under or else crushed down by her lurches. However, we managed to reach the hanging tackle below the bowsprit without misadventure; and making fast the end of the line we carried, so that it hung close on the water-line from stem to stern, we began to haul ourselves, with our knives between our teeth, up into the shrouds.

While we were doing so the ship swung round into the wind, and began to move through the water.

Spiking the guns of the mutineers on board the "Zebra."

As soon as we got our heads level with the gunwale we could dimly see the forecastle deck before us, and the breeches of the two twenty-four pounders, pointed astern. There was a man in charge of each. The two sat on the deck, with a can of liquor between them, playing dice in a quarrelsome, half-tipsy way. The rest of the company were assembled on the middle deck, and, to judge by the sounds, were deep in the discussion of their rum and their grievances.

I gave my comrade a signal, and next moment we sprang noiselessly on board, and had the two gunners overpowered, gagged, and made fast before they could utter a sound or reach for their arms.

Then without losing a moment we drove our nails into the touch-holes of the guns, trusting to the noise of the revellers and the dash of the water at the bows to drown the sound of the hammer. This done we dropped overboard, each with a prisoner, as quietly as we had come, and with the aid of the line reached the stern in safety, and found ourselves once more on the sanctuary of the quarter-deck.

Scarcely had we done so when we became aware of a movement among the enemy. So busily occupied had they been in their debauch that they had not noticed the change in the weather, or the advantage which had been taken of it to put the ship under way. As it was, they might have even allowed that to pass, supposing it only brought them nearer to Yarmouth Roads, when one of the old salts in their number pronounced that the new wind was from another quarter, and that instead of closing in with the admiral's fleet off Yarmouth the *Zebra* was running for the open sea with a strong south-wester astern.

Finding themselves thus hoodwinked, and already excited by drink, the leaders, and as many of the men as could be enticed from the liquor, came once more aft and demanded another interview.

The quarter-deck, except for the sentries, the watch, and the men at the guns, was comparatively deserted, the officers having retired below until the hour allowed by the enemy had expired.

The senior officer present was Mr Felton.

"Quartermaster," said he, as he stepped up to the helmsman, "how does she sail?"

"Nor'-east by east, sir. Making ten knots an hour."

"Keep her so.—Mr Gamble," said he, turning to a midshipman, "have the goodness to go to my cabin at once and fetch the magnet you will find lying in the drawer of my desk."

In a minute Mr Gamble had performed his errand. Mr Felton meanwhile had lifted the cover of the compass-box, into which he now inserted the small magnet, so that it pulled the needle a quarter of the circle round, and made it appear that our course was due north.

"That should give us time," said he as he replaced the cover. "The land-lubbers will know no better.—Use your pocket-compass, quartermaster, and keep her as she is.—Now, my man," said he, addressing one of the loyal marines who had been standing sentry, "what is it?"

"If you plaze, sir, the hounds beyant there want a word with yez."

"Tell them the hour is not yet up, and that Mr Adrian is below."

"Sure I told them so, and Callan, he's their talking man, says he must see yourself, or there'll be mischief."

"Very good," said Mr Felton. "Pass the word below for all hands on deck; and let every man go quietly to his place.—Marine, allow Callan on the quarter-deck."

But Mr Callan was not tipsy enough to fall into such a trap, and insisted on the honours of war and the word of a gentleman that he and three of his followers should be allowed safe-conduct, hinting at the same time that the forward guns were still in position, and that any attempt to break parole would be visited with ugly consequences.

Lieutenant Felton gravely gave the necessary assurance, whereupon, ordering their followers to wait below, Callan and three comrades, as tipsy as himself, staggered up the ladder.

"Now, sir, what is the matter?" demanded Mr Felton.

"Matter? The ship's on the wrong tack. You're sailing her out to sea; and if she's not put round at once, we'll put her about for you."

Mr Felton laughed.

"Not so easy to sail out to sea in this wind as you think, my lad. I wonder, now, if you really know what direction we are going in."

One of the four replied, "Nor'-east," unless he was mistaken.

"Bless me," said the officer, "and these are the men who pretend to speak in the name of the British seaman! I should prefer to take the word of the compass against yours in a cap of wind, my fine fellow, any day. Nor'-east, indeed!"

"The compass will say the same as us; or maybe we're a point more to eastward."

"You can satisfy yourself as to that if you please," said Mr Felton dryly. — "Mr Gallagher, take these men and show them the compass. It will be a lesson to them in navigation."

The laughter of the company succeeded in effectually damping the confidence of our amateur seamen as they slowly followed me abaft.

"Steer gingerly round these guns," said I, as we passed the two guns which had been brought to bear on the forecastle; "they're loaded. Gently now; it's not so steady walking on a deck as round the Newgate exercise-yard. Come away now. — Quartermaster, show a light on the compass here for these gentlemen. They have come to give us a lesson in seamanship."

"Compass!" said the quartermaster with a chuckle. "Ain't the stars good enough for you? Who but a landlubber ever needed to look at a compass to see which way the wind blew? However, look away; and if it's a point out of due north call me a Dutchman."

The men peered stupidly over the compass.

"It's north, sure enough," growled the only man of the party who was at all weatherwise. "I could have sworn it was nor'-east or more."

To encourage him I tapped the glass.

"We could make it nor'-east for you by putting a spring on the needle, if that's what you want," said I with a laugh.

Callan and the others looked wisely at the mendacious instrument, and then began to sheer off with the best grace they could.

"We should be in Yarmouth Roads at this rate by daybreak," said he, "provided they play us no tricks."

"We'll see to that," said the old salt. "Now we know she's sailing north we'll see she keeps so, or there'll be the mischief in it."

"Come away now," said I, "your friends will be missing you; and what will become of your first, second, third, and fourth without you?"

It did not tend to raise the spirits of the four noble mariners as they passed round the guns to hear the laughter and cries of "nor'-east by east it is, sir," which greeted their passage. Nor did they quite recover till they returned to the arms of their comrades, who bore them off with the glorious news that a fresh cask of rum had been broached, and that the lights of Yarmouth were already visible on the horizon.

Chapter Thirty
"Battle and murder and sudden death"

It was past midnight, and in two hours the summer night would be past. After that, further mystification as to our course would be impossible; but could we hold on till then, with half a gale of wind behind us, we should be well over to the Dutch side, and clear at any rate of the mutinous atmosphere which infected Yarmouth Roads and the Nore.

The men, having, as I supposed, satisfied themselves that the *Zebra* was being sailed according to their own directions, decided to wait till daylight, by which time they counted on the encouragement and company of the Yarmouth mutineers, before they finally hoisted the red flag and took possession of the ship. Meanwhile they applied themselves assiduously to the liquor, an indulgence which, in the case of a good many of the land-lubbers of their company, must have been seriously spoiled by the rolling of the ship and their first acquaintance since we left Dublin with really dirty weather.

I reckoned that we were some twelve leagues from the Dutch coast, with the wind shifting westerly and sending heavy seas over our counter, when the grey dawn lifted and showed us a waste of water, with nothing visible but a single speck on the eastern horizon.

After close scrutiny we concluded this to be one or more sail beating up against the gale; but whether they were Dutch or English, it was too soon to say.

"Keep her as she is," said Mr Adrian; "and, Mr Gallagher, pipe all hands. The sooner we come to an understanding with these fiends the better."

I obeyed. A few of the old tars instinctively turned up to the call, but seeing all decks but the quarter-deck deserted, they remembered themselves and went off to look for their comrades.

Presently an uneasy group assembled on the forecastle, many of them showing traces of the mingled drunkenness and sea-sickness of the night. We could see them scanning the horizon with their glasses, and slowly awaking to the discovery that instead of being in the arms of the confederacy of "the Republic afloat" (as one of the proclamations had called it), the *Zebra* was scudding over the high seas.

There was an angry consultation, and shouts to those below to turn up. About half the number obeyed, though many of these were fit only to lie helplessly about the deck. A more miserable crew you never beheld.

"Hands aloft! Take in the main-topgallant sail!" cried Mr Adrian, and the order was shouted forward.

Not a man moved, except Callan, who came to the forecastle rail, and holding up a pistol, shouted back, —

"Surrender the ship, or we fire!"

Mr Adrian's reply was to repeat the order just given, and draw his pistol.

One of the mutineers, sent forward by the leaders, advanced to the mainmast with a red flag in his hand, which he proceeded to fasten to the flag-lines and to hoist, bringing down the Union flag as he did so.

Mr Adrian levelled his pistol. There was a sharp, clear ring above the noise of the gale; the man flung up his arms, uttered a yell, and rolled over on the deck.

"Stand clear!" cried Callan, waving his men on either side of the forecastle guns. "Fire, my lads!"

There was a silence. No one on the quarter-deck stirred. Those on the forecastle who had stood with their faces our way, expecting to see the effect of the volley, looked round impatiently to see why the guns were mute.

Then came a cry of "Spiked!" followed by a howl of dismay as the contents of one of our quarter-deck guns crashed with a dull, savage roar on to the forecastle.

When the smoke cleared we saw a ghastly sight. Men lay in all directions—some blown to pieces, some groaning in pools of blood, some dragging themselves with livid faces to a place of shelter.

For my own part, I dreaded to hear Mr Adrian give the order to fire the second gun. The only thing which prevented it was the sudden clearing of the forecastle. All who could rushed to the main-deck, where at least they were below the range of the deadly grape.

Here Callan, who had escaped unhurt, called on his men to form, which they did in three straggling lines across the deck, howling execrations and flourishing their knives in our direction.

Before they could advance—before, indeed, those of them who carried pistols could fire—Mr Adrian, who had ranged us up behind the barricade, gave the signal to present arms and fire.

It was a volley almost as deadly as the first. Callan sprang a foot or two in the air, and fell back shot through the heart. The front rank of the mutineers went down like ninepins, and those behind fell back a pace in consternation, "Reload! Mark your men!" cried Mr Adrian, whose face was savage and as hard as a flint.

The wretches gathered themselves together after a moment's hesitation, and stepping over the fallen bodies of their comrades, advanced with a half-hearted rush for the quarter-deck.

"Present! fire!" cried Mr Adrian.

Once more man after man went down dead or wounded, and the deck was strewn with bodies. A heavy sea at the moment broke over the quarter, sweeping the deck and clashing living and dead in a heap into the lee-scuppers. A few stood still, eyeing dubiously first one another, then the quarter-deck, then the waves as they broke across the waist.

"Reload! Mark your men!" cried Mr Adrian again, with a curl of his lips.

The mutineers heard the command, and dropping their weapons, retreated in a panic to the hatchways.

"Fire!" said Mr Adrian; "and after them, some of you, and make fast the hatches."

The first order was not obeyed. It had been bad enough, in defence of the ship, to fire on one's own shipmates, but to fire on their backs was too much; and Lieutenant Adrian probably understood as much when he saw that we all preferred his second order to his first.

It was a short business making good the hatchways, after first driving below the few stragglers who lingered above board. Then we had leisure to take stock of the execution our volleys had effected. Eleven men, including Callan and two of his fellow ringleaders, were dead. Eight more were mortally wounded, and thirty-eight lay hurt, some badly, some slightly. We lost no time in throwing the dead overboard, and carrying those most in need of succour out of the reach of the waves. Tarpaulins were spread for the rest till a place could be found for them in some of the after-cabins.

The doctor (who reported that Captain Swift had breathed his last while the engagement was at its height) did what he could to dress the wounds of the sufferers, and impressed the services of one or two of the handiest of the men present as assistants.

Just then, however, with the gale threatening every moment to snap the masts, it was even more important to get hands aloft to shorten sail. The midshipmen and officers gallantly undertook this difficult task, but not in time to save the main-topgallant mast, which fell with a crash, carrying away the purser and the boatswain's mate, and fouling the rigging below with its wreck. No sooner was this cleared, and the top courses taken in, than the man who had been for some moments conning the strange sails on the horizon reported,—

"Two Dutchmen, sir, thirty-six guns a-piece, bearing this way."

During the struggle with the mutineers we had almost forgotten the presence of these strangers, and now found them not a league away standing across the wind to meet us.

It was a hopeless venture to meet them, but Mr Adrian preferred it to putting the *Zebra* about and running away.

"Let them come," said he; "they can't do worse than these scoundrels down below. Stand by the guns, gentlemen!"

We obeyed willingly enough. Had Mr Adrian only been a gentleman as well as an officer we could have cheered him. But the vision of his face as he gave the word to mow down his own crew stuck in my memory and robbed *me* of all the enthusiasm which his present courage deserved.

On we sped, and nearer drew the Dutchmen. Evidently they were cruisers on the prowl for an enemy, or sent to observe the motions of our disorganised fleet. Had we been a sound company we might have held our own against the two of them. But crippled as we were, with our guns unmanned, our ammunition lost, and part of our crew lying wounded on deck, while the rest were prisoners below, we might as well have hoped to capture Rotterdam.

Fate, however, determined our destiny in her own way. Just as we were coming about, and those at the guns were blowing their matches for a first and possibly a last broadside, the *Zebra* gave a sudden shiver in every timber, there was a dull growl, followed an instant later by a terrific explosion which rent the vessel in twain, and dimmed the sky overhead with spars and smoke, and set the ship reeling on her beam-ends. At the moment, I was in the act of firing the charge of the gun in my care, and remember nothing but the tremendous noise, and finding myself hurled, as it seemed, clear over the breech of the weapon out into the boiling sea.

Instinctively I clutched at a spar within reach, and clung to it. All else I saw and heard as in a dream—the ship heeling over further and further, and the waves leaping on her as she plunged down; the cries and shrieks of the imprisoned wretches who sought to escape from the consequences of their own desperate revenge; the sea strewn with wreckage and struggling swimmers; the first lieutenant's dying malediction flung into the wind from the quarter-deck; the looming hulls of the two Dutchmen as they hung in the wind and watched our fate. All, I say, passed like a grim nightmare. What woke me was an arm suddenly flung across me, and the white face of Mr Midshipman Gamble looking up at me out of the water.

I hauled him up on to the spar; and the effort to keep him afloat, and save myself from his wild struggles, helped me to find my wits.

"Easy, lad!" said I; "you're safe enough here. Keep quiet!"

The sound of a voice steadied him, and he ceased his struggles, and let me lash him as best I could to the spar.

The Dutchmen, who had, no doubt, witnessed with anything but pleasure their prey snatched out of their hands, were humane enough to make a show of lowering a boat for the succour of those who still lived. But the heavy sea rendered this a very difficult and dangerous task, and after very little trying we had the dismay of seeing them abandon the attempt and haul off on their course, leaving us to our fate.

You may fancy with what feelings we watched them gradually growing less on the horizon, and realised that we were at the mercy of an angry sea, with no support but a piece of broken timber, and every moment finding ourselves more and more alone, as comrade after comrade gave up the struggle and fell back among the waves.

Presently Mr Gamble, whose leg, I found, had been crushed by the explosion, groaned, and his head fell forward. Three great waves in succession washed over us with the force of a falling wall; and when they had passed, and I looked to my companion, he was dead, with the life simply beaten out of him.

Sorrowfully enough I unlashed him, and let him drop beneath the pitiless water; and then, finding my own strength beginning to fail, I lashed myself under the arms and over the spar, and hung on for dear life. In this posture I spent weary hour after hour watching the waves, and endeavouring to ward off from my head the fury of their onslaught.

About mid-day the gale eased somewhat. I looked about me. Not a sign or vestige remained of the *Zebra* or her hapless crew. Not a floating thing among the waves caused me to count on the company of a living wretch like myself. Not even a livid corpse across my track served to remind me that I, of all that ship's company, still clung to life.

Strange visions, as I rose and fell with the heaving sea, floated before my eyes. The gloomy kitchen at Kilgorman, and my mother's letter gleaming under the hearthstone—the hollow on the cliff's edge where Tim and I had once fought—Biddy McQuilkin sitting at the fireside in our cabin, setting her cap at my father—Miss Kit with the gun at her shoulder behind the hall-door at Knockowen—the unhappy old man being dragged to the guillotine in Paris—the lumbering barge floating down the Seine—Tim in the light of the lantern at the helm of the *Kestrel*;—these and many other visions chased one another across my memory, first in regular procession, then tripping one over the other, then all jumbled and mixed together in such chaos that it was Kit who was being haled to the guillotine, and Tim who lay below the hearthstone, and Biddy who navigated the barge.

Presently one vision seemed to hang in my memory longer than the others, and that was the light of the morning sun as it struck on the retreating sails of the brig *Scheldt* of Rotterdam, standing out to sea off Malin. One by one all my other fancies merged into this—the guillotine changed into a brig, the *Kestrel* changed into the *Scheldt*, the Kilgorman kitchen became a deck, and Miss Kit a Dutch skipper. Why was it? Why should everything come back to that one brig in the offing?

Suddenly I understood it. There, as I looked up from my restless raft and followed the gleam of the afternoon sun as it broke through the clouds, I perceived just such another vision in the offing—a brig, with canvas set, and the light glancing on her sails as she laboured over the waves towards me!

She may have been a mile away. By the look of her she was a foreign craft, and may have been a trader coasting between the Dutch ports. Whatever she was, the sight of her put new life into me.

I took my red scarf—the very scarf I had waved so vainly at the *Scheldt* scarce three weeks ago—and spreading it wide waved it with all the energy of which I was capable. How long the minutes seemed then! If she gave me the go-by, my last chance would go with her. Even as I raised myself to wave, my head reeled, and a dimness clouded my eyes.

Then, with a wonderful bound at my heart, half surprise, half joy, I saw the brig suddenly put about, while a flag waved at her stern showed that my signal had been seen. A minute later the welcome sight of a boat coming towards me assured me that I was saved, and with a cry of thankfulness to Heaven my weary head drooped, and the mist in my eyes became darkness.

What roused me was the consciousness of two strong arms round me, and the taste of liquid fire between my lips. My saviours, who were Dutchmen, had lifted me from the spar, and were plying me with spirits as I lay more dead than alive in the stern-sheets. I looked up. The sails of the brig, flapping against the wind, towered above me, and her dark hull as she swung over us hid the sun. The boat pulled round her stern to reach the lee-ladder. As we passed I glanced up, and my eyes fell on two words, painted in gilt letters—

"*Scheldt.* Rotterdam."

Chapter Thirty One
The highwayman on the Delft road

The next thing I clearly remember was crawling up on deck, clad in a Dutch sailor's jacket and cap (I had been stripped for action when I was pitched into the waves out of the *Zebra*), and seeing a stretch of red-tiled roofs and windmills and tall towers on the bank of the broad stream up which we sailed on the tide. Rotterdam was in sight.

I had lain in a sort of stupor since I was carried on board twenty-four hours ago. The Dutchmen had been kind to me in their rough way, particularly as they took me for a Frenchman. I thought it prudent not to undeceive them, and passed myself off to the skipper as a castaway citizen of the Republic One and Indivisible, which my knowledge of the language made easy.

But, as you may imagine, now that I stood on the deck of the *Scheldt*, my mind had room for but one thought. Miss Kit—where was she?

Even had her curiosity brought her on deck yesterday to see the rescue of the poor foreigner, she would hardly have recognised in the smoke-begrimed, swollen features of the half-drowned man her old squire and comrade of long ago. Still less would Martin, who had never set eyes on me for four years, discover me. I knew him well enough as I came upon him just then leaning over the bulwark taking an eyeful of Dutch scenery.

He turned round as I approached and nodded.

"*Comment vous portez-vous?*" said he, using up one of the slender stock of French phrases he had at command.

I replied in French that I did well, and was entirely at monsieur's service, and madame's too, for I heard, said I, monsieur did not travel alone.

Martin, who only half-comprehended, looked at me doubtfully, and turned on his heel.

Presently, as I leaned over the port watching the river, I overheard him in conference with the skipper, who spoke imperfect English.

"Convent of the Carmelite Nuns?" said the latter; "that is outside the town some distance. Is mademoiselle to be taken there?"

"Ay; those are my orders."

"Will she go?"

"She must," said Martin.

"She has not been very obedient so far," said the skipper with a laugh. "You have not received much encouragement."

"What do I want encouragement for," growled Martin, "from her?"

"Perhaps the encouragement of Mees Norah, her maid, has been enough for you. But I warn you, my young lady will not travel so easily by land as by sea. You will need a troop of horse to take her to the Carmelites, I expect."

This was said with a sneer at Martin's qualifications as a squire of dames which that gentleman did not enjoy.

"I can manage my own business," said he in an unpleasant voice. "I shall take her there in a carriage, and if she resists she will have to find out she is not her own mistress."

"As you will," said the skipper. "I thank my stars I have not the task."

Indeed, I came to learn later on that he had good reason for so wishing. For Miss Kit, as soon as ever she discovered the vile plot which had been practised on her, had retired to her cabin, and held every one on board the *Scheldt* at arm's-length except her maid, refusing to see Martin, of the skipper, or any one, and fortifying herself like a beleaguered garrison. Her cabin had a private companion ladder by which she could reach the deck without passing through the men's quarters, and after the first day or so, the poop was yielded to her as her own territory without protest.

How was I to communicate with her now? I must if possible prevent her incarceration in the convent, from which I knew escape would be difficult.

I retired below and hastily scrawled on a piece of paper the following note:—

"Miss Kit,—The half-drowned man who was taken on board yesterday was he who writes this, and who is ready to die for you. You are to be carried in a coach to-night to the Convent of the Carmelite Nuns. Make all the delay possible before you consent to go, and so give me time to get beforehand on the road, where I will find means to take you to a place of safety.—Your devoted—

"Barry Gallagher."

This paper I folded, and returned on deck in the hope of finding some means of getting it into my lady's hands.

Just as I passed the cook's galley, I came upon Norah, the maid, coming out with a tray on which was a little bottle of wine and a plate of biscuits. As we suddenly met, the tray slipped from her hand and fell to the floor, spilling the contents of the bottle and scattering the biscuits.

"Ach, but you're clumsy!" exclaimed the damsel.

It was on the point of my tongue to return the compliment in her own language; but I remembered myself, and with a Frenchman's politeness begged ten thousand pardons.

"Permit that I assist you to make good the damage, mademoiselle," said I.

This mollified her, and she bade me hold the tray and pick up the biscuits while she went for another bottle of wine.

When she returned, nothing would content me but that I should carry the tray for her to the door of her lady's cabin, which she graciously permitted, with a coquettish glance at Martin as we passed him on deck.

My agitation, if I betrayed any, was not all due to the fascinations of Miss Norah, and Martin had no cause to be jealous on that score. The truth was, that between the two top biscuits on the dish I had slipped my little note!

"*Merci bien*, monsieur," said Norah at the door as she took the tray; "and it's sorry I am I called you names."

"Any name from those pretty lips," began I, but she left me to finish my compliment to the outside of the door.

When we moored alongside the Quai, I renewed my thanks to the Dutch skipper, and offered to return him his coat. But he would not hear of it. Only, said he, if I was disposed to-morrow to lend a hand at unlading, he would consider the trouble of fishing me out of the North Sea sufficiently repaid. This I promised by all means to do; and glad to get free so easily, stepped ashore with the first to land.

As I passed the brig's poop I thought I saw a face peep from the little cabin window, and after it a little hand wave. I put my own hand to my lips as a symbol both of secrecy and devotion, and taking advantage of the bustle attending on the arrival of a fresh craft, slipped out of the crowd into the street beyond.

Here, among the first, I met a priest, to whom I made obeisance.

"Holy father," said I in French, "I beg you to direct me to the Convent of the Carmelite Nuns of this town, to which I have a message of importance from Ireland. I am a stranger here, and have but just landed."

The priest eyed me suspiciously.

"The holy sisters receive no visitors but the clergy," said he. "I will carry your letter."

"Alas! I have no letter. My message is by word of mouth, and I am free to impart it to no one but to the lady superior. Does monseigneur suspect me of ill motives in seeking the convent?"

He liked to be called monseigneur; and looking me up and down, concluded the holy sisters had little to fear from me.

"The holy sisters live a mile or so beyond the city, before you come to Overschie, on the road to Delft. You will know the house by the high wall and the cross above the gate."

"Monseigneur," said I, "a thousand thanks, and may the saints make your bed to-night;" and I departed along the road he pointed out.

I had not gone far, or reached the open fields beyond the town, when I perceived, grazing at the roadside, a horse with saddle and pillion, such as market folk rode, which had evidently broken tether while its riders were away on some errand at a neighbouring *auberge*.

Necessity, which knows no law, and made me villain enough to deceive a priest, was hardly likely to stick at borrowing a nag, especially when the safety of my dear young mistress was at stake. It went to my heart to think that the honest couple would have to complete their marketing on foot; but I promised them in my mind that if the beast was one of sense and natural affection, it should find its way home sooner or later when its present task was done.

A short ride now cleared me of the town and brought me on to the road which follows the canal to Delft. It was already dark, and as I ambled past the lofty windmills that skirt the canal, I met scarcely a soul. Presently at a junction of roads I distinguished a little way back from the highroad the roof of a building almost hidden in trees, and closed round with a high wall. A thick, nail-studded gate, surmounted by a cross, marked the entrance. Here, then, was my destination.

I reined in my horse under the deepest shadow of the wall, within view of the portal, and waited. To pass the time, I took from my pocket the pistol which had lain there all the while I was in the water, and drawing the wet charge, replaced it with powder and shot which I had taken the precaution to provide myself with before I left the *Scheldt*.

Then it occurred to me, if I was to play highwayman, I could do it more securely out in the solitary road than within earshot of the holy sisters, who might harbour within their precincts watch-dogs, human or animal, who could spoil sport of that kind.

So I rode a little way back on my steps and halted under a clump of trees at the cross-roads, straining my ears impatiently for the noise of wheels.

Nearly an hour elapsed before they came, and I concluded Miss Kit must have taken my advice and given her custodian a bad time of it before she permitted herself to be conducted from the ship to the vehicle. Now the wheels advanced rapidly, and the frequent crack of the driver's whip showed that Martin was trying to make up for lost time.

I could see as they approached that the two men were on the box, leaving the inside to the ladies. The driver was evidently pointing out the roof of the convent, dimly visible among the trees, and a face at the open window was peering out in the same direction.

At that moment I darted out of my hiding-place, and firing my pistol in the air, but near enough to the driver's ears to make him jump, shouted gruffly, —

"*Haltez là!*"

The horse came up short on his haunches. The terror-stricken men gaped round in a dazed way and tumbled off on the far side of the coach, while the maid within uttered a loud scream. But almost before any of them knew what had happened, I was bending beside the face at the window.

"Quick, Miss Kit, mount behind me." And passing my arm round her, I drew her through the window and set her on the pillion behind me; and next moment we were galloping away as fast as the beast could carry us, with her dear arms clasping me, and her breath coming and going in quick tumult on my neck.

For a mile we rode thus without a word, when I heard her give a little laugh.

"What is it?" I asked.

"What a trouble for Martin!" said she, "He has Norah to console him."

"I am not jealous of Norah."

And I thought her arms held me a little firmer.

"How well you managed it," said she in a little. "I was terrified too, just at first. Where are we going?"

"To Biddy McQuilkin's, at the Hague."

"Biddy McQuilkin's!" exclaimed she, with a start of surprise. "Surely she is dead."

"So I thought; but she is not. She keeps an inn at the Hague; and has orders from one in high authority among the Irish rebels to take care of you."

"As a prisoner?"

"Surely not; as a lady."

She sighed.

"One peril never seems to be past," said she, "but a new one looms ahead."

"Courage," said I. "Providence that saved you from the old peril will save you from the new."

"Ah, Barry," she said gently, "I begin to wonder if your name spells Providence to me. On that hateful ship I wondered often what had become of you. When I saw behind us at Malin a red flag waved on the cliff-top, I said, Could that be you, but for once too late to help?"

"It was," I replied.

"I knew it!" she exclaimed almost triumphantly, "Night by night as we sailed further and further from home, I prayed Heaven to send you. Once when an English warship crossed our path, I pictured you among the crew, and wished they might capture us. Then when I got that wonderful little letter among the biscuits I knew my prayer was answered; and I troubled myself about nothing but to do your bidding. Poor Martin," and she laughed again, "he was the sufferer by that."

You may fancy if her voice across my shoulder that night was not music in my ears! It humoured her to talk of all the perils we had encountered together, and of the ups and downs in our lots since that first day I brought her in the boat from Rathmullan to Knockowen. Then she spoke of her father and the peril he was in, and of the feuds and dangers that beset our distracted country. From that we came to talk of my adventures, and of Tim. But I could not find it in my heart to tell her of the paper under the hearth at Kilgorman, or of the villainy by which her father came into the estates he now held.

Near the end of our talk I mentioned that I had seen Captain Lestrange in Derry.

She was silent a little, and then said,—

"He is the man my father says I must marry." This was a speech I found no ready answer to, except a mumbled, "He is a fortunate man."

"He does not think so," said Miss Kit with a laugh. "He is good and kind, but he loves his liberty more than any woman."

"And what says my little lady to that?" I faltered.

"*Vive la Liberté*," said she. "Heigho, Barry, are we nearly there?"

We were past Delft, where no one supposed but we were a belated pair of market folk trudging home. Our horse had dropped into a leisurely jog, and the morning sky was beginning to show streaks of grey.

"Are you weary?" said I, putting my hand on the little arm that held me round.

"No, Barry, I am very happy so," said she; and after that we were silent till the stars began to fade and the towers and spires of the Hague loomed ahead against the northern sky.

Despite our loitering, it was still early when we found ourselves in the streets of that city, inquiring for the *auberge* of the "White Angel." After some trouble, we were directed through the town to the road that leads to the little fishing village of Scheveningen, two miles beyond the Hague, where, just as we came in sight of the sea, a little wayside inn with a swinging sign of a heavenly body in a snowy robe told us we had at last found our journey's end.

No one was astir, but our knocking brought a groom on the scene, who rather surlily admitted us to the stable-yard.

"Tell madame she is wanted at once; I bear a message from Lord Edward, tell her."

Here a head looked out from a window, and madame's voice called out in broadest brogue, —

"Lord Edward, is it? And who might you be yourself?"

"I'm Barry Gallagher, Biddy. Put on your clothes, like a decent soul, and let us in."

Biddy obeyed with an alacrity which led us to doubt whether her toilet below the shawl she wore had been very elaborate.

On the sight of me, still more of my fair charge, she broke out into a tumult of Irish welcome.

"Arrah, darlints, sure it's glad I am to see you; and it's expecting you I've been, for didn't Lord Edward send me word to look to the young leddy? Come away, honey; for you look as white as the painted angel beyant there. So they sneaked you away, did they? And all because his honour was hanging the boys. Never ye fear, dearie, you'll be safe with old Biddy, even if the whole of the United Irishmen come after you.—And you, Barry, you're welcome too, though your father Mike wouldn't let me be mother to you. Dear, oh. There's many changes to us all since then. The last time I set eyes on yez 'twas in Paris, and little I looked to see you again when they had us all to the prison. And where's Tim at all? He's the boy, and a rale gentleman."

"Give us some food, Biddy dear," said Miss Kit, "and tell us all the news to-morrow."

"'Deed I will," said the good soul, and she bustled about till the whole household was awake to give us breakfast.

I waited only to allay my hunger, and then rose.

"Good-bye just now, Miss Kit," said I.

Her face fell.

"Oh," said she, "you're not going to leave me, Barry!"

"Till to-night. I am pledged to pay the Dutchman for saving my life by working for him this day. After that—"

"Oh, go," said she, holding out her hand, "for he deserves all the thanks in the world for saving you for me."

She blushed as she saw how I lit up at the words, but left her hand in mine as I raised it to my lips.

"Farewell, my dear Barry," said she. "Heaven bless you, and bring you safely back!"

All the world then seemed turned to brightness, and I stepped out like a man who treads on air. But at the door I remembered myself enough to return and seek Biddy in her kitchen.

"Biddy," said I, "tell me one thing, as you will answer for it at the last day—which of us two, Tim or I, is the son of Mike Gallagher, and which is the son of Terence Gorman?"

She turned very white and sank into a chair. But I had no time to parley, and I urged her to speak.

"As I hope for salvation," said she, and her breath came hard and her bosom heaved fast, "the one of you that has the mole between his shoulder-blades is the Gorman's boy."

"It is Tim then," I exclaimed, and hastened to my horse.

Chapter Thirty Two
Dutch justice

I should be no better than a hypocrite were I to deny that, as I rode my weary, borrowed nag back that morning along the Delft road, there shot in and out of the turmoil of my feelings a sharp pang of disappointment.

It was no disloyalty to Tim; it was no greediness for name and wealth. It was but the dashing of a passing hope that I might find myself, after all, a gentleman, and so prove worthy to be regarded by Miss Kit as something more than a trusty servant. As a Gorman, and her cousin, I might claim her with the best of her suitors. As the son of Mike Gallagher, boatman and smuggler, myself but a plain boatswain, how durst I suppose, for all her kindness and gentleness, she could comprehend me in the ranks of her equals?

Yet to serve her was something—to have snatched her from the scoundrel Martin, and set her in a safe place, was some little triumph to set against the disappointment of Biddy's news; and as I jogged Delft-ward that morning, I fell to considering how best I could help her to her home and Tim into his estate.

More people were about now than when I rode last, and some opened their eyes to see a sailor on horseback. But I answered no questions and halted for no parleys. At Delft I hoped to find a road round outside the town, fearing lest I might encounter the owners of the nag on the streets. But I found no way except that straight through the midst of the town.

As I crossed the market-place two soldiers accosted me and ordered me to dismount and give an account of myself. As they spoke only Dutch, and I knew none of the language, it was hard for us to understand one another. But the feel of their muzzles on my ears convinced me I had better obey; and abandoning the luckless animal, I was conducted to the guard-house and there locked up until business hours.

I demanded, in the best French I could muster, on what charge I was thus laid by the heels.

My captors grunted by way of answer, and searched my pockets, from which they drew my pistol and the little leather case containing my mother's letter.

I repeated my question in English, at which they pricked their ears, spoke something to one another in which the word "spy" occurred, and clapped irons on my ankles.

Evidently then my crime was not horse-stealing, but that of being an English spy, which meant, I supposed, a volley at ten paces before noon. So here was an end to the business of Miss Kit, my sweetheart, and Tim, my brother.

I confess, as it all dawned on me, I found myself smiling over my big hopes and resolves of an hour ago. But I had long enough to wait to lose all sense of humour, and sink into the most woeful depths of despair. It always happened so. The cup was ever at my lips, and as often rudely dashed aside. My little mistress had never before spoken so gently; my mother's dying charge had never been nearer fulfilment. And now, what could be further from my reach than either? How I execrated that ill-starred jade, and the Dutch skiver, but for whom I might at this moment have been my own master.

In due time I was marched into the burgomaster's presence, and deemed it wise to make no further mystery of myself. I demanded an English interpreter, unless the magistrate would hear me in French, which latter he graciously agreed to do.

"Sir," said I, "my name is Gallagher; I am an Irishman, a servant of King George, and a sailor in Admiral Duncan's fleet. I am, as I believe, the sole survivor of the wreck in mid-sea of his Majesty's ship *Zebra*, foully blown up by her mutinous crew. I was picked up by the Dutch brig *Scheldt*, now lying at Rotterdam. I am no spy. I rode last night to visit an acquaintance—a countrywoman at the Hague—and am on my way now to fulfil my promise to the skipper of the *Scheldt* to give him a day's labour in unlading his brig in return for his kindness to me. The sailor's coat and cap I wear were given me by him."

The magistrate heard my story attentively, and not altogether unfavourably.

"Admiral Duncan's fleet," said he, "is in arms against the Dutch republic."

"It is," said I.

"How many sail does he muster?" demanded my judge.

"I cannot tell you, mynheer," said I.

"Where do his ships lie?"

"Mynheer," said I, "would you expect a Dutch sailor to betray his country to an English magistrate? I refuse to answer."

He frowned, less at my refusal than at the terms in which it was couched.

"Give me the name of your acquaintance at the Hague," said he, changing the subject.

I gave him Biddy's name.

"What was your business with her?"

"I never expected to land on Dutch shores, and so had no special business; but finding myself here, I sought her out."

This all seemed fair enough; and the burgomaster, who was an honest man and blessed with true Dutch stolidity, after consulting with his clerk and colleague, informed me that inquiries would be made, and that meanwhile I should remain in custody.

To my request to be allowed to send a letter to Biddy he returned a flat and suspicious refusal. Nor, till my case stood clearer, would he order the removal of the irons. So for the next twenty-four hours I lay in a damp cell, with black bread and water to support my spirits, and the thought of my little mistress to carry me through the weary hours.

About noon next day I was again summoned to the burgomaster's court, where, among the curious crowd assembled to see the supposed English spy, I recognised not only the Dutch skipper, but Martin. Biddy was not there.

The burgomaster wore an air of sternness and self-importance which boded no good.

"Captain Koop," said he to the skipper, "identify the prisoner."

"Most worshipful," replied the sailor, "this is the man we picked up, who said he was a Frenchman, wrecked in the French ship *Zèbre*."

"Was that true?" said the judge to me.

"Mynheer, I told you my tale yesterday. I am no Frenchman."

Then Martin was called forward, and looked hard at me with his sinister eyes. An interpreter explained the burgomaster's questions.

"Witness, you state you know the man Gallagher. Is this he?"

"Now I look at him—yes; but I did not know him before with his beard."

"Is he a sailor in the service of the English Government?"

"He is; and no friend to the Irish people, for whom the Dutch republic is fighting. More, by tokens, your honour," added Martin through the interpreter, "now I know him, I know who it was who last night carried away a certain Irish lady under my protection while on her way to the Convent of the Carmelite Nuns."

"What do you say to that?" said the burgomaster to me, with a look of horror, for he was a stout Catholic.

"I don't deny it," said I, curtly; "nor do I deny that this blackguard, instead of trying to defend the lady, tumbled all of a heap with fright off the carriage-box on to the road when I accosted him."

The interpreter smiled as he translated this, and Martin looked round not too well pleased.

"Where is the lady?" demanded the burgomaster.

"That is my affair," said I. "She was carried away from her home by this man against her will. She was rescued from him by me with her own good will, and is now safe."

"With your friend at the Hague, doubtless?"

I made no answer.

"Inquiries have been made as to this friend. She is known, but has disappeared since yesterday."

"What!" I exclaimed, "Biddy gone? And what of—"

"In company with a young lady," said the burgomaster, eyeing me sternly. "Prisoner, I demand to know where these persons have gone."

"I do not know," said I, and my own bewilderment might have answered for my sincerity.

"I do not believe that," said the burgomaster. "A messenger arrived at her inn with a letter early yesterday, and she and the lady left, it is said by boat, soon after. Do you deny that you sent that message?"

"I do."

"Do you deny that you know who did?"

"I do."

"Do you deny that you know where they have gone?"

"I do," retorted I; "and, if it please your worship, what has all this to do with whether I am a spy or not?"

"This, that a man who has lied in one particular is not to be believed in others. The same reason which induced you to pass yourself as a Frenchman may explain your refusal to say where the woman McQuilkin has gone. Her house is known to be a resort of spies and foreigners of doubtful character, and your connection with her, and the abduction of the young lady, and your refusal to give any information, are strongly against you."

I am not learned in Dutch logic, and was not convinced now; but apparently my judges were, for I was ordered to be handed over to the military authorities of Amsterdam as a prisoner of war, suspected of being a spy, for them to deal with me as they might consider best.

Before I departed, the burgomaster handed me back my mother's pocket-book, the contents of which he had had translated, and which he was good enough to say appeared not to be incriminating. My pistol he detained for the service of the Dutch republic.

The military authorities at Amsterdam were far too busy to attend to my affairs. They were in the midst of equipping an armament to land on Irish shores and strike at England with the cat's-paw of an Irish rebellion. The place was full of Irishmen, some of whom honestly enough looked to see their country redeemed by Dutch saviours; others, hungry hangers-on, seeking what profit to themselves they could secure from the venture. A few faces, even during the short time I was kept waiting in quarters, seemed familiar to me as of men I had seen in former days in the secret conclaves at my father's cabin or under his honour's roof, and one or two I was certain I had seen that day in Dublin not long since when I was present at a meeting of the United Irishmen.

Little I knew then or for months after that among these very faces, had I looked long enough, I might have seen that of Tim, my brother, or (must I say now?) my brother that was, before he became Tim Gorman of Kilgorman.

But, as I said, the authorities were too busy to inquire into my case, and, taking the word of the Delft burgomaster, locked me up with a batch of other English prisoners to await the issue of the coming war.

For three months I languished here in a dismal dungeon in dismal company and fed on dismal fare. But I who had lodged in the Conciergerie at Paris in "the terror" could afford to think my Dutch hosts lavish in their comforts.

Once and again some new captive brought us news from outside, the purport of which was that the great Irish expedition, after lying for weeks and weeks at the Texel, held prisoner there by the unyielding west wind and by Admiral Duncan, had collapsed like a burst bubble. The troops had all been landed, the ships had returned to refit, and the pack of Irishmen, seeing the hunt up in this quarter, had gone off in full cry to Paris. If the Dutch ventured anything now, it would be against England, and on their own account.

One day towards the end of September a great surprise broke the tedium of our captivity. Our jailer brought an announcement that an exchange of prisoners was in contemplation, and that some twenty of us might reasonably hope to see our native land again in a few days. Whether the fortunate score would be selected according to rank or to seniority of captivity would depend on the prisoners handed over by Admiral Duncan.

It was a pleasing subject of speculation with me, as you may guess. For were the selection to be by seniority, I was excluded; if by rank, as a petty officer in a company which largely consisted of common seamen, I might count with tolerable certainty on my liberty.

The few days that intervened were anxious and wearisome. Should I miss my chance, I had nothing to look for but a prolongation of this wretched existence, with perhaps an ounce of lead, when all was said and done, to end it. If, on the other hand, luck were to favour me, a week hence, who could say, I might be by my little mistress's side at home; for I made no doubt that when I came to inquire at the "White Angel," as I certainly would do, I should find that Biddy had taken her thither, or, if not there, at least to some safe place at which I could hear of her.

In due time came the end to our suspense. The twenty were appointed by rank, and I marched one fine evening out of that wretched dungeon a free man—stay, not quite free. There was no slipping away to the Hague and the "White Angel;" no walking through the port of Amsterdam to inspect the enemy's preparations. We were marched, under arrest, with an escort, in the dark of night, to some little fishing-station among the dunes, where we found an English lugger, attended by two armed Dutch boats, waiting to receive us. On this we embarked, bidding farewell to our captors; but not until the white cliffs of Margate appeared on the western horizon did our Dutch convoy sheer off and leave us in English waters in undisturbed enjoyment of English liberty.

Yet even so, did I still harbour a thought of returning home or seeking the lost, I was destined to disappointment. For from Margate we were marched direct to Sheerness, and there inspected by Lords of the Admiralty, who, without ceremony, told us off to fill vacancies in ships at that moment engaged in active service, promising us, when the present troubles were over, to recompense our hardships and services in some better way.

I found myself under orders to sail forthwith to Yarmouth, there to report myself on board the *Venerable*, the flag-ship of Admiral Duncan himself.

An Admiralty cutter was just then sailing with despatches for the fleet, and on it I embarked the same afternoon, and found myself in Yarmouth Roads next morning.

The admiral's fleet was all in a flutter; for news had only just come that the Dutch admiral, taking advantage of the temporary withdrawal of the English ships from the mouth of the Texel (for Admiral Duncan, after his long cruise there, had been compelled to return to refit his squadron), was setting sail at last, and determined to venture an engagement in the open. Our fleet was wild with joy at the news—as wild as the greyhound who for hours has been straining at his leash with the hare in view is to feel his collar thrown off.

Signals were flying from every mast-head. The last of the barges and bumboats were casting loose. The dull thunder of a salute came from the shore, the yards were manned, sails were unfurling, and the anchor chains were grinding apeak.

At such a moment it was that the Admiralty cutter hove alongside of the *Venerable*, and I found myself a few minutes later lending a hand to haul to the mast-head the blue flag of that most gallant of sea-dogs, Admiral Duncan.

Chapter Thirty Three
The famous fight of October the Eleventh

My readers do not, I hope, expect from me a full, true, and particular account of the glorious sea-fight of October 11, 1797, off Camperdown; for if they do, they will be sadly disappointed. Indeed, it seems to me, the worst person to describe a battle is one who has fought in it. For if he does his duty, he has no eyes for any business but his own; and as to seeing what is happening along the entire line at any time, it would take an eagle poised in mid-air, with eyes that could penetrate a cloud of smoke, to do it honestly. I am no eagle, and my eyes can carry no further than those of any other plain mortal. I can tell only what I saw. For the rest, the eagles have written their story in books, where any one can read all about the famous victory—and more than all.

There was little time to observe anything in the bustle of our putting out from Yarmouth. The ship was not yet clear of the confusion of her hurried refitting and revictualling. Stores lay about which needed stowing; there were new sails to bend and old ropes to splice; there were decks to swab and guns to polish, hammocks to sling, and ammunition to give out. Yet all worked with so hearty a will, and looked forward so joyously, after eighteen weeks' idleness, to a brush with the enemy, that before sundown all was nearly taut and ship-shape. If anything could help, sit was the kindly nod and cheery word of our admiral himself as he paced to and fro among us. A beautiful man he was—a giant to look at, and as gentle as he was tall; yet with a flash in his eye, as he turned his face seaward, that told us that there was not a man in the ship who looked forward with more boyish eagerness to the brush ahead than he. Though it was but for a week, I hold it to this day something to be able to say that I have served under Duncan.

Had I been in the mood to stand on my dignity, I might have felt affronted to find myself set to do ordinary seaman's work on board the *Venerable*. For in the hurry of our setting out from Yarmouth there was time neither to report myself nor to choose my work. I was no sooner on board than I was hurried forward to set the fore-courses; and no sooner was that done than a mop was put into my hands to swab the main-deck; and no sooner was that done than I was told off to carry stores below. At any rate, it was better than a Dutch prison, and, thought I, a common sailor under Duncan is better than a lieutenant under Mr Adrian. Time enough when prizes were towed into port to stand out for dignities.

The next day, the tenth, despite the strong north-wester, our fleet, which numbered fourteen sail of the line, held well together for the Texel, picking up one or two fresh consorts during the day, and beating about now and again in expectation of news of the longed-for enemy. We saw nothing but a few merchantmen; and the admiral was beginning to fear that, after all, the Dutchmen had given us the slip, and made off to join forces with the French fleet at Brest, when an armed lugger, flying a signal, hove in sight, and reported that the Dutch admiral was only a few leagues away to the south.

The joy on board was indescribable; and as night closed in, and we stood out on the starboard tack, the certainty that daybreak would discover the enemy was almost as great a cause for jubilation as if we had already won our victory.

Eager as we were, however, the admiral ordered all of us who were not on the watch below, charging us to get sleep while we could, and lay provender on board, for we had hungry work before us.

The first lieutenant called me to him as I was turning in.

"Mr Gallagher," he said, "I have only just had time to go over the names of the last comers in the ship's books. I see you hold rank as a warrant-officer."

"I was boatswain to the *Zebra*, sir," said I.

"So I see. It does you credit that you have worked so cheerfully at the first work that came to hand. But to-morrow we shall want our best men at their right posts. The *Venerable* has a boatswain already; but Captain Fairfax has ordered me to look up double hands for the helm. Be good enough to report yourself to the sailing-master at daybreak. We have our work cut out for us, I fancy, and much will depend on the smartness with which the admiral's signals are read and his ship handled. So you may take the duty as a compliment, Mr Gallagher; and good-night to you."

I turned in that night still better pleased with the service than ever.

At daybreak, as we came on deck, the first thing we spied to leeward was some of our own ships bearing down on us with signals flying of an enemy in sight; and not long after, the line of the enemy's fleet, straggling northeast and south-west, came into sight, hauled to the wind and evidently awaiting us. We counted over twenty of them; and with the additions that had joined us in the night, we were just as many.

The sea was rolling heavily, and a good many of our ships were lagging. So, as we were already near enough to the Dutch side, the admiral ordered sails to be shortened till the slow coaches came up, which they did not too smartly.

I reported myself to the sailing-master as directed, and soon found myself one of four in charge of the helm. After that I saw very little of the famous battle of Camperdown, for I had no eyes or ears for anything but the admiral's signals. We waited for our ships to get into their proper stations till we could wait no longer.

"Confound them!" growled the quartermaster, a fresh, cheery salt at my side, as one or two sail still dawdled on the horizon, "These lubbers will spoil all. The Dutch are shallow sailers, and they'll have us on the flats before we are ready to begin. What is the ad— Ah, that's better. Up she goes! Smart now and have at them!"

This jubilant exclamation was in response to a signal to wait no longer, but bear down on the enemy, every vessel being ordered to engage her opponent as best she could.

Up went the helm, round went the yards, and away sped the *Venerable*, and with her the rest of the British fleet, full tilt at the Dutchmen. I learned more of the battle from the ejaculations of the quartermaster at my side than from my own observation.

"Confound the mist!" growled he as we reached out for the line. "They won't see the signal to cut the line and get to leeward. Take my word for it, mate, those Dutch dogs will pull us in on to the shallows before we know where we are."

Suddenly the thunder of guns on our right proclaimed that the action had begun in good earnest.

"That's the vice-admiral," said the boatswain, "at it already, and he's making a hot corner down there. Ease her up a bit now. There's the Dutch admiral's ship the *Vryheid*. It's her we're going for."

A sudden order came astern.

"Run under her stern?—right you are," said the quartermaster. "Keep her down more, my lads.—Lie as you are, my beauty," said he, apostrophising the *Vryheid*, "and we'll blacklead you somehow."

"What's that ship astern of her about?" said I. "She's closing up."

So she was. Before we could slip through and get under the *Vryheid's* stern, she had neatly swung up into the gap, blocking us out, and leaving us to put our helm hard a-port to avoid running in on the top of her.

"Neatly done, by the powers," said the quartermaster; "but Duncan will make her smart for it. Ah, I thought so," as the *Venerable* shook from stem to stern and poured the broadside intended for the *Vryheid* into the stern of the intruder instead. "Take that, my lass, and don't push in where you're not wanted again."

It was a tremendous thunder-clap; and the *States-General*—that was the name of the intruder—with her rigging all in shivers, and her stern-guns knocked all on end, was glad enough to bear up and drop out of line before she could get a second. This suited our admiral excellently, for it enabled him to cut the enemy's line and bring the *Venerable* snugly round on the lee-side of Admiral De Winter's ship, his originally chosen antagonist.

Then all was thunder and smoke. The *Venerable* shook and staggered under the crushing fire which struck her hull. But for every broadside she got she poured two into the masts and rigging of her opponent. More than once, as the two ships swung together, with yards almost locked, we had to duck for our lives to escape the falling spars of the Dutchman. I can remember once and again, as the *Vryheid* lurched towards us, seeing her deck covered with dead and wounded men; and every broadside she put into us left its tale of destruction among our fellows.

Presently, with a crash that sounded even above the cannon, down came her mainmast by the board, and the British cheers which greeted the fall were even louder still.

But if we reckoned on having done with her, we were sorely mistaken; for three other Dutchmen just then hove up to their admiral's help, and for a quarter of an hour the *Venerable* had as hot a time of it as ship ever lived through. There was not much for us at the helm to do but stand and be shot at; which we did so well that when at last (just as the mizzen-mast of the *Vryheid* followed the example of her mainmast) the order came to haul off and wear round on the other tack, I found myself the only one of four to answer, "Ay, ay," and ram down the helm. The quartermaster, poor fellow, lay at my feet, shot nearly in two; while of our other two mates, one was wounded, with an arm shot away, another stunned by a falling timber.

It was a job to get the ship round; and when we did, there was the *Vryheid*, with her one mast left, waiting for us as saucy as ever. After that, all passed for me in even a greater maze than before; for a bullet from the enemy's rigging found me out with a dull thud in the shoulder, and sent me reeling on to the deck. I was able after the first shock to stumble up and get my hands upon the helm; but I stood there sick and silly, and of less use than the poor quartermaster at my feet.

I was dimly conscious of a din and smoke, like the opening of the gate of hell. Then, through a drift in the smoke, I could see the tall form of the Dutch admiral standing almost alone on his quarter-deck, as cool as if he were on the street at Amsterdam, passing a word of command through his trumpet. Beyond him I caught a glimpse of the low Dutch sand-hills, not two leagues to leeward. Then, away to our right, came the faint noise of British cheers above the firing. Then some one near me exclaimed, "Struck, by Saint George!" and almost directly after the firing seemed to cease, and our fellows, springing on to the yards and bulwarks, set up such a cheer that the *Venerable* shook with it. I tried to get up my head to see what it was all about, but as I did so I tumbled all in a heap on the deck—and the battle of Camperdown was finished for me.

It was nearly dark when I came to between decks, with a burning pain in my shoulder and my mouth as dry as a brick. The place was full of groaning men, some worse hit than myself, and one or two past the help of the surgeon, who slowly went his round of the berths. By the time he reached me I did not much care if he were to order me overboard, so long as he put me out of my misery.

But, after all, mine was a simple case. There was a bullet in me somewhere, and a few bone-splinters were wandering about my system. Apparently I could wait till my neighbour, whose thigh bone was crushed, was seen to. So while he, poor fellow, was having his leg cut off, and beginning to bleed to death (for he didn't outlive the operation an hour), I lay, with my tongue glued to the roof of my mouth, groaning.

"Ah, Mr Gallagher," said the first lieutenant, as he came the round, "they picked you out, did they? Nothing much, I hope? It's cost us a pretty penny in dead and wounded already."

"And we beat them?" groaned I.

"Beat? We made mincemeat of them! Haven't we the Dutch admiral a prisoner on board this moment, playing cards with Admiral Duncan in his cabin as comfortably as if he was in his own club at the Hague?"

"Could you give me some water?" I asked, with a sudden change of the subject.

"Surely; and, Mr Gallagher, I'll see you again before we land, and won't forget to put your name forward."

When at last the doctor came, I saved him a good deal of trouble by swooning away the moment he touched my wound, and remained in that condition, on and off, till I heard the anchor running out at the bows, and understood from those who lay near that we were at the Nore.

Had I wanted any further proof of our arrival in English waters, the shouting and saluting and bustle and laughter all around left no doubt of it.

"Come, lad," said the lieutenant, standing over me, while two sailors set down a stretcher beside my berth, "the tender's alongside to take you poor fellows ashore. The doctor says you must go to hospital, and they'll have another look for the bullet there. So keep up heart, man. Here are your papers, and a good word thrown in from the admiral himself, bless him!"

The pain of being lifted on to the stretcher and carried on deck was almost beyond endurance, yet I could hardly help, as I passed the cheering crowd of our fellows, giving a faint "hurrah" in time with theirs. For our noble old admiral stood on the gangway, with a kind word for every one, especially the wounded.

"Never say die, my brave lad," said he, as I was carried by; "you stuck to your post bravely.—Steady, men," added he, as the two bearers broke step for a moment; "the poor boy has had jolting enough without you.— God bless you, my fellow!"

And so I parted company with the bravest and kindliest gentleman I ever came across.

Every one ashore was wild with the news of the great victory, and we poor cripples were escorted to the hospital like heroes. I wished, for my part, I had been allowed to get there quietly, for the horses of our waggon started and winced at the noise of the shouting and music, so that my poor shoulder was all aflame long before I got to our journey's end, and I myself in a high fever.

The doctors had a rare bullet-hunt over my poor body; and when it was found, there were bone-splinters still harder to get at. The result was that when I was at last bound up and left to mend, I was so weak and shattered that for weeks—indeed, for nearly three months—I lay, sometimes in a fever, sometimes recovering, sometimes relapsing, sometimes recovering again, till I found myself one of the veterans of the hospital.

What, during those weeks, were my fevered dreams you may guess. In fancy I was hunting through the world for Miss Kit; and as sure as I found her, Tim appeared and claimed my help; and ere Tim could be helped, my little mistress had vanished again and a new search was begun—now in

Ireland, now in Paris, now in Holland, now up and down the blood-stained deck of the *Zebra*. But it all ended in naught; and I turned over wearily on my pillow, sick in body and mind, and longing, as prisoner never longed, for wings.

Glad enough I was when one day, early in January, the doctor pronounced me cured, and put me on board a ship for Dublin, there to report myself to the Admiralty, and take my new sailing orders.

"But first," said I to myself, "cost what it may, I will have a peep at Fanad."

Chapter Thirty Four
A step up the ladder

A strange thing befell me as soon as I landed in Dublin. I was prowling along the quay, wondering whether I should present myself then and there at the Admiralty, or take French leave for Donegal while I was free and had money in my pocket, when I was startled out of my wits by what seemed to be a veritable ghost in my path. Unless I had been certain that I was the only survivor out of the ill-starred *Zebra*, I could have sworn I saw Mr Felton, the second lieutenant, leaning over the rails, watching the dressing of a smart-looking revenue cutter that lay out in the water-way. The more I looked the less like a ghost did he appear, until at last I ventured to walk up to him with a salute.

"Good-morrow, Lieutenant Felton," said I.

"Captain, if you please," said he, turning round. "What! is that you, Gallagher, or your ghost? I thought I was the only man that saved his life out of that fated ship."

"I thought the same of myself, till this moment," said I.

"I hung on to a cask for close on twenty-four hours, till an English lugger picked me up. But I'll tell you of that later. Where do you spring from?"

"From hospital; I was on Duncan's ship at the battle of Camperdown—"

"You were! Lucky dog!" interjected he.

"Where I got a crack in the shoulder, and am only just out."

"And what are you going to do?"

"I am going to report myself at the Admiralty, and apply for a berth. I have my papers, and a letter from the admiral himself."

"It strikes me they'll have to build a ship for you," said he, with a laugh; "for, supposing you to be dead, I gave such an extravagantly glowing account of your conduct on the *Zebra*, that I dare swear they'll want to make a vice-admiral of you straight away. But what do you say to serve under me? Just at the time when I called at the Admiralty they had received a pressing request from the Customs to find them an officer to take charge of a cutter—there she lies," pointing to the smart craft he had been inspecting; "and they gave me the offer, and I took it. And I'm on the look-out for a few smart hands, especially a first officer."

"Nothing would suit me better," said I, "if I can get the proper step. I'm only a boatswain, you know."

"That will not be difficult with the papers you have got and your record. At a time like this they are not stiff about promotion, provided they get the proper men. So come along and beard the lions at once."

"There's one thing, sir," said I, "that I must do before I can join any ship—I must take a run home to Donegal, to—"

"Donegal! why, that's where we're ordered to, man. There's a gang of smugglers on the coast between Inishowen and Fanad that we've got to catch; and if that's near your home—"

"Near!" I exclaimed; "sure it *is* my home. I know every creek and shoal of the coast in the dark."

"That settles it," said Captain Felton, thumping me on the back; "you are the man I want, and I'm the man you want. Come away!"

As he had predicted, my papers, and especially Admiral Duncan's letter, added to the previous favourable reports of Captain Swift and Mr Felton, stood me in good stead with the authorities, especially just then when there was a dearth of men to fill all the vacancies caused by the war. I was told to call again on the following day, when, to my astonishment, I was handed a commission appointing me a lieutenant in his Majesty's navy, and a letter of recommendation to the Customs for appointment to the *Gnat*, Captain Felton's cutter.

With a bound of joy I found myself, by some strange shifting of the luck, a gentleman and an officer after all—humble and poor indeed, but entitled to hold my head with the best; and what was more—and that sent the blood tingling through my veins—no longer beyond the range of my little mistress's recognition as a suitor. A paltry distinction if you will, and one in name only; for the gentleman is born, not made by Admiralty warrants; and had I been a cur at heart, no promotion could have made me otherwise. But if at heart I was a gentleman, this new title gave me the right to call myself one, and opened a door to me which till now I had thought fast shut.

The week that followed was one of busy work; so busy that I had scarce time to wander through my old haunts in Dublin and notice the air of sullen mischief which brooded over the city. Men were watched and watching at every corner, guards were doubled, officials walked abroad only under escort. This man was pointed out as a leader of the coming "turn-out" —for so they spoke of the rebellion that was to follow—that was marked down as a traitor, and walked with the sentence of death in his hang-dog face. This man was spoken of as one to be got at and won over; and that was hooted and spat upon as he rode past in his gay equipage amid flying stones, and now and again a bullet out of space, which made him glad enough to retreat into cover. But these last demonstrations were less common than the dull, savage air of menace which pervaded the place. Something assuredly was going to happen.

Some said the French were already on their way to Ireland, and that their landing was to be the signal for a general rising. Others whispered that Lord Edward had his plans ripe for the capture of the capital, and the setting up of the new Irish republic. Many said all this suspense was just the sign that no leader was ready to fire the mine, and unless the blow was struck soon it would not be struck at all. As to the men in office and the police, they held their peace, saying nothing, but hearing all.

I encountered no one I knew, except one man, him who once had stopped me on the steps of the hotel, after my first meeting with Lord Edward, and who had offered me money for information. To my surprise he now greeted me by name.

"Good-day, Mr Gallagher; glad to meet you. How go matters in Donegal? and how is Lord Edward?"

I stared at him in amazement.

"I have not the honour to know you," said I, walking on.

But he followed, linking his arm in mine.

"Come now," said he; "you know me well enough. But be assured you have nothing to fear from me if you are open. Your name is well-known at the Castle as a leader of the conspiracy, and a friend of Lord Edward's. A word from me, and you would get free board and lodging in Newgate, if not a yard or two of rope thrown in; but I have no wish to hurt you. These are dangerous times, though."

"I tell you, sir," repeated I, "I am not the man you take me for, so kindly address yourself to some one else."

"Tush!" said he, "what's the use between friends? Tim Gallagher is as well-known a name as O'Connor's."

Tim Gallagher! Then they took me for Tim, not myself.

"And what information is it you want, and for whom?" I demanded, trying to conceal my curiosity.

"Turn up here; it's quieter," said he, drawing me into a side street, "and I'll tell you. I've no commission, mind you, but I'll undertake to say your candour will be worth a couple of hundred pounds in your pocket within twenty-four hours."

"Go on," said I, feeling my toes tingling to kick this man, who could suppose Tim Gallagher a common informer.

"It's known you're lately returned from Paris," said he, "with an important message from the rebel leaders there, and that that message concerns among other things the coming French invasion."

"Well?"

"Well! can you ask? It is presumed the leaders in Dublin know your news by this time, and are making arrangements accordingly. If so, it is worth a couple of hundred pounds to you, as I said, to let me know what is going forward."

"And if not?"

"Simply that a warrant is out for the arrest of Timothy Gallagher, at present in Dublin disguised as a naval officer, and it rests with me to put it into motion. So come," said he, halting and facing me, "make up your mind."

We had now reached the end of the street, which was a deserted one, backing on the Park. It had been all I could do to keep myself within bounds and refrain from knocking this contemptible cur on the head. Prudence, and a desire to learn something more about Tim alone had restrained me.

Now that, one way or another, the matter was come to an issue, I hesitated as to what I should do. Either I might put him off, and invent a story to please him, or I might refuse to answer anything, or I might convince him of his mistake, or I might run for it. In the first case, I should be acting unfairly to Tim; in the other cases, I should be risking my own liberty at a time I particularly needed it. Suddenly a fifth course opened before me. At the end of the street was a coach-house, the door of which stood open, and the key on the outside. It had evidently been left thus by a careless groom, for the place was empty and no one was in sight.

Quick as thought I caught my man by the scrag of his neck and pitched him head first into the stable, taking time only to say, as I drew to the door and turned the key. "Take that from Tim Gallagher's brother, you dog!" After which I walked away, leaving him kicking his feet sore against the tough timbers.

I returned straight to the *Gnat*, and told Captain Felton exactly how matters stood, requesting him to allow me to remain on board till it was time to sail.

"Which will be in two days," said he. "I'm sorry, though, you're afflicted with a scoundrel of a brother. I had the same trouble myself once, and know what it is like."

"Tim's no scoundrel," said I hotly, "though he's on the wrong side. He's a gentleman; and when it comes to that, I've no right to talk of him as my brother at all."

"Well, please yourself," said Captain Felton, who evidently did not care to discuss the matter. "That doesn't concern me, as long as you handle the *Gnat* smartly and get into no scrapes yourself. We can't afford to let private concerns interfere with the king's business."

Two days later all was ready, and, to my great relief, we weighed anchor and ran out of the bay with a brisk south-easterly breeze. The *Gnat* proved an excellent sailer, and, fitted as she was with ten six-pounders, and manned by a crew of twenty smart hands, she was a formidable enough customer for any smuggler that had to reckon with her.

We put in at Larne in expectation of getting some news of the marauders we were in search of, but found none. We were, however, warned to keep our eyes open not only for smugglers, but for foreign craft which were said to be at the old business of landing arms for the Ulster rebels, who by all accounts were in a very red-hot state, and longing anxiously for the signal to rise. Indeed, so threatening did things appear generally that the authorities gave Captain Felton peremptory instructions to allow nothing to stand in the way of his communicating immediately to headquarters any intelligence (particularly as to the expected French landing) with which in the course of his cruise he might meet.

"This puts a boot on our other leg," said the captain to me that evening, as we watched the sunset light fade over Fair Head. "It seems to me collecting customs will be the least part of our business. Never mind. I'd sooner put a bullet into a rebel any day than into a poor beggar who tries to land a keg of whisky for nothing. Fortune send us either, though!"

It seemed as if this wish were not without reason; for though we cruised up and down for a fortnight, watching every bay and creek between Ballycastle and Sheep Haven, we came upon nothing but honest fisher craft and traders.

At last, to my relief—for I was growing impatient to hear news of my little mistress—Captain Felton bade me run the cutter into Lough

Swilly. And knowing my desire, he made an excuse to send me ashore at Rathmullan for provisions, bidding me return within three days, unless I was signalled for earlier.

It was a Sunday morning when I found myself once more in the familiar inn at Rathmullan. I soon found that my host, who took little note of his customers, did not remember me; and he was civil enough now to one of his Majesty's lieutenants, and eager to execute my commissions for stores.

"Faith, sir," said he, "and it's some of us will be glad to see the luck back, for it's gone entirely since the troubles began."

"You mean the smuggling?" said I, by way of drawing him out.

"That and other things. These are bad times for honest folk."

As I knew the fellow to be an arrant harbourer of smugglers and rebels, I took his lamentation for what it was worth.

"Maybe you're a stranger to these parts, captain," said he presently, giving me another step in the service.

"I've heard something of them," said I. "I met a young fellow called Gallagher not long since, and he was talking of Lough Swilly."

"Tim was it, or Barry?" asked the landlord, with interest.

"Are there two of them, then?"

"Faith, yes; and one's as black as the other's white. Tim, bless him! is a rale gentleman and a friend to the people."

"Which means a rebel, I suppose. And what of Barry?"

"Bedad, he's a white-livered sneak, and he'd best not show his face in these parts. There's a dozen men sworn to have the life of him."

I laughed.

"It must have been Tim I spoke to, then, for he spoke well of you, and said you had some excellent rum in your cellar. Maybe he knew more about it than the Custom-House, eh?"

This put mine host in a flutter, and he vouched by all the saints in the calendar he had not a drop in the house on which he had not paid duty. And as Tim Gallagher had mentioned the rum, would I be pleased to try a glass?

"Where is this Tim now?" I inquired, when the glasses were brought.

"'Deed, captain, that's more than I can tell you. He was wanted badly by the boys here, who chose him their captain for the turn-out that's to be; but it's said he's abroad on the service of the country, and we'll likely see him back with the Frenchmen when they come."

"Ah, you're expecting the Frenchmen, are you? So are we. I may meet this Tim Gallagher over a broadside yet."

"If you do, dear help you, for Tim's got a long arm, I warn you."

As I was about to go, I inquired,—

"By the way, you have a magistrate living somewhere near here, haven't you a Mr Gorman, whom I am to see on business."

The landlord's face fell.

"Ay. His honour's house is across the lough yonder at Knockowen. But you'll get little value out of him. He's a broken man."

"How broken?"

"Arrah, it's a long story. He's run with the hare and hunted with the hounds too long, and there's no man more hated between here and the Foyle. His life's not worth a twopenny-piece."

"Was he the man whose daughter was carried off?" I asked as innocently as I could.

"Who told you that?" said he, with a startled look. "Not Tim. If it had been Barry now, the scoundrel, he could have told you more of that than any man. Ay, that's he."

"Did he ever get her back?"

"'Deed, there's no telling. He says not a word. But he hangs every honest man that comes across him. I'd as soon swim from Fanad to Dunaff in a nor'-westerly gale as call up at Knockowen."

"Well," said I, with a laugh, "get me a boat, for I must see him at once, and take my chance of a hanging. Give me oars and a sail; I can put myself over."

So once more I found myself on the familiar tack, with Knockowen a white speck on the water-side ahead. What memories and hopes and fears crowded my mind as I slid along before the breeze! How would his honour receive me this time? Should I find Knockowen a trap from which I should have to fight my way out? Should I—here I laughed grimly—spend the night dangling at a rope's end from one of the beeches in the avenue? Above all, should I find Miss Kit there, or any news of her? Then I gave myself up to thinking of her, and the minutes passed quickly, till it was time to slip my sheet and row alongside the landing-stage.

"Halt! who goes there?" cried a voice.

"A friend," said I; "first officer of his Majesty's cutter *Gnat*, with a message from the captain to Mr Gorman."

"Pass, friend," said the sentry, grounding his gun with a clang.

"Ah," thought I, as I walked up the well-known path, remembering the half-hour I had been kept waiting at my last visit, "it's something to be an officer and a gentleman after all."

Chapter Thirty Five
His honour escapes his enemies at last

It was less than a year since I had seen Knockowen. But all seemed changed. Weeds and grass were on the paths, the flower-beds were unkempt, the fences were broken in places, damp stains were spread over the house front. Everywhere were signs of neglect and decay. Had I not known his honour to be a wealthy man, I should have supposed him an impecunious person with no income to maintain his property. As it was, there was some other cause to seek, and that cause I set down to the absence of Miss Kit.

Twice between the pier and the house I was challenged by sentries, and when I reached the door I noticed that the lower windows were shuttered and barred like those of a prison.

I announced myself to the servant who answered my summons as I had done to the sentinels, without giving my name, and was presently shown into his honour's room at the back of the house, which, as all the shutters were closed, was lit by candles, though it was still daylight.

I was shocked to see how Mr Gorman was changed. The sly, surly expression had given place to a hunted, suspicious look. His face was haggard and pale and his beard unkempt. He started at any little sound, and his mouth, once firm, now looked weak and irresolute. Worse still, there was a flavour of spirits about the room and the man which told its own tale, and accounted for his bloodshot eyes and shaking fingers as he looked up.

"Gallagher!" he exclaimed, rising to his feet in evident panic; "what brings you here in this disguise? What have I ever done to you?"

"It is no disguise, your honour," said I, in as reassuring a tone as I could assume. "I am Lieutenant Gallagher now."

"And what do you want here? Why do you come in this sudden way? Go away, sir, and come when you are wanted! Where is my guard?"

And the poor man, whom the landlord at Rathmullan had well described as broken, actually put out his trembling hand to reach a pistol that lay on the table.

"You mistake me," said I, paying no heed to the gesture. "I came merely on business, and if you like you can call your guard in. I've nothing to say that they need not hear."

"You're a good fellow, Gallagher," said his honour, reassured. "I'm a little shaken in the nerves, and your coming was so sudden. I know you could mean no harm to your old benefactor."

It made my heart bleed to hear him talk thus miserably, and I resolved to shorten the interview as much as I could.

"Stay and dine with me," said he, as eager to keep me now as he was to be rid of me a minute ago; "it's lonely, night after night, with no one to speak to and nowhere to go. You've heard, no doubt, I am a prisoner here."

"How so, sir?"

"There's a sentence of death out against me—not in the king's name, but in the name of Tim Gallagher, your brother, captain of the rebels here."

"In Tim's name!" exclaimed I. "It's false! I swear he never signed it; he is not even in the country."

"Don't be too sure of that. Anyway he's their chosen leader, and they do all in his name. I daren't go outside my own doors after dark for fear of a bullet."

"The scoundrels!" cried I, starting up; "and they dare drag Tim's name into their vile machinations. I tell you, Mr Gorman, Tim would no more wink at murder than—than Miss Kit would. And, by the way, sir, what of Miss Kit?"

He looked round with his haggard face.

"What is that to you, Gallagher?"

"I love her," said I bluntly, "and so I have a right to know."

"You! the son of Mike the boatman, and brother of Tim the rebel! You dare—"

I cut him short.

"See here, Maurice Gorman; understand me. With or without you I will find her, if I have to seek her to the world's end. I've done so before now; remember how we parted last."

"Oh," said he, "I know all that, and of your meeting her in Holland and placing her in Biddy McQuilkin's care. She wrote me all about that; and it's little I owe you for it. Biddy belongs, body and soul, to the rebel faction."

"But she wouldn't let a hair of Miss Kit's head be hurt for all that."

"How do you know that, so long as I could be made to suffer by it?"

"Where are they now, then?" I asked eagerly.

"Till lately she was in Dublin, in the family of Lord Edward, who, traitor as he is, is at least a gentleman, and a distant kinsman into the bargain. She was happy there; and what sort of place was this to bring a girl to? But look here," said he, getting up and fumbling in a drawer among some papers, "what do you say to this?" and he put a letter, written in a delicate female hand, before me. It read as follows:—

"To Maurice Gorman, Esquire.

"Sir,—With great sorrow I inform you that Miss Gorman, while walking yesterday evening in the Park with her attendant McQuilkin, was surrounded by a gang of masked men, and they were both carried away, whither we know not. We are in terrible distress, and sparing no effort to find the dear girl, whom Lord Edward and I had come to love as a sister. Be assured you shall receive such news as there may be. Lord Edward's wrath knows no bounds, and he even risks his own liberty (for he is a marked man) in seeking for them.—I have the honour to be, sir, your obedient servant, Pamela Fitzgerald."

"That is from Lady Edward," said his honour. "Now read this."

The paper he handed me now was a dirty and illiterate scrawl, without date or signature.

"Maris Gorman,—Take note your doghter is in safe hands, and will not be returnd till you take the oth of the Unyted Irishmen and pay 5 hundred pounds sterling to the fund. Allso note that unless you come in quickly, you will be shott like a dog, and the devil help you for a trayter to Ireland."

"Now," said he, with a gloomy smile, "you know as much of my daughter's whereabouts as I do."

"This is terrible news," said I. "How is it you are not in Dublin at this moment, moving heaven and earth to find her?"

He laughed bitterly.

"It's easy talking," said he. "In the first place, I should be shot before I reached my own gate; I have been practically a prisoner here for weeks. In the next place, what could I do? Even if I took the oath, where is the money to come from?"

"Five hundred pounds is a small sum to a rich man like you."

"Whoever calls me rich, lies," said he testily, and with an uneasy gesture which explained to my mind the dilapidated state of the place. Maurice

Gorman was not only a poltroon but a miser, and five hundred pounds were worth more to him than his own daughter.

"Is nothing being done?" said I. "Have you shown the letter to the authorities, or to Lord Edward?"

"What use?" said he. "I am on too ill terms with either to expect their help."

"And so you intend to leave that poor girl to her fate?" I cried. "But if you will not move, I will!"

"What can I do?" said he wearily. "You know how I am fixed. Perhaps when I am shot they will let her go. Maybe that will be the simplest way out of it, after all."

I could not help pitying him, much as I despised him, so miserably did he speak.

Then he began to talk about the state of the country, and of the bad odour he had fallen into with his brother magistrates.

"They suspect me of being in with the rebels, Gallagher, as if I had cause to love them. On my soul, if I'm to be suspected, it sometimes seems I might as well be so with reason as without. Suppose, for the sake of argument, Gallagher, I took their precious oath—suppose it, I say, how should I stand then? By all appearances, Ireland is going to be delivered; and it will be a bad day when she comes into her own for those who withstood her. Should I be worse off by joining them? I'm told they are ready to welcome any man of position and landed interest on their side. It might be an opportunity of doing some service to my fellow countrymen. Besides, when a daughter's liberty is at stake, one does not stand at sacrifice. They hate me now because I have been instrumental in thwarting them. By winning me over they would be rid of an obstacle; and all the favour I have shown them in the past in the matter of the arms, and allowing some of them to slip through the fingers of the law, would stand to my credit. Why, Gallagher," added he, growing quite excited at the vision, "in the new Irish Government I should be a man of mark; and my fortune, instead of being confiscated, would be my own, and at the service of my friends. Why, you and Tim—"

"Are you so sure that fortune is your own now?" said I, losing my self-restraint at last.

He turned a little whiter as he glared round at me.

"You mean that improbable story of the changeling at Kilgorman," said he, with a forced laugh. "As pure moonshine as ever was, and beyond all proof even if it wasn't."

"You forget Biddy McQuilkin has been found."

"Did she say anything?" he demanded.

"She did, on her oath."

"And, pray, what was her version of this wonderful story?"

"She told me all I needed to know—that is, which of us two was Terence Gorman's son."

"And which is, pray?"

"That is my secret. Time will show."

"What!" exclaimed he, "some new conspiracy to rob me? And one of the conspirators a man who presumes to my daughter's hand! Come, Gallagher, let you and me understand each other. I defy you, or Biddy, or any one, to make good your story. But if you are frank with me, you won't find me unreasonable. Let me see the documents."

"In good time, sir," said I. "Now, as to the smugglers."

And we proceeded to talk about the object of our cruise. I found he had little news to give me, or else he chose to give little, and after a while I rose to go. He pressed me to stay the night, urging his solitude; but I had no desire to prolong the interview.

"We shall meet again," said I; "and you may rely on hearing from me if I have any news of your daughter."

We were out on the doorstep by this time. It was a beautiful, fresh evening, with a half-moon hanging above the opposite hills and sending a broad track of shimmering light across the lough.

"It's a tempting night," said he. "I've not taken the air for days. I've a good mind to see you to your boat."

For all that, he looked round uneasily, with the air of a man who suspected a lurking foe in every rustling leaf.

"Two of you men follow," said he to the sentries at the door. "Keep me in view. Ah, how fresh the air is after that close room! Yes, Gallagher, you were speaking of my daughter. Since she left me—keep in the shade, man, it's safer—this place has been a hell to me. What's the use of—what's that?" he exclaimed, catching my arm; "it sounded like a man's breathing. What's the use of keeping it up, I say? I've a mind to—"

He got no further. We had emerged from the shady walk into the moonlit path leading down to the pier. The two sentinels were just discernible ahead, and the footsteps of the two behind followed us close. There was no other sound in the stillness but his honour's quavering voice, and nothing stirring but the leaves of the trees and the waves of the lough as they broke gently on the beach.

Suddenly there rang out from the water's edge the sharp crack of a gun, followed by a wild howl. Mr Gorman staggered forward a pace and fell on his face. There was a rapid swish of oars, two hurried shots from the sentries, and the phantom of a little boat as it darted out across the moon track and lost itself in the blackness of the shadows.

In a moment I was kneeling beside the body of the poor dying man. The shot had struck him in the breast, and the life-blood was oozing away fast. He was conscious as we tried to lift him.

"Let me lie here," said he. "I'm safe here now."

But by this time the soldiers had him in their arms, and were bearing him gently towards the house.

It was little a doctor could do if we had one, but a soldier was sent to Fahan to bring one, and to take word of the murder. Meanwhile we laid him on his bed, and I did what I could to stanch the bleeding and ease his suffering.

For half-an-hour he lay in a sort of stupor. Then he said,—

. "Gallagher, I want to speak—Send the others away—no, keep one for a witness."

We did as he desired, and waited for what was to come.

Several minutes passed; then he tried to lift his head, and said,—

"It is true that one of you is Terence Gorman's boy, I knew it, but only Biddy knows which it is. I had no hand in Terence's murder, nor had Mike Gallagher, though I tried to put it on him. Write that down quickly, and I'll sign it."

I wrote his words hurriedly down, and read them over; but when it came to putting the pen in his hand, he fell back, and I thought all was over. But after a few minutes he rallied again.

"Hold me up—guide my hand—it all swims before me."

The paper with his woeful scrawl affixed lies before me at this moment as I write.

"Gallagher," said he, more faintly yet, "be good to Kit, and forgive me."

"God will do that, your honour," whispered I.

"Pray for me.—Ah!" cried he, starting suddenly in bed, and throwing up his arm as if to ward off a blow, "I'll take the oath, boys. You shall have the money. God save—"

And he fell back, dead.

Next day an inquiry was held which ended in nothing. No trace of the murderer was to be found, and no evidence but that of us who saw the tragedy with our own eyes. Plenty of folk, who had given him a wide berth living, crowded to the place to look at the dead Gorman; but in all their faces there was not one sign of pity or compunction—nay, worse, that very night, on Fanad and Knockalla bonfires were lit to celebrate his murder.

The next day we buried him. For miles round no one could be found willing to make his coffin, and in the end we had to lay him in a common soldier's shell. Nor would any one lend horse or carriage to carry him to his grave, and we had to take him by boat to his resting-place, rowing it through the gathering storm with our own arms. The flag half-mast on the *Gnat* was the only sign of mourning; and when we bore the coffin up to the lonely graveyard on the cliff-top at Kilgorman, and laid it beside that of his lady, in the grave next to that of the murdered Terence, not a voice but mine joined in the "Amen" to the priest's prayer.

When all was said and done, I lingered on, heedless of the wind and rain, in the deserted graveyard, full of the strange memories which the place and scene recalled.

Eight years ago I had stood here with Tim at the open grave of her whom we both called mother. And on that same day her ghostly footstep had sounded in our ears in the grim kitchen of Kilgorman, summoning us to a duty which was yet unfulfilled. What had not happened since then? The boatman's boys were grown, one into the heir of half the lough-side, the other into a servant of his Majesty. Tim, entangled hand and foot in the toils of a miserable conspiracy, was indifferent to the fortune now lying at his feet; I, engaged in the task of hunting down the rebels of whom he was a leader, was eating my heart out for love of her who called by the sacred name of father the murdered man who lay here, to whom we owed all our troubles. Was the day never to dawn? Was there never to be peace between Tim and me? And was Kit, like some will-o'-the-wisp, always to be snatched from my reach whenever I seemed to have found her for my own?

I lingered beside his honour's grave till the daylight failed and the waters of the lough merged into the stormy night, and the black gables of Kilgorman behind me lost themselves against the blacker sky. The weather suited my mood, and my spirits rose as the hard sleet struck my cheek and the buffet of the wind sweeping the cliff-top sent me staggering for support against the graveyard wall. It made me feel at home again to meet nature thus, and I know not how long I drank in courage for my sick heart that night.

At length I turned to go, before even it occurred to me that I had nowhere to go. The *Gnat* lay in the roadstead off Rathmullan, beyond reach that night. The cottage on Fanad was separated from me by a waste of boiling water. In Knockowen the bloodstains were not yet dry. Kilgorman—yes, there was no place else. I would shelter there till daylight summoned me to my post of duty on the *Gnat*. Looking back now, I can see that destiny led my footsteps thither.

As I turned towards the house, I thought I perceived in that direction a tiny spark of light, which vanished almost as soon as it appeared. Still more remarkable, a faint glimmer of light appeared in a small gable-window high up, where assuredly I had never before seen a light. It may have been on this account or from old association that, instead of approaching the place by the upper path, I descended the cliff and made my way round to the cave by which so many of my former visits had been paid. Fortunately the gale was an easterly one, so that the water in the cave was fairly still, and I was able in the dark to grope my way to the ledge on which the secret passage opened.

All was quiet when at last I reached the recess of the great hearth and peered out into the dark kitchen. By all appearance no one had looked into the place since I was there last a year ago and left my note for Tim, and found the mysterious message which warned me of the plot to carry off Miss Kit. I wondered if the former paper was still where I left it, and was about to step out of my hiding-place in search of a light, when the crunching of footsteps on the path without and the flitting of a lantern past a window sent me back suddenly into retirement.

A moment's consideration told me that it was easy to guess who the intruders might be. The night that Maurice Gorman had been laid in his grave would be a grand night for the rebels of Fanad. And who could say whether the object of their meeting might not be to consider the fate of Miss Kit herself, who, now that her father was dead, was no longer a hostage or the price of a ransom in their hands? There might at least be news of her, and even of Tim.

So I stood close, and waited as still as a mouse.

Chapter Thirty Six
The fight in Kilgorman

I had not long to wait before the footsteps sounded in the long passage which led to the kitchen, and a dim streak of light appeared at the doorway. Two of the company, rather by their voices than their faces, I recognised — one as Martin, the other as Jake Finn, the treasurer of the rebels, whom I had last seen in this very place on the night that Paddy Corkill was appointed to waylay and shoot his honour on the Black Hill Road. The other two, who carried cutlasses at their belts, were strangers to me, but seemed to be men of importance in the rebel business. Evidently a fifth man was expected.

"Sure, he'll come," said one.

"It's myself met him this blessed day no farther than Malin, and he promised he'd be here."

"Did he know this about Gorman?"

"How should he? Sure, I didn't know it myself. Besides, he's just from the Foyle, and our news doesn't travel east."

"How will he take it?"

"Whisht!" cried Martin. "There he is."

Three low taps sounded at the window, and Martin, taking the candle, hurried down the passage to admit the new arrival.

The other three men advanced to the door.

A quick, jaunty step sounded down the passage. The door opened, the men drew themselves up and saluted, Martin held the candle above his head, and there entered—Tim! At the sight of him the great fount of brotherhood that was in me welled up and nearly overflowed.

Tim was in the dress of a merchant sailor, and very handsome he looked, although the cut of his beard gave him a half-foreign look. His frame was knit harder than when I saw him last. His open face, tanned by the weather, was as fearless and serene as ever, and the toss of his head and the spring of his step were those rather of the boy I had known on Fanad years ago than of the dangerous rebel on whose head a price was set.

"Well, boys," said he, as Martin replaced the light on the table, "what's the best of your news?"

"Faith, that you're welcome, Tim Gallagher," replied Finn; "and it's right glad we are to get our captain."

"'Deed if it pleasures you to call me captain, you may," said Tim; "but I've no time to spend in these parts. I have business that won't keep. How goes the cause since I was here last?"

"Badly enough," replied one of the men. "The boys are slack, and we've been desperately thwarted by traitors and dirty informers and the English gang."

"And, saving your presence," said Martin, "we've to thank your own brother Barry for some of that same trouble. It was him who thwarted us on the Black Hill Road, and nearly spoilt our trip to Holland—"

"Barry?" said Tim sharply. "What of him? He's no 'dirty informer.' What's all this about Black Hill Road and Holland?"

"'Deed, Tim," said Finn, "it's an old story, and has been righted by now. You mind his honour, Maurice Gorman of Knockowen?"

"Mind him? of course I do—a coward that blew hot and cold, and led the boys on to mischief only to betray them. Yes; I mind Maurice Gorman."

This invective seemed greatly to encourage the men present, who had evidently feared Tim might for some reason have harboured a regard for their victim.

"It was him was to be settled with on the Black Hill Road a year ago; and settled he would have been but for Barry."

Tim's anger, I could see, was rising.

"Settled?" he said; "do you mean murdered?"

"Shot, any way. He got off that time; and a purty use he made of his chance, hanging boys by the dozen, and giving us no peace at all, at all. But since the young lady was lost to him—"

"What?" exclaimed Tim again; "how lost?"

"Didn't we have her over the seas to Holland for a hostage? And ever since he durstn't do a hand's turn against us. But he wouldn't come in for all that, or pay the money. It was Barry as nearly spoilt that game for us too; for he spirited the girl away in Holland, and if it hadn't been for some of the boys who got hold of her again in Dublin, she'd have been clane lost to Ireland for all our trouble."

"You dogs!" cried Tim, starting forward with his hand on his sword. "You mean to say you carried away an innocent girl to spite her father? You're a shame to your country!"

They looked at him in amazement. Then the speaker went on,—

"Sure, all's fair in war. The girl's safe enough." (Here Martin laughed in a sinister fashion.) "And now that all is settled up with Maurice Gorman at last—"

"Is Maurice Gorman dead, then?" asked Tim, controlling himself with a mighty effort, as was plain by his white lips and flashing eyes.

"He is so. We had him watched day and night, and on Sunday came our chance. He's gone to his account; and it's not six hours since he was put out of harm's way under the turf. By Saint Patrick, but it's a grand day for Ireland this."

"And you mean to tell me," said Tim, in a voice which made his hearers shift on their feet uncomfortably—"you mean to tell me that you dare to commit murder and outrage like this in the name of Ireland?"

"Why, what's amiss? Wasn't it yourself was saying with your own lips the Gorman was a dirty coward?" retorted one of the group testily.

"And that means the same to you as saying a man should be shot in the dark without a word of warning, and his innocent daughter carried off, who never did a hand's turn in the place that wasn't kindly and good?"

Guess who it was that loved Tim as he spoke those words?

"It's no time to be squeamish," persisted the man who had first spoken. "It's a blow for the good of the country, and there's them will give us credit for it, if you don't."

"You curs! I give you credit for being the meanest cowards unhung. And I don't mind telling anybody as much. Pray, is it you and the like of you I'm captain to?"

"When we chose you, we thought you were for the people," snarled Martin.

"Then take back your choice, you crew of blackguards," cried Tim, now in a towering rage. "I've nothing to do with such as you. No more has Ireland, thank God!"

"That's well enough," said Finn savagely; "but what's done is done, and in your name too, whether you like it or not. You should have let us know in time if your stomach wasn't strong enough for the work."

"My name! The girl carried away in my name, and her father murdered. How dare you, you dirty whelp, you!"

And he struck Finn across the cheek with his hand.

Instantly the scene became one of wild uproar. The blow was all the men had wanted to give vent to the bitter resentment which Tim's contemptuous reproaches had called up. As long as the quarrel was one of words, they were sullen but cowed. Now it was come to blows, events befell rapidly. Ere I could push my way into the room, sword in hand—in truth, more rapidly than I can narrate it—Tim, my brave, impulsive brother, had sent one of the rascals to his last account, and had stepped to the wall, with his back there, holding the others at sword's point.

Martin—that malign spirit, fated to thwart and injure me at all points—more cunning than his comrades, had stepped back behind the other two while Tim was engaged with them, poised a long knife above his head, and at the moment when Tim was lunging at the nearest of his assailants, I saw the brute, as in a nightmare, strike with all his might. The cowardly blow struck Tim full on the forehead, and brought him down with a crash on the floor. I had sprung at Martin's raised arm, but, alas! had just missed him by a flash of time.

"Take *that* for many an old score!" I shouted, as I brought him down on the instant with a cut which laid him bleeding and prostrate at my feet.

Then stepping across Tim's senseless body, I let out at the other two.

My sudden appearance—for I seemed to have dropped from the clouds—amazed and paralysed them. They were too terror-stricken to show much fight; and it was as well for them, for I was in a killing mood, and could have sent them to their last reckoning with a relish had they invited me. As it was, with white faces they backed to the door, and presently howled for mercy.

"It's Barry himsilf!" exclaimed Finn. "Be aisy now Barry darlint, and don't harm a defenceless man." And he dropped his weapon on the floor.

The other man laid down his knife and tried to edge through the door; but I stopped him.

"Now you are here," said I, "you shall stay here till I please. Help me to lift Tim; and the first of you that stirs for anything else is a dead man."

We lifted Tim tenderly—I could see, now that the heat of passion was cooled, that the men really respected him and deplored the upshot of the unexpected encounter—and we laid him gently on the table. My heart almost stopped beating as I noted the ghastly pallor of his face and saw the blood running over his temple. He opened his eyes in a dazed way for a moment; but if he saw me he did not know me. I bandaged his wound as best I could, and soaking my kerchief in a pool of rain-water, which had oozed through and on to the window-ledge, moistened his parched lips.

"Now," said I, sternly enough, stooping over Martin, on whom—with hardly a ray of pity for him in my heart, I fear—I could see the hand of death was laid, "one question for you: where is Maurice Gorman's daughter?"

Martin half opened his eyes. I think he saw the gleam of my pistol, which, though still in my hand, I had no intention of using. A convulsive look of terror passed over his face as he muttered thickly,—

"Take that thing away, for mercy's sake, and you shall know all. We took her and Biddy to the priest's at Killurin; but Father Murphy would have nothing to say to us. We didn't know *what* to do. So we—we—we—ah, Lord, forgive all."

There was a painful pause. For a moment I thought his secret would die with him. Then he murmured, pointing to the ceiling with his thumb, "We brought her *here!*"

"What?" I cried in amazement; "Miss Kit is in this house now?"

Martin raised himself with difficulty on his elbow, fumbled feebly in his belt, and handed me a rusty key. Before I could seize it he fell back on the floor, and I had to take the key from his dead hand.

In the midst of my woe a wild throb of joy shot through me as I realised what this unlooked-for news meant.

As I looked from Martin to his dead comrade, and from him to my poor bruised Tim, from whom, as I feared, life was rapidly ebbing away, my mind was filled with the pathos and a sense of the useless suffering of it all. Addressing the two men who only a minute or two ago were his assailants and mine, but who now stood with downcast faces, I said,—

"Boys, I don't doubt that ye are both acting from what ye consider to be a sense of duty to old Ireland, and maybe even to your Maker, in all this terrible bloodshed and unhappiness. To my thinking it's a sadly mistaken sense of duty, and will only land you and the dear country in shame and misery. But that is not here or there. Let us part without hatred. You will find a passage here to the sea," said I, showing them the opening by the fireplace through which I had entered the room; "and in a cave at the end of the passage you will find a boat. Carry your dead to it, and see them taken to their places."

Both men said gravely, as in a chorus, "God save Ireland!" to which I could utter, though in a different sense from theirs, "Amen!"

Then they did as I bade them, and laboriously carried away their dead comrades.

I turned to Tim. He was stirring slowly and feebly. I took off my coat and rolled it into a pillow for his head. Presently he opened his eyes, and a smile like the smile of an angel passed over his face.

"Barry," said he, "dear old Barry, and is it you, my brother?"

I bent over him and kissed his cheek.

"Methinks, Barry dear," said he, "I have struck my last blow for beloved Ireland. God bless her! But it has been a paltry, poor bit of work—all that I have been able to do."

"Cheer up, Tim, my boy, keep up your heart; we'll soon have you right again," said I, though my own heart misgave me as I spoke. "Do you know, Tim, that I have just heard that Kit is here, in this house, now—"

"Kit? Dear old Barry!" He took my hand in his and held it there, but all the strength was gone from his grip. I saw that he read my secret. "Now that her father is dead, Barry, this is *her* house," he said, trying to smile.

"No, Tim. This house and these lands are yours."

His face seemed to flush at this.

"Is that so? are you sure?" said he. "As sure as that I am here."

"And it is I who am heir to the estates?"

"It is. You are a rich man, for your father besides had land in England with your mother."

Tim's eyes were wide open. He lay silent for a time. "Barry, boy," he said, now almost fainting for lack of blood, "we have always been brothers, haven't we? even when we differed and fought when we were boys, eh? Nothing, nothing can unbrother you and me, Barry. I hand on all my rights to you and Kit—God bless ye both!"

His eyes closed wearily, but on his face there came again the happy smile of boyhood.

"Tim dear, shall I bring Kit down?—if, indeed, she is here."

"No, Barry, no; this is no place to bring a lady to, nor am I in a condition to see any lady."

As I looked at the blood-stained floor and table, and the walls which bore marks of the fray, I could not but agree with him. It was easy to see also that poor Tim's moments were numbered. His eyes were sunk deep in his head, his face was pallid, and his breathing became more and more difficult. His lips moved in broken utterance, but I saw he was not addressing me; there was a far-off, unworldly expression in his eyes. I could hear him murmur,—

"Ah, the tragedy! ah, the farce of it all!—I dreamed of a free, happy country, of a free, happy people prospering and blessed when the tyrant was overthrown—I thought I could help on this glorious time; and what happens? I am struck down by the hand of a friend in a miserable squabble; inglorious, farcical!—O Ireland, Ireland! the follies of your own children may be a greater curse to you in the days to come than have been the crimes of the stranger who has usurped your rights."

While I held his hand, stooping over him, with a heart too full for speech, he opened his eyes again, and said,—

"Barry, brother, you have forgiven me for that stone I threw at ye on Fanad Head?—ay, and the poor old mother is gone, and father too—and the guns are in Kilgorman—and Wolfe Tone is coming—and the French are preparing to deliver us; yes, they are on the way—and a time of joy is coming to Ireland—Barry, Barry, do ye hear the rustle of silk by the hearthstone? Do ye think the ghost is here?—I hear something—put but the light, boy, and lie close—there, there—my God, it is mother!" and he swooned away.

I thought he was dead, and I began to pray, when I heard him murmur,—

"Barry, are ye there, dear?—I can't see ye at all, at all. Why don't ye light the lamp?—there is no air!—open the window!—light, light, give me light!" and he fell back dead.

It was the bitterest, saddest moment of my life. Yet I felt a curious envy of him. He was out of the whirl and confusion and chaos of our unhappy time! Peace be with him! I loved him as my own soul, with a love which was not weakened but made only more pathetic to me that his ideals for the happiness of our loved country were not my ideals.

But there was comfort for me—of a kind I perhaps little deserved—close at hand. When I had drawn my coat over Tim's face, I rushed upstairs, calling aloud as I went,—

"Kit, Kit, I am coming! where are you, Kit?"

Then by-and-by I heard, far off, from a remote attic up in the roof of the rambling old building to which I had never before penetrated—I heard, faintly, a voice calling me by name, which fell on my heart like sweetest music. And when the rusty key had turned in the rusty old lock, and the crazy door was pushed open, I found a pair of arms flung tightly about my neck, and a pair of lips pressed close against mine, with cries of "Thank God, Barry! thank God, Barry! you are here at last."

It was a meeting of smiles and tears, of most delicious joy, with a background of infinite sadness.

Kit and Biddy McQuilkin were quickly brought by me to more comfortable quarters in Knockowen, and where they were more likely to have better protection. Captain Felton, on my signal, came ashore from the *Gnat*, and I found in him a friend indeed. He urged me to take Kit and Biddy to the house of his aunt (the widow of one of the canons of Salisbury Cathedral), who lived a peaceful life in one of the quaint old houses in the Close of that lovely cathedral city—at any rate until quieter times for Ireland. Not only this, but he managed so that Kit and Biddy and I were landed at Stranraer, on the Scottish coast, bearing letters from him to his aunt, who received us hospitably, and in whose care I was content to leave my beloved one, with a lighter heart concerning her than I had experienced during all the years I had known her.

I am not going to detail here all the bloody work of the next few months in our loved country. The wars of brothers are best left untold. Of the terrible doings in the north and south and west, but especially in County Wexford, at Enniscorthy and Vinegar Hill, where blood was spilt like water, we had enough, and more than enough, in the public prints, and on the loud tongue of rumour, at the time. But I was in the sea-fight off Lough Swilly, when we made mincemeat of the French squadron in October of that black year 1798, and pluckier fighting against enormous odds than was done on that day by the French frigate *Hoche* I had never seen, nor ever again wish to see. It was courage worthy of a better cause.

It was for the part I had in that affair that, later on, to my joy, I received my promotion, and gained the coveted right to place the honoured word "captain" after my name. With the defeat of the French expeditions in the west and north, and the capture and subsequent tragic death of the heroic if erratic genius Wolfe Tone, and after many weary days of suffering on the part of Ireland's noblest sons and daughters, there came gradually a modifying of the brutal spirit of hatred and bloodshed throughout the land. And with the better and more kindly understanding between the peoples there came by-and-by a measure of peace and prosperity and a calm after the long period of storm and disturbance.

In the spring of 1799 Kit and I were wedded in Salisbury. My friend Captain Felton was my "best man." At first our home was in Belfast, but we made frequent expeditions to Knockowen and Kilgorman as the countryside became more settled; for the place, in spite of all that had passed, had a fascination for both of us. And as the painful associations died away, we have long since returned to Donegal. There for many a day we and our little ones—beloved Tim and Kit and Eileen—have made our home by the side of our lovely lough, as happy a home as any to be found throughout Ireland, in a renovated and regenerated Kilgorman.